"Kiotski!" the commanding officer shouted. He snapped something to the other soldiers, and they started laughing and jabbing at the group of women, making them back toward the sea. "I think they just want us to go someplace else," the woman with the tiny topknot said. "God knows where, but let's pretend to swim back to Singapore."

The women waded into the surf. The soldiers stayed above the waterline. As Gloria got in above her knees, she looked back just in time to see the line of soldiers raise their guns. "Duck!" she screamed to the others.

She heard the first gunshots as she flung herself forward and felt something like a fiery knife slice through the outside of her upper thigh. . . .

GUESTS
OF THE
EMPEROR

Janice Young Brooks

BALLANTINE BOOKS • NEW YORK

Library of Congress Catalog Card Number: 90-93035

ISBN 0-345-36198-9

Manufactured in the United States of America

First Edition: September 1990

Dedicated to

Ilsa Corfield, Natalie Crouter, Betty Jeffrey, Agnes Newton Keith, and all the other women who risked their lives to keep diaries so that we would know

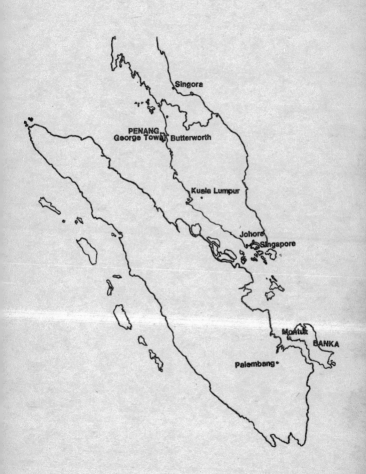

PART I

Under the Noonday Sun

Sumatra

1955

The battered jeep struggled through a mud-mired trough in the steep road. It slid sideways, the nearly bald tires spinning before they caught on solid ground. The jeep lurched forward. The young native driving the vehicle wiped the sweat out of his eyes and muttered a curse.

The handsome, redheaded American woman sitting next to him thought to herself, *He's figured out that we're not going to be very profitable to him. He's used to the rich old widows who come out here and want to be taken shopping and touring to look at waterfalls and quaint native villages. All his charm and flattery are wasted on us.* The engine sputtered and Hazel said, "You ought to check the spark plugs. I think that's the problem."

In the back of the jeep was a pretty, younger woman wearing a bright floral-patterned dress and a wide-brimmed hat. She had long, loose hair and bare legs. She seemed happier, easier with this journey than the other two and was carrying a big bunch of flowers wrapped in paper.

The one sitting behind the driver, the tall, plain woman with the dark hair and the ugly, sensible missionary shoes, seemed downright grim. "This can't be the right road," she said. "It was much wider."

"It was a long time ago and we were walking," Hazel said without turning around.

The driver took a curve faster than he should have and had to brake suddenly when a monkey ran across the road. The back of the jeep slid and bumped into the steep embankment. None of the women cried out or showed any alarm. The destination was all that mattered to them.

When the jeep crested the next hill, the driver had to swerve suddenly around a branch in the road. The redhead said, "That's enough. Stop." When he'd done so she said sternly, "Trade places. I'll drive."

"But no, missus. My boss, he only let me drive jeep."

"I'll take better care of it than you do. Move."

As he walked around the front of the jeep, he glanced at the pretty young one who was smiling behind her hand. The missionary was fanning herself and looking around as if expecting to see something familiar. The redhead was studying the hand-drawn map on a little scrap of paper, faded and smudged. What in hell did they want to come out here for anyway? the driver wondered. There weren't any temples or shops or gardens to see. No place to spend money. And it was damned hot. The road actually steamed where the equatorial sun was full on it, and these women didn't even seem to care.

The redhead took the wheel with competent hands, let out the clutch, and said over her shoulder to the others, "It must have been along here that Dinki caught the bird. Remember how mad she was when we made her give it to Spike?"

"Good old Spike," the young woman said with a bitter laugh.

The missionary lady said, "The sadist bastard."

They came to a tiny village with a cluster of stilted, atap-roofed huts and a central building with a saddle-shaped roof and buffalo horns decorating the high-gabled ends. A rickety tourist bus was stopped by it, and half a dozen foreign tourists were taking pictures. The women in the jeep paid no attention. They passed through the kampong and a mile or so beyond it the redhead slowed down, glanced at her map, peered into the bush, and took a turning that was barely more than a path. The jeep bumped and jolted in spite of her skillful driving. Parrots flew out of the brush, squawking at this invasion, and once they nearly ran over the end of a very large snake that was slithering out of the way.

Eventually they stopped. "This is it," Hazel said, giving the hand brake a firm pull and getting out.

The young man hopped out and offered his hand to the pretty woman in the back, but she didn't notice. "This? There's nothing here," she said.

"Hazel's right. See the buildings?" the plain one said.

The three women stood at the side of the road together, looking down a small incline to an area that had once been cleared but was now covered with low growth. Around the edges of the one-time clearing there were the decayed remnants of several buildings. Of bare wood construction, they'd been eaten by wood borers and strangled with vines. One still sat on two of its stilts and leaned at a rakish angle. In the center of the clearing a pile of flat rocks had supported a big iron pot that had toppled off and lay on its side. This had once been the coolie quarters of a Dutch rubber plantation.

Hazel took a step down the incline and picked something up. "Barbed wire," she said, dropping it and brushing the rust off her hands and rejoining the others. "Barbed wire," she repeated sadly.

As she stepped back onto the road, the woman with the sensible shoes took her hand to help her and kept her grip. "Hazel, do you remember . . ." the words trailed off as their eyes locked.

"Yes—oh, yes, everything," Hazel said softly. "Where are the flowers?"

"I'll get them," the young one said. She took the bundle of wilted blooms from the jeep and the three women walked off into the jungle. They went through the low growth without even looking down for snakes. Slowly, purposefully, with heads cocked as if expecting to hear voices, the women passed like a processional through the center of the clearing, between two of the disintegrating buildings and up a slight rise. There they stopped and stood together for a long moment.

Hazel was the first to speak. "There's nothing. No sign at all." She unwrapped the flowers and laid them reverently on a fallen log.

The missionary lady put her arm around the young one. "That last day, when we were all getting ready to leave, I came here. To say good-bye to them. I swore I'd never come back. But here I am."

"It's not right," the young one said in a shaky voice. "Someone should know they're here. There should be a memorial."

Hazel said, "*We* are their memorial—whether we want to be or not."

Chapter 1

Singapore

December 7, 1941

". . . world without eh-eh-eh-nd, ah-ah-ah-men."

Hazel Hampton sat up very straight, willing herself to stay awake. It wasn't easy to combat both the smothering Malayan heat and the long Church of England service. Somebody near them was wearing a pungent green scent that made the already oppressive air nearly impossible to breathe. If only some women wouldn't wear so much scent to church, Hazel thought. She tried to concentrate on the service, but the words ran together into a comfortable, meaningless drone. She had a paperback mystery novel in her handbag, a new one that seemed to be whispering seductively to her. She wondered briefly if there was any way she might sneak a look at a few paragraphs without anyone noticing. She put her hand to the clasp, and as gently as a butterfly her mother's hand settled on hers as if she'd read her daughter's mind.

Hazel glanced sideways. Roberta Hampton, with her blond hair and white silk suit, seemed carved in marble. The impression was intensified by the pleasantly blank expression she always adopted in church. She was small and pale with dainty, sweet features, the sort of angelic-looking woman who astonished people when she smoked a cigarette or asked for a gin and tonic. In church she was most deceptive; she always looked like her thoughts were on "higher things," but Hazel knew that behind that angelic face, a sharp mind was rewriting recipes or mentally replaying favorite bridge hands with which she had annihilated opponents.

On Hazel's left her sister, Barbara, and Barbara's friend Emmy

Wadsworth were passing notes back and forth and silently giggling. They didn't think to pass the messages to her.

To look at the two of them, nobody would suspect Hazel and Barbara Hampton were sisters. In fact, that was a comment Hazel had heard far too many times and never liked. Physically, Hazel was her father's daughter with his fair, freckled English skin and reddish hair. Tall for a woman, tending slightly toward overweight ("It's just baby fat, darling," her mother had frequently assured her until she was twenty, then stopped mentioning it), Hazel looked sturdy and faintly athletic, as if she might have been a good wing on a girls' hockey team in high school. In spite of beautiful teeth and lovely blue eyes, she had a square, sensible, reliable look—and she hated it.

Barbara Hampton, in startling contrast, had inherited her American mother's delicate physique and curly blond hair, but not her tranquility. Barbara was full of "bounce" and "go," as people said admiringly. She could flounce and flirt and tell amusing stories with charm and vivacity. She had everything—perfect skin, great legs, a small waist, generous breasts, and tiny, beautifully shaped hands with long, painted fingernails.

Just looking at her made Hazel feel like a plowhorse.

Her father was the only person who knew and understood Hazel's envy of Barbara—envy that didn't impinge on affection. "You mustn't care so much, my dear," he'd told Hazel when she was sixteen and fourteen-year-old Barbara had stolen the show at her birthday party. "You're going to be a fine, dignified woman and Barbie will be a girl until she's forty."

He was right and he meant it lovingly, but the last thing a self-conscious twenty-two-year-old aspired to was dignity. What passed for that quality was usually just paralyzing shyness anyway. She still wanted to be able to skip down the stairs with her skirts swirling like Barbara did so wonderfully. But if Hazel skipped downstairs, the windows rattled and people looked up in alarm.

"Wake up, Hazel!" Barbara said, digging a sharp little elbow into her sister's ribs. "Service is over. Emmy wants us to go to Raffles for an early luncheon with her."

"I've promised to put in some extra hours at the hospital," Hazel said as they made their way outdoors. "I've fallen a little behind on the filing."

"You said at breakfast that you weren't going until two and you don't get paid anyway." Barbara turned to Emmy and pulled a pouty face. It was attractive on her. "Do they call you 'Sister' at the hospital, Hazel?"

"Of course not. I'm not a nurse."

"But the nurses aren't nuns and they're called Sister here. I think it's very odd. Emmy, can you imagine going halfway around the world and right away finding volunteer work to do? Isn't Hazel admirable?"

"Barbara, don't talk about me as if I don't understand English," Hazel said. She wasn't sure if the compliment was sincere or a joke.

"Come along, please," Barbara insisted. "Mommy, will you come, too?"

Roberta Hampton smiled at her—a real smile, not the recipe version. "No, darling. You girls go along. Johnny and Milly Leighton have offered me a ride home in their new car. Hazel, don't forget we're expected there for a late supper."

"Mother, I don't know—"

Roberta took her arm. "You don't have to come, darling. But it would be nice—"

"You just want a fourth at bridge."

Roberta grinned. "Why do you think I had *two* children? To create a table of four. You girls are a sorry disappointment to me, neither of you knowing the difference between clubs and spades. I should have just gone on having babies until I got the right ones."

"Daddy'll be back in a week or so," Hazel reassured her. "He'll play bridge with you and the Leightons."

They saw their mother off, and Barbara and Emmy took a rickshaw, even though the big hotel was just a block away. Hazel walked, and quickly regretted it. Though still early in the day, the sun was out and even a leisurely stroll seemed a battle against the thick, hot air. She soon felt like a sweaty elephant. Her blouse was sticky and kept coming untucked. Her linen skirt was wrinkled and drooping. Even the light veil on her hat seemed suffocating. In spite of her turtle pace, Hazel reached Raffles first. Her sister and Emmy must have detoured. She stood in front of the hotel, waiting. A slight breeze off the sea made a rustling sound in the gigantic royal palms towering over her. "It's not much like home," she said under her breath.

Home. Frank.

She was momentarily so homesick it made a pain in her stomach. Chicago would be cold now, with crisp, pine-scented air in sharp gusts that took your breath away. The streets would be busy with Christmas shoppers. If the Hamptons were home in Evanston, she'd be holding the stepladder while Dad put the lights on the blue spruce by the front door. Barbara would be assembling her wardrobe for a round of dinners and dances. The prize item was the fox stole she'd received last Christmas. Mother would be in the kitchen baking dozens of cookies and writing out invitations to holiday card parties. And Frank would be coming home from law school for a few weeks and they'd hold hands and walk along the lakefront on the crunchy, icy sand and talk about plans for their wedding next summer. Frank was a big man, a full seven inches taller than Hazel. When she was in his arms she felt little and delicate. That was the first thing that had attracted her to him—his size.

Barbara and Emmy arrived at Raffles, still giggling. Boyishly slim with black hair and pale blue eyes, Emmy Wadsworth was a perfect foil to Barbara. While Barbara seemed to skip adorably through society, Emmy floated on a cloud of English gentility. "I'm sorry we kept you waiting. We stopped to buy some sweets," she said to Hazel. "It's my great failing, Daddy says. Let's get out of the sun. How divine!" she said, popping a piece of candy into her mouth after offering some to Hazel.

Hazel liked Emmy; or, rather, she was fascinated by her. Emmy affected a fragile vacancy of mind that was, surprisingly, charming. She was as pretty and restful as one of those glass paperweights with falling snow inside. Even here in the tropics she wore a lightweight blush-pink twin set and pearls—the uniform of the well-brought-up English girl who was above mere climate. Hazel wondered if Emmy had sweat glands.

They got settled at a shaded table in the courtyard, removed their gloves, and ordered lunch. "Have you heard from your father?" Emmy asked Hazel politely. Emmy *did* aspire to dignity and was secretly in awe of Barbara's older sister, though Hazel never suspected the admiration.

"Mother got a letter yesterday. He got to Penang without any difficulty and was going up to look at the plantation this week."

"How lucky you are to have inherited a whole plantation," Emmy said. "It's probably terribly grand. Many of them are. With Daddy being career army, we've lived everywhere and never actually owned a place of our own."

"It remains to be seen if the plantation is an asset. That's why he went to look it over. He'll probably sell it."

"Then you don't think you'll move there?" Emmy asked, looking at Barbara out of the corner of her eye.

"Oh, Emmy! Bite your tongue!" Barbara said, reacting just as Emmy expected. "Live on a smelly old rubber plantation in the jungle? Me?"

"But you'd come to Singapore all the time and we could have such good times. Of course, Hazel wouldn't stay anyway. Being engaged and all. I bet you miss your fiancé."

Miss him? So much it hurts, Hazel thought, but she said, "I do, but I'm enjoying this vacation. It's the last time the family will be able to take a trip together." How priggish and sensible she sounded, even to herself. Couldn't she have made some kind of joke instead? She often thought of funny things to say, just never in time.

A Malay waiter brought three plates of curried shrimp salad. The lettuce around the plate was already wilting. Emmy took a bite of salad, chewed thoughtfully as if deciding whether or not to keep the chef, and said, "It's quite good today. Seriously, I think you should leave as soon as your father gets back. I'll hate it and miss you both dreadfully, but Daddy says the Japs are going to start a war any day now and that will be the most awful bore."

The only thing that agitated Emmy into breaking out of her perfect boarding school manners was her father. Having finished school in England the previous spring before returning to the family, she was going through a stage of having a rather innocent crush on him and became quite animated when she parroted his opinions. Emmy's father was a British army colonel serving under Lieutenant-General Arthur Percival. It was through her reporting of her father's opinions that Hazel understood a little of what was happening around them—or was about to happen, if Colonel Wadsworth was to be believed. The newspapers certainly didn't talk about the possibility of war. Barbara thought Emmy's military gossip was boring, but Hazel was interested and a little alarmed.

Hazel and Barbara's father didn't talk much about the war either because it was the only thing that could be counted on to cause a raging argument with his wife. Ronald Hampton was British born and had taken American citizenship some years before, but his loyalties were being torn now. Like most Americans, he didn't really want to become involved in Europe's war, even though he said it was clearly inevitable. "If France and

England come under Hitler's yoke, America will be next," he said. "He has to be stopped, and it will require American aid, before he can take Europe. It's in America's interest, not Europe's."

But he hadn't said it often. Roberta Hampton, the most non-political person in all other respects, was a fanatic isolationist. "We gave the Europeans the lives of our men, and won their last war for them. Then we loaned them money to rebuild—money they never paid back—and set them back on their feet. For all that, they still regard us as crude and laughable. They should have stopped Hitler a long time ago, but they were too stupid, and now they want us to send our men to die again!"

After a few such fights, they both found it better not to discuss the war. But though Hitler and Europe were dangerous topics, neither of them considered Japan a threat. Japan wasn't even worth bothering to have an opinion about. Oh, they were going to cause some sort of trouble sooner or later, but unlike Emmy's father, Ronald Hampton didn't believe the Japanese would attack anytime soon. Clearly hostile toward the Western powers, the Japs didn't have the military strength for actual attack—so he believed—and told his wife and daughters while this trip was being planned.

"Daddy says the Japs will probably make their move on a Sunday morning because that's when Europeans have their guard down. Isn't that marvelously clever of him to figure that out?" Emmy said.

"Then we're safe for another week," Barbara said. "Don't you like bamboo shoots, Emmy? Can I have yours? Anyhow, you said those two big British ships will take care of anything the silly Japanese might try."

"Yes, I think Daddy did feel better when the *Prince of Wales* and the *Repulse* got here, but still, the Japs could interfere with shipping lines for a while and then you'd be here for six months or so until they're put down. And there could be shortages, too."

"Oh, Emmy, must you go on about the Japs? I want to know about that dress you wore last night. Did you have it made here?"

"No, I bought it last week at Robinsons—"

Hazel ate her salad while the younger women talked about clothes. She was beginning to wish her father would return quickly from Penang. Although, if it weren't for missing Frank and worrying a bit about a war, Hazel would have rather liked being trapped in Singapore for another six months. This life was so fascinatingly foreign to her, so unlike good old comfortable Evanston, where everyone was plain American and spoke plain English and did ordinary jobs.

Here in Singapore virtually everything was exotic. It was like living in one of the novels she was always reading. Europeans were a minority and Americans even more so. The people were mainly Chinese, Malay, and Indian, and they spoke a deafening multitude of languages, none of which Hazel understood. Going out on the streets was like listening to a verbal jigsaw puzzle. The only drawback was the weather; the climate was either hot and damp or hot and wet. The monsoon was starting, and there had already been a number of heavy rains; everybody said it would get much worse. And such rains! They came down in a savage deluge that was almost frightening in its intensity.

The contrasts to the existence Hazel had always known were astonishing and went far beyond climate, however. Though the Hamptons were well off, the work ethic was deeply ingrained in Hazel. But for Westerners, life in Singapore was lush and idle with languorous rounds of cricket, dining at Raffles or the Adelphi, shopping at the Cold Storage or Robinsons, strolling through the Botanic Gardens, or sightseeing in the Chinese section. Nobody seemed to work; nobody white needed to. Mornings were for tennis and cricket and golf; afternoons were for long naps under big ceiling fans; evenings were for dining and dancing and concerts. The big, palm-shaded stucco house the Hamptons had rented came with a cook, a serving girl, two cleaning girls, a chauffeur, a personal maid, three gardeners, a laundress, a bossy little Chinese majordomo, and one boy whose only job was to go about with a basket on a pole and get the *chichak* lizards off the ceilings so they wouldn't drop down on the American *mems*' heads. Even those on the lowest steps of the Western hierarchy had servants.

All of which was why Hazel had immediately found something to do when they arrived and her father prepared to go upcountry to see the plantation an English great-aunt had left him in her will. It certainly wasn't that Hazel liked sick people or had any great calling to help the unfortunate. It was a desperate need to keep busy so that homesickness wouldn't overcome her. It was also a need that amounted to a virtual hunger to do something well. For Hazel, in spite of her athletic appearance, wasn't much interested in sports and was easily bored by the social round. As it turned out, helping at the Kandang Ker-bau Maternity Hospital was a pleasure. Nobody was ill, the mothers were happy, and the babies were adorable. Hazel's abil-ity to file and sort and keep a decent inventory of supplies wasn't a glamorous skill, but it was a useful, satisfying one.

". . . and no one took much note, which Daddy says is a shame," Emmy was saying.

"I'm so sorry, Emmy. I was daydreaming," Hazel said. She'd finished her lunch without hearing much of anything the two younger women had said. "No one took much note of what?"

"I was saying that last month a Japanese ship left Singapore with hundreds of Japs on board from all over the island and the peninsula. All sorts of people—grocers, barbers, geishas" (this on a hushed note), "fishermen, mine workers. If you'd been here two or three months ago, you'd have seen a difference. There used to be Japs everywhere and they've all just disap-peared. Daddy says he thinks they were spies, sent to check out the British defenses, and they'd been called home to make final reports before the invasion."

"Invasion!" Barbara scoffed. "Everybody knows Singapore can't be invaded. That's why all those people from Borneo and places like that are coming here. There are all those guns at Fort Canning and now the big warships in the harbor. Even I know that!"

"But Daddy says those are all sea defenses. There's no land defense at the north of the island."

"I would think the peninsula itself is the best defense. I hear it's almost solid jungle except for a few roads. And I understand the only good road is on the protected west side. Nobody could bring an army down through it," Hazel said, repeating what she'd read in the papers.

"Probably not," Emmy admitted. "Certainly not a bunch of stupid little Japs. Still, you should get your father to come back and take you home, just in case."

"What about you, Emmy? If your father is so alarmed, why doesn't he send you and your mother home to England?"

Emmy looked at her with genuine surprise. "Oh, *we* couldn't go, Hazel. It would look unpatriotic. Terribly bad form."

"I see," Hazel said, offended and not sure why. "Well, I think I'll go to the hospital now."

"Don't you want to come to the Tanglin Club for a bit of tennis first?" Barbara asked.

s heat?''

azel, we don't *play* tennis. We just watch all the men
y,'' Barbara said.

"Just the same, no thanks. See you later.''

Several hundred miles to the north, at a small military hospital on the west coast of the Malay Peninsula, Australian nursing sister Gloria Denk came on night duty at eight. It was a
sleepy backwater of a post, where nothing much ever happened.
Most of the medical cases were men who forgot to take their
daily quinine and came down with malaria, or those who un-
derestimated how treacherous the jungle roads were and got into
accidents.

Gloria stood at the side of a soldier's bed, taking his pulse.
The soldier, Captain Niles Atchison, studied her admiringly as
she gazed at the watch pinned to her starched uniform bodice
and silently counted his heartbeats. She was about as cute as
they came, with short sandy hair (what a shame to cover it all
up with that silly nunlike headgear), sea-blue eyes, and an almost (but not quite!) tomboyish figure. Most surprising, she had
a deep, husky voice that was about the sexiest sound he'd ever
heard. Besides all this, she was a swell sport, he thought. He
asked her out nearly every chance he got, and once in a while
she accepted. She could drink half the men he knew under the
table and tell jokes that made the other half blush, but when she
was on duty, he was discovering, she was a damned fine nurse.

"If you boys had something worthwhile to do with yourselves, you wouldn't have time to get drunk and fall off porches,''
she said quietly so she wouldn't disturb the man sleeping in the
next bed. "You're lucky that leg wasn't broken instead of just
cut up a bit.''

"What's a poor soldier with no war to fight supposed to do?
Besides, if you'd been with me, it wouldn't have happened,
Dinki,'' he said.

"Why? Do you think I'd have thrown myself to the ground
and cushioned your fall? Not bloody likely, Niles.''

"When do you get off tonight?''

"Sooner than you,'' she said, making a note on his chart.

"Let's run off together, Dinki.''

"Run off? You can't even get up.''

"Part of me can,'' he said, glancing down at the tent his
erection was making under the light sheet that covered him.

She looked, too, and laughed. "I've seen better than that on men who are under anesthesia. Give it up, Niles."

"Come on, you like me, don't you?"

"Sure. I like lots of people. So what?"

"So if you didn't come out to get a man, what are you doing out here in this godforsaken jungle? Pretty girl like you ought to marry some good-looking bloke like me and settle down back home."

Sister Denk looked around to see if Matron was watching. Satisfied she wasn't, she sat down on the side of the bed. "May I point out that you're 'out here,' too?"

"Yeah, but only for another four months, then it's back to Adelaide. We could have a good time for a bit, get hitched, and go home together."

"Uh-huh. You go back and have a hell of a swell life riding all over some sheep station in the back of beyond with your friends while I settle down in some ramshackle cottage with no hot water and torn screens in the windows and the loo out in the yard. I know what you have in mind: I'd get busy having a bunch of brats and you'd drop in from time to time for a quick poke to give me another one. No thanks, Niles. I saw my mum dry up and die that way. Not for me. You men are all alike. A smart Aussie girl gets out and all you bastards want to do is drag her back."

"I get it. You'd rather marry some pommy bloke who owns half of Devonshire."

She grinned. "Hell, no. That's the same thing, just with better plumbing. Or maybe not. They probably pee in the moat. Anyway, every rich Brit I've ever met looks like he's got a loony aunt hidden in the attic."

"So what *do* you want, Dinki? To stick around out here forever?"

"Oh, I don't know, Niles. Something—"

"Sister Denk!" Matron snapped.

"Yes, ma'am, just checking a hole in the mosquito netting," Gloria Denk said, hopping up and looking very efficient. "Captain Atchison, I think that was just a shadow you were seeing. The net is intact." She reached up and pulled the flap of netting down and tucked it under the mattress.

Matron knew Sister Denk was lying and she also knew she'd stick to the story to the death. Getting this girl had been a distinctly mixed blessing. When she heard they were getting a nurse who'd been evacuated from one of the beleaguered Shanghai hospitals a year earlier, she'd felt they were going to get a cool, competent professional. It turned out she was all of that, but she was also a troublemaker, a rule questioner, a practical joker when off duty. "It's hardly necessary to crawl into the patient's bed to check the netting."

"Yes, ma'am. I mean no, ma'am," Gloria said, winking broadly at Niles.

Hazel returned at ten that night. Her mother was sitting on the balcony outside her bedroom, wearing a light wrapper and high-heeled satin mules. She was nibbling from a bowl of fresh strawberries, and the scent from a vase of fresh roses hung in the still air. "Hazel dear, you look hot and tired. You shouldn't work so hard. There's no need."

"I wasn't working hard and it's hot everyplace. We had twins born this evening. They were adorable. Where's Barbara?"

"She and Emmy are at a dinner dance. You were invited; have you forgotten? Sit down, dear."

Hazel took off her shoes, rolled down her stockings, and pulled her long, unruly red hair up off her neck as she sunk into a big wicker chair. Roberta fixed her a gin and tonic and they sat quietly for a while. Finally Hazel said, "Emmy was gabbing at lunch about the Japanese again." She repeated the pertinent bits of the conversation. "I don't mean to scare you, Mother, but I thought you should hear."

"I know," Roberta Hampton said, delicately tapping the ash off her cigarette into a cloisonné ashtray. "It's very indiscreet of Emmy to be telling everybody what her father says, but Johnny and Milly Leighton were talking about nothing else all afternoon. Of course, being British, they discount it all as quite silly alarmism and repeat the cautions only in order to sneer at them and be terribly superior. Still—I'm going to write your father in the morning. I don't think we ought to take chances. It's so hard to know what to believe. Most people say the Japanese are in so far over their heads with their war with China that they can't possibly spare the effort to attack anyone else, and that does make sense. It's what everybody at home said. It's what your father believes. We wouldn't have come out here at all other-wise—"

"That's probably true," Hazel replied.

"It could be. But then the few who think otherwise chime in

and scare the stuffing out of me,'' her mother continued. "And the papers are full of all sorts of alarming things—Americans being evacuated from Japan, diplomatic sniping. And that atlas business. Did you hear about that? Some Japanese atlas they've just printed with new Japanese names for islands that aren't theirs. Yes, I'll wire your father first thing in the morning.''

"We've got until next Sunday,'' Hazel said, smiling in the darkness. A little breeze had sprung up, cooling the back of her neck. "Emmy's father says they'll attack on a Sunday.''

"I wonder if they know that.''

"Niles, wake up! Niles? Goddamm it, wake up!'' Gloria whispered harshly.

"Huh? What—Dinki?''

She lifted the mosquito netting and put her head next to his. "Do you think you can walk?''

Fuddled as he was, he sensed the urgency and sat up quickly. "I think so. Dinki, what's wrong? What time is it?''

"One o'clock. Listen . . .''

At first all he heard was the muted chorus of snoring that was the usual sound of the darkened ward at night. Then he picked out another sound. "Thunder,'' he said with a laugh. "You afraid of storms, cookie?''

"Don't 'cookie' me, you dumb bastard. That's gunfire. What kind of soldier are you? We just got word—the Japs are at Kota Baharu.''

"Kota Baharu? That's only—''

"Just across the peninsula—a few miles north of here.''

"Don't you worry. They can't take it. Heath's Indian regiment is there,'' Niles said, slipping his legs carefully over the edge of the bed. It wasn't nearly as painful as he'd feared it would be.

"They *have* taken it, Niles. It took them less than an hour. They're coming this way.''

"Jesus God! You've got the wrong end of the stick somehow, Dinki.''

"Then your commanding officer must have it wrong, too. He ordered us to throw anybody halfway able-bodied out of bed and tell them to report for duty. We need you out of the way in case we need to pack up to evacuate. Now, get your ass off that bed and get dressed.''

He stood, leaning heavily on her shoulders. Flexing his knees in turn, he said, "Shit! I guess Adelaide's going to have to wait for me a little longer. You'll wait for me, won't you?"

"Oh, sure. Now put your clothes on. And Niles—be careful, will you?"

Hazel was dreaming of home when the sirens started. She sat up in bed, disoriented. Fumbling in the dark, she nearly knocked the lamp off the bedside table before she got it turned on. The clock said it was four-fifteen. Why would they blow the sirens in the middle of the night? The practice drills were always in the daytime or early evening. She threw on a light robe and went to her mother's room. Roberta was standing at the door to the balcony. "What's going on, Mother?"

"Some overeager civil servant pushed the button just to keep us on our toes, I imagine," Roberta said, lighting a cigarette. Her tone was very don't-frighten-the-children, but her hand was shaking and the flame danced. She put the cigarette down and started nervously taking out her pincurls.

Barbara stumbled into the room, attractively disheveled. "What is that noise?"

"Nothing, dear. Go on back to bed," Roberta assured her.

But in the moonlight Hazel could see the look of concern creasing her mother's forehead. Below them in the sideyard they could hear several of the servants chattering excitedly. Barbara mumbled something and curled up on her father's empty bed to go back to sleep. As Hazel and Roberta stood listening to the sirens, they noticed the flash of headlights against the hedge.

When they got downstairs, Johnny Leighton was at the door. His blazer was buttoned crooked and his silk ascot was askew. "Just thought I ought to pop over and see how you're doing." He was the living embodiment of the aging "second lead." Good-looking, good-natured, something of an ass, he'd appointed himself to look after the Hampton women while Ronald was upcountry. Until now it had meant escorting them to dinners and bridge parties.

"What is it, Johnny?" Roberta asked.

"Nothing to worry about. Some fool reported Jap planes twenty-five miles away and lost his head. Probably some of our R.A.F. boys out for a midnight spin—"

As he spoke the last word, the sky lit up, and a second later a bomb blast nearly deafened them. A few flakes of plaster fluttered down from the ceiling. Johnny Leighton turned and ran back out the front door. "Damn!" he said, looking at the sky. There was another flash of light and explosion of sound. He stood gaping like a fish out of water. His script didn't tell him how to handle something like this.

"They're bombing Singapore," Roberta said in a dead voice. "Dear God!"

"They can't! They just *can't*!" Johnny said. "Throw some things together and come with me. I've got to get back to Milly."

Hazel waited for her mother to respond, but Roberta's attention was on the sky, so Hazel replied. "Thanks, Mr. Leighton, but we'll stay here."

From upstairs she heard Barbara scream. Roberta went inside without another word.

"Right-o. Suppose our chances are the same wherever we are. I'll get back to you as soon as I can," he said, running over and jumping into his sporty new car.

Hazel stayed outside, reasoning that if a bomb were going to get her, she'd rather it just *got* her at once instead of knocking the house down on top of her. The bombing went on for a while longer, then stopped as suddenly as it had started. Nothing had struck near them, though the heavy tropical air was full of smoke. When the wind shifted slightly, Hazel thought she could hear faintly the screams of the injured and bereaved.

She put her hands over her ears and whispered, "Please, Daddy, come back and get us out of here!"

Chapter 2

When the sun came up, the pall of smoke still hung over the city. Hazel sat down to breakfast on the veranda. Her eyes were

gritty from lack of sleep and her hands kept shaking. Up until
the day before, all the talk of war had been theoretical, as interesting and impersonal as the books she was always reading. Last
night was real—and terrifying. Roberta joined her just as Johnny
Leighton returned. Sartorially correct now, he nevertheless
looked vaguely frazzled. He took a seat and sighed heavily. "It's
not good news, I'm afraid. I've been having a bit of a chin wag
with a friend at army headquarters. Strictly off the record, of
course."

"What's happened?" Roberta asked.

"It's the Japs, as we knew. They've just sprung up everywhere
like mushrooms. All but knocked out your American base at
Pearl Harbor. Thousands of servicemen killed. Most of your
Pacific fleet sunk—"

"Dear God!" Roberta whispered, horrified. Their next-door
neighbor at home had a son stationed there, and the posh posting
had been something of a joke between them. "That bastard
Roosevelt has finally gotten what he's been wanting!"

Johnny was clearly shocked by both the sentiment and the
vehemence. "It does mean you Americans are finally at war
along with the rest of us, of course."

He sounded downright smug when he said this. It irritated
Hazel but it set Roberta off like a firecracker. "You mean we
have to get into your damned war now! The Americans can save
you like we saved you in the last one. My father died saving the
British, and I'm not going to lose my husband!"

"Really, Roberta—" Johnny Leighton said, rising.

Roberta suddenly realized what she was saying. "Oh, I'm so
sorry!" she said, leaning forward and clutching at his arm. She
looked sincerely stricken. "I shouldn't have said any of that. I
don't mean it, you know. It's just all so upsetting. Please forgive
me."

"Of course," he said, seeming to enjoy being magnanimous.

"It wasn't supposed to happen on a Monday," Hazel said.
She hadn't meant to speak; in her distress the words had just
come out.

Leighton looked at her oddly. "It *was* early Sunday morning
at Pearl. The international date line, don't you know. We've got
more than fifty dead in the Chinese district and a couple hundred
injured," he went on. "Of course Singapore was lit up like a
great beacon. Our own fault, really. They hit Hong Kong hard,
too. People are saying they bombed Guam, Wake, and the Phil-

ippines as well, but I don't know if that's true. How could there be that many of them? The worst of it is, they actually came ashore at Kota Baharu. And took a place called Singora.''

''Where is Kota Baharu?'' Roberta asked.

''Upcountry about as far as Penang, but on the east side of the peninsula. The *Prince of Wales* and the *Repulse* are being readied to set out to Singora.''

''Penang!'' Hazel exclaimed. She and Roberta instinctively reached out and grabbed each other's hands.

''No cause to worry about Ronald. They can't get cross country. It's too dense and mountainous and the roads are hardly more than paths. The best they might do is creep along the beach a bit south until our boys get there, then we'll pick them off like ninepins.''

Ignoring his comforting remarks, Roberta summoned the Chinese majordomo and jotted down a message on a scrap of paper. ''See that this wire is sent to Mr. Hampton in Penang, please. Your other duties can wait.'' He stuffed the paper up his sleeve and trotted off, his face a worried frown.

''Excuse me, Mr. Leighton,'' Hazel said. ''I've got to get to the hospital. They'll be short of staff.''

''No, Hazel,'' her mother said. ''You mustn't leave the house.''

''Mother, they'll need me at the hospital, and I certainly couldn't keep anything from hitting the house if I were here.''

''Oh, very well, but you must call and check in with me every hour. Do you hear? Every hour.'' She seemed to be making a real effort not to lose her head again.

''Yes, Mother,'' Hazel said, preoccupied with thoughts of Frank. If the United States went to war, as surely they must, what would happen to Frank? He had only five months of law school to finish. Certainly he wouldn't quit so near the end to join the service—or would he? That would ruin all their careful plans. If only he'd stay in school, it would probably be all be over by the time he finished. She'd get home and the wedding would go on as planned.

The hospital was full when Hazel arrived. Convalescent patients from other Singapore hospitals had been moved there to make room for the injured from the Chinese section to be treated where the facilities for such wounds were best. Hazel was put to work on the tedious business of sorting and filing the influx of forms. Midmorning her period began and she started having cramps, an affliction she seldom suffered. For some reason, that was the final straw. She went to the bathroom and had a good cry before getting back to work. It was after one o'clock when she got a chance to sit down quietly with a hot water bottle on her stomach and dash off a note to Frank. Fearing that the newspapers in the States would report the bombing of Singapore, she wrote to assure him that they were safe and would come home just as soon as her father returned from Penang.

When she got home late that afternoon, however, the word on her father wasn't what she had hoped. "I haven't gotten any reply to my wire," Roberta admitted. "But I'm sure it's just because the telegraph people are busy."

"Do you know that your wire got through?" Hazel asked.

"Oh, I'm quite certain it did. He'll be here in a day or two, you'll see," Roberta said brightly. "He's probably already on his way."

The Hampton women had a quiet dinner alone. No one wanted to talk about the situation they were in, and none of them could think about anything else, so long silences stretched between them. After dinner Barbara did some sewing, Hazel read for a while, and Roberta laid out solitaire hands and scooped half of them up, unplayed. At every little creak of the house, they jumped. At dusk they turned off the lights. "Isn't there somewhere we should go?" Barbara asked. "Someplace safe?"

Neither Hazel nor Roberta answered.

It was a long night of anxiety, made worse in a sense because nothing happened. Though their nerves were strung as tightly as violin wires in horrible expectancy, there were no bombs, no whine of planes. They went to bed early and slept fitfully in their clothes, ready to—to what? They didn't know, but it seemed better to face whatever might happen fully dressed. Barbara had a nightmare about Frank; he was wearing a military uniform and was carrying a bomb in his arms that she knew was about to explode, but she couldn't make him hear her warnings. In the morning they were all tired, snappish, perversely disappointed that all their fearful anticipation had been for nothing.

After breakfast the next morning Roberta blew out a long stream of cigarette smoke and announced very firmly, "I do believe this is a tempest in a teapot."

"What?" Hazel asked, setting down her glass of orange juice.

"I think those nasty little men just bombed Singapore to

make some sort of crazy point. If they were serious, they'd have come again last night. I don't believe they'll be back again."

"I'm so glad," Barbara said, as if her mother's opinion were proven fact.

Barbara's immediate, grateful acceptance made Hazel understand why her mother had made the optimistic and totally uninformed remark. It was simply the maternal instinct to reassure them. The way Roberta nervously puffed on her cigarette belied the words. This firm-minded assurance was what Hazel had craved, and now found it impossible to believe. It was the first time Hazel had been able to step back and see her mother as a woman. A frightened woman, at that.

"I think you're absolutely right," Hazel said.

Roberta gave her a long look and a spark of understanding leapt between them. "I'm going to do a little packing so we're ready as soon as your father gets here, then I believe I'll call Milly Leighton and set up a bridge party."

Life goes on as usual, Hazel thought. And then: well, why shouldn't it? What good was a sleepless night of fear? It hadn't made them healthy, wealthy, or wise, as her father was fond of saying. And it certainly hadn't made them happier—or safer.

"Sister Denk, have you folded those linens?" Matron asked sharply.

"In the cabinet there," Gloria answered without looking up from the leg wound she was cleaning. "That's going to heal up quickly," she reassured the soldier who had all his facial muscles clamped against the pain. He relaxed a little at the soothing sound of her voice and almost managed a smile.

There was the now-familiar rumble of a lorry outside the window. First the trucks had rolled out, filled with young men eager to finally start doing the job they'd been trained for. They'd been cocky and brazen, covering their fear with brash self-assurance. They'd saluted smartly, shouted cheerful vulgarities, and even struck up a song here and there as they disappeared up the road to Kota Baharu. But within a day and a half the lorries had started coming back, filled with painracked, groaning, blood-crusted boys.

Now, after fourteen straight hours on duty, Gloria finished wrapping the dressing, pulled the sheet up to the soldier's chin, and gave him a quick smile before heading briskly for the front entrance of the hospital. The driver, his own uniform blood-spattered, leapt out and ran around to let down the back flap and started shouting at the passengers in a broad Australian accent. "Come on now, mates, get your asses out. I got my schedule to keep up or the bus company will dock my pay. That's it. Right into the pretty nurse's arms. Hell of a way to get a bit of a cuddle, if you ask me."

Those who could get around on their own, the ones with head or arm injuries, crawled, jumped, or fell off and several stayed back to start helping the more seriously injured. A man with his right arm so severely shattered that shards of the bone showed through was handed down and draped over a nursing sister half his size. She supported his weight without apparent strain as she led him inside. The hospital orderlies started sliding the stretcher patients out. An officer with his head bandaged so that only one eye showed swayed and nearly fell as he got out of the lorry. "I'm a medic," he said. "We lost three on the way."

Gloria put her arm around his waist. "Inside with you," she said. "Good thing Aussies have such damned hard heads. I'll bet all you need is a haircut and a bit of stitching."

She got him inside under a good light and unwrapped the makeshift bandage. Her stomach churned. In her years of nursing, she'd seen a lot of disease and a good many accident victims, but that was nothing like the horror of unwrapping a bandage and finding the raw damage of war. The right side of this soldier's head was so covered with blood that it was impossible to guess the extent of the damage. Once he was lying down, he started fading away, slipping in and out of consciousness. "Where are you from?" Gloria asked as she started rinsing his face and scalp. He might well have a concussion. She had to keep him talking while she found out how bad it was.

"Melbourne—" he mumbled.

"Pretty place, I hear. I've never been there. Tell me about it." There was a long, open gash from the center of his forehead that ran down diagonally across his eye and deeply into his cheek. There was no sign of imbedded debris.

"Real pretty. Lots of flowers. My mother grows—"

"What does your mother grow?" Gloria asked loudly. "Turn your head a bit this way. That's it."

His eyelid was cut, but had already started swelling shut the gash. Impossible to tell if it was cut through. She gently lifted the swollen flesh and examined the eyeball. Extremely blood-shot, but no apparent surface damage. "You're luckier than you know, my friend,'' she said, smiling at him. ''Close the other eye. Can you see me?''

''Blurry—'' he breathed. ''You're pretty, too.'' His voice drifted off.

''That's all right. You'll be chasing us around the ward by tomorrow. You get a bit of a rest now.''

One of the doctors looked over her shoulder. ''Condition?'' he snapped. Gloria reported that the wounds were extensive but surface. ''You'll have to stitch him up, then,'' the doctor said.

''I'm not a doctor and this is his *face*,'' she objected.

The doctor glared at her. ''I've got a boy over here with half *his* face gone, Sister, and another with an arm that's hanging by a thread. Can you do this, or shall I ask someone else?''

''I'll do it.''

It took her nearly two hours. Matron had stopped twice to see how she was doing, but was too busy to help. There had been no sign of a doctor, as all four of them were in the operating theater. When Gloria finally finished the last stitch and tried to stand up straight, she realized she was nearly frozen into her half-bent position. ''Lean the rest of the way down, then stand up,'' Matron said from behind her. She peered at the sleeping medic's face with the dozens of tiny neat stitches. She nodded a curt and somewhat grudging approval. ''They need you in the operating theater.''

Gloria scrubbed hastily, donned mask and gloves, and slipped into the room. Dizzy with fatigue, she swayed and leaned back against the wall for a moment, closing her eyes and trying to dredge up some hidden source of energy. There were four tables set up with four operations going on. She could hear the harsh buzz of a saw cutting through bone, the hiss of the sterilizer, the clank of nickel-plated instruments, the crisp snap of rubber gloves, the shuffle of feet as exhausted doctors and nurses shifted from one leg to the other. The room stank of blood and ruptured bowels and sweat and was inhumanely hot from the glare of the big overhead lights. There was a clank as a severed limb was dropped into a metal bucket.

''Dinki? Is that you?'' a young doctor whose face was as white as his mask shouted across the theater at her. ''Get the hell over here with some more hemostats.''

Gloria pulled herself together and fished instruments out of the sterilizer. Laying them out on a sterile, towel-covered tray, she edged her way through doctors and nurses to the far table, where there was a man's body that looked like an explosion in a meat market. Intestines had been pulled out of the gaping wound in the abdomen and were looped over the sterile field of white cotton. Two sisters were carefully picking over the glistening mass, cleaning and searching for further perforations to be stitched shut. The surgeon was trimming away ragged edges of the man's stomach, trying to find a way to piece as much as possible of it back together. He flung small, rubbery bits into an enamel dish on the patient's chest. "I can't find his pancreas," he muttered. "I don't know where it is! I just hope to hell it's in here someplace."

A chaplain who was moving quietly through the theater stopped at the head of the table and put his fingers lightly to the patient's forehead. He murmured a prayer and moved on. The anesthetist suddenly bent over the rubber cone that covered most of the patient's face and with quite urgency said, "We've got a problem. His breathing—"

The surgeon stopped and hastily moved the enamel basin. It slipped out of his hand and bounced on the floor, spraying pieces of stomach tissue. He put his ear to the soldier's chest. "Shit!" He raised his fist and gave the sternum a sharp smack to shock the heart back into action. The blood that had welled in the abdominal cavity spurted up in clots on the nurses. The surgeon listened again, tried again, listened again. The anesthetist was already turning off the valves on his tanks and taking off the patient's mask.

"Dammit!" the surgeon said, his voice trembling with fury and defeat. "Dinki, get him out of here and send the next one."

The other sisters quickly dumped the intestines back into the body cavity and went to the corner of the room to strip off their gowns and throw them on the growing pile of blood- and feces-soaked linens. Gloria went to the foot of the wheeled table, let up the brake with her toe, and maneuvered the table through the wide doorway to the makeshift morgue. There were bodies there in rows. An orderly met her. "Help me, please, Harry. I've got to get this table back," she said.

It wasn't until she went to the head of the table to lift the dead man that she saw his face.

"Niles!" she gasped.

"You knew this guy?" the orderly asked.

Gloria had to gulp back the bile rising in her throat. "He proposed to me. Oh, no, not Niles—"

"Sorry, Dinki, but get a move on," the orderly said. "You take his feet if you'd rather."

There was no word from Ronald Hampton on Tuesday. But Wednesday morning a wire finally arrived. "Transportation muddled. Coming soonest. Keep safe. Xmas at home, loves. Ronald."

"Thank God!" Roberta said, handing Hazel the telegram and collapsing into a chair.

That evening they heard the news that the *Prince of Wales* and the *Repulse* had been sunk. "They couldn't be," Barbara said. "They were British warships!"

"Mother—" Hazel began.

"No! There's no need to panic about this," Roberta said, her voice shrill. "If there were any real danger, the government would be making arrangements to get people out. You know that's true. And look at this!" She waved a copy of that day's *Straits Times* in Hazel's face. "Do you see anything in this saying anybody should leave now? Besides, if the Japanese are all over the Pacific like some people are claiming, it would be far more dangerous to leave."

"Of course. You're absolutely right," Hazel said, deeply shaken by her mother's nearly hysterical tone.

"I have *such* a headache!" Roberta said, marching out of the room.

On Friday night Johnny Leighton came to call. His normally boyish face was drawn. "Hazel, have you heard from your father yet?" he asked in a hushed voice.

"Yes, didn't Mother tell you? She got a wire on Wednesday saying transportation was a mess, but he'd get her as soon as he could. We expect he ought to be here by tomorrow or the day after at the latest. Why?"

He put a finger to his lips and motioned her to come outside. "Don't want to alarm your mother. Know she's having a bit of a bad time as it is. Ought to tell you though before the papers do."

Hazel's heart was pounding in her ears. A small, unworthy part of her was thinking, why tell me? Why not let my mother protect me instead of the other way around? "What is it, Mr. Leighton?"

"I've just heard—well, the Japs have crossed the peninsula upcountry."

"Penang—?"

"And Butterworth. They say they've bombed George Town yesterday and there are hundreds dead."

"Yesterday? But there was nothing in the papers or on the radio. Surely this can't be right."

"Christ, Hazel! I hate to be telling you this. It could very well be wrong. We have to pray it is, but maybe it's true and there's some reason the government won't let the papers print it. If that's the case, you ladies have to get out of here."

"No." Roberta's voice came from the open doorway. She wasn't shrill now. Her voice was flat and dead. "I'll send the girls on the next ship, but I'm not leaving without Ronald."

"Roberta, you've got to be sensible. Ronald wouldn't want that," Leighton said. "It looks damned bad. The British and Dutch have withdrawn all their aircraft from Penang to defend Kuala Lumpur and Singapore. I've heard the Japs have taken the American garrison at Peking and they're landing in hordes on the Philippines. The Scots, Canadian, and Indian troops are rumored to be trapped on Hong Kong island. They've taken Guam and Thailand and God knows what else. This is the real thing and you're right in the middle of it."

"No, my husband is in the middle of it and I won't abandon him. Just as he wouldn't abandon us. But I would be grateful if you'd help me get the girls out."

Johnny Leighton made a wide, helpless gesture. "Roberta, I don't mean to be harsh, but you don't seem to understand yet. It's possible Ronald is d—"

Roberta cut across the word. "It's just as possible he wasn't even in George Town. He could have been out on the plantation. Or, more likely, he's just a few miles from here now on his way back. His wire said he'd come as soon as he could. Johnny, I appreciate your concern, but I absolutely will not leave here without my husband. If you'll just help me with the girls—"

"No, Mother," Hazel said. "We're not leaving without you." And as she was saying it, a frightened child's voice in the back of her mind was crying, *Make me go home. I don't want any of us to stay here.*

Johnny Leighton threw up his hands in a gesture of despair. "I'll come back tomorrow morning. I just hope by then you've come to your senses. All of you." He was thoroughly disgusted with these American women he'd taken upon himself to protect.

"Now, Hazel—" Roberta began as they went back inside.

"Mother, I see your point about waiting for Daddy. I'm not sure you're right to stay, but I do see why you feel you have to. But understand, we feel the same way about both of you. At least I assume I'm speaking for Barbara. We can't leave you behind."

Roberta slammed the door. "Hazel, I won't be spoken to in that manner by my own child. You and Barbara are leaving Singapore and that's that."

"We aren't and that's that," Hazel said calmly.

The battle between them raged furiously for two days, then less furiously for several more. And all the while there was no further word of or from Ronald Hampton. By that time soldiers and civilians who had been wounded in the attempt to defend Penang and Butterworth began to arrive at hospitals in Singapore and the newspapers finally reported the attack. It had been ferocious; hundreds killed, thousands more wounded. There had been no warning, no shelter, and no defense.

Hazel combed the hospitals, spending hours and hours trying to find her father or anyone who knew him or had any idea of his fate. She met with almost complete failure. Only one man, a British rubber plantation manager, had met him in Penang. "He came to look over our operation, miss. Very nice gentleman—for a Yank."

"When was that?"

"The day before the bombing."

"So he was there still. Did he say anything about leaving? Or about having received word from his family?"

"No cause to. I was just asked to show him our latex go-downs. Talked business."

Hazel pressed him, trying to make him recall every word of the conversation for any clues to her father's plans or whereabouts, but got nothing more except for the fact that Ronald Hampton had seemed worried and quiet. "But he could have had a train ticket for that very evening, couldn't he?" Hazel asked.

"Of course. I did, and I didn't mention it to him. No reason to."

Roberta was encouraged by this. Hazel suspected her mother would have found a way to be encouraged by anything she found out. "I'm certain now that he must have been out on the plantation, safely away from the bombing in the city. Naturally he'd be unable to contact us—a visiting American businessman would have very low priority on overloaded communication lines. I'm sure he's with the civilians we're hearing about who are working their way down the peninsula."

Hazel didn't remind her that what they were hearing was that the civilians were fleeing down the length of the peninsula being hotly pursued by the Japanese. Though a part of her was more of a realist than Roberta, Hazel wanted just as badly to believe her father was well—and much of the time she succeeded in convincing herself. After all, there are hundreds of people pouring into Singapore from the towns, mines, and plantations up-country; most of them were disheveled, frightened, and missing many possessions, but unharmed.

The hotels filled quickly with the upper-class Western refugees and those with large homes started taking in the overflow. Roberta agreed to take in two families, and when they moved in, they brought good news.

"Mrs. Hampton? We met a Donald Hampton at the train in Butterworth," one of the women said cheerfully when she was introduced.

"Are you sure it wasn't *Ronald* Hampton?" Roberta asked.

"Yes, I believe you're right. Is he your husband?"

"Oh, yes! Tall, with reddish hair and a space between his front teeth? Did he come on the same train, then?"

"No, sadly enough, he did not. We offered to share our compartment with him, but just as we were about to pull out of the station, some army officer put him off and gave us the most dreadful Indian soldier with a broken leg. An Indian, if you can believe it! In a first-class compartment—well, I suppose in times of crisis one has to let certain standards slip a bit, but—"

"But he was well? My husband. He wasn't injured?"

"Not a bit. I imagine he got on the next train. I wouldn't worry a bit about him, Mrs. Hampton."

Roberta burst into tears of relief, and their guest watched her emotional outburst with much the same disdainful expression she must have given the wounded soldier who threatened to bring down the Empire by polluting a first-class compartment with his presence. Fortunately, this guest stayed only two days before locating an old friend to move in with. She did manage, however, to convey in nasty, subtle ways that in her opinion this whole war was the fault of the Americans. In what way wasn't clear.

As the days passed, it became easier to accept Roberta's statement that this was a tempest in a teapot. After the first night of bombing, there had been no more attacks on Singapore. And following the announcement in the papers of the sinking of the two British warships, there had been little news of the progress of the war. A few of the more astute readers were able to trace the approach of the Japanese by the newspaper announcements of the Hong Kong and Shanghai Bank telling which branches upcountry had been "closed until further notice," but most of these people kept this ominous insight to themselves. Emmy and Barbara resumed their busy social round, but Emmy was no longer giving out tidbits from her father. Whether he had stopped talking in front of her or warned her to keep quiet didn't know.

Hazel received two letters from Frank, both written before December 7 and therefore comfortingly innocent of alarm. They were full of plans for their wedding, complaints about the weather, and talk about a professor who had given him trouble over a paper. He mentioned world events only fleetingly. "All this war talk has gotten to a couple of the guys here. They're thinking about trying to get into the army in a legal position. Good way to have a job and serve your country at once. Still, I think they're jumping the gun. I don't think we're going to get into Europe's war, no matter what the newspapers would like us to think. After all, their job is to sell news, so you can't blame them for blowing things out of proportion."

Hazel read the letters over and over and wrote back to him nearly every day, wondering just how many of her letters would get through—and when.

Life did go on. If it hadn't been for worrying about why Ronald still hadn't turned up in Singapore or wired them about his whereabouts, the Hampton women would hardly have known there was a war going on at all. There were no shortages of food or gasoline. House agents were still busily soliciting business, invitations were issued to Christmas parties, dressmakers ran up silk frocks for holiday entertaining. Shiploads of Western goods and mail from home entered Keppel Harbour unmolested. Every morning the Cold Storage van stopped to deliver milk. Virtually the only signs of war were the Australian troops who poured in through the city and immediately set out for the north.

And there was the well-meaning but disastrous attempt on the part of the municipal engineers to dig air raid trenches on the sports grounds. Johnny Leighton, restored to good cheer, reported on this effort. "They sent out a coolie crew to dig these great long trenches," he said. "Then the engineers came and looked and threw their hands in the air because the trenches were in neat, straight rows. Said they were traps in case of machine guns and had to be staggered. The coolies filled some in, dug new ones, then some hospital bloke came along and started carrying on something terrible about rain and mosquitoes breeding and whatnot, so the engineers ordered that all the trenches be filled *halfway* up. As if only half as many mosquitoes can breed that way. Bloody waste of a good field, I say. It'll be months before they can get it leveled out enough for a decent cricket game. As for polo—"

Hazel knew Johnny Leighton was something of a fool, but it was actually soothing to have someone around whose greatest concern was the well-being of polo ponies' legs. Neither he nor anyone else mentioned leaving Singapore. "Much more dangerous out at sea" was the accepted philosophy as frequently voiced by Johnny, who had conveniently forgotten his own warnings to them to get out. "Besides, we can't appear to run away, can we? The Japanese are stupid, backward little people who just got a bit of luck on their side when they attacked. It'll all be over in a month or so, you'll see."

They put Ronald's presents under the small Christmas tree and convinced themselves he'd be there to open them. They no longer pretended that they'd be home in the States by then.

Chapter 3

Christmas day was bleak. The Japanese army was flowing over Southeast Asia like lava. Penang and Butterworth had been lost; the American garrison in Peking had been taken prisoner; the Philippines were being overrun as were Borneo, Wake Island, and Burma. Thailand had already signed a treaty of alliance with Japan. On Christmas Eve there were air attacks on Rangoon, and when the Hampton women turned on the radio the next morning, they heard the report that Hong Kong had surrendered. This was a terrible morale blow. Everyone had believed that Hong Kong, like Singapore, couldn't be taken by the inferior little yellow men.

Roberta Hampton was beginning to look haggard. She'd lost weight and lines were appearing in her face where Hazel had never noticed them before. She was smoking twice as much as ever. Her temper had grown short and sharp. Normally serene in her outward manner, all the nervous energy she usually kept concealed had come to the surface and she was jumpy, frequently in tears. Hazel often came upon her pacing her bedroom or the long balcony, a cigarette in one hand, a drink in the other.

Barbara had changed, too. In her, fear and anxiety took on extreme selfishness. Still young and untried and never terribly sympathetic to the needs or feelings of others, she now became obsessed with her appearance and social life to the exclusion of all other considerations. Fortunately for her, there were still parties galore and she scurried from one to another like a crazed chipmunk in a roomful of peanuts.

Hazel found herself becoming increasingly irritated with both of them and felt guilty for the irritation. Still, if they would only occupy themselves with something worthwhile, they might be better able to cope with the situation. Her own work at the hospital, now taking ten or more hours every day, left her exhausted but satisfied and gave her little time for pointless speculation about her father or worry about Frank.

They opened their gifts listlessly that Christmas morning, in spite of Hazel's rather hectic attempt to create a cheerful atmosphere. But Ronald's gifts, unopened, sat under the tree like accusations. It would have been better to ignore the holiday entirely, Hazel thought as she tried the perfume Barbara had given her. Hazel loathed heavy, sweet perfume. Her mind kept going back to the last Christmas day. The house full of family and friends, wrapping paper and gifts strewn everywhere. There was political talk, of course, of Hitler and Poland, but Hazel had ignored it at the time and now preferred to remember the smell of the crackling fire and the cold gusts every time the door opened, and Frank kissing her under the mistletoe. That had been important, a sign that their affection was real and legitimate. Frank wouldn't have kissed her, not even a polite little peck, in front of her family unless he were serious. It was a month later that he'd proposed. She hated this Christmas for reminding her of that one.

"Mother, if you wouldn't mind too much, I'd like to pack up my dinner and take it along to the hospital," she said when the hideous gift business was done.

"Hazel! Not today. It's Christmas."

"I know, Mother, but I'm needed."

Barbara snorted.

"What does that mean?" Hazel snapped at her.

"Barbara probably fails to see why you feel those strangers need you more than we do," Roberta said, crumpling a ball of wrapping paper into a small knot.

"What on earth good will it do for me to sit around here all afternoon?" Hazel said, goaded beyond good sense. "You'll just pace around or play solitaire and Barbara will be off with her friends the minute she can get away. You'd both be far better off doing as I am—helping somebody else instead of wallowing in—"

"Wallowing! How dare you!" Roberta exclaimed. "Have you no concern whatsoever for you father?"

"Mother!" She came perilously close to asking how sitting

around knocking back gin slings illustrated a greater concern, but was glad she managed to bite back the words.

Roberta stubbed out a cigarette and said, "Oh, Hazel—I'm sorry. I don't know what I'm saying. Yes, of course, you must go on to the hospital."

The reconciliation was only a thin crust over a searing mass of discontent, but they took great care to preserve it. Hazel carved the turkey in her father's absence, and resented even that. *Why am I expected to do these "head of the family" things?* she thought to herself. She made her own share into a sandwich to carry along and eat on the way to work. The meat was dry and stringy and it was all she could do to choke it down.

Late that night, when she returned home, Barbara was waiting at the front door for her. "Barbie, what's wrong?"

"Nothing's wrong. Keep your voice down. I want to talk to you."

"Is it Mother? Father? What—?"

"Hazel, shut up! Just listen. Emmy's father is sending her and her mother to the States to a cousin or something—"

"The Conscience of the Empire? Letting down the side?" Hazel said, amazed.

"What are you talking about? Emmy's aunt is sick and her mother's afraid she might not get to see her again if she doesn't go to her now. The point is, there's a ship leaving the day after tomorrow and he can get tickets. He can get them for us as well, but only if we let him know first thing in the morning. Come out in the yard, where mother can't hear us."

It had rained heavily, but now the skies were clear as they picked their way to the little gazebo. Barbara spread her handkerchief on a wicker chair and sat down. Hazel, her khaki hospital uniform already sticky and dirty, didn't observe such niceties. "Have you talked to Mother about this?"

"I tried, but somebody was here earlier—a planter from George Town. He's been all this time working his way down-country."

"News of Father!"

"He said he'd met Daddy the day after the bombing and had brought a message to us. Just that he was unhurt and would be here as soon as he could. He was helping the army people get some damaged trucks repaired."

Ronald Hampton owned a highly lucrative family company that made railroad engine parts, but his hobby was restoring old cars. They'd left three of them in various stages of repair in the big garage in Evanston. There were probably few people better qualified to help get a disabled fleet of trucks moving again.

"And Mother is determined to stay and wait for him?" Hazel asked.

"More than ever. This afternoon she actually talked for the first time about leaving. I think she meant it, but after that man came—"

"Why didn't he send her a message to get out?"

"She wouldn't have listened to it. You know that. Besides, the man who came here said he had no idea of the real situation, how bad it is. We don't get much news, but apparently they'd gotten even less up there. Hazel, you've got to make her see that we have to get out of here. We've got a chance now. You know Daddy wouldn't want us to stay here."

Hazel rummaged in her purse and brought out a crumpled cigarette pack. She smoked only two or three cigarettes a day, but this called for one. She lit it and inhaled deeply. "Barbara, it's just as dangerous, probably more so, on the open sea than here."

"Maybe, but I'd rather take my chances in the hope of getting someplace safe, wouldn't you?"

"Yes, I would, but dammit! You know I can't make Mother leave any more than you can."

Barbara was silent for a long moment. The only sound was that of her long fingernails tapping nervously on the little table between them. "Hazel . . . why do we *all* have to stay?"

Hazel looked up sharply, but Barbara's face was in shadow and she couldn't read her expression. "Are you suggesting that we should go off and leave Mother here alone?"

"Well—not both of us."

"But you should go?"

"Or you. We could flip a coin."

"That's a hideous thought. People don't decide important things by flipping coins."

"Have you got a better way?"

There was a soft *clink* and Hazel looked down at the shiny American dime Barbara had put on the table. So Barbara had already planned out this whole conversation. Hazel didn't touch the coin. "I don't know. Let me think—"

"Hazel, there's not that much to think about. You know there's no way to get Mother to leave—"

"True."

"And there's no reason both of us must wait with her."

A monkey, startled out of sleep by some unseen disturbance, scampered across the yard in front of them. Barbara shivered. "I hate those nasty little things."

"I don't see how either of us can go. I've got work to do. I know you and Mother don't think it's important, but it is. And you—you're too young to be scuttling across the world by yourself."

"I wouldn't be my myself. Emmy and her mother—"

"You want to go, don't you?" Hazel asked.

Barbara looked at her with genuine surprise. "Of course I do. I'm not crazy! There's a war and we're in the middle of it. You want out, too. You can't pretend you're so noble that you like it here."

"Yes, I want to get out, but not this way."

"This way? Hazel, we aren't being given a lot of choices. This is the only way there is."

She's right, Hazel thought. *I want to be the one who goes home, but I couldn't live with myself if I did. And it's up to me.* Barbara was silent, waiting for Hazel's opinion. She was the older one, the sensible one; Barbara would go along with whatever she said, even if it meant staying in Singapore.

Hard as she tried, it was impossible to justify leaving Barbara—dithery, self-centered Barbara—to be their mother's comfort and support. Roberta was too distraught to make intelligent choices, and Barbara was too impractical. God only knew what sort of muddle they'd get into by themselves in a foreign country in the middle of a war. But there was no reason for both of them to stay. In fact, Mother might be easier to manage without Barbara flitting around, Hazel thought, sighing wearily. If only it weren't so damned hot, maybe her mind would clear. "All right. One of us should go home."

"Which one?" Hazel could hear the hope in Barbara's voice.

"You."

Barbara let out a long breath. "What about Frank?"

"Don't talk to me about Frank!" Hazel all but shouted. She hesitated, getting a grip on herself. "Look, Barbara, I'm not volunteering to stay here forever: if this man who came to see Mother just got to Singapore, there's every chance that Father is only a day or two behind him. We'll all get home, but there's no reason we have to go together. You should be the one, since you've got the opportunity to go along with Emmy and her mother.'' She didn't believe a word she was saying.

"I still think we should flip a coin. It's the only fair way."

"It's a stupid way. Barbara, go along and tell Mother what we've decided. I'll be in shortly."

Barbara started back to the house, but got only a few steps before running back and hugging Hazel. "Thank you," she whispered, her voice shaking.

Hazel sat for a long while, pushing the dime around the tabletop with her finger. Finally she picked it up. "Heads I go. Tails Barbara goes," she said to herself as she dropped the coin. It bounced, rolled in a big circle, then toppled over with a tiny whirring sound. Hazel bent over to look at it.

Heads.

Emmy's father worked a wonder for them. Not only did he manage tickets for his wife and daughter and Barbara on a ship sailing for Australia, he got them places on an army transport plane that was to leave for Los Angeles the day they were to dock. Barbara would be home—or at least in her home country—in a matter of days. Once there, the Wadsworths' relatives would see that she got safely to Chicago and Roberta's brother and his wife would look after her there. "I'll probably have to ride the airplane in a crate," Barbara said as she stuffed the last of her dresses into a trunk.

"Barbara, I'm sorry I can't come to the ship with you, but I've got to work today," Hazel said, handing her a pair of stockings that had been left out.

The younger woman rolled them into a ball and tucked them into the toe of a pair of pink satin pumps. "It's just as well you and Mother aren't coming to the ship. I hate good-byes and Emmy's father says the docks are a madhouse. Hazel, is there anything you want me to tell Frank when I see him?"

"Nothing I haven't said in my letters to him. Anyway, I'll be along right behind you." Hazel looked away, as if searching for anything else Barbara might have forgotten to pack.

The matron was fuming when Hazel got to work. "I had no idea you weren't going to be in at your usual time," she said. She was standing at the door of the storeroom in the midst of a vast pile of cartons and paper-wrapped parcels.

"I did call and leave a message. I was saying good-bye to my sister."

"Well, the message wasn't delivered, but this was. All of this!"

Hazel felt herself flushing unattractively with humiliation. *At least she can't fire me, since I'm a volunteer,* she told herself. "Don't worry, I'll get it all put away."

"No, you won't. It's not ours. That's the point. It's linens for the Tan Tock Sen and the First Malayan General at Johore. If you'd been here, you'd have known that and made the driver take them on where they were meant to go. As it is, I can't get anybody to come back for them."

"Maybe the other hospitals—"

"Tan Tock Sen doesn't have people to spare and the First Malayan is afraid they might have to evac at a moment's notice and don't want any of their vehicles out of sight."

"Don't we have anybody who can take them up?" The Tan Tock Sen, Hazel knew, was at the north of the island of Singapore and the First Malayan General was just across the causeway to the peninsula, no more than twenty or thirty miles, if that.

"We have more vehicles than anyone knows what to do with, but the only person I could spare as a driver is that horrid Cedric, and I can spare him only because he's too stupid to be of any use. I couldn't trust him to find the way. Miss Hampton, I'm sorry to be brusque with you. I know this isn't your fault—"

"In a way it is. And I think I have a solution, too. Send me."

"You? A young woman alone on the roads? Certainly not."

"Why not? You can send Cedric along as the brute force. I can drive a truck and follow a map."

"You might be able to drive it, but there's too much danger of a breakdown and with everything at such sixes and sevens—"

"But I could fix it. Honestly. Matron, my father's hobby is fixing up old cars, and I've helped him since I was little. I've spent hundreds of hours with my head in an engine."

It took a good deal of further argument, but at last Hazel convinced the matron. And all the while a plan was forming in the back of her mind. At first she tried to ignore it, but it grew in appeal.

Another one of them had died. That was three of the fourteen of them gone. Gloria Denk cursed under her breath as she folded the once-handsome young man's hands over his chest. The lorry jolted through a pothole and the hand dropped. Gloria glanced around the dim interior. The rest of them were sleeping or unconscious. Dear God, this was a terrible thing to be doing to already-dying men. She ought to be using her skills to try to save them, or at least comfort them in their last hours instead of dragging them about in this hideous lorry down this long, hideous road. But then, the alternative would have been far worse. Another twenty-four hours and the hospital would have been taken by the enemy. They'd have probably all been shot in their beds if they'd stayed.

If only she could get one good solid night's sleep, then maybe she'd feel less depressed and unraveled. Exhaustion and nerves were making her shaky and even confused. She'd lost track of days since they'd been on the road and sometimes got the men's names wrong. That made her feel the worst: when a man was dying, his name was all he had left. It was sacrilege to get it wrong.

The lorry lurched again, pulled to the left, speeded up for a moment, then ground to a groaning halt. Gloria stumbled to the back and opened the khaki flaps. They'd pulled out of the crawling line of traffic into a small lay-by. They'd be another hour squeezing back in, but they all needed a rest. The driver, a Malay medic they called Joe, came around and gave her a hand down. As she jumped, she felt as if every bone in her body was protesting. "Lorry, it not working right, Sister. I look at engine."

"Flag down someone else in our convoy, Joe. We have to keep together."

"Other all ahead, Sister. Sorry."

"We're the last in line? Damn. Well, hurry up and look it over, Joe. We have to catch up by this evening."

She looked back into the lorry. No one needed her attention for the moment. Several needed more than she could give, and at least one was beyond anyone's help. She bent over hoping to pull some of the twists and cricks out of her back, but it didn't help.

She walked away into the small clearing. A big log had rolled off some lorry and was lying alongside the edge of the clearing like a bench. It hadn't started the inevitable, voracious rotting process yet, so she sat down on it. At least it wasn't raining at the moment, she thought, trying to find something good about the situation. The rainy days had been by far the worst. The rain always found a way to pour into the lorry through the canvas roof and drip on the men in shock or those shivering with malaria, never cooling the feverish ones who needed it. It had added the reek of mildew to the stench of death and sickness.

Gloria could hardly focus her eyes, but couldn't afford to fall asleep. Instead, she forced herself to concentrate on the traffic inching by. There were other lorries like hers, big, lumbering, canvas-clad ones full of wounded and ill soldiers, but most of the vehicles were private cars—planters from upcountry with suitcases and crates strapped on top, station wagons stuffed to bursting with clothing and dishes and children's toys. Every little gap in the procession was filled with top-heavy bicycles, rickshaws, hand-drawn carts, and native wagons being dragged forward by carabaos—the big, slow, water buffalo of Malaya.

Gloria found her mind wandering into trivialities. It seemed, watching this desperate parade, that the whites were ill equipped for flight. They didn't know how to efficiently pack up their worldly goods. The Malays were better at it, and the Chinese who passed were the best. They appeared to be able to load up a wagon with everything they might ever need in this or the future life and then stick two or three tiny children on the top of the tottering heap to cling like little moneys as the wagon lurched along. Or maybe the children were tied on—she hoped so.

Where on earth will they all wind up? Will *we* all wind up? she wondered, closing her eyes for just a moment against the glare of a sudden shaft of sunlight that found its way through the dense jungle cover. Just so long as she didn't end up back in Australia. She wasn't sure she had the strength to get away from there twice.

She woke suddenly when Joe shook her. She'd toppled over sideways and the bark of the tree was biting into her cheek. The sun was gone and a drizzling rain was falling. "Sister, *mem*, the lorry is broken good."

She sat up, disoriented for a moment. "Joe, you *must* fix the lorry."

"Too much broken, Sister. Big hole in petrol tank. Cannot fix, *mem*."

It was too much. Gloria stood up, blinking back tears of frustration. They must have hit a rock in that last big jolt before they stopped. "Do you mean to say it's just standing there in a pool of petrol? The first boy who lights a cigarette is going to blow us all to kingdom come. Dammit, Joe!" She raced back to the lorry and hoisted herself up. Only one man was awake and well enough to smoke. Gloria snatched the cigarette away from him and handed it out to Joe. "Take it far from here and put it out. Private Colley, if you light up again, we'll be knocked clear to Singapore."

"Not sure that's such a bad idea," the boy said, smiling weakly at her. "Get the ride over with."

Gloria went to the road and managed to stop the next military transport that passed. "We need some help here," she told the driver, who grinned down at her. "I've got a body and eleven casualties and my lorry is sitting in a lake of petrol."

"Put those fags out, boys," the driver shouted back as he pulled the vehicle over to the side and climbed down. He commandeered three other men to help push Gloria's lorry out of danger and took four of her most severely injured soldiers into his. He didn't have room for the rest.

Gloria spent the next two hours alternately tending her soldiers and stopping traffic. An overloaded ambulance pulled over and waited for her to fill out the paperwork of death, then took the dead soldier. A staff car took two of the live ones. A woman doctor with a carload of Malayan orphans took another. That left Gloria with four soldiers, Joe, and a broken lorry. And it was growing late.

As she stepped back to the roadside, she heard a commotion beyond the curve in the road. While this was theoretically a two-way thoroughfare, both lanes were now taken up with south-bound traffic, but there were troops going north, and every time a convoy came along, there was a terrible din of horns and shouts and all the traffic had to squeeze back onto one side to make room for them to pass. People started pulling over, fenders grated, tempers flared, shouts were exchanged, and in a few minutes the huge lorries started to lumber past in a long chain. Gloria waited for the last in the line and all but stepped in front of it, waving her arms and shouting. "I need help. I'm stranded with injured soldiers," she said to the glowering driver.

"I ain't turnin' 'round, Sister," he replied.

"No, I know that. But I've got to feed these boys tonight and I've lost my convoy along with our food."

"Awright, but get your ass out of my way, toots." As the gears meshed and the lorry rumbled back into motion, a crate of rations was heaved out the side and onto the lay-by.

Behind Gloria there was another cacophony of horns and

shouting, but she paid no attention. It wasn't until she'd pried the lid off the box that she noticed there had been a small lorry squeezed in behind the big one and it had now pulled off the road. "Don't stop there," Gloria shouted. "The ground is soaked with petrol." The small lorry backed up and the driver got out. It was a young woman with thick reddish hair and a rumpled khaki uniform without any insignia. *God help us, another do-gooder volunteer,* Gloria thought.

"Can I help you?" the woman said, walking forward with long strides.

"Not the direction you're going."

"I'm turning back."

Gloria looked up. "Oh?"

The redhead extended her hand. "I'm Hazel Hampton."

"Gloria Denk. Sister Denk. Glad to meet you, Miss Hampton," Gloria said, rising and taking Hazel's hand in a firm grip. "What's that uniform and what are you doing on this road? You talk like a Yank."

Hazel sighed. "I'm a civilian hospital volunteer. Supplies, not nursing. I was—well, I was looking for my father, but I had no idea how hard it was going to be to go upcountry. I'm going back. Do you need a fire to heat this stuff up? I'm a good fire-builder."

"I'd rather have a good mechanic, but a fire would help. Is that lorry of yours full?"

"Empty. What do you need a mechanic for?"

Gloria explained her predicament and was astonished when the redhead offered to crawl under the lorry and take a look at the problem. Heedless of the wet ground, she lay down and scooted under the vehicle. "No, there's no fixing it here," she shouted back out a moment later, her voice echoing oddly. "Has to be drained and put on a lift to be welded."

There was a muttering and communal groan from the four men remaining in the truck who'd been listening to this exchange. "Can you take me and my blokes back to Singapore, then?" Gloria asked as Hazel reemerged, her hands greasy.

"Of course. Now, let's see about a fire. I hope you'll feed me—and Cedric," she added, remembering her doltish companion who'd been patiently sitting in the truck all this time. She motioned to him to get out and join her.

They got a meal together and sat in a row along the log to eat. Gloria's four remaining soldiers were the most fit of an unfit lot, and the break from the jolting traffic had revived them some-what. One of them started humming and the rest joined in a few songs. "If we wait about an hour, the traffic will thin out some. It usually does after dark," Gloria told Hazel. "I don't like to push someone who's doing a favor, but I need to get these boys to Singapore as soon as possible. Do you mind if we drive all night? Joe can help out. He's a good driver."

"I don't mind at all. In fact, I need to get the truck back. I'm probably in a lot of trouble about it. You see, I was supposed to go only as far as the First Malayan General in Johore, but—"

"—you *stole* that lorry!" Gloria exclaimed admiringly. "There must be more to you than it looks like."

"If that means I don't look like a thief, I consider it a com-pliment, but I didn't really steal it, I just—just—well, yes. I guess I stole it."

"That's bloody grand of you!"

Hazel smiled. "I don't think Matron will feel quite that way, but thanks."

"So, where were you going with it?" Gloria asked.

"I was hoping to meet my father coming down the road. He was in Penang when it was bombed and my mother is frantic with worry. I suppose I thought there would be fifty or a hundred people along the road, and I'd just give him a lift. It was awfully naive of me, and now my mother is probably on the verge of nervous collapse because I've disappeared, too. I sent her a note, asking for a change of clothes and saying I'd be gone a day or two and it's been four."

"I guess you didn't find your father—" Gloria was beginning to revise her impression of this Yank and warm to her. She'd been taken in at first by her awkward, overweight shyness and assumed she was one of the helpless, interfering sorts. But she appeared to be a pretty nervy, determined woman.

Hazel gestured helplessly toward the tide of humanity crawl-ing past them. "In this? No. For all I know, we passed each other. Who *are* all these people? I wouldn't have thought there were this many people in the whole of Southeast Asia."

"The Europeans are planters, engineers, tin-mine owners, clerks, secretaries, teachers—anything a white man can do to make money in the jungle. The Indians are mainly civil ser-vants, and the Malays and Chinese are the people who work the plantations and mines. Then there's us—the wounded and their nurses coming back from the front and falling back to Singapore for investment.''

"Investment?''

Gloria glanced at her with some pity and lowered her voice to a whisper. "It's the army word for siege. We're not supposed to use it. You didn't hear me say it.''

Hazel looked out into the soggy twilight. "Is that what's going to happen?'' she asked softly so the soldiers wouldn't hear.

"Probably,'' Gloria answered bluntly.

They set out about nine in the evening. Joe and Cedric helped them get the soldiers and all their gear into Hazel's "borrowed'' truck. Joe took the first driving shift while Hazel and Gloria got naps in the back. Hazel's last bemused thought was that she was sleeping with four men. What *would* her mother think to see her daughter stacked like cordwood with a truckload of soldiers? This was one of the adventures she probably wouldn't tell Frank about.

They stopped again about three in the morning and Hazel, after relieving her bladder in the jungle at the side of the road (at a dangerously modest distance from the traffic), took over the wheel. Gloria, having changed some bandages, dispensed medicines, and ascertained that her charges were doing as well as could be expected, joined her in the cab of the truck, but soon fell back asleep. When the sun came up, she came back to life and offered to drive, but she handled the truck with such wild abandon that Hazel feared for the lives of everyone on the road.

"Sister Denk, I don't mean to criticize, but''—Hazel paused as they brushed by a cart, dislodging some pots and pans strung along the side—"you're scaring me to death.''

Gloria took it well. "Then I'll ride back with the boys for a while. It's time again for medications anyway.'' She pulled over and Hazel thought for a second that the truck was going to go over onto its side in the steep ditch.

Gloria disappeared, Hazel scooted over, and a moment later one of the soldiers joined her. "I'm Private Colley, ma'am. Dinki said I could come up here with you,'' he said, his voice dim and flat with illness.

Hazel found just how ill he was five miles later when he suddenly clawed at the door as if trying to get out. Clutching the wheel with one hand, Hazel grabbed him and pulled him back. He turned to say something and, instead, threw up all over her. Retching, Hazel cranked the steering wheel and stomped on the brakes. The truck following too close behind bumped into them, but she didn't even notice. Somehow, in spite of her own nausea, Hazel managed to pull him out of the truck and was holding him up by the waist like a rag doll as he continued to vomit when Gloria took over. The soldier was cleaned up and put back onto the bed of the truck, then Gloria, Joe, and Cedric formed a circle and held up a sheet to form a tiny dressing room for Hazel to change in. Changing, of course, merely meant putting back on her alternate set of clothes that were already filthy. Bathing wasn't an option.

Their hopes of reaching Johore by that night were fulfilled, but since Hazel had dropped off the misdirected linens, the hospital had packed up and evacuated to the Selerang Barracks at Changi on Singapore island. There was, therefore, no medical aid for the soldiers, but at least the utilities were still functioning and they were all able to bathe and sleep for a few hours on clean sheets before moving on.

Gloria was in a desperate hurry now. Her supplies of medicine were running low, and one of her patients had developed a septic arm, which was swelling alarmingly. "I think it's gas gangrene," she told Hazel. "It means slicing into the muscles to let the gas escape. I don't have the scalpels or the anesthetic, not to mention the skill. I have to get him to a doctor."

They set out before dawn and got across the causeway onto the island itself before stopping for a short rest. It would have normally been an hour's easy drive. It had taken them six hours and brutally aggressive driving on Joe's part. After a hasty lunch they crowded back onto the road and started on the last stretch with Hazel at the wheel. The soldier who'd gotten so sick the day before asked to ride with Hazel again. "I'm awful sorry about yesterday, Miss Hampton. I'm better now. Really better. I promise. But I'm near to crazy looking up at that canvas. I want to look at the road."

"Hop in," Hazel said with a forced smile. She kept glancing uneasily at him for the first mile or two. *If he does it again, I'll just throw myself out the door into traffic and end it all,* she thought. But eventually she relaxed. His color was good today, and he did genuinely seem to be better.

"I feel bad taking up the room with these guys," he said. "They've all got wounds; I just got some damn bug in my guts."

"You weren't in the fighting, then?" Hazel asked, maneuvering around an open truck full of young Chinese men with grimy, frightened features. Tin miners, she assumed.

"Yes, I was. But I got off lucky. I'll tell you, Miss Hampton, it was scarier than I thought anything could be. I ain't no military man, never wanted to be, but even I can see there's things wrong. I mean, look at all this stuff going up the road—"

"What do you mean?"

"Look at our men. They've got six layers of clothes; big, heavy weapons; packs full of mosquito netting; and more food and water than they'll ever have a chance to get down their gullets. I came out from Winnipeg, and was given a hundred-pound pack and a rubber rain poncho. I nearly died inside the thing, what with the heat. But the Japs—the Japs don't have nothing but nerve. Our guys sweat and strain and trudge along like pack mules, but the Japs are practically in their underwear. They don't care about the rain or the heat and they ain't scared of snakes and tigers and all in the jungle. Swear to God, Miss Hampton. Me and some buddies got pinned down and a bunch of Japs came along this plantation road. They was wearing shorts and singlets and little caps. That's all. Each of 'em had one gun and a canteen and they were riding bicycles."

"Bicycles? Through the jungle?"

"Right. The tires had busted, so they just went along on the bare rims. Made a godawful noise on this sort of gravel path, but it didn't bother them none. I never heard a noise like that and I hope I never do again. Miss Hampton, if you ask me, white people don't belong out in this place, not so long as they think like white people."

"But it's your duty to obey orders," Hazel pointed out.

"Yes, ma'am, and when I'm over this bug, I'll do what I got to do, but that don't mean I have to think it's smart."

"Private Colley, you aren't meant to be a soldier. You're a philosopher. You just summed up for me what I'm doing here. I've been wondering."

Hazel left Gloria and her charges at Changi, and as she was climbing wearily back into her stolen truck, Gloria caught up with her. "The doctor thinks he can save Private Robinson's arm. I thought you'd want to know and I wanted to thank you for helping us out. I can tell you're not used to this sort of thing."

"Is anyone?"

"No, I guess not. But you did a fine thing, bringing us back.
A couple of boys owe you their lives. If you get in a dust-up
about the lorry, you just say that. I hope we'll meet again."

"I hope it's in happier circumstances."

"Bound to be."

Chapter 4

Singapore had been spared more bombing in December after
the initial attack on the eighth, but throughout January it became
a disheartening daily occurrence. At first the raids happened
only at night, and the daily round could go on as usual, but by
mid-month the enemy was brazenly attacking at all hours. They
focused on military installations and the Chinese district of the
city, so life for Hazel and the other non-Asians in the suburbs
continued much as it had, except for the blood-chilling whine
and concussion of the bombs. As Hazel traveled around the city,
however, she saw ample evidence of what was happening to the
rest of Singapore. There were hundreds of funerals a day, hospitals and orphanages filled and overflowed, and whole neigh-
borhoods had been reduced to smoking, tangled debris.

A doctor who was treating Sister Denk's soldiers had actually
taken a moment to call at the Kerbau Kerbang Hospital and
praise Hazel's efforts before her interview with Matron Wins-
low. Because of that, she hadn't been in nearly the trouble she
anticipated over "unauthorized use" (as Matron put it) of the
truck. Instead of being sent back to her little office and storeroom, Hazel was given a new assignment. Now her primary job
for the hospital was to help set up and periodically arrange to
move the clinics that were improvised to dispense free typhoid

innoculations. With the elaborate and desperately needed drain-
age and sewage system damaged in places, disease posed a
greater immediate threat to the citizens of Singapore than the
Japanese.

She didn't get off so easily with Roberta, however. "For four
whole days I had no idea where my husband or either of my
children were!" Roberta raged tearfully. "Didn't you even think
for a moment what you were doing to me, Hazel? Someday
you'll be a wife and mother and perhaps you'll understand how
horrible that was for me."

"I'm sorry, Mother. Really sorry. I just thought I could find
Father for you."

"But you *didn't*!"

"No, I didn't," Hazel replied.

On the nineteenth, a sodden Monday morning, Colonel
Wadsworth phoned with the news that Barbara, Emmy, and his
wife were safely in the U.S. "It's time for us to go, Mother,"
Hazel said.

"You know I can't, Hazel. There are still people arriving
from George Town."

"Mother, I've gone up to the causeway twice this week, asking people who come across for news and they're all from Kuala
Lumpur and Kuantan now. Those are far south of Penang. The
British Far East fleet headquarters have been moved to Java, and
all the bombers on the island are being taken to Sumatra. Don't
you see what that means?"

It meant, of course, that Ronald Hampton was either dead or
captured, but Hazel couldn't put it into words.

Roberta couldn't even think it. "Hazel, you're just being an
alarmist. If there were actual danger other than the stray bomb,
the government would have ordered an evacuation. Isn't that
true? Isn't it?" she demanded.

"I know—it seems true. But can't you see that you're not
helping Father by staying here. If he knew we were in danger,
he'd be frantic."

Roberta folded the newspaper she'd been reading, then folded
it again, carefully creasing the edges with a fingernail. Hazel
noticed her nail polish was chipped, a cosmetic flaw Roberta
would never have allowed in the past. Hazel felt a wave of panic
over that one tiny detail that seemed suddenly to symbolize the
disintegration of the family. "Hazel, don't you see what you're
doing to me? I must be here when your father returns. I must.

But there's no reason why you should stay. Go home, Hazel. Go back to Evanston and your dear, dear Frank. Let me look after myself. I'm perfectly capable.''

"I know you are," Hazel lied, "but just as you feel it's your duty to stay and wait for Father, it's my duty to wait for you.''

They'd been over this ground so many times that they were like a pair of worn-out old actresses mouthing words from a script that was so familiar it barely had meaning anymore. Neither had anything to say that hadn't been flung back and forth with varying degrees of heat a dozen times, but they finished the dispirited argument anyway. As always, it ended in a draw.

That afternoon's mail brought a letter from Frank, the first Hazel had received that was written after the war started. The tone was a mixture of panicked concern for her and boyish enthusiasm for going to war himself. "I know people in our circle are calling this Roosevelt's war, but after all, those were our men killed at Pearl Harbor. Your own friend next door was on the *Arizona* and Roosevelt didn't kill him, the Japs did. Nobody can say of that 'It's just politics.' It was a terrible act that America has to avenge.''

He had, as Hazel feared, signed up for the navy the Monday morning after the bombing, but to her great relief there was something wrong with one of his ears and he was distressed that he might not be approved for overseas duty.

"Thank God," she whispered before reading on.

As for their marriage plans, he said, they would have to be changed somewhat. He didn't know how soon he'd be able to get a leave or for how long, but they'd manage it somehow. "I'm sorry to have made this important decision without being able to consult with you, but I was certain you'd have wished me to join up and do my duty to my country.''

For a moment Hazel felt a sense of regretful superiority to Frank. He was saying these things from a position of safety and insulation, not in the midst of the actual fiery fact of war. He hadn't seen people's homes turned into smoldering ruins in an instant; he didn't know what a young soldier with his arm blown off looked like or felt like. Frank had never awakened in the middle of the night to the thunder and acrid stench of bombing or heard the terrible wailing of women who'd seen their children killed.

And yet, had she been at home instead of here and merely heard of the atrocity of the attack on Pearl, she would have agreed with him—she would have felt a proud sense of romantic martyrdom at being "the girl he left behind" to fight for his country. She'd read the text of the President's speech to Congress asking for a declaration of war. The way he'd put it, there was no question. The United States had to fight back. It didn't matter what had provoked the Japs, if anyone really had. What mattered was what they had done.

She reread the part of the letter about his ear, then put the letter down and stared out the window. For the first time since this horror began, she felt a mild sense of relief. An almost lawyer with an ear problem would certainly be given a safe posting—wouldn't he? Maybe a Washington office job. She'd be home in a few months and they could marry wherever he was stationed. It didn't matter if they had a big wedding, though she'd been looking forward to filling the big house in Evanston with friends and family. Nor did a honeymoon matter. A weekend alone in a house of their own would be fine, and then they'd get on with life. If only Father would turn up and they could get home, everything would work out fine.

If the navy didn't cure his ear.

Nobody could quite understand how Sister Denk managed to get all her patients on the ship to Australia and miss getting on it herself. The other nurses thought it was mildly funny; Matron Eagleton was furious, certain that Gloria had done it on purpose. Although a reason why the girl would *want* to stay in Singapore instead of going home eluded her.

"I just don't know," Gloria said. "One minute the ship was there and the next time I looked—it was just gone."

"Sister Denk, you make a great mistake in assuming I'm a fool," Matron Eagleton said coldly. "A troop transport ship doesn't just drift away silently in a few seconds."

"I'm certain you're right," Gloria said with an expression of perplexity. "Still, I'm sure you can find something to do with me since I am still here."

"Yes, I'm sending you to Singapore General Hospital."

"But that's civilian. I'm army."

"A distinction that no longer applies. They're being overwhelmed and need all the help they can get. I'll see that you're evacuated with the next sailing of wounded."

Once she was dismissed, Gloria went to the hospital canteen for a cup of coffee. Grinning, she sipped on the hot brew. "They aren't getting me on a bloody boat to Australia while there's a white woman left in Singapore,'' she said to herself.

Every morning when Hazel awoke, she glanced first at her little desk calendar on her dressing table. It seemed that she'd been looking at the January 1942 page forever. The air was so wet from the driving monsoons that the paper had actually begun to crinkle from the humidity and heat. That single page of paper grew to have a certain symbolism in her mind. When it was time to tear it off, they would go. She didn't know how she'd make it happen, but she and her mother would leave. In her desperation, she was starting to have desperate ideas. She might have to find a lawyer and get her mother declared incompetent and haul her home as a mental patient. No, Roberta would never forgive her that. Perhaps some doctor could prescribe something that would lay her low physically without actual harm and she could get her on a ship strapped to a litter.

Hazel knew that her father wasn't going to get to Singapore. She hadn't any proof, any news, but she had the certainty that he loved them as much as they loved him, and if there were any way he could have gotten back, he would have by now. It had been seven weeks, almost eight since the war started, and they'd had only two messages from him, early on.

On Saturday, January 31, she rose as always and said to herself, *This is the last day.* But by that night she still hadn't come up with a way of convincing, or forcing, her mother to give up waiting. She went to bed late but couldn't sleep. There was heavy bombing that night, and the noise plus her nerves kept her twitching and thrashing. Thoroughly awake before dawn, she got up and paced the garden next to the house for an hour. Then she dressed and made one more trip to the causeway. She had a premonition—a phenomenon she didn't believe in—that there would be some news of him there today. Somebody would come across the long road to the mainland with a letter from him, or perhaps Ronald himself would be among the throngs that were always crowded onto the road.

But she was still some miles away when she realized that this morning was very different. Not only was the sun shining from a clear blue sky, the likes of which hadn't been seen since before the war began, but the traffic coming toward her today was of a different composition entirely. There were practically no civilians. It was all military traffic—truck convoys, ambulances, staff cars, tanks. She was moving against a tide of thousands of soldiers. An overloaded troop train rolled south along the railway next to the road.

This was a vast military retreat.

Investment . . . siege. The words kept running through her mind as she struggled to drive the little rented Morris along the very edge of the road.

Finally the density of the traffic forced her to abandon the car. She pulled onto a soggy, grassy area a few hundred feet from the causeway and walked. As she got close enough to see the water of the Johore Strait and the long, low landbridge, a heavily armed soldier stopped her. "You can't go any farther, miss." He was no more than eighteen and looked like he'd never shaved. He was trying to sound tough and official, but his voice quavered a little. *He's as scared as I am,* Hazel thought.

"What's happening here?" Hazel asked, but it was a silly question. She knew the answer; she had to hear it anyway.

"This is a withdrawal from the mainland, ma'am."

"Then Singapore's cut off—?"

"In about half an hour it will be."

"What's that?" Hazel asked, turning her head to hear better. It was the heartbreaking skirl of bagpipes.

"That's the commander and pipers of the Argyll and Sutherland Highlanders, ma'am. They brought up the rear of the retreat. They're the last to cross."

The last to cross.

Hazel stood by the young man for a long while, feeling that perhaps he needed her support as much as she needed his at this terrible hour. As the pipers came into view, the soldier spoke again, almost as if he were talking to himself. "There were almost nine hundred of them a month ago. Now there's only ninety left. A smart bloke in my outfit says that's what decimated really means. One in ten left."

Just ahead of the pipers, men hurried along, unrolling wire. The pipers finally reached the island and the pipes died with a mournful groan. As Hazel watched, everyone turned to look back, and at that instant there was a terrific explosion at the middle of the causeway. A great cloud of dust and debris rose into the air. Sections of railroad track and ties hurtled outward like matchsticks. Jagged blocks of cement flew up, tumbling end over end before landing in the water with huge splashes.

Hazel and the soldier stood watching for long moments, then she put her hand on his arm. "Good luck to you," Hazel said.

"And to you, miss," he said.

As Hazel recounted what she'd seen that morning to her mother, Roberta stood at the door to the balcony, staring out at the sunlit garden and listening impassively.

". . . and then the causeway was blown up. The road and the railway. Nobody else can come into Singapore now," Hazel finished. She was braced for anything—argument, outrage, tears.

But Roberta surprised her. Closing the louvered doors carefully, she came back and sat down across from Hazel. She crossed her legs and laced her fingers together on her knee, then she said with composure, "Then that's it. We must go home. I'll call Johnny Leighton and ask how best to go about getting away."

Hazel could have danced with relief. This was her old familiar mother back again at last.

Unfortunately, once the decision was made, the implementation of it was much harder than Hazel had anticipated. Normal passenger service on the shipping lines had been seriously disturbed, and in some cases curtailed. Keppel Harbour was full of big ships, but most of them were the gigantic Australian troop ships that disembarked soldiers, then loaded back up with wounded soldiers and the few lucky civilians who could get places. Unfortunately, they were all headed for Australia, by way of Java, one of the few countries in Southeast Asia that was still free of Japanese.

"Will we be able to get to the States from Australia?" Hazel kept asking of the authorities.

The answer was always a shrug. "Sooner or later. Probably."

"Will they attack Australia, too?" Roberta asked Johnny Leighton when he stopped by.

"It would be a nice prize," he said.

"But it's a whole continent," Hazel said.

"Size and distance haven't bothered them so far," Johnny said. "Of course they can't take it, but they might try."

That's what you said about Malaya and Hong Kong. And Singapore, Hazel thought.

By Monday morning they'd decided they'd have to go to Australia, and Hazel set out to book tickets. All evacuation was being handled by the Peninsula and Oriental Line, which had moved its office out of the city and into the manager's house at Cluny, about five miles away. A long line of women and children with a few men snaked up the long driveway and moved so slowly that it seemed not to be moving at all. There was a good deal of daylight bombing now, and every hour or so everyone had to duck to relative safety in the deep ditch alongside the drive. Then they would crawl back out, muddy, frightened, and disheveled and try to reconstruct the same order. There were disputes, tears, and occasional slaps. P&O clerks did their best to keep order among the terrified women and cranky children. The sun rose higher and they fanned themselves lethargically.

The whole thing made Hazel think of *Gone with the Wind*— a defeated, overrun (or about to be) population milling in sweaty, frantic crowds. Like Scarlett, Hazel wanted only to get back to her own Tara, but unlike Scarlett, she was on an island on the other side of the planet. There was no hopping in a wagon and charging through the flames for her. Nor was there a Rhett.

By the time Hazel finally reached the house itself, after seven hours in line, she felt sweat-drenched, ragged, and furious at fate. In spite of the emergency nature of the situation, the P&O people were being exasperating models of slow-moving bureaucracy. Every passport was examined with unnerving care. That of the woman in front of Hazel turned out to have expired a few days earlier and the clerk refused to issue her tickets. She was a big woman and she leaned over the clerk menacingly. "Look at me, you fool! Do I look like a native or a Chinese? Do I sound like one? I'm white and I want out. I've got two children! You must give me tickets!"

"I'm sorry. Next?"

The woman was all but dragged away, crying and shouting abuse at the clerk. Hazel stepped forward in fear. Suppose there was something wrong with her documents or Roberta's? The clerk looked at the passports and up at her. "American—" he mused, as if that alone were highly suspicious. "Where are you trying to go?"

"To the States, of course."

"Impossible."

"I was afraid of that," Hazel said, forcing a smile. "Then Australia."

"Hmmm." The clerk flipped through a pile of paperwork. "I think I can get you on a cargo ship to Melbourne. They're working now on unloading it before they start knocking together some berths in the meat lockers.''

"Meat lockers!''

He looked up at her again, frowning. "Miss, there are people grateful to be taking places in the holds of oil tankers.''

"Yes, of course. I'm sorry. Two berths in a meat locker will be fine.'' Imagine what a place like that was going to smell like in the tropics! She wanted more than anything on earth to slap his smug, pasty face. He began filling out forms in slow motion, mumbling in a prissy way to himself the whole time while people crowding behind Hazel jostled and muttered impatiently. When he finally handed her the passports and two tickets, she said, "But this says February thirteenth is the sailing date. That's nearly two weeks from now. We can't wait that long.''

The impatient mutter behind her took on an ugly tone.

The clerk snatched back the tickets with a disapproving sniff. "Then I'll have to send you to Sumatra or Java if you have to leave sooner.''

Hazel paused. She wasn't altogether sure where either of those places were or how they'd get away from them if that's where they went. She grabbed the tickets back before he could start over. "No, I'll take these.'' *Two weeks!* she thought frantically as she pushed her way back out through the crowd. What would Scarlett do? Seduce someone, of course. Hardly an option.

On the morning of February 10, Sister Denk was assigned to the operating theater that had been set up in the Adelphi Hotel. After several frantic hours she was given a twenty-minute break, and used it to have a cup of coffee and take her shoes off. As she slumped back into one of the chairs in the lobby, she heard her name being called by a familiar voice. Matron Eagleton. Dear God, if the woman had hunted her down here, she must be in big trouble. But for once she couldn't imagine what for.

"Ah, there you are, Sister Denk.''

"What is it, Matron?'' Gloria said, dragging herself into a respectful upright position.

The matron, limping and looking utterly drained, came over and sat down. She glanced at Gloria's stocking feet, but made no comment. "We've had orders from General Percival to evacuate half the nurses today. No, don't get that look. We drew lots. You're staying, though heaven only knows why you'd want to. I'm to take half our girls and half Matron Deeping's. She'll be in charge of the rest of you. I wanted you to know to whom you are to report.''

''Thank you, Matron.''

''The rest of you will follow right behind. I understand the Japs are already on the northwest of the island. It should be only a day or two longer.'' The Japanese had demanded the surrender of Singapore. General Percival had refused, saying the city would resist to the last man. The intense bombing that followed his reply had been a living nightmare. Patients, military and civilian, were lined up in the hallways of all the hospitals; mothers and children shared beds until they ran out of beds, then people were put in rows on the floors of the corridors. Hotels like the Adelphi and Raffles, once the scene of dancing and drinking and romance, now had operating theaters in their ballrooms and mortuaries in their dining rooms.

Even Matron Eagleton was a casualty. As she went home one morning after an eighteen-hour shift, she received a shrapnel wound in the calf that had required twelve stitches, but she hadn't missed so much as a minute of duty. ''Sister Denk—I want you to know something. You are one of the finest nurses I've ever worked with.''

''Thank you, Matron.''

''That's not to say you don't have your failings,'' Matron quickly added. ''But if you could learn to accept authority, there's no telling how far you might get in the nursing profession.''

Gloria accepted the warning with a straight face, then stood up and dug a tiny notebook out of her pocket. ''Matron, will you take something for me? When we ran out of admission forms and death certificates, I started keeping the names and home addresses of the boys in my care who died. Will you write to their families as soon as you can? There's no guessing when the army will tell them, if they ever do.''

Matron took the small pages Gloria tore from the book and added them to a pile of similar notes she'd collected from some of the other nurses. ''I'll take care of it,'' she said.

Gloria took her outstretched hand. ''Don't worry. I'll go when it's time. I don't want to get stuck here.''

''I'll be waiting for you, Sister Denk.'' It was part assurance, part threat.

Friday the thirteenth.

Hazel wasn't superstitious, but under the circumstances the

significance of the date could hardly be overlooked. She tossed the calendar into the suitcase, then changed her mind and put it into the wastebasket. As she did so, there was a deep ominous *boom* and she instinctively ducked down to avoid flying glass, even though most of the glass in her room was already shattered.

Her impulse was to simply throw everything close at hand into the luggage and get the hell out, but they'd been warned that they could take only one case each, so packing had to be done very carefully. Thank God they were only visitors to Singapore, not residents. All their real family treasures were safely home in Evanston. If this were home, instead, she'd be having to weigh the value of clothes against scrapbooks and family records. It was hard enough as it was; they had no way of knowing where they were going or how long they would be there before they could get the rest of the way home.

If they landed in the south of Australia, they would need some warm clothing. She'd packed a pair of wool slacks and a heavy sweater, but replaced it with a lighter one for the sake of space. Five dresses, including a beautiful rose-colored knitted suit, were already laid flat on the bottom of the case. Then there were three pairs of cotton slacks and three skirts along with eight blouses. Certainly she could get by for several months on that. And it wasn't as though she couldn't purchase more clothing in Australia, if need be. She also had purchased some lovely batik shawls as gifts when they first arrived in Singapore and a good deal of very fine silk underwear she'd never worn. It was to be part of her trousseau. That could all go, since it took little space.

The one thing she didn't think she could acquire on shipboard and certainly couldn't do without for a long journey was sanitary napkins. She'd laid in quite a large supply and had flattened them down and tied them in tight bundles with stout twine to save space. She wasn't sure that they'd ever fluff back up and be of use, but it made her very uneasy to contemplate running out of them in the middle of the Pacific. She'd also packed quite a bit of soap and shampoo, but questioned the weight—they'd probably have to carry their own bags for the first part of the journey.

The other heavy item she knew she couldn't do without was books. Half a dozen as yet unread novels and a few favorite classics added significantly to the weight of the suitcase, but she couldn't bring herself to leave any of them behind.

"Are you ready?" her mother asked from the doorway.

"Almost. You?" Hazel asked, experimentally trying to close the suitcase. Something would have to go.

"All but my jewelry. I don't know what to do with it." Roberta sat on the bed, a teak box on her lap. "I'm afraid to put it in the suitcase, for fear it might get lost. I wouldn't mind if I never saw my clothes again, but my jewelry—your father will never forgive me if I lose any of it. Most of it came from his side of the family."

"We should hand-carry it. Wait, I've got an idea." She pulled a long white silk scarf out of the suitcase. "If we tie or sew it all into this, one of us could wear it around the waist like a money belt. No chance of losing it or dropping it that way. I'll take care of it."

Roberta went back to her packing and Hazel got out her sewing kit and began to baste rings, brooches, earrings, and necklaces down the center of the scarf. She tied it around her waist, tucked her blouse in over it, and realized she didn't dare bend over for fear of stabbing herself. Oh, well, it wouldn't be for long and it was the safest way. She put Frank's letters in the suitcase along with an extra deck of cards for her mother, a sewing kit, a manicure set, a package of airmail stationery, and a first-aid kit. She had to remove three of the books before she could force the top down.

Dragging the heavy bag, she went downstairs and took a last look around at the rented house that had been home for almost three months. The owners weren't going to be happy about what had happened to their property. Most of the windows had been broken by the bombing and one of the servants had left in the middle of the night earlier in the week, taking a number of valuable ornaments and most of the silver with him. The mattresses had all been hauled down to the ground floor and stacked up against the heavy dining room table, making a sort of cave, where Hazel and Roberta had been sleeping since the bombing got so terrible. For a moment Hazel felt guilty, thinking they ought to put everything right, but then reality overcame her. In days, if not hours, this house would belong to the Japanese, if they didn't blast it to tinder with their damned bombs first.

She heard the toot of a car horn, and called, "Mr. Leighton is here, Mother."

Roberta came down the steps, dragging a case that looked even heavier than Hazel's. "From the upstairs window I can see smoke from the direction of the harbor."

"It doesn't matter," Hazel said with a great deal less confidence than she felt. "We've made it this far and we're *going* to get out of Singapore."

Roberta laid an envelope on the hall table, then said somewhat guiltily to Hazel, "For your father. To tell him we've gone home. Just in case—you did wire Barbara which ship we're going on and when, didn't you?"

"Yes, Mother. Two wires and two letters."

As they were getting into the car, there was the now-familiar drone of planes. "Quick! Over here!" Johnny Leighton shouted, dragging them toward the trench the servants had dug in what was once a lovely flower bed. They all jumped in, heedless of the mud as they ducked down, covering their heads with their arms.

There was a blast that shook the earth, and dirt started falling around them. Then nothing but a crackling silence. Cautiously, they peered over the top of the trench. The gazebo was gone, a crater marked where it had been, and a section of the back of the house was in flames.

Hazel suddenly understood what it meant to be sick with fear. Her stomach heaved and her mouth filled with the saliva of nausea, but she managed to crawl out and help her mother to the car. Johnny Leighton, his hands shaking so badly he could hardly hold on to the wheel, started the engine, and they sped up the long driveway without looking back.

Chapter 5

Gloria and the other five sisters were nearly thrown out of the jeep when the sirens started and the driver made a sudden turn so they could take shelter in the cathedral. Before the jeep was at a full stop, they'd jumped out and run for cover. Now, ten minutes later, they were sitting with dozens of other women, mostly nurses like themselves, and listening to the hollow echoes of the ack-ack guns outside. Most were in uniform, a few wearing their caps, others in their Sunday-best hats and a few with ridiculous-looking tin helmets. Some of the sisters, relieved of the responsibility of being courageous in front of their patients, were crying quietly. Others knelt in prayer. Some, like Gloria, just sat still, glad for a moment of rest.

For the first time since it all began, Gloria was genuinely frightened. She'd been busy, angry, exhausted, and exhilarated before, and she'd put on a hell of a brave face for the soldiers she'd cared for. They never even saw her flinch when the bombs blew the windows out of the hospital. But until this moment she'd never been outright frightened. *I might actually die here*, she thought with a fleeting sense of terror that was foreign to her nature. She rummaged in her shoulder bag for her packet of loose papers on which she'd recorded yet more names of dead soldiers. She nudged the nurse beside her. They'd been working together the last two days. "Do you have these, too?"

The sister, a very large, blond, buxom woman of about thirty named Caroline Warbler, glanced at the papers, then pulled some of her own out of her bag.

"Sister Warbler, what if we—"

"Don't make it out? I was thinking about that, too, Dinki," Caroline Warbler answered. She had a tiny, whispery, feminine voice completely at odds with her large physique.

"Let's collect them from everybody and hide them here. Certainly at least one of us will make it out safely, then when this is over, we can come back for them."

They went quietly along the aisles, explaining their errand. They met at the front of the sanctuary, each holding a fat handful of paper scraps. Gloria looked around, then motioned to Sister Warbler. "Behind the organ. The Japs won't think of looking for anything there."

By the time they'd hidden their papers, Matron Deeping was motioning them to get their things to continue their journey. Gathering their suitcases and handbags, they filed out of the cathedral and back into the jeeps and lorries they'd been traveling in.

They had to get to the harbor by back roads. The Japanese

were already swarming in some of the main roads and the traffic to the harbor was jammed to a congested halt. Though it was midday, the sky was as dark as a stormy twilight from the smoke of thousands of fires. As they passed behind Raffles, they saw a half dozen employees of the hotel flinging bottle after bottle of the finest liquors against the side of the building to break them. "What a terrible waste," Caroline Warbler whispered.

"Can't have the little yellow bastards getting drunk on good British booze," Gloria said. "Sacrilege."

Everything that might be of use or pleasure to the invaders was being destroyed. At one pier, a line of luxurious automobiles was inching forward. At the head of the line, a small group of men in shirt-sleeves was methodically pushing them off the end of the pier and into the sea. Everywhere the air reeked of the petrol that was being flushed away. As they approached the harbor, they saw relays of workers removing crates and barrels of unknown goods from the godowns that lined the road. They, too, were being shoved into the ocean.

Gloria and the others had to walk the last few blocks through a living nightmare. The crowds were too thick for vehicles to move. It was almost impossible for people to move. Buildings were blazing all around them, hot sparks making brown holes in their clothing and burning off bits of their hair. Rubble blocked the roads; newly landed troops struggled to unload military equipment while civilians fought desperately to escape. People were being pulled out of the wreckage of buildings, and it took at least six men to bully their way through the crowds with each stretcher. The sirens wailed, barely audible over the screaming and shouting, but there was no question of taking cover now. For the thousands of terrified civilians on the docks, the only possible safety now was in escape.

The crush of human bodies was as dangerous and frightening as the bombs. Gloria struggled forward, holding her suitcase against her chest like a piece of armor. Head bent, she concentrated on keeping her feet on the ground and getting air into her lungs. Both took her full concentration. Suddenly everyone started screaming even more loudly. Looking up, she saw the low-flying Japanese plane, the "poached egg" on the wing clearly visible. She raised her suitcase over her head and crouched down just before the bomb struck the building on the other side of the street.

When she stood up, she found herself facing a young man

with frizzy blond hair. He was holding a crying baby and his mouth was working wordlessly. At his feet, a young woman— his wife—lay sprawled with a hideously huge shard of wood sticking out of her chest. Gloria stepped over her and gave the man a rough push. "She's dead. I can't help her. You can't either. Get the baby out. Save the baby." The people behind her tripped over the woman or stepped on her.

The young man didn't want to abandon his dead wife, but Gloria shoved him forward relentlessly. He'd lost his suitcases someplace, but belongings weren't worth going back for, even if one could have moved against the tide of hysterical humanity.

Finally, more by fate than design, Gloria found herself in a line that was being funneled down a long gangway to a waiting barge. The man at the head of the gangway was checking tickets. *Checking tickets!* Gloria thought furiously. "This isn't a ship!" she complained. "We can't go all the way to Australia on this!"

"I'll bet you could if you tried," the man said coldly. Then, mainly for the sake of a distinguished-looking old gentleman behind her, he added, "The ships are down harbor. The larger ones can't get in around this mess."

Gloria looked out to sea and realized what he meant. The harbor was full of debris, much of it burning. Masts of sunken ships stuck up here and there. Gloria stumbled along, her suitcase bashing against her shins as she struggled to keep from falling into the water. Finally, the barge was loaded, and a tug started hauling it down harbor. Gloria upended the suitcase and sat down on it, breathing heavily. She was sick with heat and fear and still couldn't believe she was actually leaving Singapore.

The barge wallowed through the oily water for what seemed like hours before reaching a small, battered coastal steamer that was already full far beyond its intended capacity. Rope ladders were flung down and those on the barge began to climb up. Other ropes with hooks on the ends were used to haul up baggage. As Gloria reached the top of the ladder, a familiar voice said, "Well, I see you made it, Sister Denk."

"Matron Deeping! Am I on the right boat, then? It's a miracle!"

She heard the laughter of other nurses, including Caroline Warbler, who had somehow managed to get to the steamer ahead of her. But Matron Deeping was no more amused by Gloria than Matron Eagleton had been. "We have a number of wounded on board and may have more before we get to safety. I'm pairing the sisters up. You're with Sister Cassini and your medical kit is in the captain's cabin waiting for you to sign for it."

"No rest for the wicked," a young woman with a neat cap of dark hair and piercing blue eyes said to her. "I'm Sister Cassini. Have you got your suitcase yet?"

"It's just coming up."

"Then I'll meet you at the captain's cabin. It's up there," she added, pointing forward before disappearing.

Gloria stood at the rail, looking back. Beautiful, luxurious, glamorous Singapore. The sparkling, priceless jewel of Southeast Asia—nothing but a smoking, heat-stunned wreck now. Flames leapt along the waterfront, silhouetting the skeletons of buildings. Great roiling clouds of smoke billowed up, obscuring the sun. The whole city seemed to be screaming. For the first time since leaving home, Gloria looked forward to setting foot on Australian soil.

When the tugboat Hazel and Roberta Hampton were on reached the ship, it was turned away. "I'm sorry, but they can't take you," the captain of the tug told his passengers after a long consultation with the captain of the transport.

"What can you mean? We have tickets," a Frenchwoman asked in heavily accented English.

"Tickets or no, they're filled up to the rafters. Another ship went down out here an hour or so ago, and they had to take on her passengers. We'll find you something else."

"But—" Roberta started to say, but Hazel took her arm and spat out, "It doesn't matter, Mother. As long as we get out of here, it could be on a sampan."

"But you wrote Barbara that we'd be on this ship," Roberta insisted.

"It makes no difference. Barbara's back in Evanston. She wasn't going to meet us at the docks in Australia anyway. When we get there or to Java or wherever we end up, we'll wire her about the change in plans."

"Yes, of course. You're right. I'm acting like a fool," Roberta said.

It took an hour of chugging around in the ocean traffic to find a ship that would take them. Most of the big transports had already left. The sky was darkening, and the tug captain had given up on getting rid of all his charges at once. He was disposing of them in ones and twos. Finally, he pulled alongside an oversize yacht. It must have originally belonged to some sort of local royalty, because it was large enough to comfortably accommodate twenty or thirty people, plus a crew. "Can you take on four extra?" he shouted up.

A Malay sailor called back, "Got one hundred now. Take no more or we sink."

"Just two, then?" the captain asked.

The sailor glanced over his shoulder, then nodded. "But quick-quick. Captain say we go now."

Only two men, clerks to judge by their age and manners, remained besides Roberta and Hazel. They gestured that the women were to go on board. Hastily thanking them, the Hampton women scrambled up the ladder the sailor had lowered. He snatched it up quickly behind them, as if afraid the others might follow them, then he brought up their suitcases. The other passengers stood silently glaring at them, as if they were somehow responsible for the whole horrible situation.

With a low growling and thumping, the engine of the yacht came to life. "We'd better try to find someplace to stake out as our own," Hazel said.

That was far easier said than done. The sleeping rooms were full to overflowing; women and their children were sleeping four to a bunk and in rows on the floors. Hazel and Roberta finally managed to get just enough space to stretch out on the floor of the companionway belowdecks. It was stifling hot and reeked of the sweat of frightened humans, but Hazel was too tired to care. She rolled her jacket into a wad to use as a pillow and squeezed herself flat along the wall in the hope that she wouldn't get stepped on. Nearly hypnotized by the drone of the engines and weariness, she fell soundly asleep while Roberta was still talking to her.

Sometime during the night the sailors brought around cold corned beef sandwiches—"bully beef" to the British—and mugs of strong, sweet tea, but Hazel slept through it. She also missed some bombing nearby that alarmed everybody else nearly out of their wits but did no actual damage. When she did wake, at dawn, the ship had stopped and was eerily silent. A child sleeping along the wall above Hazel's head had managed to slip a warm little bare foot down the back of her blouse. She wriggled free without waking him and stood up, stretching. She was stiff and achy and had a terrible crick in her neck, but at least she felt slightly less stupefied than before her long sleep. Why weren't they moving? she wondered. Maybe someone else was awake she could ask, she thought, but first things first. She got her handbag, in which she had fortunately thought to stash her tooth powder and brush along with some lipstick and face powder, and went in search of a lavatory.

The one she found had once been opulent. Mostly highly polished mahogany with brass fittings, the outer cloakroom had fancy mirrors and mirrored tables along one wall, and brocaded benches where the ladies entertained aboard the yacht could freshen their makeup. There were lovely Chinese dressing screens folded against the walls and crystal lamps. Now there were women sleeping on the carpeted floors and one very glamorous blonde seated by one of the mirrors applying lipstick. She took no notice of Hazel. Hazel went through to the toilet, which was mercifully unoccupied, then washed her hands and face. She needed to change her clothes, but the thought of trying to get anything out of her suitcase just now was daunting. There had been a very fat man sleeping on it when she awoke.

Instead, she went on deck. Here, too, some people were sleeping—a few civilian men in rumpled and stained tropical suits and battered straw hats, Chinese and Indian servants, and some Eurasian women and children. The captain and one of his officers were at the rail, talking in low tones. They stopped guiltily when Hazel approached. She walked on past them and they nodded politely, but couldn't disguise their alarm. Hazel felt her stomach churn. She went on forward, picking her way carefully around the sleeping passengers. The sky was still gray and hazy from smoke though she couldn't detect a particular source. Looking down, she could see that there were things floating on the surface of the water—the lid of a wooden valise with a crimson and gold scarf caught on it, a child's doll with yellow hair, planks of wood, and many dead fish. The water also had a shimmering rainbow glaze, as if there were a great deal of oil or gasoline on it. She turned away quickly.

They were stopped in the shelter of a small island cove. As she headed back to her space in the hallway, the engines came to life and they began to move again, but slowly, stealthily. By eight everyone was awake and the crew had come around again with food—tea and thick slabs of buttered bread. There was also some sliced bacon, but not enough for everyone. While the distribution was going on, the ship's sirens began to sound and they were ordered belowdecks. They could hear the drone of aircraft and the muffled *whollop* of bombs striking the water nearby. Then, unnervingly, the planes left.

A woman along the hallway was screaming—from fear, Hazel assumed—until the words came through clearly. Someone had stolen her slice of ham during the confusion and she was demanding to see the captain to bring legal charges.

The morning went on. Hazel made her suitcase into a table, and she and her mother sat cross-legged on the floor and played gin rummy for an hour. They both kept forgetting the score. This wasn't unusual for Hazel; it was unheard of for Roberta.

Finally Roberta put down the cards and said, "I keep thinking I'll wake up in a moment and I'll be home in Evanston. You and your father will be out in the garages, puttering with car parts and ruining your clothes. Barbie will be talking on the phone and none of this will have been real. I wish we'd never heard of goddamned Singapore. I hadn't, you know, until your father inherited that land. I thought it was in Africa someplace. I was happier thinking that."

Hazel shuffled the cards, surprised at her mother's swearing. One of the cards got loose and flipped across the companionway. "What shall we have for dinner when Daddy comes back?"

Roberta smiled. "Lamb, I think. He loves it, although it does smell up the house. With a nice mint jelly. We'll make lots of mint jelly this summer, shall we? Gallons. We'll go to Marshal Field's and buy some nice little glasses, then we can give away jars for Christmas next year. Get that eight of diamonds back, Hazel. We may need it again."

Gloria and Sister Cassini were up most of the night caring for the mothers and children aboard the steamer. Packed in like olives, they were terrified and many were seasick. The young man whose wife had been killed on the docks had retreated into some private hell in his own mind and Gloria had to find another nursing mother to take care of his baby.

This boat, too, had taken shelter near a small island. At dawn, a number of the men went ashore to gather some firewood and fruit. Breakfast was hot tea and mangoes. Gloria made sure the children in her charge were fed after they had set out again, then found a spot to sit down and lean against a wall for a few minutes sleep. It was still relatively cool, but as the sun rose she'd have to dispose of some of her uniform. Like most of the nurses, she was in full dress—down to girdle, corset, thick white hose, and starched cap. It gave her a certain assurance, almost protection from the hideous alien situation, but it would simply be too hot on the open sea in broad daylight.

She'd barely nodded off when a sailor started shouting, "Take cover! Take cover!"

"How does the bloody fool expect us to do that?" Sister Cassini, slumped beside her, asked.

Still, both young women rose and started organizing the children, making them crouch down and cover their heads with their arms. Gloria regarded the whole episode as an inconvenience until the first plane came over and there was a horrific explosion. "Dear God! We're hit!" someone shouted just as another explosion knocked them off their feet.

The steamer was already listing. "We're going down!" voices called in rising hysteria.

Matron Deeping went past at a trot and called out, "Girls, get your people on lifeboats. Quickly."

The pitifully inadequate boats were already being lowered. Gloria managed to get the women and children she was responsible for on one of the first boats to be released. She tossed her medical kit in after them. The ship was burning now, and gusts of wind kept sweeping choking smoke over them. Everywhere people were scrambling blindly, coughing, crying.

"My daughter!" a woman screamed at Gloria. "I can't find my daughter." The side of her face was badly burned, but she seemed unaware of it.

"We've got all the children off now. She's on one of the boats. Now you must get on this one. It's the last." The woman was still sobbing and trying to cling to Gloria when the boat was lowered. It scraped the side of the steamer, broke loose at one end, and started sinking as soon as it met the water below. Those still on board began throwing down anything at hand that might float. One of the other lifeboats came back and picked up those who were still floundering.

A sailor came along the deck, stumbling under a load of life vests. Gloria started strapping people into them and shoving them off. "Jump as far clear as you can and mind you hold the vest down or it'll crack you in the chin when you hit," she told each, but could tell she wasn't being listened to. One after another they leapt and their heads snapped back as they landed.

The evacuation had taken ten or fifteen minutes, and now there were only a dozen people left on the ship, mostly nurses and a few of the crew. There weren't enough life vests left. "I'm a good swimmer. You take this one," Gloria said to a Malay sailor who was literally shivering with fear. He snatched it from her.

Sister Cassini put her hand on Gloria's arm. "Let's jump together."

"Good. But let's get a fair run at it."

The decks were clear now. Hand in hand they dashed down the sloping deck to where the gangway would have been, and went flying out into the sea. Sister Cassini came up grinning, oil streaking her face. "I'll race you to shore," she said, spitting out some seawater as she spoke.

"Right. Where's that?" Gloria replied. If only she'd had the sense to get rid of some of this clothing before jumping. She felt that it was dragging her down. Too late now. They had to get away from the burning ship, then she'd worry abut getting undressed.

Sister Cassini gestured toward the line of lifeboats and people in life vests—all of whom were far ahead of them. "That boat's going to cause an awful drag when it goes down. We'd best hurry."

Fortunately, they were a safe distance away when the steamer suddenly upended and slipped down into the water. The drag pulled them back a little, but also provided them with a section of planking that shot up out of the sea a few feet away. "A raft. Especially for us," Gloria said, swimming toward the ragged piece of deck.

They scrambled on top, one from each side to keep it from turning over. Their weight caused it to sink just below the water level, but it supported them well enough that they could lie back and recover their strength. After a while Gloria sat up. The makeshift raft rocked alarmingly for a moment, then settled. She leaned over and took off her heavy, white, laced shoes. "I hate the waste," she said, "but I can't swim with these things on." Sister Cassini was removing her shoes, too. They let them bob away on the waves. Ahead of them, the lifeboats were barely visible, and the water between them was dotted with people in life vests and in groups clinging, as they were, to floating wreckage. "Do you think they know where they're going?" Gloria asked.

Sister Cassini shrugged. "There's got to be land somewhere.

The place is full of islands, and Sumatra shouldn't be far. Listen! What's that?''

It was the distant drone of planes.

"Jesus Christ! They aren't coming back, are they?" Gloria said, but without further discussion both young women slid off their makeshift boat into the water. The small Japanese planes were coming from the direction they were going. A bomber in the lead dropped a string of bombs down the middle of the scattered stream of survivors. Other planes behind it swooped low, shooting everyone in sight. "Quick! Under the raft!" Gloria shouted before taking a deep breath and diving.

The bomb concussions were crushing. Her ears throbbed with the pain and her chest was on fire with the effort of holding her breath. She came up briefly for more air, then submerged again, fearing she was losing consciousness. But the Japs must not see her white uniform and use her for a target. She had no idea where Sister Cassini was. When she came up the second time, she couldn't tell if it was over or if she'd gone deaf. There wasn't a sound. Then she sensed the lapping of wavelets against the raft. She clung to the edge, taking deep, rasping breaths and trying to identify just where the pain was. It was everyplace. Her stomach, her head, her limbs. Even her fingers and face hurt.

"Are you alive?" Gloria whirled around as her companion came swimming toward her. "I lost my grip somehow. Have you ever seen so many dead fish?"

Gloria looked around. "Oh, shit! That one looks like a shark."

"If it is, the Japs did us one favor. Do you think we could row with some of these planks that are coming loose around the edge?"

They climbed aboard and tried it. But their progress revealed a horror. Most of the people who had been just ahead of them were dead now. They passed body after body, and many parts of bodies. A man's arm, still wearing a watch and wedding ring, got caught on Gloria's "oar" and Sister Cassini started gagging at the sight of a dead child, half her face gone and her long red hair streaming out into the water.

"How could they hit everyone?" Gloria asked.

"They probably didn't. It was the bombs, I think. The concussion can implode your lungs and intestines. Just like it does the fish. I helped treat the men from the *Repulse*, and the doctor told us that.''

"But why not us?"

"We were farther away and we're wearing girdles and corsets. At least I am. I never thought I'd be grateful for the damned harnesses."

Somewhere farther ahead they could hear voices calling, but they couldn't see anybody. Nor could they see land. There was nothing but dead fish, dead bodies, and oily, stinking debris all around them, some of which was still burning. It was worse than any nightmare. But at least they'd survived.

Hadn't they? Gloria had the sudden skin-crawling thought that maybe she hadn't survived. Maybe she'd died back in the strafing and this was hell. If it wasn't, it was certainly the next worst thing.

I'll never complain about Australia again, God, if You just let me get back there, she thought.

The sirens started again in the midafternoon. But this time there was no drone of planes or crackle of bombs. Hazel and Roberta sat huddled in the companionway, waiting for the inevitable blasts. There were voices above, but they couldn't distinguish the words. Finally the sirens stopped wailing and a pair of shiny black boots appeared at the head of the stairs. A trim, handsome Japanese officer stepped down and looked around at them with vast contempt.

There was a collective gasp and everyone drew closer together. Hazel felt that her heart had nearly leapt out of her chest with the shock. Up until that moment the Japanese had been almost an imaginary, theoretical enemy—invisible pilots of the planes that wrought such destruction, not living, breathing individuals only a few feet away. The sudden physical reality of this man stunned all of them.

The officer glared at them a moment longer, shouted something over his shoulder, and ascended the steps. A babble of frightened conversation broke out behind him. "Have we been captured?" Roberta asked needlessly.

A woman standing next to her took her hand and patted it comfortably. She was in her sixties with an all-knowing face as weathered as the side of barn. Hazel remembered her introducing herself earlier as Mrs. Hill. "Don't worry, dear. They'll just rob us and let us go. I've been out here in the East a long time and flatter myself that I know these people well. You see, they want the lands they're trying to conquer for the resources, the rubber and tin; they want the peasants to work it; but they certainly don't want a bunch of white women and children to guard and feed and take care of. Just give them anything in your handbag that they want, bow respectfully, and they'll go away. You'll see.''

''Handbag?'' Hazel said suddenly. Where was hers? She'd left it in the fancy cloakroom when she went back there an hour or so before. Dear God! It had Frank's picture in it. The Japs could have anything else they wanted out of it, but she didn't want somebody just tossing it overboard. Leaving her mother talking to the expertly reassuring Mrs. Hill, she pushed her way along the companionway.

The women in the cloakroom were babbling with fright. Hazel tried to pass on what Mrs. Hill had said while she searched for her handbag. They were somewhat comforted by her words but couldn't help her with her search. The only place left was the toilet. Hazel knocked, heard no reply, then opened the door.

A handsome woman of about fifty with carefully waved graying hair and a controlled but terrified expression was tearing up pieces of paper and flushing them down the toilet. One of the items was an American passport. The rest looked like the paper covers of books. ''Oh, I'm so sorry—''

The woman didn't look up. She went on tearing the papers into small bits. ''I'll be through here in just a minute.''

''I was looking for my handbag.''

''Is that it in the corner?'' the woman asked. She dumped the last of the papers in the toilet and flushed it once more, watching to make sure every shred disappeared. ''You didn't see anybody in here,'' she said to Hazel firmly, meeting her eyes for the first time. It wasn't a threat or plea, only a remark made with complete confidence that it would be obeyed.

''No, I didn't.'' Hazel grabbed her handbag and hurried back to her mother, pondering not only what was going to happen to all of them, but what the woman had been throwing away and why.

⊠ Chapter 6

The Japanese were ordering everybody up on deck in groups of twenty. They were told to bring all their belongings. Hazel and Roberta were in the first group. Standing in the middle of the line, Hazel leaned forward to see what was going on at the end. A young, fat soldier with pimples was shouting at an elderly woman and her husband. They obviously had no idea what he was demanding, but were eager to comply with whatever it was. He gave the man a shove and the lady shrieked. Then the soldier slapped her soundly across her wrinkled cheek. She subsided into a heap. Hazel was appalled. She'd never actually seen an adult strike another adult except at the movies. The soldier jabbed his bayoneted gun at the suitcase in front of her. The old man opened it with one hand while patting his sobbing wife's frail shoulder with the other.

The soldier rummaged in the suitcase with the point of the bayonet, then bent over and picked out what was apparently a jewelry box. Another soldier stepped forward with a lidded basket and the first one dumped the old lady's jewelry into it. Then he grabbed the old man's arm and screamed in his face. The old man, hands shaking, unhooked his watch and dropped it into the basket. The soldiers' superior officers stood by, watching with approval. The yacht's crewmen, Japanese guns pointed at their heads, stood at rigid attention, terrified and impotent.

Hazel took off her engagement ring with shaking fingers and furtively slipped it down the front of her brassiere.

The soldiers moved down the line, taking rings, necklaces, watches, earrings, money, checkbooks, money clips, passports, and any document that looked official—Hazel suspected that they couldn't read them and took them just in case they might be valuable. She was terrified that they might be searched and had the awful sense that the scarf full of jewelry at her waist was bulging obviously. It was the Hampton women's good fortune that they hadn't changed clothing and hence, looked too poor, wrinkled, and disreputable to be suspected of harboring anything more worthwhile than the scant money in their purses and the watches they wore.

Their suitcases were torn open, torn apart, and kicked aside. The soldier held up one of Hazel's tightly packed bunches of sanitary napkins and giggled foolishly. One of the Japanese officers spoke sharply at him and he threw it back into the case, glaring at Hazel. When everyone had been searched, they were told to take their things back down the stairs and send the next group up.

"You see," the woman who'd reassured Roberta said when they returned. "They'll let us go on our way when they've finished, and we'll all have an adventure to tell the people at home about."

It was finally over. Mrs. Hill, a self-appointed lookout and eavesdropper, came down the stairs and reported to those in the companionway. "The Japs have gone back to their ship with our belongings. They told the captain to sail on to Sumatra. Like I said, they don't want to be bothered with us."

As she spoke, the ship gave a lurch and began to move. Everyone sat around in a stupor of relief for the rest of the afternoon. They were hungry and tired and many had lost valuables, but they were all so glad it was over that such things didn't matter. At dusk they came within sight of land. "Is that Sumatra?" Hazel asked Mrs. Hill as they stood at the rail with the others.

"No, it's probably Banka Island—it's a big island off the coast of Sumatra. We may have to ferry over to the mainland and cross to the other side to get transport to India or Australia. I don't think this boat could make such a long journey. Tedious, but still . . ."

Her words trailed off and she squinted against the afternoon sun. The others along the rail grew quieter as well. The long pier was busy, with trucks and people and several boats disembarking along its length. But what had riveted their attention was a flag being raised over a building on the bank. It fluttered in the torpid tropical wind, then as it reached the top of the flag-pole, a spotlight was shone on it. After a moment of heart-stopping silence, a breeze took the flag and held it out as if for display.

It was white—with a large red-orange circle in the middle.

Gloria and Sister Cassini stayed on their raft all day. Every wave and swell loosened it and bits gradually fell away. Along the way they took several bodies out of their life vests and tied the vests underneath the raft to try to keep it above the water, but it still kept disintegrating, splinter by splinter. At one point they took on a woman and her child who had been hanging on to a large wooden crate, but the child, about three years old and already unconscious when they found her, died within minutes and the mother, crazed by thirst and salt and fear, slid off the edge of the raft and disappeared an hour later.

They found a floating canteen about half full of fresh water around noon and took turns taking tiny sips. A picnic hamper floated by and Gloria tried to swim out and snag it, but it gurgled and sank before she could get it. They were terribly hungry, their skin was waterlogged, sunburned, and full of splinters, and they still ached all over from the bombing, but they kept on paddling toward a shoreline they could occasionally glimpse. Now and then someone would call to them, but they could never get close enough to make real contact.

When night fell, they were in despair. They cried quietly for a while, then, "I won't just die out here for no sodding reason!" Gloria said furiously. Sister Cassini started giggling. Gloria began singing "God Save the King," and a man somewhere in the darkness took it up with a feeble voice which gradually faded away.

Eventually it became fully dark. Sister Cassini was quiet for so long that Gloria became alarmed. "You can't go and die on me, Sister!" she said.

"I saw an elephant on the shoreline. Look. Just there," Sister Cassini said in a soft voice.

There was nothing to see. No shoreline. Certainly no ele-phant. Gloria shivered with apprehension. It was all very well for one of them to start hallucinating so long as the other one knew it, but what if she went crazy, too? Then where would they be? Gloria stared into the darkness and for a second she could see the fierce orange glow of the elephant's eye.

"Dammit!" That's a campfire. It has to be. We must be near the beach and somebody has a fire going. Hey! You lot onshore! Can you hear me!" Gloria screamed at the top of her lungs. Sister Cassini got a grip on herself and joined in. Finally, voices wafted back to them. They couldn't tell if it was men or women's voices or what the words were, but it didn't matter. The two young women slipped into the water and got into water-saturated life vests. They abandoned the remaining bits of their raft and started swimming with all their strength.

But as hard as they tried to head directly for the flickering campfire, they couldn't keep on course. A strong current kept pulling them southward. They were probably getting closer to land, but at a debilitating diagonal which was sapping their energy. There was also the chance that they were already at the south end of whatever island it was and would bypass it entirely.

Gloria kept swimming, singing "God Save the King" inside her head and kicking to the rhythm of the music. Sister Cassini kept right alongside her. Suddenly Gloria felt something touch her foot. Her first thought was that she'd attracted a shark, and then she realized it was something solid. "Stand up!" she shouted, fighting for her footing on the rocky bottom. "We're there!"

They staggered ashore, yelping encouragement to each other. Stumbling, they cut their hands and knees and bare feet, and they'd been in the water so long they couldn't get their land legs for a while, but they were so thrilled to be on solid ground that the pain didn't matter at all. They lay silent and exhausted on the beach for a long while, soaking up what warmth was left from the sun and reveling in the sensation of land. After a while it started drizzling.

"We need to find the others. The ones with the campfire. And we need fresh water," Gloria said.

"If we walk along the beach, we're sure to come to someplace where a stream runs into the sea, aren't we?"

They didn't find a stream, but they had good fortune. The drizzling rain blew up into a sudden tropical rain squall. By sitting in the open with big leaves held out in front of them, they were able to funnel a good amount of rainwater into their mouths. "Much healthier than a stream, anyway," Gloria said, smacking her lips. Their thirst temporarily satisfied, they walked up into the edge of the jungle to find shelter from the rain. They didn't want to go very far into the brush for fear of the deadly snakes and spiders that inhabited the jungle, not to mention the furred and clawed menaces. They found a relatively dry spot under a squatty, broad-leaved tree and curled up back to back. Inevitably, both young women fell soundly asleep.

Gloria woke up with her stomach growling ferociously and the sun full in her eyes. She shook her companion awake. They collected a few greenish bananas from a tree nearby and set out to walk up the beach to find the others from the shipwreck. All along their way the beach was covered with wreckage, and there were natives out picking through it. They disappeared as soon as the young nurses approached. As they progressed, they realized this represented a good deal more than a single shipwreck. Suitcases and clothing littered the beach. There were bodies, too. They checked each one for signs of life, but all were dead. Finally, they found a lifeboat in which there was a single passenger—a dead sailor. Sister Cassini crossed herself and muttered a quick prayer, as she had done for the others, then they looked over what else was in the boat.

"This is some woman's suitcase," Gloria said, opening a large, expensive leather case. "We can put on clean clothes. Oh, look! Medical supplies. A whole crate."

They dumped the clothing out, taking what they wanted to wear. They stripped off their wet, filthy uniforms and put on some strange woman's day dresses. The rest of the clothing they dumped out and replaced with the bandages, bottles, vials, and tubes of medicine. "I'm not really me in this—" Sister Cassini said, looking down at the dress she'd put on. It probably cost what she made in a month.

They shook out their uniforms and laid them on top of the medical supplies before closing the case. Then they continued down the beach. Rounding a bend, they spotted a group of people huddled in the fringe of the jungle. All women and children, a good many of the women in nurses' uniforms. It felt like coming home. The others welcomed them and shared some fresh water and fruit. They even had a can of tinned beef, which tasted like heaven.

There were ten nurses and eight civilian women and children. One of the women, a horsey, commanding sort with a tight button of a bun on the top of her head that looked like the knob on top of a cookie jar, explained the situation. "We're on Banka Island. There's a town a few miles along. Muntok, one of the men said he thought it was. The Japs have the island, of course—''

"Oh, no!" Sister Cassini exclaimed.

" 'Fraid so, m'dear. There are natives about. Keep peeking at us, but they're afraid to help us. Nothing to do but surrender. The men have gone into town to ask someone to come pick us up. No point in the women and children walking all the way."

"Surrender!" Gloria exclaimed.

"What else? The natives can't help—or won't. We haven't any way to get off the damned place. Might as well make the little yellow devils feed us. It's their fault we're here. It won't be long, girls. Might as well give in with good grace and get it over with."

Much as Gloria was loathe to accept this pragmatic view, she realized it was the right one. If the enemy had taken Sumatra, they'd probably taken Java as well and everything else within a thousand miles. Damned filthy place to sit out the war, but there it was.

She and Sister Cassini surveyed the medical supplies they'd found, then closed the suitcase back up and settled down for a nap. They awoke to the rumble of a lorry. Canvas-covered and belching oily smoke, it pulled down a path toward the beach, then stopped while a dozen Japanese soldiers leapt off like clowns from a tiny car at the circus. But there was nothing amusing about them.

They dashed up to their captives, screaming and barking incomprehensible orders. "Now, see here!" the bossy woman with the bun said, but one of the soldiers jabbed the point of his bayonet at her and she clamped her mouth shut quickly. The soldiers surrounded them and suddenly fell silent as well when a skinny, bowlegged soldier—apparently their commanding officer—approached. Gloria despised him on sight. His face was narrow with close-set little eyes and a terribly pocked, jaundice-yellow complexion. He walked with a slight limp that he managed to make into a swagger. There was madness and loathing in his study of them.

"Does anybody talk Nip?" one of the other nurses muttered under her breath.

"*Kiotski!*" the commanding officer shouted. The women looked at him and at each other. They had no idea what he was saying. It was obviously a command but to do what?

He snapped something to the other soldiers, and they started laughing and jabbing at the group of women, making them back toward the sea. "I think they just want us to go someplace else," the woman with the tiny topknot said. "God knows where, but let's pretend to swim back to Singapore."

It was so silly it would have been laughable in normal circumstances. But this was a long way from normal for any of them. One of the women tried to go for her suitcase, but the soldiers wouldn't let her take it. "Leave it. We'll come back when they've left," Gloria told her.

The woman waded into the surf. *Much more of this and I'll grow fins,* Gloria thought with disgust. The soldiers stayed above the waterline. As Gloria got in above her knees, she looked back just in time to see the line of soldiers raise their guns. "Duck!" she screamed to the others.

She heard the first gunshots as she flung herself forward and felt something like a fiery knife slice through the outside of her upper thigh.

The bastards! The bloody, despicable bastards, she thought as she scraped her forehead against the bottom. In spite of her fury and terror and the pain in her leg, she realized she couldn't possibly swim out of range. The only thing to do was to pretend to be dead. She let herself float back up to the surface, using every ounce of willpower to keep from thrashing in the water. The gunfire was still going on. She forced herself to roll sideways with excruciating slowness, like a dead body might roll in the waves. She took a quick gasp of air, then made herself go utterly limp.

Roll. Breathe. Relax. Don't listen to the sound of slaughter, to the screams and gurgles.

Roll. Breathe. Roll. Breathe. Relax.

Finally the gunshots stopped. With the next wave Gloria contrived to get herself turned sideways to the beach so she could see them. They were going back to the truck, the leader's limp making him distinctive even from this distance. Gloria continued to lie motionless in the water until she could no longer see the truck, then she stood up. Even waist-deep in the water she could hardly support her weight at first. Her leg was throbbing horribly. But step by agonizing step she dragged herself through the crimson water, checking all the victims. Someone had been shot in the abdomen and watery feces streaked the waves.

The woman with the cookie-jar topknot: dead.

The pair of nurses who looked enough alike to be sisters: dead.

The fat lady with the two babies: all three dead.

Sister Cassini: dear God in heaven! A hole the size of a shilling through her forehead and another through her larynx. Dead.

All of them: dead.

All but Gloria Denk.

She knelt in the shallow water, racked with spasms of horror, saltwater washing the gaping wound in her thigh.

"I never even asked her what her first name was!" she cried to the empty beach. She could still picture the limping, pock-marked commander. "I'll get you for this, you bastard!"

The passengers on the yacht stayed on it all night. Heavily armed soldiers were posted alongside. Several of the men attempted to make contact with Japanese officials to determine their status, but were not allowed to leave. Nor did anyone come aboard to explain the situation. Hopes rose. Perhaps they'd be allowed to sail on to Java in the morning. The Far East Allied Command had been moved there as well as the R.A.F. They'd be safe.

Midmorning an officer finally arrived and ordered them to disembark. Clutching their belongings, the passengers filed off the boat. Hazel, fearing that her mother was dangerously near hysteria, put on a great show of unconcern which she was far from feeling. "Don't worry, Mother. I'm sure Mrs. Hill is right. What would they want with us? We're not anybody's idea of valuable spoils of war. I imagine they just want our boat. It's quite nice."

Japanese soldiers lined the pier at intervals, their faces either completely blank or angry, as if these European and American civilians had done something to them. When they got to land, they were lined up again, shoved into three straggling rows. A soldier went along the front counting them. "*Ichi, ni, san, shi, go, roku, shichi, hachi*—no, no move, wimmens! *Ichi, ni, san, shi, go, roku*—" It took him four tries and the help of three of his comrades to get a figure that satisfied him. "We go town now, wimmens."

The glamorous blonde Hazel had seen earlier in the fancy cloakroom was now in the row in front of her. She had three suitcases. "See here, you'll have to get someone to carry these things for us," she said.

This threw the soldiers into a babble of confused consultation. The one who fancied that he spoke English stepped up to her, barely coming to her chin. "You lazy white wimmens. Nobody work for you now. You cally, you leave. No matter."

"I can't carry all this!" she said.

The soldier shrugged and turned away. She grabbed his arm to continue her demands, but he whirled instantly, landing the flat of his hand on her face so hard that she was catapulted backward over her collection of luggage. Her hat was askew and a bright patch was already discoloring her cheek. "Why you little—"

Before she could scramble back to her feet, she was instantly surrounded by bayonets.

The other women quickly picked up their things and tried to look agreeable and cooperative. Two of the men in their group helped the blonde with her luggage. They walked a long way along a tarmac road to the outskirts of a small town with signs in Dutch on the shops. Hazel, accustomed to exercise, didn't fare too badly, but Roberta and many of the other older women weren't fit for such a walk. Hazel carried her mother's suitcase after the first mile, but that didn't save Roberta from getting horrible blisters from her stylish shoes. She was limping badly by the time they were allowed a rest.

Their group of about a hundred people was herded into a small parklike area. A group of Dutch nuns, apparently from a nearby school or convent, came around with bandages and iodine and did what they could for the captives' injured feet. There were also natives who passed among them with balls of rice rolled in banana leaves. "Good grief!" Roberta said, looking with distaste at the offering. "I despise rice."

"Mother, it's food. Eat it. We may not get anything else," Hazel said.

After eating, they lined up at a trickling tap at the corner of the park and, cupping their hands, got drinks. Then they were ordered to pick up their things and set out again. Passing through the town, they were marched along another road. This time they walked for only about an hour. Hazel tried to keep her mind off her present circumstances by thinking a movie. She concentrated on remembering *The Philadelphia Story* scene by scene, but somehow the cool, luxurious, upper-crust tone of it was hard to capture, or care about under these circumstances. They finally came to a vast collection of dreary tin-roofed huts surrounding a concrete court and in turn surrounded by barbed wire. "What in the world—?" they asked each other before the realization sunk in. This was a jail.

Still Hazel felt the obligation to reassure. "Mother, they have to put us someplace until they can arrange to ship us back out."

"Oh, Hazel, will you stop being Little Miss Sunshine? We're prisoners of war. You know that as well as I do."

Hazel just nodded, relieved of the responsibility of pretending. They might just as well face the worst and deal with it. But there was a small, optimistic part of her that still refused to believe what was going on. This sort of thing just didn't happen to ordinary, harmless people like the Hamptons from Evanston. This sort of drama was for books and movies, not real life.

They entered the jail in a long line past a battered table staffed with clerks. They were asked their names, their "born place," their husband's or father's jobs, their ages, and how much money they had with them. Since they'd all been robbed aboard ship, this seemed an extremely pointless question, but as they explained they had none, they got progressively angrier responses from the clerks.

"Money? You already took our money!" the man in front of Hazel said.

"Honorable Nipponese soldiers not thiefs like Western imperialists," the clerk said in a loud, grating voice. "How much money you have in pockets?"

"None." The man sighed wearily. "None at all."

Their luggage was searched again, and this time they took Hazel's manicure set and one of her books—a travel book about Southeast Asia. They also removed a pad of unused stationery from her suitcase and the fountain pen from her handbag. "You go there now," the clerk said, pointing toward a hut at the northern corner of the compound.

"I want to wait for my mother."

"No wait! No talk back. Do what *Nippon heitai* say or I slap!"

"Go on, Hazel," Roberta said.

Hazel gathered her things and entered the jail compound. It was quite the most depressing sight she'd ever seen. There were hundreds of people here, milling about, talking, crying, arguing, even laughing. The men were all being herded into one area, the women with babies and small children into another. The building she'd been directed to had a patch of shade in front, where a number of women were sitting. Hazel dragged her suitcase over and joined them. Leaning back, she watched the table where her mother was being asked the same questions she'd been asked. She tuned out most of the babble of conversation going on around her until a strange tone of voice got her attention.

"But Dr. Sutherland, we met at Veronica Lacey's tea in your honor—"

The person to whom these words were spoken was the woman Hazel had seen destroying her passport in the lavatory on the yacht. "I'm terribly sorry, but as I say, I'm afraid you've mistaken me for someone else. My name is Bright. Peggy Bright. I'm not acquainted with any Dr. Sutherland."

The other woman was getting angry. "I don't understand why you're saying that. We met. We talked about colleges and I told you my son was at Harvard—"

"How nice. I'm sure you're very proud of him, but the fact remains—"

"Now, look here, Dr. Sutherland—"

Hazel thought she heard an undertone of panic in Peggy Bright's—or Dr. Sutherland's—voice. With a fleeting thought that it was bad enough enduring what the Japanese were doing to them without doing wrong to each other, she turned and said, "Peggy! Peggy Bright! Is it really you? Oh, I'm so happy to see a familiar face. Oh, pardon me. Did I interrupt your conversation?"

She turned and smiled at the other woman. "How do you do. I'm Hazel Hampton. Peggy is my second cousin and we haven't seen each other for years. Or is it first cousin twice removed, Peggy? I can never get these things straight."

"I—but I thought she was Dr. Sutherland," the woman said, completely perplexed.

"Oh, really? I met a Dr. Sutherland in Singapore. Is that the same person? You know—I think there is a similarity, now that you mention it. I think it's the way you're wearing your hair these days, Peggy. When did you get it cut? I always envied your long hair."

The woman who'd been questioning her so belligerently drifted away. Peggy took Hazel's hand and said, "I owe you my life. Thank you."

"You know you're stuck with being my cousin Peggy for as long as we're here?"

"It will be an honor—Cousin Hazel."

* * *

It was an ugly wound but not a serious one. Gloria had crawled up the beach to the leather case full of medical supplies and examined her injury. The bullet had entered her upper thigh on the outside of her leg and gone clear through. It hadn't struck bone or muscle, but had split the skin open along the length of its track. Gritting her teeth and twisting at an awkward angle, Gloria got it stitched shut and bandaged. She also gave herself a cautiously small dose of morphine. Then she lay back in the sand, shivering with shock and pain as the sun set.

Early in the morning she woke suddenly to the sound of a lorry backfiring. Momentarily forgetting her leg, she scrambled into the jungle for cover. To her surprise, she was quite close to a road. The lorry rattled past. It was an open troop transport vehicle driven by Japanese soldiers. In the back was a crowd of bedraggled shipwreck survivors. They must have been picked up farther down the beach. Gloria sat back to think out her situation. Apparently not everybody on the beach was being executed. Some were being picked up and taken somewhere. But where? And why? Just to be shot someplace else? Not very likely. Probably to be fed and housed as prisoners.

Not me! she thought bravely.

Then she looked around. Could she survive out here on her own? There was plenty of food—fruits and small animals she might catch. Water was a problem, but there were natives living on the island, so there must be fresh water someplace. Of course, the natives would be there, too. They certainly hadn't shown any willingness to help the miserable whites washed up on their island so far. Wouldn't they turn her in for whatever reward the Japs were bound to offer?

She'd have to hide from everybody. And everything. The awful truth was nibbling at her. This was a tropical jungle, crawling with wildlife—poisonous snakes and spiders and big dangerous predators like tigers. Not to mention the little things—the mosquitoes that carried malaria, the hookworms. If she got seriously ill or injured again, she'd have no one to care for her.

Sodding Japs.

An hour later she heard another lorry approaching. Pulling her skirt down over the bandage on her thigh, she picked up the suitcase with the drugs and uniforms and hid behind a tree at the side of the road. When she was certain it was another load of prisoners, she limped into the road and waved her arms. The truck stopped and the Japanese soldier got out. He was a huge, muscular boy of about seventeen with a wide, happy face.

He approached Gloria, made a quick, awkward bow and pointed a hammy hand at his chest. "Masamichi Asakawa," he said.

"Okay, Mickey, old boy. I'm all yours!" Gloria said.

He took a battered tin of American cigarettes out of his shirt pocket and gave them to her, then politely picked up her suitcase and handed it up into the truck for her. Gloria stood in the road, staring in amazement at the cigarettes in her hand.

PART II

Under the Rising Sun

Chapter 7

Dear Jim,
 *Did you think your mother would ever be writing to you
from a prison camp? You probably didn't guess that I would
be stupid enough to get caught in such a situation, did you?
Historians study the past for a reason—to learn from it and
have a sense of future. Well, I certainly let down the side,
didn't I? The worst of it is, I can't even talk about you because
I'm supposed to be Peggy Bright, a maiden lady schoolteacher.*

This is all Dennis's fault, Audrey St. John thought to herself
furiously as she lugged her three suitcases across the cement
quadrangle to the tin-roofed dormitory hut. A guard gave her a
shove and one of the cases bashed painfully against her Achille's
tendon, making her lose her balance and fall on her knees. One
of her silk stockings ripped clear through. Damn him! How
could she have been stupid enough to believe him that Singapore
was safe? She'd learned a long time ago not to trust men; it was
one of the guiding principles of her life. But after all, he was a
Brigadier, for Christ's sake! He should have at least been trustworthy on a military judgment. The old lecher probably knew
all along and thought that if he couldn't get out, neither should
she.
 She tried to comfort herself with the memory of all the cash
and jewels he'd lavished on her in those last frantic weeks—
valuables she'd quickly stashed away safely for her retirement.
Of course, they wouldn't do her much good here. But then, she
wouldn't be here long. She couldn't be. She had something very

important to take care of. Something she should have taken care of sooner.

"Are you in here with us?" a big, disgustingly fresh-faced redhead sitting in front of the wretched little building said. "I saw you on the yacht. I'm Hazel Hampton. This is my mother, Roberta, and our cousin Miss Peggy Bright."

"How do you do, Mrs. Hampton, Miss Hampton, Miss Bright," Audrey said in her pinched, upper-class accent. "I'm Audrey St. John." Dear God, all this bridge-party chumminess. How could she endure it?

The other women were taking their things into the hut. She might as well go on in and stake out a good bed. When she first stepped from the glare of the sun into the gloom, she was unaware of anything but the wave of heat and the stench. "Oh, dear God!" she said, stumbling back a little with her lace-edged linen handkerchief to her nose.

"Let's get those outside flaps up first," Peggy Bright was saying. "Maybe if it airs out a little—"

Audrey went back out and sat down on her largest suitcase while the other women worked on cranking up some shutterlike planks that went down both sides of the hut. She rolled off her good stocking and put it in her pocket. The one with the knee out got thrown on the ground. After a few minutes she tried going inside again. Audrey was appalled by the interior. There was no question of getting the best bed; there weren't beds, only wide bamboo platforms along both sides of a center aisle. The air was so full of dust, it was hard to see at first, but as it began to drift away and settle, the rat droppings, dead lizards, and roaches became dreadfully visible.

I can't live like this! Audrey thought with a deep sense of panic very like claustrophobia. *Not again!*

"I don't understand," Hazel Hampton was saying. "Are we supposed to sleep on those lumpy boards?"

"I'm afraid so," Peggy Bright answered. "In which case, we better get it cleaned up a bit." There was a ragged broom lying on the floor. She picked it up, gave an experimental whisk, and said, "Let's start at the far end and put everything out the front. I'll sweep. If the rest of you will improvise some rags, you can come along behind and catch what I miss."

"Good God! I'm not a housemaid!" Audrey exclaimed.

"It may have escaped your attention, but neither are we," Peggy replied coolly. "But if you'd like to claim your space first, we'll be happy to leave it undisturbed until you can get to the employment agency and find better help.''

Hazel grinned. Whoever this woman really was, she was going to like her.

''Bitch,'' Audrey muttered under her breath.

At dusk a flat wagon pulled by a couple of oxen was brought into the center of the compound. On it were five or six natives and several huge iron pots full of overcooked rice. The prisoners were summoned to line up, but quickly realized that only rice and about two hundred half coconut shells were provided; the rest of them were to be given no containers or implements with which to eat. There was a mad scramble back to the huts to find something to serve as a plate or bowl. People turned up with teacups, face-powder tins, hats, leaves ripped from the few trees at the edge of the compound, and some just accepted their food in cupped hands only to discover that it was too hot to hold. Those who dropped their rice were told they could have no more and would have to eat it off the ground. Most of them preferred to go hungry.

When it became dark, four big, harsh spotlights were turned on in the corners of the compound and a single low-wattage bulb hanging from the center of each hut came flickeringly to life. Audrey paced around the compound, loathe to return to the hut. *If this lasts more than a week, I shall go starkers!* she told herself. *Damn Dennis Stacton.* Her instincts not to get involved with military men had always served her well. She should have stayed with them. If only she hadn't been beguiled by his money—or his wife's money, more accurately—she'd have been safely away from here.

A guard approached her, spouting orders and making jabbing motions with his gun. She didn't understand the words, but the meaning was clear. Giving him her haughtiest look, she turned and walked back to the hut. ''Where is the lavatory?'' she demanded of the group of women sitting by the door.

Mrs. Hampton looked up from her bridge hand. ''There's a wash hut, Miss St. John. Turn left outside the door. Last hut. It's not exactly the ladies at Raffles.'' She said this with an odd smile, then went back to her game.

Audrey followed the directions, making sure she didn't run into the same guard again. Stepping into the wash hut, she discovered the worst. There was a long tin trough along one side with a faucet at the end, dripping a rusty trickle of water. Another trough was sunk into the concrete running through the center of the hut. The water that ran through it wasn't enough to thoroughly wash away the lumps of excrement. This, unbelievably, was the toilet! One was actually expected to simply straddle the trough, and squat down like a coolie in plain view of anybody who might walk in. Audrey turned away, gagging. Going around behind the building instead and finding a dark spot, she hurriedly urinated in the dirt.

She returned to the sleeping hut and crawled onto the platform as far from the bridge players as possible. They'd probably been laughing with each other about her while she was gone. She wouldn't give them the satisfaction of knowing how appalled she'd been. She lay down gingerly, realized it was impossible to rest without some padding, and got back up to go through her things. By arranging a coat and several of her heavier dresses properly, she was able to make a relatively soft place. Reclining, she looked over her companions with despair.

The hut was only about half full. There was the redheaded American girl, somebody Hampton, she thought she remembered, sitting directly under the light bulb trying to read a book in the gloom. No common ground there. She was one of those wholesome, girl guide types. You could spot them a mile away. She'd probably be organizing nature study groups or sing-alongs by morning. The fragile blond woman who was apparently destroying the other bridge players was her mother. Utterly boring. Too American for words and Americans were always so vulgar. Even the ones with a sophisticated veneer.

The Bright woman was looking through her suitcase for something. Audrey hoped she wouldn't find it, whatever it was. American, too. Well-spoken, if nasty, and not at all bad-looking for her age. Probably a secretary to some high-powered rubber or tin executive. She was obviously the sort who was accustomed to organizing things and having people jump to her words. *Well, not me!* Audrey thought. *I'm nobody's goddamned skivvy.*

Another truly lost cause was across the aisle from her. A tall, angular woman who could have been anywhere from twenty to forty. She was too plain and ghastly to guess. Dark, stringy hair that had never touched a curling iron or had a good cut. Thin, severe mouth and eyebrows that could use hedge clippers. And those clothes! Nobody here looked her best, but that one was wearing the sort of things that tacky people put in the church mission box—a baggy skirt, a shapeless, faded blue blouse, and sturdy, resoled shoes. She had to be a missionary. Nobody else could contrive to look like that if they tried.

This homely specimen was leaning back against the wall, looking at nothing. Looking perfectly miserable, in fact—like she'd been hit in the side of the head and was still stunned. But she glanced up suddenly and caught Audrey's gaze. There was a glint of intelligence that surprised and disconcerted Audrey.

"Hello. I'm Nancy Muir. Miss Muir," she said in an uninflected voice that matched her appearance.

Audrey introduced herself, then looked away quickly before the poor thing could decide they had something to talk about. Probably spouts scriptures at the drop of a hat! There must be *somebody* amusing here, she told herself. She peered into the semidarkness. The rest of the women in the hut were either in the shadows or turned away from her, but from what Audrey could see, there wasn't anybody particularly interesting. At least, thank God, they didn't have any children in here. The camp was lousy with the sounds of babies crying. Bad enough to be surrounded by the noise of the brats without having one right under your nose.

The light suddenly went out. The bridge players groaned and fell into a discussion of whether they'd try to finish the game in the dark from the memory of what they held or leave it for morning. Somebody in the dark started crying, and made some perfectly horrid snuffling noises trying to get a grip on herself. Others apparently had gotten up and were crashing around in the dark, trying to find a place to sleep.

A soft voice in the darkness said, "Don't you think we should say a prayer?" When no one answered, the individual took the silence for assent and started the Lord's Prayer. Several others joined in.

Damn you, Dennis Stacton, Audrey thought as she turned over and tried to get comfortable.

Two hours later the light went back on and some guards came crashing in. They prodded everybody awake, shouted things at them in Japanese, slapped a woman who was crying, then left as unexpectedly as they'd come. "What on earth was *that* about?" Audrey demanded.

"It was about being Japanese," the missionary woman across

the way said. There was enormous contempt in her voice, whether for the guards or for Audrey was impossible to tell.

An hour after that they were disturbed again. This time it was more prisoners. An exhausted, rain-soaked group of five women were shoved in the door and their suitcases thrown in after them. Two of the younger ones were wearing only native sarongs. They must have been helped by natives before they were caught. A third was an elderly lady who spoke only French and became hysterical because nobody could understand her. The other two were nuns. Finally the newcomers found places to lie down and it got quiet again.

Toward dawn two more women were put in the hut. One was a heavy matronly sort with her arm hanging at an odd angle. It was obviously broken and she was in shock. Some of the women fussed over her in the dark, but it did no good. She moaned for the next hour, then got very quiet.

They were awakened again at first light—or what would have been first light if it hadn't been raining—by a terrible clanging. The women in the hut hardly had time to sit up before a guard was screaming in their faces. The gist of it seemed to be that they were to assemble outside.

Nancy Muir was the only one to respond. Stepping up to him, she said, "Need doctor. Understand?"

"No doctor. No doctor. No wimmens get sick."

"Not sick. Dead. That woman is dead." She pointed to the heavy woman with the broken arm. She was, indeed, dead.

He looked at her, then back at Nancy Muir. "Not dead. No wimmens get dead." He turned on his heel and left.

"What are we to do?" Hazel asked, panicked. She'd never been in the same room with a dead body except at funerals, and that was very different. Flowers, soft music, everyone dressed in their best—not a filthy jungle hut with a fat, dead stranger!

"What we're told, I suppose. Certainly there will be somebody here who can understand."

They filed out into the quadrangle, most making a quick dash to the hideous wash hut first. Once assembled, they spent the first half hour standing in the rain being counted. Over and over again the guards tried to arrange them in such a way to account for them all, but the concept of tallying seemed to elude them. They got more and more confused, and several times the guards themselves nearly came to blows over their various results.

"They aren't the cream of the crop, are they?" Hazel said under her breath to Nancy Muir, who was standing next to her.

"Probably Formosan or Korean or crazy. The ones they can't trust at the front," Nancy whispered back.

Finally they were dismissed and shooed like chickens back to their huts. Hazel and Nancy Muir lagged behind. "You seem remarkably cheerful, under the circumstances, Miss Hampton," Nancy said.

"Not cheerful, believe me, but I do feel a strange sense of—well, I suppose it's relief."

"Relief!"

"It's hard to explain, but my mother and I have been living in a constant state of anxiety about what was going to happen to us. I suppose that's true of almost everyone here. Every hour of every day since December I've been wondering if we'd get away safely or not. And now I finally know. We aren't. It's certainly not the answer I wanted, but at least it's an answer."

"But it's only replaced with a lot of new questions. Like will we survive this? And if so, for how long?"

"That's true. I suppose I just haven't had time to get obsessed with the new questions yet. No doubt I will. What are you doing out here, Miss Muir?"

It had become the standard conversational opening among the prisoners, and Nancy had a standard answer ready. "My father was a missionary. He died a few months ago and I went to Singapore to think things out and decide where to go next," Nancy answered. It was the truth, after all, just not the important parts of the truth.

"Where are you from?"

"Sacramento, California. But I haven't been in the States since I was a child. And you, Miss Hampton?"

Hazel also had an abbreviated form of response ready and gave it, by which time they were back to the hut. The dead woman was gone. Nobody knew where. Hazel joined the rest of the women in trying to find dry clothing to put on. In spite of the tropical heat, most were shivering from standing out in the rain for so long. Hazel, like the rest of the ladies, changed quickly and with as much modesty as possible in such close confines, then surreptitiously watched Audrey St. John, who had simply shed her wet clothing in a heap as if a maid would be along later to pick it up. She was wearing a beautiful aqua lace brassiere, the likes of which Hazel had never seen or even imagined, and aqua lace panties that matched. Her figure was as stunning as her underwear.

"What are you all staring at?" Audrey demanded suddenly, and Hazel realized she wasn't the only one who'd been fascinated by the sheer spectacle of Miss St. John getting undressed.

Nancy Muir answered her. "I was just wondering, since you have so much clothing and these two ladies have nothing but their wet sarongs—?"

"I'm terrible sorry, but I do not loan my things. It puts a terrible strain on relationships, don't you know."

A dreadful silence followed this announcement.

Then Peggy Bright spoke coldly. "Haven't you noticed yet where you are? This isn't the dressing room of Robinsons."

"I have some blouses and skirts I can share," Hazel said quickly to avert a further confrontation between Miss St. John's values and everyone else's. But at that moment the clanging began again and in the hopes that it meant food, they all dashed outside.

After another meal of rice and vegetables with a few vaguely suspicious bits of meat, they all returned again to the hut. The earlier conversation had left everybody wary, and most of the women simply curled up in their allotted spaces to try to catch up on their sleep. Only the bridge players talked as they shuffled and dealt.

Around noon, when the rain stopped and the sun was blistering, they were again summoned into the compound. This time the men prisoners were not in their usual ranks. As the women and children assembled, three trucks pulled into the center and the men, stuffed like sardines into two huts, were brought out and told to get on the trucks. Hazel felt a sudden overwhelming sense of sorrow for them. A woman was allowed to cry or express fright without being less of a woman. But a man was not. These men, from teenaged boys to elderly retirees, had to be "manly" at all costs. It was their patriotic duty. Some of their wives and mothers rushed forward and tried to cling to them, but the guards beat them off and other women pulled them away to keep them from being seriously hurt.

"Allan, don't go! I'll die without you!" one young woman sobbed over and over.

Her young husband tried to get to her, but a guard hit him in the face with his rifle butt. He fell, bleeding and unconscious, to the ground. Other men picked him up and put him on a truck. Hazel turned away from the sight, faint and sick at both the physical and emotional brutality.

The trucks eventually rumbled out of the compound and an awful quiet fell over them. "I didn't even know any of those men, and yet I feel lost without them," Hazel whispered to Nancy Muir. Then she realized that Miss Muir had tears rolling down her face. "Was one of them—someone—to you?"

Nancy shook her head. How could this girl understand what she herself couldn't understand or admit to? She didn't even know his name—how could he be "someone" to her?

The guards began again with their tedious and ill-conceived attempts to count the women. As they did so, another truck came into the compound. After a few words between the driver and one of the other guards, it pulled over to the hut where Hazel and the others were assigned and the women on it started to climb down.

"Oh, my God!" Audrey murmured. *Beryl Stacton! Of all the people on earth. And in the same hut!* It was simply too much to bear.

Hazel, too, thought she recognized someone, but at this distance it was hard to tell. When they were finally dismissed, she hurried back to the hut and approached the bedraggled blonde in the oversized navy and white dress. "Aren't you Sister Denk?"

The young woman turned and winced from some invisible pain. "Yes, I—oh, you're the girl who stole the truck. Miss Hampton, isn't it? Did you find your father?"

"No, I'm afraid not. Are you unwell?"

Gloria was swaying in place. She sat down carefully. "Is there a doctor here? I need to see one, but I can't let the Japs know. You see—" She told Hazel, in hushed tones and with the omission of the horrible details, about the massacre on the beach. "If they knew I was a witness to such a bloody atrocity, they'd kill me."

"Stay here. Rest. I'll find help for you. Oh, Miss Muir, this is Sister Denk. Do you know where a doctor might be?"

"They're apparently setting up a hospital of sorts right now in one of the huts the men were in. I'll go find somebody."

The doctor she returned with, a Belgian woman, was delighted to receive the medicines Gloria had found, unharmed, in the lifeboat. She was also complimentary about Gloria's job on her own leg. "Ziz is no so bad. I could stitch it better, but too many people, they would know. Better to leave it as it is. Zere is no sepsis. Keep covered away from zee flies—and zee eyes of others."

When she'd gone, Hazel said, "I don't understand. Why conceal it from the others?"

Nancy Muir, who had been sitting in on the "house call" replied, "Because we don't know how long we may be here, Miss Hampton, or what information may become a useful commodity."

Hazel was shocked. "You don't mean somebody would tell the Japs? We're all in this together."

Nancy hesitated. "There are people who are not good keepers of other people's secrets, especially if they are hungry or desperate. Not everyone feels the togetherness. We're all terrified individuals, especially the mothers with small children to look after. And, if you don't mind my advice, Miss Hampton, you shouldn't call them Japs. They hate that. They call themselves Nipponese."

Audrey was pretending to take a stroll outside the hospital hut that was being set up. The doctor who was in there was too busy organizing things to pull her aside for a chat. Audrey had already tried. As the other doctor approached, on her return from calling on Gloria, Audrey caught her. "You are the doctor, are you not?" she asked. "I have something I must discuss with you."

"Very well. Are you sick or injured?"

"Not precisely. I'm—with child."

"Ah, zis is a bad place for you, then. I will ask that you, as the other pregnant women, be given extra foods. Come in. I have vitamins. Not enough, but—"

"I'm afraid you don't understand. I want to get rid of it."

"Zis cannot be done."

"I know it can't under normal circumstances. But we're not under British law now."

"I do not speak of law. My calling is to save lives, not take them. Zis matters not where I am or whose law prevails."

Audrey's eyes narrowed. "You can't tell me you've never done an abortion. Doctors do them all the time."

"Yes, sadly, this is true. I have—but when zere is something terribly wrong with fetus or mother is to die otherwise. Even if zese things were the case, I have no way to do it safely. Not here. Ze chances of infection are too great. No, miss, I will not do as you wish.''

She went into the hospital hut before Audrey could pursue the conversation any further.

''Well, somebody will do as I wish!'' Audrey said to herself. ''Somebody *must!*''

Beryl Stacton had just returned from her first memorable visit to the wash hut and was lying down, trying to get her breath back and let her stomach calm down. Her heart was racing, her corset was biting into her ribs, and she was appalled at how she smelled. Sweat, seawater, and a faint but distinct odor of mildew hung around her, embarrassing and disgusting her. She'd been so meticulous in her personal habits for so many years that she was astonished to realize that she could smell bad. She had found her own suitcase on the beach, which was a small miracle, but it was waterlogged and probably everything inside was ruined. She hadn't the strength, now that she was prone at last, to get up and find out.

Why on earth hadn't Dennis known this might happen to her? How could he have let it happen? She had, naturally, been the good military wife, agreeing to stay on to be by his side—not that his ''side'' was around much of the time—but she'd assumed that before it was actually dangerous he'd send her away to India or Australia. Just as it had been her duty to leave England and live all over the world with him, it was his duty to protect her.

The bridge players in the corner finished a game. ''Do you play?'' a frail-looking middle-aged blonde asked Beryl.

''Not as well as I wish,'' Beryl said modestly as she sat up.

''We've lost our fourth to the wash hut. Would you care to join us? I'm Mrs. Hampton, by the way.''

''I'm Mrs. Stacton. I believe I would, if you don't mind waiting while I try to find something clean to put on.''

She rose and dragged her heavy suitcase onto the sleeping platform. As she feared, everything inside was quite damp. ''Oh, dear.''

''Here, let's just hang these things out for a bit,'' Roberta Hampton said. ''And in the meantime, someone else left a suitcase with some dry clothing. It might fit you well enough.''

"But I can hardly do that without the lady's permission."

"I'm afraid you'll have to. She died last night."

Beryl gulped. "Oh, I see—"

The others helped her hang up her wet dresses in such a way as to create a sort of dressing screen, behind which she peeled off her stinking apparel and got into a dead woman's clothing. She joined the others and was dealt quite a nice hand. A little too heavy on low spades to be all she might wish, but given a good partner, she could overcome that.

She had just taken her third trick in a row when someone else walked into the hut. Glancing up automatically, Beryl was suddenly frozen with shock. The cards dribbled from her fingers.

"Oh, I say! Are you ill?" the player to her right said, putting down her hand and placing a supportive arm around Beryl.

That woman! It was that woman! Dennis's whore. The doxy he'd been bewitched by. All her good British "pluck" drained away. She could cope with being a prisoner. She could even adjust to smelling common and wearing a dead woman's clothing, and upper-class moral indignation could get her back to the horrid wash hut. But this—this was too much! Having to actually be in daily contact with her husband's mistress was more than she could bear. She put her face in her hands and sobbed uncontrollably.

Audrey looked down her long, patrician nose at the spectacle of fat, old, frumpy Beryl Stacton going to bits. Then, with long, graceful strides, she turned and left the hut.

In spite of her words earlier in the day to Miss Muir about her sense of relief, Hazel's deliberate good cheer failed her that night when the flickering light bulb went dark. She lay on the hard platform in the steamy darkness and felt her anxiety wrap itself around her chest like a snake. When the men were taken away, she'd begun to realize how utterly dependent they all were on the whims and motives of the Japanese—people none of them could begin to understand, people who obviously despised all of them. Then, when Gloria Denk told her story, Hazel had realized that those whims were deadly. Their lives were precariously balanced.

But something trivial and personal that happened in the evening was what really brought her spirits down, and it wasn't something their captors had done; it was something Hazel herself had done. One of the young women had come into the hut and said, "Rats! I've got the curse. Has anybody got a few napkins?"

And what Hazel had done was nothing. She didn't speak up.

Now, in the oppressive darkness, surrounded by foreign smells and the sounds of misery, she picked at the incident like a hangnail. A day or two as a prisoner and she was already seeing selfishness in herself. If this went on for long, what else might she find? What dark traits might surface in a week, or a month? Or longer?

Please, God, get us out of here before we learn the worst about ourselves, she prayed.

Chapter 8

Dear Jim,

I've never been much interested in food, as your experience with my cooking will attest. And yet, in the last couple days I've become nearly obsessed with it. What I wouldn't do for a nice Virginia ham! Cloves stuck in those little diamonds on the skin, a big bowl of cheese-crusted scalloped potatoes like your aunt Eileen makes—heaven. And I want it served on a long, damask-draped table, with real silver and pink candles. And while I'm dreaming anyway, I want you and your father there. And me with my hair freshly washed and my shoes shined—

They were jarred awake by a hideous noise the next morning. The Japanese guards had hooked up the primitive loudspeaker system and one of them was clanging a cowbell into the microphone. Children screamed with fright, babies cried, and several of the women, worn down by fatigue and injuries and fear, had hysterics. But most of the women simply staggered to the wash hut and then to the center of the compound. Those few who thought the summons could be ignored and went back to sleep were dragged out of the huts by guards shouting "*Tenko*. You come *tenko*!" Once again they were ordered to form up in ranks to be counted and, as before, the enumerating process defeated their captors.

As they were muddling through it, shoving people into line, out of line, and trying to find a way to count in multiples, one guard went into the hut they were apparently using for an office and came out shouting a name. The woman he was summoning stepped forward and raised her hand. Two of the other guards grabbed her by the elbows and quick-marched her to a staff car. "No! Where are you taking me? What are you doing?" she protested.

No one answered her. The other women strained forward, feeling like a part of them all was being torn away even though most of them didn't even know her. The staff car was driven off and they could hear her frightened objections through the open window.

After an hour the guards got some figure that satisfied them and a new individual came forward from the guards' hut.

"Jesus! What's that when it's at home?" Gloria said under her breath to Hazel.

"Lord! I can't imagine!"

A young woman was standing before them on a makeshift podium. She was a dumpy little Japanese in a drooping black bag of a dress that appeared to be some sort of uniform. An apparent attempt to have her hair cut into a Western style had resulted in disorderly black spikes sticking out all over her head like a very cheap wig.

"Western women! I am Nurse Royama. I am translator for the Imperial Nipponese Army in these camp. I say to you messages from Colonel Ienaga." She spoke in an excruciatingly high, loud, singsong voice that grated on the nerves every bit as badly as the cowbell. The officer for whom she was speaking stood in the doorway of the guards' hut, watching with a bored expression. "I am now here teaching you to bow," Nurse Royama went on. "Western women, observe! When an honorable soldier from the Nipponese army approaches, you do thus—"

"Only when an honorable one approaches? That ought to be easy," Gloria muttered.

Nurse Royama demonstrated a proper bow, then explained it. "Firstly, you put all carrying things on ground such as package or handbag. Then remove all head clothing, such as scarf, hat, or sunglasses. Discard cigarette. Bend forward with feets together and hands at sides thus. Being silent, remain. Now I will show again. Thus. Now, Western women, you bow!"

She raised her arms in a conductor's salute and watched with something between alarm and disgust as some of the women attempted to follow her directions. "No, no, no! This is not very good." She repeated her directions and tried again with the same results.

Ienaga had lost interest and disappeared.

"I'm not bowing to the bloody nips!" Gloria said, standing quite straight.

"They'll beat you senseless if you don't," Nancy Muir, on the other side of her, said as she executed a perfect bow. "When you're lying on the ground unconscious, I guess that'll show them."

"I'm not afraid of them!" Gloria persisted.

"Then you're a fool and you'll soon be a dead one," Nancy commented.

"We are their prisoners! Just bow, Sister Denk," Hazel advised.

With stiff reluctance Gloria did so, hating herself, the Japanese, and her companions equally. They practiced it again and again. The children and some of the younger women made something of a game of it. Others were not so resilient. When a woman two rows in front of them continued to refuse to bow on command, Nancy Muir's prediction was proved true. Two of the guards, coming only up to the tall, dignified woman's chin, struck her first in the stomach, causing her to double over, then sharply across the back. She fainted, and when the women near her tried to come to her aid, they were shoved back at the point of a bayonet.

"Dear God—" Hazel murmured, nearly faint herself. It wasn't only that the soldiers were doing such terrible things, but that the women were helpless to do anything about it. She looked away, determined to concentrate on something else. Down the row from her, Audrey St. John had just bowed. Somehow, though doing it just as they'd been told, she managed to make it look like an insult. Hazel studied her intently, wondering if she could imitate the arrogant, mocking manner, but decided she lacked something vital to carry it off.

When Hazel looked back, the woman who'd been knocked down had finally struggled back to her feet and reluctantly bowed. Nurse Royama's high, shrill voice went on and on, instructing them over and over, pulling good examples out of the ranks and further humiliating them by praising them. As she walked among the women, Hazel got a closer look at her. She nudged Gloria. "Get a load of her teeth," she whispered.

Nurse Royama had tiny, even teeth that were all silver-capped.

"Christ!" Gloria whispered, suddenly grinning. "The family must have sunk their entire fortune into the bitch's mouth! Maybe they thought no one would notice the rest of her face that way."

Eventually most of the women were cowed into performing a bow to Nurse Royama's minimum standards, and she got back onto her podium and addressed them again as a car pulled into the prison compound. "Now, Western women, you will bow to Commandant Natsume."

It was apparent from her tone that this was somebody she considered terribly important, much more so than Ienaga, who'd come back out of the hut and was standing at rigid attention. Royama looked around at them in a way that suggested that they were probably as impressed as she was, or they should be.

A dapper military man in his fifties got out of the car and looked around the compound with an utterly unreadable expression. Slowly, almost regally, he walked to the small podium upon which Nurse Royama had begun her lecture. She had gotten down from it and kept bowing to him and gesturing for the prisoners to do the same. Most did, though not with the enthusiasm she hoped for.

Commandant Natsume took a step up and continued to study the prisoners. He was rather tall for a Japanese, with very fair skin and black hair only slightly streaked with gray. His uniform was covered with medals and ribbons. There was something slightly unnatural in the way he held his left arm. Hazel stared at the black-gloved left hand and decided that either the arm was paralyzed or it was a prosthesis. There was something compelling enough in his stance and presence to command silence—if not respectful, at least intensely curious silence.

Finally, he spoke. His voice was deep and clear, almost melodic. He addressed them in perfect American English with only the slightest trace of an accent. "You will learn much while you are here. It is your duty to learn, as it is the duty of the Imperial Nipponese Army to teach you. For centuries your husbands and fathers have come to Asia and have raped the land and its people. This cycle of history is now completed and has come full circle. Thanks to the wisdom of the Emperor, Japan has now returned Asia to the Asians. You British, Dutch, Australians, and Americans are now members of fourth-class nations. You are fourth-class women. As you have made coolies of the Asians, now we shall make coolies of you. You will live and eat and obey as the Asians did when they were enslaved by you."

"Then we are your slaves? What about the Geneva Convention?" a woman in the ranks called out loudly enough for everyone to hear.

Three of the guards started to descend on her, but Natsume waved them off with a curt gesture of his right arm. He stared at the speaker for a long moment, then said, "You have much to learn. You have been proud and arrogant and you shall be cured of it. In future, such outspoken rudeness will not be tolerated and you would do well to learn that. In the meantime, I shall answer you. All of you. As you must know, Japan did not ratify the Geneva Convention documents which are to govern the treatment of prisoners of war. We have no obligation to observe them. Nor are you prisoners; you are guests of the Emperor."

"Guests, hell! He makes it sound like a sodding tea party," Gloria said.

"Shut up!" Nancy Muir warned her.

But Gloria wasn't about to take that advice. She spoke up, addressing Natsume as boldly as the other woman had. "How long do you intend to keep us before we are repatriated?" she asked loudly.

Hazel cringed. Why couldn't Sister Denk keep quiet?

This time Natsume didn't hesitate. "This is forever."

A profound silence now fell over them, broken only by the insane chattering of a pair of squabbling monkeys just outside the barbed wire of the compound.

Natsume let the silence stretch out unbearably before continuing. "The sooner you accept that, the better your life will be. The Nippon army has been victorious throughout Southeast Asia and the Pacific. All countries and islands are under our control and wise administration. Resistance has been eliminated. Escape is impossible, and any attempt will result in death. We have entered a new era, and you must quickly learn your new role in this world. You will be obedient, hardworking, respectful, and orderly."

Someone else started to speak, but this time he made a quick, sharp gesture and the guards silenced the woman. "That is all I have to say to you at this time."

Nurse Royama, with a frenzy of arm waving, tried to lead the Western women in another round of bowing as Natsume stepped off the podium and went back to his car. As he was driven away, the women were dismissed and both Colonel Ienaga and Nurse Royama disappeared as well.

"Where do you suppose they put her when she's not out here flashing her horrible teeth?" Hazel asked Gloria.

"Probably back into her jar of formaldehyde," Gloria answered.

"Don't you feel a little sorry for her?"

Gloria whirled and faced her angrily. "Sorry? For her? You can't mean it!"

"I don't know. She's such a pathetic thing. Ugly as mud— and I think she's as scared of them as we are."

"Speak for yourself. I'm not scared of them."

"Come on!" Hazel said, gesturing toward Gloria's injured leg. "If you're not afraid of them, you're insane. You, more than most of us, have cause to know just how frightening they are."

"Oh, stop harping on it!" Gloria said harshly. She turned and limped away.

"Sister Denk, I'm sorry. I just—" Hazel was left standing alone, feeling lonely and abandoned. She went back to the hut, thinking she could talk some of this over with her mother and feel better. But Roberta was already engaged in another bridge game. "Here, darling. You can sit by me and watch," she offered.

"No, thanks." Hazel went to her allotted portion of the sleeping platform. She'd read for a while, she decided. But try as she might, she couldn't keep her mind on the words on the page. She'd try to think a movie. Something with Bette Davis, maybe. Disjointed scenes flashed through her mind, but she couldn't seem to get a fix on any of them. Finally, she put the book down and looked around the hut. Miss Muir was curled up on her side, sleeping, or pretending to. There were the two nuns, one very old, the other in her twenties. They were kneeling together, mumbling prayers as they went through their rosaries. Miss St. John, extraordinarily enough, had managed to find a servant. She'd brought a bedraggled girl of about fourteen into the hut and was telling her how she wanted her clothes brushed and folded and put away. Amazing, Hazel thought. A prisoner with a servant. Mrs. Stacton, currently sitting out the bridge game, was watching Miss St. John with an expression of utter hatred.

I can't just lie here and do nothing all day! Hazel thought. But what was there to do? She had only a few books along, and if she raced through them and they really were stuck here for weeks or even months, she be sorry she hadn't spaced them out. Two of the women were mending and one was knitting something, but Hazel didn't enjoy that sort of thing. There was bridge, of course, but she hated that. What she really wanted was to just talk to someone. Perhaps if she got out of the hut—

As she was leaving, Gloria Denk came in, towing a very large woman by the hand. The large newcomer was dressed only in her corset, a short half slip, and a huge man's overcoat. Her fair skin, of which a great deal was exposed, was bright pink with sunburn. "Everybody!" Gloria said. "Meet Sister Caroline Warbler. She's just gotten here and she's going to be in with us!"

Beryl Stacton looked at her with horror. "Young woman, where is your clothing?"

"I used my dress for a sail to bring a little boat in," Sister Warbler answered in her surprisingly tiny voice. "I got to shore and took a little nap and my boat—and my uniform—drifted away. Luckily, I found this coat on the beach. I've been walking all over the island, trying to find somebody to turn myself in to. The natives were afraid of me. I don't believe they'd ever seen a white woman my size." She laughed, and her substantial bosom jiggled in waves.

"I have an extra uniform you can have to wear home, but you'll have to do a bit of slimming first," Gloria said. "It was Sister Cassini's."

"Was? You mean—?"

"Yes, come sit down and I'll tell you about it."

They brushed past Hazel.

Hazel picked up her plate and wandered into the compound.

She was among the first to get her rice allotment when the truck came. This time the gluey rice had been cooked in old ten-gallon kerosene cans and tasted of kerosene. Hazel was hungry enough that she didn't care. There were very small bits of some kind of light-colored meat in it, but it was so bland she couldn't tell if it was chicken or fish. She took her plate as far as she could from the crowd and sat down in the shade of one of the huts.

She ate as slowly as she could, just to make this one small activity last as long as possible before long, useless, anxious hours again stretched out in front of her. As she was finishing the last grains of rice and shreds of mysterious meat, she was joined by Peggy Bright.

The older woman sat down on the ground and ate a few bites of her rice. She made a face. "Everyone—and I include myself—is holding up better than I expected," she said in a conversational tone. "I've been thinking about us—all of us. We look like a cross-section, and I suppose we are in a way. There are the very wealthy and the high-ranking military clear down through the middle classes—"

"Yes?" Hazel encouraged her to go on. This was just what she'd been longing for—someone to talk to about ideas, not the emotions that were ravaging them all just beneath the surface.

"But last night I realized we aren't entirely representative. For one thing, we don't have any of the lower classes of European or American society. And even if you rounded up the first five hundred upper- and middle-class women and children you could get your hands on in the streets of London or Chicago, I don't believe they'd cope as well as this group will in the long run."

"It doesn't seem we're coping at all well."

"Look again—"

Hazel gazed around the compound. There were several groups of women standing and talking pleasantly—almost normally—while they ate. Others, mainly the younger women and nurses, were sitting on the ground, obviously having a good gossip over their kerosene-flavored rice. Some of the children had already chalked in a hopscotch pattern on the concrete, and others were playing cat's cradle or games with dolls they'd managed to get ashore with. A pair of Dutch nuns was leading a group of very small children in a song. Once Hazel listened for it, she actually heard laughter here and there.

"Well, I suppose we aren't all having breakdowns every moment—" she admitted. "What is your theory to account for it?"

"Ah, the theory. It all hinges on the fact that we were out here where we could be caught," Peggy said. "With a few exceptions, we are the adventurous ones, the adaptable ones. If we weren't, we'd all be safely at home listening to the radio and knitting socks for the Red Cross, not out flitting around the world. We are the people who read about Asia and said to ourselves, 'Ah-hah, that looks interesting and different. I think I'll give it a try.' And that same adaptability is what will allow us to survive. Maybe even thrive."

"But it's not true of everyone. Me, for instance. I'm not out here from any sense of adventure. I merely accompanied my parents. And there are many young children who had nothing whatsoever to say about it. Many of these boys and girls were born out here."

"—born to the adventurous, adaptable parents who pass their attitudes on with the pabulum. As for you, I've watched you with your face buried in a book most of the time since you've been here. That proves you have the other necessary quality—a deep curiosity and desire to learn things. Now, this awful place isn't anything you'd choose to learn about, but while you're here, I've no doubt you'll learn all you can."

"How? What on earth is there here that's worth knowing?"

Peggy Bright put her empty plate down. "Why, everything there is to know about human nature."

"You make it all sound like a big intellectual challenge. But it's not. It's a tragedy."

"It's both. And the longer it lasts, the more of our intellect we had better bring to it," Peggy said with an intensity that had been lacking in her previous talk.

Hazel felt a chill down her back. "How long do you think it will be?"

Peggy thought for a moment. "It could be a good long while. The American fleet has to be practically rebuilt if what we hear about Pearl Harbor is true. Four or five months at the least for that. Then another three to six to actually get back into the fray and push the Japanese back."

Hazel was appalled. "You mean we could really be here— *here*—for a whole year!"

"Probably not, but it's possible. Of course, they're apparently stunned by the sheer numbers of us. I don't think they expected to have so many captives. They might just ship us all off to Australia to get rid of us, but it's unlikely.''

"How will we survive?" Hazel said despairingly.

"I don't know, but we must. Consider the alternative. You won't give up. Neither will I."

"I'm more likely to die of boredom."

"That's the worst of it, isn't it?" Peggy said thoughtfully. "When the rest begin to realize this isn't just something we're stuck with for a few days, we'll tend to that. Boredom is truly the enemy of the human soul."

Hazel stared at her. She'd never heard expressed something she just now realized she felt so deeply. "You're right. Miss Bright."

"Good heavens! We're supposed to be cousins—not Miss Bright and Miss Hampton."

"Yes. Peggy, what are you doing here? What kind of adventure brought you to Asia?" Peggy looked at her intently, as if trying to see into her character and assess it. "You can trust me," Hazel said, sensing her thoughts.

"Yes, I think I can. But let's move over there by the fence."

They picked up their empty coconut shells and strolled over to a clear area near the barbed wire where no one could overhear them. First allowing a silence while she gathered her thoughts, Peggy finally said, "I was Peggy Bright—that's my maiden name, which is why it came to mind when that awful woman started going on at me. Many years ago I went to Wellesley, where I was assigned to tutor a young Chinese girl who was a student there. As it turned out, she needed very little tutoring. Her English was impeccable and her mind quick. Her name was Meiling Soong—"

"Soong? Didn't she become Sun Yat-sen's wife?" Hazel asked.

"No, that was one of her sisters. Meiling is the generalissimo's wife. She's Madame Chiang Kaishek now. I don't know how much you know of recent China history, but they've been attempting to fight off the Japanese invaders for many years now. The Japanese have taken much of the coast, but the Chinese still hold most of the vast inland. Chiang Kaishek is probably the one man in the world the Japanese hate the most."

"But I don't understand—many people must have known her. What has she to do with you?"

"Everything at the moment. You see, I'm the president of a

small women's college in Missouri, but I've also written a number of books, political biographies—"

Suddenly the name Dr. Margaret Sutherland clicked into place in Hazel's mind. "Oh—oh, I know! I read your book about Eleanor Roosevelt on the ship on the way to Singapore. It was wonderful!"

"How nice of you to say so."

"And your picture was on the cover. I remember now. That's why you were tearing up the dust jackets on the ship, wasn't it? But I still don't see—"

"When the war started, I was in Singapore on my way to Chungking, where the Chinese government was centered, to begin research on a book about Meiling. In spite of the war with Japan, it sounded like an exciting thing to do, and I was eager to work closely with my old friend. I was taking copies of my books to her. The difficulty is, I made no secret of my plan or my relationship to her. In fact, I mentioned it in several of the interviews I did in connection with the Roosevelt book. While my name isn't exactly a household word, I'm probably known to the Japanese and am a marked enemy. Think of the propaganda they could make of me—or make of my death or alleged renunciation of my Chinese friends."

"They would kill you for your connection with the Chinese government?"

"Killing me might be the least unpleasant of the options."

They were facing the jungle beyond the barbed wire and suddenly turned to see what the commotion was behind them. Roberta Hampton dashed up. "Quick, Hazel, you must hide! They're looking for you!"

But a soldier was practically on her heels. "Hazer Hammon? You Hazer Hammon?" he barked. Taking her stunned silence for an answer, he grabbed her by the arm and started to drag her away.

"Mother!"

Roberta and Peggy Bright were right behind her. "Where are you taking her? What do you want her for?" Peggy demanded. Roberta was crying.

All Hazel could think of was the woman who'd been dragged away earlier in the morning. What had either of them done?

The guard turned and, with his free hand, shoved at Peggy and Roberta. They kept a few paces behind, just out of his reach.

He dragged Hazel to the hut that was being used as an office. Shoving her in the door, he turned and screamed at the other two women. The door closed behind her, and Hazel found herself facing a desk behind which Colonel Ienaga sat smoking a cigarette in an ivory holder. The silver-toothed Nurse Royama was standing beside him, holding a sheaf of papers. "You are Hazel Hampton?" she asked.

No point in denying it. "Yes, I am." She tried to stand up and pretend to calm dignity.

"You bow!"

Hazel bowed.

"Where is your birth place?"

"Evanston, Illinois. In America." What did that matter? She'd already given that information.

Nurse Royama studied a sheet of paper covered with Japanese characters. She spoke to Ienaga in Japanese. He nodded. "Why are you in Asia?" Royama asked.

"I came with my parents." Her knees were shaking so badly she could hardly keep upright.

The Japanese nurse continued to study the top paper. She mumbled something to herself and nodded. Then she opened the desk drawer nearest her. "This is yours," she said, holding out Hazel's manicure set that had been taken from her when she was brought to the jail.

Hazel took the case. "Thank you," she whispered. "Is that all?"

"Of course that's all!"

Hazel started to turn away, but remembered just in time to bow first. Nurse Royama smiled her silver smile.

Opening the door, Hazel's knees finally gave out and she fell into her mother's arms. "My manicure set," she said. "They gave me back my manicure set! Excuse me. I think I'm going to be sick."

Chapter 9

Dear Jim,
You probably don't remember this, but once when you were about four years old, we took a trip to New York just before Christmas and I took you to Macy's to see the Santa Claus. You studied him with caution, but when you were put on his lap, you went wild with fright. Scrambling away, you ran to me and started hitting me. We're all struggling against that impulse. When we're terrified, we often don't lash out against those who frighten us, but against our own. We are perched on emotional TNT. A single spark at the wrong moment, and we would all go quite mad and uncivilized and tear one another to shreds. How arrogant I've been, thinking I knew so much about people, and knowing so little about people under stress.

There was another long *tenko* that afternoon. Several of the women, upon consideration, had decided it was clearly unpatriotic to bow to the enemy and were prepared to stand up for themselves. They were also prepared to take the consequences of their action, which was admirable, but to everyone's surprise they were not beaten this time for their disobedience.

Instead, Nurse Royama announced quite calmly that they would all wait for the intractable women to change their minds. In one sentence, she'd made the entire camp responsible for the few rigid consciences. So they waited. Standing at attention in the fierce tropic sun of midday, the women sweated, got leg and back cramps, and waited. And waited. Several women got nauseated, but they were not excused. Two of them bent forward and vomited on the ground and had to remain standing over the mess. The guards brought Nurse Royama a chair, upon which she sat, holding a parasol, calmly reading a newspaper and occasionally glancing up to see if the nonbowers had come to their senses. When the children began to get fretful and cranky, she stood up and said they—the children—could go back to their huts. The mothers of the smaller ones got frantic at this. They didn't want their children running about without supervision.

"For God's sake, just bow, you bitch!" one of the mothers said to the woman in front of her.

"Yes, please think of the rest of us, especially the children," another woman urged her.

"Just because you have no pride in your heritage is no reason I should knuckle under to these savages!" the woman replied.

"It isn't a question of pride!"

"Western women. You will not talk!" Nurse Royama said, sitting back down.

Nancy Muir was standing in the back row. The woman in front of her fainted, wetting herself as she collapsed. Nancy knew better than to try to come to her aid. She waited patiently until the guards' attention was elsewhere, then she leaned forward and pulled the unfortunate woman's skirt down where it had hitched up, letting her pink rayon panties show.

They have no idea what this is all about, Nancy thought. *There isn't one in ten who comprehends the extraordinary depth of racial and personal hatred these people have for us or the grave danger we're in. Should I tell them? No. How could I? There's no way to compress years and years of hard-earned comprehension into a short lecture. Nor would they believe me. They can't afford to. I wish I didn't know what I know of them. How could I inflict that deadly knowledge on these innocents?*

A woman down the row from her was one of the proud, patriotic ones. She was swaying on her feet but still had her chin high. Nancy gazed at her, hoping the intensity of her thoughts might be conveyed. *You will bow. You will all bow or we will all die waiting. The Japanese culture is ancient and patient. Minutes and hours mean nothing to them. Years—centuries mean nothing. They'll wait until we all bow. If it takes all day, if we have to all be dead on the concrete, they will wait.*

"I will have some tea," Nurse Royama announced to the women, then conveyed her request in Japanese to the guards.

One of them fetched it for her, and she sat slurping it noisily and watching the Western women with their dry mouths swallow and look away.

Nancy closed her eyes, trying to let at least her mind escape from this horror. She was back at the mission. . . .

Mama had died years before, when Nancy was only six. Nancy had a photograph of her, but no actual memory. Papa had died the previous May, but he'd been ill for a long time and the church had already sent out his replacement. Dr. Ivan Jake arrived the day after Nancy buried her father and he insisted that she stay on for as long as she liked. She made a great fuss and bother about being prepared to leave right away, knowing all the time she hadn't an idea in the world where she'd go. She had cousins in the States, but she'd never even met them, and what would they want with an old-maid missionary! But Dr. Jake— Ivan, as he insisted she call him—had been adamant that she remain for at least a month or two.

He'd been so kind to her. Accustomed to her father's stern, religious fervency, Ivan's breezy friendliness had been intoxicating. He sang boisterously and off-tune. He told religious jokes and laughed uproariously. Before a few days had passed he was calling her "Nan," as though they were old friends, even intimates. His Japanese was textbook, learned at the seminary and unused during his medical training, so she had to accompany him everywhere.

She sensed the truth at first—before she became intoxicated by the looks and sound and touch of him. The truth was that she was the only native English-speaker and the only white woman for fifty miles. And even a plain, scrawny old maid was better company to a gregarious man like him than the incomprehensible Japanese women, mainly elderly or outcast, who frequented the mission. But she was eager to forget that.

Ivan was so bright and brash and handsome—so handsome it broke her heart to look at him. His mop of unruly sandy hair, his broad, square shoulders, and long, loping stride suggested an Anglo ruggedness she thirsted to see while his almost transparently light blue eyes and delicately curved lips meant a sensitivity she was positively starved for.

The first time he touched her, he'd been there a month and they were walking back up the hill to the mission after seeing a woman whose baby had died. "Awful shame. I never know what to say that could really make a difference," he confessed, casually putting his arm around her shoulders.

It was as though a jolt of electricity had shot through her. Except for a few instances when a Japanese had reluctantly taken her hand or elbow to help her across difficult terrain, no man had ever touched her. Ever!

"Are you cold? You're shivering," Ivan said.

"A little. It's nothing," she said, afraid her trembling voice betrayed her emotions.

But he must have known.

That night, in the parsonage, as they sat across from each other in the deeply upholstered American armchairs her father had brought to Japan, Ivan kept glancing up from the medical text he was reading and catching her eye. She tried to concentrate on the hem she was mending, but there was a current in the room that seemed to lap at her in waves. She'd never felt this way before, and it embarrassed and unnerved her. She retired early. She was jittery, headachy, and kept feeling that she might suddenly giggle stupidly. It was as though something deep in her abdomen were uncoiling like a fern and she was powerless to stop its ferocious growth.

She dismissed the maid who always slept in her doorway as chaperone. "Yuriko, you may go to your family in the village tonight," she said, attempting to sound natural and casual.

"Yes, Miss Muir," Yuriko said gleefully, clapping her hands together as if she'd been promised a gift.

Nancy blushed furiously and turned away. By morning the whole village would know what she had done—or planned to do. It was now clear in her own mind what course she'd set. She was like a person who knew a *tsunami* was rushing toward her. The choice was to attempt to run for higher ground or to simply lie on the beach and let it crash over her.

He came to her room as she had expected.

"Nan, we're a long way from our world and we need each other," he said softly, taking her in his arms.

She rested her plain, thin face against the crisp hair of his chest. "Yes, Ivan."

He cupped her breasts through the thin fabric of her worn blue kimono, and as he bent to pull the cloth away and kiss them and suck gently on her nipples, she felt voluptuous. All her bony angles had turned to curves. In the darkness, with his hands roaming her body, she was beautiful and shimmery and certain that if she were to look in a mirror, she wouldn't recognize her own image. She felt a hot pulsing between her legs that she only dimly remembered from a few dreams she'd tried to forget.

It was she—homely spinster Nancy Muir—she who led them to the high feather bed that the Japanese staff stared at with wonderment. It was she who plunged her hands down the waistband of his pajama trousers and boldly, frantically, guided his penis as though she knew what she was doing. And somehow she did know. She bit into his shoulder as her maidenhead was pierced and she exulted in the pain. Writhing under his body, she wrapped her long legs around him, wanting to devour him, to encompass him, to make him an internal, eternal part of her body.

It was wonderful. So wonderful she couldn't imagine words for it. When he gave one last savage plunge and cried out, she couldn't bear to release him. He rolled onto his back, sweating, panting, and she crawled onto him. She laid her body along the length of his and moved back and forth, back and forth, savoring the texture of skin and hair against skin and hair. She tucked her knees up and rubbed against his now-flaccid penis, faster and faster, harder and harder, needing hardness, needing the pain again. Finally, he twisted away, grimacing, and slid his big hand to her crotch. She cried out and shuddered with pleasure. It wasn't until he had his fingers inside her and was rhythmically kneading the soft flesh that she finally found release. She was only half aware that the shuddering, ecstatic cry was coming from her own throat. Her muscles knotted and froze and shuddered violently, as if in death throes.

She had fallen into an exhausted sleep, very nearly a faint, immediately afterward and awoke at dawn, thinking it was only seconds later. But he was gone. She was lying alone in the tangled, sticky bedclothes. Still in the lethargic afterglow of passion, she rose slowly and stretched luxuriously before going to her tiny dressing room. Yuriko wasn't there to bring her hot water, so she bathed with cold, appreciating the brisk sensation.

Wrapping herself in the old blue kimono, she went to look for him. She found him in the kitchen. He was dressed and had made tea and was pouring a cup. His back to her, he didn't hear her approach. She slipped her arms around his waist and let one drop caressingly. He turned suddenly, startled. "Nancy! I didn't know you were awake."

"What are you doing?" she asked softly.

He stepped away from her and put on a coat she hadn't noticed lying across the table. "I've—I've got to be gone for a day or two. Apparently there was some sort of fight between some of the village boys. Or maybe with some soldiers. The message wasn't clear. I might have to patch quite a few of them up."

"You should have told me sooner. It will take me only a few minutes to get ready."

"There's no need. I can manage on my own."

"But the language—and if you're going to be gone for several days, you'll need food, and you shouldn't risk getting involved with soldiers. They hate us—"

"I'll manage." He fumbled with the buttons of his coat.

He's afraid of me, Nancy thought.

But that wasn't when she lost God.

Not even when he grabbed his medical bag and all but ran from the mission house. It was later that morning when a boy brought a package from the mission headquarters in Yokahama. These boxes came about every four months and Nancy, as was her habit, unwrapped it. Inside, as always, were the medical supplies and the American magazines she always devoured the very day they arrived. At the bottom was an envelope with the missionary's salary, formerly her father's, now Ivan's. When there was mail, which was extremely rare, it was in the same large manila envelope with the money. This time there was only one piece, a square, pale lilac envelope addressed to Dr. Ivan Jake in lovely, flowing handwriting. But it was the return address that riveted Nancy's attention. Liana Jake. It could be his mother or sister, Nancy told herself. She put the envelope on the battered old desk her father had used and now Ivan sat at to make his medical records. Five minutes later she went back and looked at it again.

A few minutes after that, she opened it.

My darling Ivan,

I have the most wonderful news. The doctor says my leg is entirely well and I'm fit to travel whenever I want. The break has healed perfectly and I can gad around without even a trace of a limp. I've booked passage already and shall be with you very soon. I have other wonderful news, too. I want to keep it a secret and see your face when I tell you, but I just can't keep it to myself for all the weeks until we're together. Ivan, my beloved, we are going to have a child at long last. I

*suspected it before I had that fall and got hurt and I didn't
tell you then because I knew you were already worried enough
about leaving me behind to get well . . .*

There were several pages more, but she didn't read them.
Instead, she went outside to the small, exquisite garden she and
Yuriko had laid out the previous spring. The maid, now returned
from her night at home with her family, saw her through the
kitchen window and came out. "You need tea, miss?"

"No, Yuriko. Not tea. But I need a cart hired and loaded.
Get two village boys. Pack my clothes and books and my armchair."

"But miss—"

"Do as I say, Yuriko. Now."

Nancy went inside and gathered her personal belongings,
photographs, a few treasured gifts Japanese friends had given
her over the years, and the small fund of money she'd saved.
Papa had never known about it. She raised chickens and, through
Yuriko, sold the eggs. After giving Yuriko her share, she gave
half the remainder—which Papa thought was all the money—to
the mission and squirreled away the rest. Now it amounted to
the equivalent of about four hundred dollars American.

She went back to the mission package and took out the magazines and the envelope with Ivan's quarterly salary. She put the
cash with her own and closed the small case. Then she took her
Bible down from the shelf above her bed and methodically
shredded it into tiny pieces and left them strewn on the bedcov-
ers. As she finished, she glanced up and caught sight of herself
in the mirror across the room. There she was—just as plain and
angular as ever.

There wasn't room to sit next to the driver, so she sat in the
armchair on the bed of the wagon. Facing backward, she looked
at the mission and the parsonage as the cart went down the hill.
"Good-bye, God," she said through clenched teeth. She wanted
more than anything to set fire to that house, the only one she
ever remembered living in.

Her father had loved God with such intensity that he couldn't
find room in his heart for his own motherless daughter, and
Nancy—thousands of miles from her own kind and surrounded
by people who made no secret of their amused contempt for the
crazy foreigner—had tried to emulate his adoration. But she had
never fully succeeded, and now she had lost even the wish. That

God—if there was one—had sent Dr. Ivan Jake to the mission, and that same God had filled her with the desperate, lonely lust that had made her make an utter fool of herself.

God had made her desecrate herself. No wonder Ivan had been afraid of her—a desperate spinster, made incredibly bold and wanton by decades of starvation for affection. How disgusted he must have been with her by the light of day, the old maid playing the slut in a worn-out kimono; how terrified he must have been of the obsession he'd unleashed. But no matter what she accused herself of, it did not excuse him. He was a married man and had concealed it from her. Though he'd not sinned with the explosive abandon that she had, his sin was the equal or greater.

As she rode through the countryside sitting in her armchair looking the fool and being laughed at as they passed through villages, Nancy Muir decided that she was through with God and would never get involved with a man again either. And that resolve had lasted undimmed during those long, aimless months in Singapore while she used up her savings and the stolen mission funds. It had lasted, too, through the bombing and the volunteer nursing and even the mad flight to evacuate the burning city. But it had cracked when she was on the ferryboat plowing through the debris in Keppel Harbour. They'd struck something and the jolt had thrown her to the deck. A man with thick glasses and thin blond hair had helped her to her feet.

"You've scratched your arm," he'd said with apparently genuine concern.

"It's nothing."

"In this climate it could be serious. Let's get you a bit of iodine and some cotton lint," he said with a shy smile. "Must get you out of here in one piece, don't you know?"

Nancy's heart was wrung by his small kindness, and she told herself fiercely that she was just a sex-starved old maid. But all the while another faint voice in the back of her mind was saying, "This is different. This is a nice man."

But she refused to listen.

Nancy suddenly felt herself falling and realized she'd gone to sleep standing up at *tenko*. She recovered her balance and glanced at her watch. It had been four hours.

"There will be no food brought into this camp tonight if

Western women do not all bow," Nurse Royama was saying in her grating voice.

This had gone on long enough. As loathe as she was to draw attention to herself, Nancy raised her arm.

"What is it?" Nurse Royama called out.

"It is well known among civilized people that the Japanese are good to children," Nancy said. "Certainly the children may be fed and the mothers allowed to go to them, to care for them?"

Royama puffed up. "What you say is trueness. However, the children are most loved by their mothers and it is the duty of the mothers to make a good life for them here. The mothers must make these few proudful women see their error."

"I understand," Nancy said respectfully, and bowed. Bending over felt quite good after standing for so terribly long. She hoped what she'd said would have the result she'd intended.

And it did. "You are not going to starve *my* child!" one of the mothers screamed at one of the "proudful" women.

Nancy raised her hand again. "May I speak to the proud women?" she asked Royama.

Obviously the squat, silver-toothed nurse was getting sick and tired of this charade, too, but having made her demand, she couldn't back down. "If you think you can instruct them," she said with a curt nod.

Nancy, stiff and awkward from standing, walked down to the nearest troublemaker. She spoke quickly and quietly. "You must live with these women, and it's foolish to make them hate you as they hate you now. They will make you even more miserable than the Japanese will. We are prisoners. Doing the minimum to survive isn't the same as collaborating. Much more important, Royama will let us drop dead right here before she lets you off. Believe me. And the children will be the first to die. Your loyalty to your country doesn't include letting its children die at your hand."

The woman she addressed sagged against her. As Nancy had hoped, she was eager for someone to give her a face-saving excuse to get out of the mess she had caused. She took a deep breath and then called out to Royama, "For the sake of our children—" and bowed.

Everyone's eyes went to the other women. One at a time they grudgingly followed suit. "For the sake of the children—" each of them repeated.

Finally satisfied, Nurse Royama said, "Very good. You are dismissed."

Many of the women, their bladders painfully full, tried to run for the wash hut, only to find that the blood had pooled in their feet and legs and made them stumble and fall when they attempted sudden motion. Some took a few steps and fainted. Others just sat down abruptly where they stood. A few wept, and one woman took advantage of the chaos to soundly slap one of those who'd subjected them to the extended *tenko*.

Nancy wandered back toward the hut she was assigned to. Hazel Hampton caught up with her. "Miss Muir, that was very brave of you."

"It wasn't brave at all," Nancy said, uncomfortable with praise because she'd received so very little of it in her life. "I just didn't want to stand there forever."

"Still. It was brave. How do you know so much about the Japanese?"

That set off a silent alarm in Nancy's mind. "I don't know a thing about them except what I've read in books."

She spoke curtly, much too curtly. She could see that Miss Hampton went away feeling she'd been snubbed, but Nancy had already determined that she wasn't going to let herself become known as an expert on the Japanese, either their psychology or their language. That was the sure road to end up in the middle of all sorts of unpleasantness. No, it was far better to let the guards continue to believe that none of the white women understood what they were saying when they spoke to each other. And the only way to keep a valuable secret was to not share it with anyone. Not even someone as nice as Miss Hampton.

But still, she felt sad at having offended the young Miss Hampton. Nancy had never had a woman friend, and it might be very nice. Of course, she'd never had a man friend before Dr. Ivan Jake, and that had caused an excruciating unhappiness that was far worse than being lonely. No, it was probably better to stay as she was.

"Do you play cards, Miss Muir?" one of the women in the hut asked as she entered.

"No."

"Oh, I'm sorry. I suppose it's against your religion, isn't it?" Nancy didn't answer.

* * *

Gloria stared at Caroline Warbler for a long moment before bursting into laughter.

Sister Warbler had, to everyone's surprise, made it through the long *tenko* in the big overcoat she'd walked into camp wearing, but she'd disappeared just after they'd had their evening ration of gluey rice and weak tea. Gloria had asked around for her, but no one knew where she'd gone. When Gloria finally found the other nurse, she was in the wash hut with the young nun from their sleeping hut. Caroline was now dressed in a nun's habit—or the major part of a habit. "What in the world—?" Gloria tried to say before dissolving back into giggles.

"Sister Maria loaned it to me. It's her extra. They make these things quite large. It's the only dress in the place likely to fit me," Caroline said defensively.

"But it—it doesn't exactly fit!" Gloria shrieked, pointing out the hem, which would have modestly swept the ground on Sister Maria but came only just below Caroline's knees.

Sister Maria put her hand over her mouth, but couldn't hide the smile in her eyes.

Caroline looked down and said, very seriously in her sweet, small voice, "The great advantage, which you have obviously overlooked, is that I can merely sit down anywhere and disguise myself as a tent that got left behind. You, Dinki, poor bloody unfortunate that you are, are unable to do anything half so clever."

At this, Sister Maria lost the battle and shrieked with laughter.

![] *Chapter 10*

Dear Jim,

I'm afraid it's going to be a long visit. I hope those who say the Japs didn't want us and will repatriate us as soon as possible are right, but I doubt it. I think giving us back to our countries would cause them to lose face. Maybe that's what this war is all about to them—face.

"That's all I can stand!" Gloria said from the door of the sleeping hut the next day. Her face was pale. "That wretched wash hut is impossible. There isn't enough water running through the trough to wash away the—"

"Please!" Roberta Hampton exclaimed.

"Well, I'm sorry about your delicate sensibilities, but it's time we talk about it."

"Of all things!" Beryl Stacton said, turning away and fussing with the meager bit of mosquito netting she'd managed to beg or buy from someone to hang over her section of sleeping platform.

Gloria was getting mad. "Look, you pommy ladies may be above discussing such vulgar things, but you aren't above the germs that are breeding there. Cholera and dysentery don't give a damn about what la-de-bloody-da class you are. The doctor just told me she has three more down with the squitters this morning. We've got to make the Japs clean the place out. Now, who's the best one of us to go complain to the little fat thing with the silver teeth?"

Audrey St. John left off picking through a box of hard candies

124

she pointedly hadn't offered to share. "Since you're the one so fascinated with the subject, I think you should go, Sister Denk," she drawled.

"No!" Hazel exclaimed.

"Why not?" Gloria demanded.

Hazel hesitated over how to put her objection tactfully and quickly decided there wasn't any way. "Because you'd just make her mad."

"You may be right. Well, you're nice and polite. How about you?"

"I'm too scared of her. I'd throw up or faint."

Gloria could see the justice in this, too. "Then Miss Bright—?" she suggested.

"No!" Peggy and Hazel said in unison, but before anyone could ask for an explanation of why Miss Bright needed to stay as far from the attention of the authorities as possible, Hazel went on. "I think Miss Muir would be an excellent spokesman."

Nancy had been sitting quietly in the corner, trying to mend a run in her only pair of decent stockings. She was astonished— and not at all pleased—that the conversation had turned to her. She was used to being ignored and rather liked the safety inherent in it. "I have no more desire than any of you to have a confrontation with Nurse Royama. Or any of the rest of them, for that matter."

"Miss Muir, it isn't a question of who *wants* to talk to her," Hazel said. "Nobody wants to. What matters is who could be most effective. She's already impressed with your diplomacy over the bowing business."

So they see me as their dogsbody, Nancy thought. Helping to resolve the bowing problem had been a mistake. Still, if she refused, the brash, mouthy Sister Denk might appoint herself and all hell would break loose if she tangled with Nurse Royama. "Very well, I'll ask to speak to her, but I don't think anything will come of it."

She went to the office where Nurse Royama and Colonel Ienaga spent their time when they weren't roaming around harassing the prisoners. She was surprised she was even allowed to speak to Nurse Royama, but she was. Fortunately Ienaga wasn't around.

"Who are you?" Royama asked first, going through the sheaf of records.

"Nancy Muir. Miss Nancy Muir. American."

"And what was your purpose in Asia?"

"My father was a Baptist missionary. I took care of his house."

"Where?"

"Kuala Lumpur," Nancy lied.

"So your father is coming out to interfere in the spiritual life of the Malay people, then abandoned them when he found himself in danger!"

"No, he died before your people invaded," Nancy said.

It was the wrong way to put it. "Invaded! No, no, no! The Nipponese Army liberated the people of Malaya from their white oppressors."

Liberated them with bombs and guns and bayonets, Nancy thought, but she bowed respectfully and said, "Just so."

Royama relaxed, having won the first round. "What is it you wish to speak to me regarding?"

"The wash hut. It is quite filthy and needs to be cleaned so there will not be disease. We would request that the guards hose it out."

"You are suggesting that honorable Nipponese soldiers clean the effluvium of Western women?"

Oh, dear. Wrong again. "Then perhaps some natives—?"

"The natives of this island and the others in the Greater East Asia Co-Prosperity Sphere are no longer the coolies of Western oppressors."

"But they fix our food."

"That is because they are ordered to by the Nippon army," Royama said, as if there were an obvious difference. "If the Western women have fouled their sanitation, they must clean it up themselves."

Since this was exactly the answer Nancy had feared she would get, she was ready. "Very well, but we need tools. Some brooms, a hose, a shovel with which to bury—'effluvium.' "

"That can be arranged."

"And we need paper."

"No, no paper. No writing allowed!"

"Not for writing. For sanitary purposes. Toilet paper. Loo paper." Nancy was frustrated. She could have explained herself so easily in Japanese if she weren't so determined to keep her knowledge of the language secret.

Royama puzzled over this for a long moment, then suddenly

got it. "Ah!" She got up and went to the corner of the office, where there was a stack of old Japanese newspapers. "You may take this to your women." She beamed, as if having conferred a great gift. Nancy supposed it was, given their desperate lack.

Nancy left the office carrying the newspapers. Gloria and Hazel were waiting for her outside. "*We* have to clean it out?" Gloria exclaimed in horror when Nancy reported her conversation with Royama.

"Yes, and I've given myself the job of cutting up the newspaper into small squares," Nancy said before Gloria could make any job assignments of her own.

Not surprisingly, Gloria found no willing volunteers for the wash hut clean-up, but she did manage to coerce Caroline Warbler and two others nurses into helping. Caroline left her borrowed nun's habit outside to keep from soiling it and worked in her underwear. Gloria said the blue dress she'd been wearing ever since she found it on the beach was so filthy a little shit wouldn't hurt it a bit. Besides, she was getting a new dress when she was done with this job, she told Caroline.

Nancy Muir borrowed a pair of scissors and got on with cutting up the newspapers. Hazel offered to help. "I could crease them and tear strips even without scissors," she said.

"No, thank you. I'd rather do it myself," Nancy said.

"I—I thought perhaps you'd like the company," Hazel said.

"Thank you, but I'm able to manage on my own."

"Fine. You do that!" Hazel said, turning on her heel and storming off. *What an odious woman that missionary is*, Hazel fumed. *That's the last time I bother trying to be friendly to the bitch.*

Nancy watched the younger woman go, feeling something twist painfully in her chest. *Why didn't I just admit I want to read the newspapers before I cut them up?* But she knew the answer. She had so little to contribute to the welfare of the group—only her knowledge of the enemy and her secret ability to eavesdrop on them. It wouldn't be a secret if she told so much as one person.

While the clean-up was under way, four big empty troop transport trucks pulled into the center of the compound. They were Dutch army property, but driven by Japanese soldiers. The guards started turning the women and children out of three of the sleeping huts to be loaded onto the transports. Once again the big table was brought out, reams of forms were shuffled, questions asked, luggage searched. Hazel wandered over as near as she dared, hung about for a while, and returned to Peggy Bright, who was sitting on the doorstep of their sleeping hut.

"They aren't given a hint as to what it's all about," she told the older woman.

"They're probably just starting to spread us out around the countryside in other camps," Peggy said.

"But it could be repatriation."

"—or they could be on their way to being shot," Audrey St. John said coolly from the doorway, and having delivered this comment, she wandered off into the compound to get a closer look at what was going on.

"She's right, isn't she?" Hazel said.

"I doubt it, but—" Peggy didn't finish.

The process of removing about a hundred and twenty women and children took the better part of two hours. As the last truck pulled away, Gloria came strolling over from the wash hut. Hazel and Peggy could smell her coming. "Dear God! Would you stay downwind?" Peggy exclaimed.

"Don't worry. I'm going to clean up in a minute. I just wanted to point something out to you. See that shed behind the office?"

"Yes. It's storage or something, don't you imagine?" Hazel asked.

"You'd think so to look at it, but it's actually Nurse R's quarters. It's got a window around the back side and I looked in. There are the most extraordinary pair of green taffeta knickers hanging out on her wash line. Royama must have quite an interesting private life."

"Sister Denk," Hazel said, feeling nauseated, "would you mind moving away a little farther?"

"Sure. You just keep sitting here and glue your eyes to the door of Royama's shed."

Gloria went into the sleeping hut and came out in a few minutes with a bundle under her arm. She disappeared into the wash hut with it. As she'd suggested, Peggy and Hazel watched the shed. When the departure of the truckloads of women was completed twenty minutes later, Nurse Royama went to the shed and stepped inside. She came reeling out a few seconds later. She ran for the office, holding a handkerchief over her nose and mouth, then returned with three of the soldiers. They got close to the shed, then drew back, holding their noses.

"What do you suppose they're carrying on about?" Peggy wondered out loud.

"I'm not certain, but—"

Gloria came back and joined them. She was sparkling clean and her short hair, fluffed around her face now, looked several shades more blond. She had on an emerald green linen dress and matching short-sleeved jacket. She was wearing lipstick and a touch of rouge over her freckles, and she even smelled beautiful.

"What a transformation!" Peggy exclaimed.

Gloria sketched a quick curtsy of acknowledgment. "Do you think Queen Mary would approve? Probably not. No hat," she said, then sat down by the others. She watched Nurse Royama and the guards, still blundering about the shed in confusion, and said dreamily, "The great problem, I believe, is that they know so little of Sumatran building techniques."

Peggy and Hazel looked at her.

"You see, the shed, like the other buildings, is on short stilts, but the facing boards come clear to the ground. A person who looked closely might discover that there's about eight inches crawlspace under the shed and several of the facing boards on the back side are quite loose—"

"You didn't!" Hazel said, laughing.

"Didn't what? I didn't do a thing," Gloria said with leering innocence.

"Everything from the drain?" Peggy asked, smiling in spite of herself.

"No, just selected aromatic bits," Gloria said.

"We'll all be in trouble for it," Hazel said, suddenly seeing the other side of the situation.

"They won't figure it out, but even if they do, there isn't any paper in it. We'll say that the monkeys hereabouts like to crawl under things to do their business. They don't know anything about the tropics."

Audrey St. John had come out of the hospital hut while they were talking and started to step over them with her characteristic arrogant unawareness. But she stopped midstride, her aristocratic nose in the air. "Perfume," she said. "My perfume. Somebody's been into my perfume." Suddenly she looked down at Gloria and her eyes grew wide. "That's my dress! You're wearing my dress!"

"Yes," Gloria said calmly. "I needed one and you have more than anyone in camp."

"You—you *Communist*!" Audrey shrieked.

"That's as may be, but I'm the Communist who cleaned up your shit." Gloria remained absolutely calm, almost pleasant.

"Well, I'm just not having it! It's common robbery, and I'm going to see to it that you're punished!"

"By whom?" Peggy asked with clear-eyed curiosity.

Audrey turned and glared at her. "You stay out of this, you old busybody. I'm going to report this to the guards." She whirled on an elegant foot and went off toward the office.

"That ought to entertain the Japanese," Hazel said. "Imagine her reporting a theft to the same people who robbed all of us. They're going to be awfully unhappy to hear that she had something worth stealing and they missed it."

"Wait until she figures out about her shampoo and silk underwear," Gloria said, smiling.

The guards failed to turn off the lights as early as usual that evening, and Peggy used the opportunity to continue the letter she'd been writing to Jim for days. She knew she'd probably never have a chance to send it to him, but it made her feel good to write it. Suspecting that the enemy wouldn't approve of letter-writing, she composed in the very smallest possible handwriting on sheets of fine airmail stationery they'd overlooked in her luggage.

> *Jim darling,*
>
> *A group was taken away this morning and there was much speculation about why. Late this afternoon, however, another group was brought in to replace them. I think this place is a clearing house which all prisoners must pass through. Heaven only knows where we'll go from here.*
>
> *This was a coolie jail the Dutch planters probably set up. I believe the Japs find a certain joy in the irony of it, putting all the white wives and daughters of the oppressors in the jail their men built. Of course, it wasn't the Japs being oppressed and I don't sense the natives are any more thrilled to have them here than we are.*
>
> *Let me tell you about some of my "roommates." There's*

a nice young woman named Hazel Hampton from Chicago. I wish you could meet her. She's a little awkward and unsure of herself and no glamour girl, but a healthy, attractive young woman of potential. After all my years of teaching, I can spot character, and this girl has it although I don't think she knows it yet. She seems especially lost here. Her mother, one of those brittle, sophisticated, impeccably groomed, chain-smoking types, looks like I imagine Jean Harlow would have looked at her age, had she lived. She's abdicated motherhood.

Hazel's in her twenties—not a child by any means—and a bright, sensible individual. But I don't think Mrs. Hampton realizes that Hazel wasn't yet ready to be set free of the maternal bonds. Anyway, Hazel's at loose ends. She's not one of the brassy, breezy types who make a great show of their unconcern. And she isn't one of the nurses, all of whom knew each other or knew people each other knew before. That, and their profession, gives them a bond. Nor does poor Hazel fit in with the missionaries—there are a lot of them here and some are most peculiar.

Poor Hazel is a thinker. Some aren't. First among them is a girl named Gloria Denk. Dinki, her nurse friends call her and it suits. Dinki is little and energetic and is one of those people who plunge through life. I suspect her "take-charge" attitude makes her a good nurse, but she hasn't got that outlet. We have a few very ill women and children—some have already died—but we've got more nurses than patients at this stage. We even have three or four woman doctors here, so Dinki isn't needed to do what she probably does best. So she causes trouble.

You know I've seen my share of "troublemakers" in my years with girls. They seem to be of two types: the bitter, unhappy ones who want to make everyone as miserable as they, and the overenergetic ones who just want something interesting going on all the time so they don't have to fall back on their own thoughts. Dinki is one of the latter. I don't think her thoughts run much more than about a half-inch deep, but her personality is as open and honest and straightforward as the Australian outback.

Today she took on a filthy job which ruined the only dress she had (except her uniform, which she's saving to go home in) and she decided that someone who hadn't helped and who had a great many clothes should share them with her. The *problem was, she didn't consult with the owner of the clothes. Dinki just stole what appealed to her. There was a great schism caused by this and a meeting with impassioned speeches on both sides of the issue. I could have wept at the thought of being condemned to spending weeks with a group of women who could mistake this for an important or intellectual debate. And yet I think many of them thought it was.*

The owner of the clothes was a Miss St. John. A stunningly beautiful woman "of a certain age." She's terribly continental with an accent so upper class that she sounds like she's got a mouthful of pebbles. The gossip is that she's the illegitimate daughter of some terribly important English (or was it German?) duke or baron who had no legitimate heirs and left her his money. She's been married—perhaps that's where the German baron comes into the story, I'm sure I've muddled it—to a man who killed himself. I doubt the whole German part, as she wouldn't have been interned if she had German citizenship. It seems she's been swanking it around this part of the world for some years—Shanghai, Hong Kong, Singapore—being a decorative fixture in the highest levels of society.

The fascinating thing is that she seems to have been a mistress (my informant was a little fuzzy on the exact relationship) to an army man in Singapore. This man's wife, a Mrs. Stacton, is also in our hut and, my dear Jim, the looks that are exchanged! Mrs. Stacton is one of those excessively well-permed and -corsetted middle-aged adherents to "the done thing" who see themselves as the defenders of Victorian morality. Her loathing of her husband's—whatever she was—practically makes her come out in a rash.

Another difficult person we're saddled with is a missionary. Actually, there are three or four of them in our hut, but this one seems representative of the worst of the type. Poor Miss Muir. A tall, plain woman, Miss Muir casts her brooding presence over all of us like a pall. While the others are always trying to urge us to excesses of prayer, Miss Muir doesn't appear to think we're even worth it. She just watches, silently, and with a vague aura of disappointed superiority. I shouldn't think of her so unkindly, because she saved us all from dying on our feet at a tenko—which is what the Japs call lining us all up to fry in the sun. But even that was done condescend-

*ingly. Miss Muir obviously wants nothing to do ith any of us.
Any number of people, including Hazel, have tried to make
friendly overtures to her, out of a sense of courtesy, and she
rejects all of them.*

*I wish we could all get over the feeling that we're waiting
for something that's just about to happen. Nobody is willing
to say to herself, "This is it. This is where I am and where
I'm going to be for a long while, so I'd best get on with ren-
ovating my life to fit these circumstances." That would be a
mark of giving up, a sign of downright disloyalty to our countries, and, in some strange way, to ourselves. Perhaps we'll
be fortunate and never have to admit such a thing. If the
optimists are right, the war will be over the day after tomorrow!*

 Chapter 11

Dear Jim,

*From fearing that we'll be taken away to the unknown,
most of us have come to hope we'll be moved almost anywhere, just to escape the crowding and attendant filth. Anyplace has to be better than this. Garbage and sewage are
collecting at an alarming rate in spite of the Japanese soldiers' attempts to make the local natives carry it off, and it
seems every rat on the island had gotten news of the white
women's relatively affluent presence. Voracious, the creatures
eat not only food, soap, toothpaste, shoe leather, and candles, but sometimes even gnaw through lip rouge containers
and clothing. One infant has been badly bitten and is still
hovering on the brink of death.*

During the next three weeks numerous groups of women, and a few men, had been moved through the jail, but the people in the hut with Hazel and Gloria had stayed pretty much the same. Occasionally one or two would be taken out to leave with a departing group. At various times individuals who fell ill were taken to the medical hut. More often than women left, newcomers were put in with them as the jail grew more and more crowded.

When two new groups containing women who refused to bow to the enemy came to the camp on consecutive days, resulting in long *tenkos* for all, a self-appointed committee started calling on new internees. They made suggestions that amounted to threats, and the problem wasn't repeated again until one evening three weeks into their incarceration. An idealistic young missionary whose fervor verged on the unbalanced refused to bow on religious grounds. Over five hundred women and children stood for four hours until she finally had some sort of hysterical fit and relented.

The next morning a physician from the latest group called on their hut. An elderly woman with a lilting voice and an accent that spoke of Scottish upbringing overlaid with many decades in Asia, she introduced herself as Dr. Claudia Millichope. She explained that she'd been court physician to the wives and children of an upcountry rajah until her retirement due to failing eyesight several years before. Spectacles with lenses like the bottoms of bottles attested to her handicap. She moved carefully, with one hand outstretched for obstacles. Rather than seeming an awkward gesture, it appeared more of a stern benediction as she lightly touched things along her way.

"Still, I can poke around and be of some use," she told the women matter-of-factly. "One of your other doctors asked me to come to talk to you and see a Sister Denk."

"Doctor, could I speak to you alone for a moment," Audrey St. John said, taking her arm in a proprietary and highly condescending gesture.

Dr. Millichope disengaged her gently but expertly. "Later, my dear, if you don't mind. I wanted to give all of you a bit of a biology lesson." Audrey rolled her eyes, and although Dr. Millichope couldn't have seen the expression, she reacted to it. "It might save your lives. I'd advise you to listen."

"We'd be pleased to," Peggy Bright said, and glanced

around, "gathering eyes," as she'd done so often when she taught school.

"Very well," Dr. Millichope said. "When you move, your muscles contract and that contraction squeezes, or 'milks,' the blood along your veins, helping the heart with its circulation job. But when you stand upright for a long period without moving—as we did yesterday—gravity gets ahead of the heart's ability. That is, the heart continues to pump blood to the extremities, but it begins to pool in the legs and feet. That causes the muscles to cramp and it also causes a decreased blood and oxygen flow to the brain. That's why you get nauseated, confused, and faint and eventually become unconscious."

"All this is certainly interesting, but—" Roberta Hampton said coolly. She'd awakened with a splitting headache and was in no mood for vivid medical lectures.

"Is there anything we can do?" Hazel interrupted, embarrassed that her mother should be so rude.

"Yes, it takes some subtlety, but we may get a good deal of practice. You see, it's possible to alternately contract and relax the muscles of the legs and arms without moving and without it being awfully apparent. In fact, working your way around the body mentally, as it were, is a healthy diversion. Work especially on the feet, as they get the worst of it. Flex your toes, one at a time, if you can, and rotate your ankles. Here, young lady, stand up here by me and try it," she said, picking Hazel out of the group that was listening.

Hazel got up and tried completely relaxing one leg while tensing every muscle in the other. It gave her an odd, rocking motion, which Dr. Millichope said she must work at avoiding.

"Thank you, Doctor. We appreciate the advice. Is there anything else?" Peggy Bright asked.

"No, except that you might as well go right on and faint if you feel like it. After all, falling down and resting a moment before rising again is a nice bit of exercise, too."

"Are you suggesting that we pretend to faint?" Beryl Stacton said, suddenly red-faced. "That's just what they want—to humiliate us and prove their supposedly superior strength. I think pretending to faint is downright unpatriotic. And you an Englishwoman!"

"I'm a doctor, trained to help people stay alive," Dr. Millichope said in an almost pitying voice. "I have no politics."

"That's just what I mean," Beryl rolled on. "Without moral purpose and standards there is no point in life. No point at all."

"Speak for yourself, Mrs. Stacton!" Audrey said, once again trying to take the doctor's arm. But the old physician neatly dodged the grab.

"Apparently I am, Miss St. John," Beryl Stacton persisted. "One cannot hope to inculcate a sense of morality into those who have none."

"Now, which of you is Sister Denk?" Dr. Millichope said, cutting in before the discussion could rage further.

Gloria, who had been listening to her with a smile, stepped forward. "I'm here, Doctor."

"I'd like to examine your leg wound, if you please."

"It's quite well now."

"Still, I want to see for myself."

"Doctor, it's too dim in this light and I can't show you outside. The guards might notice and—"

"Yes, I know the story. But I don't need light. Sit down here."

Gloria sat down on the edge of the sleeping platform and pulled her skirt up past the injury. The flesh had grown together healthily but unevenly, leaving ugly puckers. The old physician felt the scar gently, moving soft fingertips around and over the wound. Then she leaned down and smelled it. "Yes, it's healing very nicely. You did a nice job on the stitching, considering the angle from which you had to work and the fact that it was your own leg. Yes, quite nice. You'll want to have it fixed up when you get out of here. A young woman like you should be free to wear a short bathing costume without embarrassment."

Hazel, listening, was suddenly engulfed in homesickness— and longing for Frank.

The past summer, after they became officially engaged, her parents had thrown a day-long celebration party for them on the lake. Friends from all over Chicago and even some cousins from out of town had come. Ronald and Frank had gone out in the morning to build a big fire on the beach, and Roberta and the cook had worked for days to prepare a huge, extravagant picnic luncheon. Hazel salivated at the memory of the hot ham with the crispy crackling, the fat, juicy hamburgers, the charred hot dogs in their toasted buns. There had been jars of homemade watermelon pickles with their tender pink edges, and huge bowls of tangy potato salad—Roberta had a secret ingredient she'd never told anyone, not even the cook. Ronald had arranged for a keg of beer and a big tin vat full of Coca-Cola bottles nestled in ice.

Late that afternoon, they'd all eaten until they were nearly sick with repletion, then sprawled about the beach on blankets and towels until a hardy few got up a game of tag. One by one they'd joined in the romp, which gradually worked its way into the water. One of the guests had come by boat, a small yacht that was moored offshore. The young people got up teams and had swimming races out to it. Barbara, naturally, stayed on the beach, looking gorgeous and voluptuous in her green and white polka-dot swimming shorts and halter top, and being greatly admired by Frank's college friends, but Hazel joined Frank in a swim. They waded in, hand in hand, and swam out in a leisurely way. The sun had nearly set by then, and there was a full moon, still huge and orange near the horizon.

"I'd like to stop life right here and make it last forever," Hazel said, turning onto her back and floating.

Frank murmured agreement, then dived and came up underneath her, lifting her up and flipping her over. She laughed and sputtered. "I'm being romantic and you're being a rowdy!" she complained.

"Oh, I can be romantic, too," he said in a suddenly throaty voice that made her shiver deliciously. He came around behind her and pushed her legs forward with his so that she was once again floating, but with his body beneath hers. They drifted silently, rocked by the waves for a moment, as Frank hummed some melody she didn't quite recognize. Then, as if it were entirely natural, his hands came around and cupped her breasts— but only for a surprised moment. "Dear God! What is all this?" he exclaimed.

Hazel giggled. "It's the boning that holds the top of my swimming suit up."

"How uncomfortable for you," he said, slipping one strap off her shoulder, and then the other. "Now, isn't that better?"

She pulled her arms free and spread them wide as he peeled down the front of the suit. Her generous breasts, nipples hardened, shimmered on the surface of the moonlit water. His big hands cupped them again, gently kneading and stroking. After a moment he ducked under the water, turned her slightly, and blew bubbles against her left breast before sucking for a moment on the taut nipple. Hazel trembled with pleasure. Frank came up with a gasp for air, then kissed her long and hard. She put her arms around him as he treaded water. "Oh, Frank, let's just get married now. Just swim back to shore and demand that somebody perform the ceremony this minute."

"We don't need to wait for the ceremony, you know. Not for what we both want now."

"Oh, Frank—"

"Don't say anything," he cajoled. He took her hand, guided it to the front of his trunks.

Hazel was stunned at her own reaction to the hard maleness she felt through the fabric. She was a modern girl; she knew about human anatomy—even male anatomy—of course, but in a theoretical way. She'd never really thought about touching that part of a man. Nor had she imagined it so large and firm and wonderful in the hand. She rubbed her palm against him and he shuddered. "Oh, Hazel darling, that feels great."

"Yes, it does," she said with pleased surprise. "It really does."

She kept rubbing, and after a minute Frank pulled his trunks down enough that the fabric wasn't in her way. It was so smooth and soft but hard at the same time. He guided her hand to wrap around it and move up and down and groaned as she began to do so. Hazel was excited by touching him, but even more by his reaction. She felt a sudden surge of something like power. Holding him this way, she felt she had control of him, of his essence. Frank was always the dominant one, the strong one who was in control of every situation. Now, in the most remarkable way, she had control.

They bobbed in the water, gasping for air, her hand working faster and faster, his breath and hers coming more raggedly. She got some water up her nose, but she hardly noticed the burning sensation. Paddling with one hand, he grasped her breast with the other, pinching her nipple almost painfully. She liked the slight hurt and felt a great need to return it. She held him even tighter in her hand and he suddenly gave a great shudder and a watery cry of pleasure. She felt something hot rush over her hand.

"Hey, who's out here?" a voice called across the water.

Hazel nearly choked on a mouthful of water. They bumped elbows and knees against each other as they scrambled to get their swimming clothes back in order. Frank jerked up his trunks and tried to help her find the straps of her suit to put her arms back through.

"Just a mermaid I found out here," he answered the caller, trying to put a casual laugh into it.

"Yeah, I'll bet!" the voice called back. It was a fraternity brother of Frank's. "The water's full of 'em."

There was a feminine giggle, then, "Oh, Bill, you're so fresh."

They'd gone back to shore, to rejoin the guests. Frank had been the life of the party the rest of the evening. He was back to being the man she'd always known, self-assured, in full control. But Hazel was jangling with undischarged longing. People asked to see her ring again, talked to her about their plans, and eventually the whole party sat around the dying campfire and sang songs late into the night, but all Hazel wanted to do was go back into the water with Frank and finish what they'd started.

Now, sweating, dirty, and hungry in an internment camp halfway around the earth, Hazel felt that longing again, and something else as well, something she'd been miraculously spared feeling until now—a deep, frantic sense of helplessness so severe it was physically painful. She'd thought about Frank a great deal since the capture, but never with such desperate need.

Save me, Frank, come take charge and save me! she wanted to scream. *If you really love me, don't let this happen to me!*

That night a guard came to the door of the hut moments before the light was turned out. "Tomollow, you go 'way," he said. "You take things. You go. All go." And with that the flickering bulb went out and he disappeared.

"Tomorrow!" Audrey St. John exclaimed with angry disbelief.

"Tomorrow," Nancy Muir said faintly in the dripping tropical darkness.

A woman in the far corner starting crying hysterically. No one spoke to her or made any attempt to calm her. She gradually got control of herself and was quiet. "Well, they're not taking *me* anywhere!" another woman said. "Me neither!" someone else agreed. Nobody bothered to point out to them that they had no choice.

In the morning they rose and began packing. No one spoke except when necessary. As Hazel put the last of her things into her suitcase, Gloria came into the hut carrying a long-handled mop. "What's that for?" Hazel asked her. "Are you going to tidy up the countryside?"

"It could use it. No, I thought we could put this through the handles of a couple of suitcases and two people could carry each end on their shoulders."

"What a good idea!"

"Thanks, but I didn't think of it. Dr. Millichope did."

That was when it occurred to Hazel that Sister Denk had no belongings at all of her own but the medical kit—the contents of which she'd turned over to the camp doctors—and her uniform and that of the other nurse who had died on the beach. Hazel suddenly felt quite guilty about her self-pity. At least she had some personal things of her own, and that was a comfort of sorts. She thought back to all the times in the past few weeks when she'd gone through the pictures in her billfold, reread parts of her books, fiddled around with her manicure set and hairpins. *Maybe our belongings help us validate our being*, she thought.

The horrible *tenko* cowbell started clanging and they went outside. Hazel noticed that Miss St. John seemed in unusually bad spirits that morning, which was really saying something. While the rest of them lined up with the growing placidity of habit, she barged about as if looking for someone. A guard finally caught her by the elbow and flung her into place. "You bastard!" she exclaimed. "I have to find someone!" He didn't understand or didn't care and merely made a threatening gesture with his gun.

As much to keep her mind off her own worries as anything, Hazel watched her, speculating on her unease. Naturally they were all disturbed at the upheaval and their unknown future, although few of them really believed they'd been kept all these weeks just to be taken out to be killed. But Miss St. John wasn't just nervous. She was actively, busily distressed. When *tenko* was over, she shoved her way through the crowd and caught up with a woman standing near Hazel.

"We have to leave this morning," she said.

The other woman, a haughty-looking middle-aged Eurasian, looked down her shapely nose and said, "Is that so?"

"There isn't time for—for what we planned."

"I see."

Audrey stared at her a moment. "Well, you must also see, of course, that I must have my money back."

"I'm sorry. I already spent it."

"But you must give it back!"

"Most unfortunate, *mem*," the Eurasian woman said. The last word dripped with sarcasm.

"See here! I won't have this! I gave you a hundred dollars, and it's not my fault the Japs chose today to move us!"

The woman shrugged and smiled. "Karma," she said.

"Karma, hell!" Audrey grabbed her arm, but before she could say anything more, the woman used her free hand to deliver a sharp slap to Audrey's flushed face.

A passing guard, apparently feeling that slapping women was his privilege, not theirs, dragged Audrey away. Barking orders, he prodded her back to the hut. Walking backward, dodging the bayonet point and tottering on her fashionable high heels, Audrey shouted back, "I'll get my money back. You can't get away with this! You chi-chi bitch!" Her accent wasn't nearly as proper as usual.

The other woman just smiled serenely and ostentatiously pretended to brush out the wrinkles Audrey's grasp had made in her sleeve.

Hazel, having stopped to listen to the exchange, stepped up to the stranger. "What did she pay for?" she asked bluntly. A few weeks ago good manners would have forbade her even thinking of asking something that was so clearly none of her affair.

"Why, an abortion. What else? You don't have any 'little problem' I can help with, do you?"

"No! No—"

She walked slowly back to the hut. How extraordinary to be offered an abortion as openly and casually as one might be offered a cigarette or a section of the Sunday newspaper.

When Hazel got back to the hut, everyone was being herded out. She got her suitcase and handbag and joined the rest. Something more than a hundred women and about twenty children were lined up and once again went through the tedious business of being questioned and checked against the ubiquitous lists. This time they were also weighed, and that information was added to the paperwork. The only one who was happy about this was Caroline Warbler.

"Good Lord! I've lost nearly a stone," she said cheerfully. "Another few weeks and I'll look so much like Hedy Lamarr you'll mistake me for her." This was so patently ridiculous that everyone around her laughed.

This enraged the guards. One of them shoved her off the scale so roughly that she fell painfully against the table edge and cut her arm. The laughter died suddenly. Sister Denk tore a strip off the hem of Sister Warbler's nun's habit and wrapped it around the injury.

Hazel has lost ten pounds, but unfortunately, so had her mother, and Roberta Hampton hadn't weight to spare. Several of the mothers became terribly distraught at their children's weight loss.

Finally they were all "approved for transport," as Nurse Royama put it, but they had to stand around waiting another hour for the trucks to arrive. When they did show up, one was missing. It had broken down somewhere and they had to be crammed into the remaining ones so closely that they couldn't sit down. "At least the canvas tops are off," Caroline Warbler said, straddling someone's luggage awkwardly and getting a firm grip on the overhead bar that was intended to hold the canvas up. "Otherwise we'd all suffocate."

"Must you be so bloody cheerful!" Miss St. John snapped.

Caroline Warbler ignored the fact that this was a rhetorical question. "Yes, I think probably so," she replied softly.

The trucks started up with violent lurches that threw the women against each other and the corners of their suitcases. "Where do you suppose the stupid bastards learned to drive? At a circus?" Gloria asked, rubbing her shin.

"They're going to burn out every clutch in Sumatra before this is over," Hazel commented.

She said this so seriously that Gloria hooted with laughter. "Maybe that's part of their grand scheme. The Greater East Asia Co-Prosperity and Clutch-Destruction Sphere."

"That's got a nice ring to it," Hazel said, grinning. "Perhaps with a little music—?" They put it to "When Johnny Comes Marching Home Again" and sang it over and over until some of the older women begged them to stop.

It turned out that they were being taken back to the pier where Hazel and those with her had started. The journey that took a full day's walk should have taken only minutes to drive, but the Japanese managed to drag it out to hours. Several times the trucks stopped with a jolt, and the drivers leapt out and conferred in their staccato way, shouting and gesturing wildly at each other. Twice the women were all made to get off the trucks, stand in ranks, and be counted before being put back on the trucks.

"Do they think we're leaping off into the underbrush every time they turn their backs?" Gloria asked the third time they stood in the road.

"Actually, I think someone did," Peggy Bright said. She'd been on another truck, and during the lull when everyone was milling around, she'd joined them. "She didn't hurl herself over the edge, but I haven't seen her since the first time they got us out of the trucks. I think she slipped away."

"What a bloody stupid thing to do!" Gloria said. "A white woman couldn't survive in this jungle. Even if she could, she'd be caught and turned in."

"She was Chinese. She might stand a chance. I hope so," Peggy said.

Hazel managed to get a place at the outside edge of the truckbed on the last leg of the ride and was able to watch the lush countryside flash by. Her mind knew that this wasn't freedom, just a different stage of imprisonment, but her senses were overwhelmed with the illusion of liberty. For a few hours, at least, there was no barbed wire, no tall, slatted fences to baffle the breeze. The air, though hot and humid, smelled clean and fresh, and there was the occasional refreshing fragrance of tropical flowers instead of the hideous wash hut. Away from the jail the sky seemed a more intense shade of blue and the trees were greener and more clearly delineated.

But she, like all of them, kept wondering what it would be like wherever they were going.

Wherever they were going—

Oh, Frank, she thought.

Chapter 12

Dear Jim,

Had I guessed this was going to happen to me—an impossibility, to be sure—I'd have been certain that we women would have been, in some mystical way, "bound" as women. That there would have been a strong sense of sexual common cause between us. But there is none. We are aligned against a common enemy. Several, in fact. The Japs, the climate, the food, etc. But even then we aren't a united front by any means. Some are already "adjusted," some are still frantic with denial, and the rest of us fill in the gap between. I suppose what this means is that women aren't women, they're individuals.

Why should this surprise me?

By late afternoon they found themselves back at the long pier where Hazel's group had arrived on Banka Island. The women and children were ordered off the trucks and lined up along the pier and once again, they were inexpertly counted. The guards seemed to sense they'd lost someone, and kept taking tallies to confirm it. First the prisoners were lined up in threes, and in all the shoving two women were pushed into the water. There was great consternation, the guards behaving as though the floundering victims had tried to escape. Dripping and near hysteria, the women were fished out and counted again. The guards conferred. Papers were shuffled, laid out in stacks, chased down when a breeze snatched a few away. Meanwhile, legs and backs aching and nerves frayed, the women stood in line.

"Can't the stupid bastards count anything?" Dinki muttered under her breath to Hazel.

Apparently the guards couldn't reach a consensus of opinion. The prisoners were rearranged again, this time in fours. The guards chattered and bickered among themselves. At one point, they pulled Peggy Bright out of line and, waving papers in her face, shouted at her for a few minutes.

"Good God! What are they talking about?" Hazel asked wildly. "Doesn't anybody understand Japanese?"

Nancy Muir was silent.

Dr. Millichope finally stepped forward and, with a bow, put a question to them in Malay. The guards muttered between themselves, and one came over to her and answered brusquely in a mangled version of the same language. Dr. Millichope nodded and turned to Peggy. "I think he wants to know how many were on your truck."

"I didn't count them," Peggy said, trying very hard to keep the internationally understood tone of sarcasm out of her voice.

Dr. Millichope translated to Malay and the guard translated to Nippongo. The rest nodded and as suddenly as the interrogation began, it was over. Peggy was pushed back into line.

"Ijo arimasen!" the guard called down the length of the pier to the clerks at the end.

Nancy hid her smile. As long as they thought everyone was present and accounted for, who would dispute it? Where *had* the Nippon army found so many stupid soldiers! Of course, they would of necessity be the dregs. All the men of honor and intelligence were fighting the war. Those left the degrading task of caring for dishonorable women prisoners were the ones who couldn't be trusted at the front, either because of their stupidity, ill health, or questionable loyalty. In a purely intellectual sense she regretted that the rest of the women were naturally being misled into thinking these men represented Japan. But in her heart she despised them as much as anyone else standing on the pier.

Finally, they were ordered onto a boat. Hazel hardly realized at first that it was the same yacht she'd been on earlier. In the intervening weeks, it had been stripped of its elegance. The mahogany paneling and brass and crystal accoutrements had been ripped out to adorn who-knew-what temporary Japanese billet. The yacht, like some of the women, had aged ten years in a few weeks under Japanese control. The decking was gouged and scraped and what couldn't be removed had been defaced. She was among the group of women herded into what had been a piano lounge, but the piano was gone and the big mirror that had covered one wall was now a pile of dangerous shards of glass on the floor.

"Somebody's going to get hurt on that," Dinki said in her bossy, practical manner. "Let's clean it up and throw it over-board."

"Look here, young woman," Beryl Stacton said, "if you think I'm going to become a cleaning maid for the Japs—"

Gloria rounded on her. "For Christ's sake! When are you going to realize this isn't some bloody tit-for-tat game?"

"Now, Sister Denk—" Dr. Millichope said softly.

"I'm sorry, Doctor. Look, I wouldn't lift a finger to pick my nose for the filthy Japs' sake, Mrs. Stacton, but we are the ones in this room," she said through gritted teeth. "The children could get hurt. We could all get hurt. The bloody Nips don't care what happens to us."

"Sister Denk is right," Peggy Bright said in her firmest schoolmistress voice. "We must look to our own safety because no one else will. I'll help. Who else will join us?" Her glance commanded several women to pitch in. If they, like Hazel, were helping less for the sake of safety than to avert further confron-tation, it didn't matter, so long as the job got done. Beryl Stacton was noticeably absent from the group.

After characteristically long and unexplained delays, they set out from Banka Island. One woman with three small children kept insisting that they were being repatriated. "They're taking us to Java, you'll see."

But they proceeded west, to the mainland of Sumatra. To stop the woman's weeping, Peggy said, "It's not such a bad thing, really. When the fighting to recover the area starts, the small islands will be the most dangerous place. We'll be far safer on the big island until they can come for us." She believed it her-self, so it was easy to speak with comforting conviction.

Crossing the Banka Strait, they went south along miles of mangrove swamps to the mouth of the Moesi River and then the battered yacht turned upriver. Progress was slow, as there was so much debris in the waterway. Using spotlights, the Japanese attempted to continue as darkness fell, but soon gave up and moored the vessel. "When are we going to get some food?" the women started asking each other. No one had an answer.

They could smell something cooking. Something with onions in it, a smell that made their stomachs cramp with hunger. Gloria disappeared for a while and came back to report that she'd sneaked around to the dining room, where she'd seen the soldiers and sailors were eating. There was no sign of food being prepared for the rest of them.

"But the children! They can't let the children go hungry!" the mothers cried.

Once again Peggy took charge. "I believe it's up to us. Many of us have bits of food tucked away. Candies and such. Not very nourishing, but better than nothing. I picked up some fruit along the way. How about the rest of you?"

With clear reluctance the women started unearthing their preciously hoarded food. All but Audrey St. John. "What about those hard candies you're always nibbling on, Miss St. John?" Peggy asked.

"Too boring, all this rash altruism, darling," Audrey drawled, glancing up from a fingernail she was filing. "What is mine stays mine."

Peggy walked away fuming and repeated the conversation to Hazel, who said, "Never mind her, Peggy. She's pregnant. In a way, she's feeding one of the children."

"*What* did you say?" Beryl Stacton, sitting behind them, grabbed Hazel's arm.

Astonished by the vehemence in Mrs. Stacton's tone, Hazel repeated what she'd said. The older woman stared across the crowded room at her enemy, her eyes narrowed with loathing. Hazel suddenly remembered the gossip she'd heard earlier about the relationship between the two women. She had no reason to like Mrs. Stacton, but she suddenly felt very sorry for her. The awful Miss St. John was probably pregnant with Mrs. Stacton's husband's child. Hesitantly, she said, "She probably won't have the baby, actually. She's trying to get rid of it—to have an abortion. I heard her talking to a woman at the camp—"

"Abortion!" Mrs. Stacton's double chins trembled with emotion.

Peggy, listening to the exchange, said, "It's not something any of us would normally condone, but under the circumstances—"

But Beryl was gone. She walked across the room and out onto the deck.

"Shouldn't I have said anything?" Hazel asked Peggy.

"I don't know, dear. I'm fresh out of moral judgments," Peggy said wearily.

Sumatra had been a thriving Dutch colony for many years. It was an island rich in oil and therefore of extremely high value to both sides of the conflict. In mid-January, when it became apparent that Singapore might fall, some troops and most of the British bombers had been evacuated to Sumatra. But on the day after the mass civilian evacuation from Singapore, Japanese parachutists landed at Palembang, Sumatra, where the Dutch garrison was forced to retire. The very next day, a fleet of Japanese ships arrived in Palembang, and the Allies, before moving their aircraft to Java, torched everything of potential value to the Japanese. The sprawling refineries of Sumatra's most industrial city were turned into twisted, charred wreckage. The big tankers were taken to the middle of the Moesi River and bombed by the departing planes, both to destroy their contents and to blockade the river.

Now, more than a month later, the sight was devastating. Riverbanks that should have been lush jungle or ugly but profitable industry were a blackened, dead landscape out of nightmares. Everything was burnt wreckage. Tankers had spilled their burning oil, which washed downstream burning the natives' stilt houses that formerly sat out in the water. What wasn't singed was coated with oily muck. There were so many dead fish in the water that the stench was appalling. Holding handkerchiefs over their mouths and noses, some of the women stood on deck as the yacht plowed through the thick water. Some cried for the desolation of a country they'd never seen before. Others simply cried for themselves because they were hungry, hot, frightened, and desperately homesick.

They docked at midmorning a few miles past what remained of the city. It had taken them a full day to go eighty miles, a day without any food and very little water. Once again they were lined up, counted, and generally harassed before being loaded onto captured Dutch troop transport trucks. After a bruising ten-mile journey, they pulled into what appeared to be a recently abandoned church and school compound. Once again they smelled food cooking. Sister Maria, who had the best vantage point, called out, "Look at the building the smoke is coming from. I think there are men in there. I saw some at the window."

"Revolting little yellow ones?" Audrey said with a yawn.

"No, white men. I'm sure of it."

This immediately perked everybody up. Skirts were smoothed down, cheeks were pinched, combs were passed around. "They'll save us!" one woman said.

"Don't be an ass. They're prisoners, too. But if they just speak English! I haven't heard a real man's voice for weeks!" Audrey St. John replied, applying lip rouge with the tip of her little finger.

It was another hour and a half before they were allowed to eat the food the Dutch and British soldiers had prepared for them. In the meanwhile, they were once again counted and made to stand in long lines while they were checked off lists. And again they were weighed and this time photographs were taken of them. Nobody knew what the pictures were for, but Hazel managed to get photographed twice; once as herself and once as Peggy Bright. Eventually, the bureaucratic tedium completed, they were told to sit in rows on the ground. Most of the children were crying with hunger.

The cookhouse door opened and the men who'd been kept inside all that time came out carrying pots and kettles and platters of steaming food to put on long trestle tables. Hazel gazed at them hungrily, hoping one of them would look a little like Frank. One almost did. They were a luxurious sight, all the tall, straight-limbed, fair-skinned European men. The women sat in awed silence, devouring them with their eyes.

At long last one of the Japanese guards gave an order, which the women took to be permission to go eat. They were on their feet in an instant, like a flock of ducks rising from a pond. Some of the women went straight for the food, others for the men.

"Do you know my husband? Karl Hooven is his name."

"Is there a woman with you named Susan Hatcher? Mrs. Susan Hatcher?"

"Is this meat of some kind?"

"—Robert Waterton?"

"Genevieve Bolt. Petite with blond hair—"

"What have you heard about Java?"

"—Australia?"

"—California?"

"—boiled shark fins. A bit oily, but good."

"—my father, Colonel Haverford—"

"—more rice?"

"—awfully sorry. Died in the invasion—"

"—haven't got any sulfa, have you?"

"Harry! Oh, thank God you're alive—"

Nancy Muir hung back. The man dishing up the rice at the end of the trestle table was the nice one from the boat, the gentleman who'd shown such solicitude about her cut arm. At the sight of him, she'd gotten an odd feeling in her stomach that had nothing to do with being hungry.

You're a disgusting, sex-starved old maid! she told herself brutally. She'd go without food rather than let herself get any closer to him. Put into practice what Papa had always preached about the benefits of mortifying the flesh. Of course, Papa did it for God. Nancy was doing it for herself.

But still, she couldn't make herself move way, and as she stared at him, he glanced up and caught her gaze. His pale, round face brightened and he smiled broadly. "Hello, there," he called, gesturing for her to come forward. "Have you a bowl? I have a few coconut shells back here if you need one."

"I—thank you," she said as he lobbed a spoonful of rice into one of the shells and handed it to her.

"Sorry I can't offer you a spoon. Fresh out, don't you know. How's that arm? Healed up nicely, I hope."

"Yes, thank you." *He remembered her.* Such a nice voice. She'd forgotten that about him. Rather high, as though he would sing in a good clear tenor. And with the slightest hint of cockney under the precise British consonants.

"Any idea where you're going?" he asked.

"No, none."

"Nor do we know. They started to move us out yesterday, then changed their minds, such as they are—I suppose because they learned you were coming through."

"Have you heard any news from outside?" Anything to keep the conversation going.

He shrugged. "A great deal. Java's been taken. Java hasn't been taken. Both bits of news proclaimed with equal authority."

"Are they treating you badly?" Nancy asked, noticing a bruise on the side of his face.

He looked embarrassed. "Well, rather badly—" he admitted.

"Darling, this little tête-à-tête is too precious for words," Audrey St. John interrupted, "but could you move along so the rest of us could get our food?" She dug a sharp elbow into Nancy's ribs as though by accident.

Mortified, Nancy turned away, nearly tripping and spilling her rice.

They were allowed to stay only a few hours and spent most of the time eating voraciously. It was the first meal they'd had since their incarceration which was varied and filling if not appetizing by outside standards. The fish tasted oily and slightly spoiled, the fruit was overripe, and the rice overcooked. But there were small, bitter soya beans and sliced Chinese cabbage in the rice, and someone had managed to get a whole bottle of vinegar to splash over it. Even those who'd never liked vinegar fought for a teaspoon because it had a strong, tangy taste and they were so sick of bland rice. There was even a big roasted chunk of beef, or something that resembled beef. It was stringy and tough and was sliced paper-thin, but those who were first in line and got some savored it and talked about it for days afterward.

Late in the afternoon the women and children were put back onto the trucks. Several families had been temporarily reunited, and their parting was so heartbreaking that the other women had to turn away to hide their own tears. As the trucks rumbled off into the shadows, the occupants were silent for a long time. "It seemed almost like freedom for a while, didn't it?" Hazel finally said quietly to her mother. Hazel had spent her time in a harmless but exhilarating flirtation with several young men, one of whom had lived briefly in Chicago and wanted to compare memories. She'd told herself she had to keep in practice for when she saw Frank again.

"I don't know that I'll feel free again until I can have a professional haircut and manicure," Roberta answered distractedly. "It's odd all the things I used to take for granted—even complain about—that would be so welcome now. Like pork chops. I never liked them because there wasn't a neat way of eating one. So greasy. Now I'd knock down anybody who stood between me and a pork chop."

"That's your body telling you that you need fat in your diet," Dr. Millichope said.

"A chocolate-covered cherry. That's what I want," Gloria said. "With that sticky juice that always tries to run down your chin."

"Does that mean you lack sweetness?" Hazel asked, smiling.

"Please stop this talk!" somebody at the back of the truck said. "It's not fair to the children."

They fell silent again.

After a few miles of driving along a road that ran parallel to some railroad tracks, the trucks pulled over and stopped at a tiny station. "Hmmm, looks like we're going to take a train ride," Gloria said. "Can't be any worse than these damned lorries."

"I like trains," Hazel said. "I'm going to close my eyes and pretend I'm on the *Super Chief*."

"I doubt that you'll get a first-class sleeper, but if so, I want the lower bunk—and I want Clark Gable in it with me," Gloria said.

After an hour wait they saw the light from an approaching train. It was now fully dark and the surrounding jungle was alive with ominous animal noises—wild dogs barking, something in the distance that sounded like a gigantic cat fight, and thousands of frogs and crickets—or something that sounded like frogs and crickets. As the train strained and screeched to a stop, the women stared in disbelief. It consisted only of an engine and four rackety boxcars.

"They don't mean to make us ride in those, do they?" Caroline Warbler whispered.

"They *can't* do this to us!" another voice said quiveringly.

Unfortunately, that was precisely the plan. They were shoved in like cattle and the sliding doors thumped shut behind them. "Wait a minute! Where's Clark Gable?" Gloria cried. Nobody laughed. It was pitch black inside and smelled strongly of citrus, so strongly it was to give them all headaches within a few hours. Somebody in Hazel's car started shrieking, and there was the sharp sound of a slap.

Peggy Bright's voice suddenly overrode the other conversation. "Look here, there isn't room for luggage to take up sleeping space, so I suggest we put all the bags down flat—like an extra layer of flooring. Then if we all lie down with our heads toward the front of the train, we should all fit well enough to get a little sleep. Leave an open place along the right side, and we'll improvise some sort of lavatory at the back."

A quarrelsome voice came out of the darkness. "Just who do you think you are to order us around this way?"

The anonymous answer came promptly. "Somebody with a

good deal more common sense and better grammar than the rest of us—especially you! Now, do be quiet and do as she says."

There was murmur of agreement as they started shuffling their persons and belongings. Eventually everyone got settled on a relatively level plane. The layer of suitcases had another benefit, that of insulating some of the deafening sound of the wheels just beneath them. All of the children and most of the women fell asleep immediately. A few, their digestive tracts in upheaval from all the food they'd eaten earlier, spent the night crawling back and forth to a leaky bucket in the back corner, which was unspeakable by morning.

As the sun rose, shafts of it sliced through the cracks in the old boxcar and women started haggling for the opportunity to get nearer the cracks, where there was some fresh air. It was already getting warm in the car. The citrus odor and that of the bucket, mingling, were already taking their toll. As it got warmer, it all combined with the rocking of the boxcar to give them motion sickness. Finally, the brakes screamed again and they slowed down to a gradual stop. There was some shouting outside as the Japanese gave orders to somebody. When the doors slid open, the women jumped and tumbled out in a rush.

They were stopped at a village where food had been prepared. The natives were standing sullenly in their doorways while the guards prodded the prisoners forward to the big black cookpots full of rice.

"We have different guards now," Hazel observed to Gloria. "Look at that huge one." He was enormous, especially for a Japanese. Though he couldn't have been more than seventeen or eighteen years old, he was well over six feet tall with wide shoulders and a round face and a wide mouth exposing some of the biggest, crookedest teeth Hazel had ever seen. He was trying to look fierce and soldierish, but it was apparently an effort. His was a simple face, made for laughter.

Gloria turned. "Oh, that's Mickey."

Hazel stared at her with amazement. "How do you know him?"

"He was driving the truck when I turned myself in. Gave me a pack of cigarettes, Mickey did."

"And formally introduced himself?"

Gloria laughed, drawing several critical stares. "Yes. Some long Nip thing—or maybe he was telling me to haul my ass into the truck. Dunno—but there was a 'Mickey' in it someplace."

As they spoke, he had lumbered over and approached them. Glancing around at the other guards and finding himself unobserved, he bowed slightly. "Itohay Masamichi Asakawa," he said.

"See? What'd I tell you? Hello, Mickey," Gloria said. Returning his bow, she added, pointing to herself, "Gloria Denk—Dinki."

"Herrow, Dinki."

They both looked expectantly at Hazel. She bowed and said her name. "Herrow, Hazer Hammon," Mickey said courteously.

At that instant the pleasant interlude was interrupted from two directions. Behind Mickey, another guard barked an order. Behind Hazel, Roberta Hampton said coldly, "Hazel, what in the world are you doing?"

Before turning to her mother, Hazel surprised herself by winking at Mickey. "Just learning a bit of Japanese, Mother."

Roberta flushed. "I'm not pleased at this sarcasm."

"Sorry." Hazel really was. "He was being polite, so I thought I should be, too."

"Then you must think again. He is one of the enemy!"

"But—"

"No buts, Hazel. Even if there are a few of them who have decent manners, you dare not risk the slightest hint of collaboration. Even if it does mean forgetting our own good manners in some circumstances."

"Collaboration!"

"He *is* one of the enemy."

"He's a big, stupid boy, Mother."

"Hazel—!"

"Yes, Mother," she said. But as she got her bowl of rice and cabbage and sat on the ground cross-legged eating it, she thought about the exchange. She'd always regarded herself as a good, loyal American, but she must not be much good at patriotism. She could easily regard the screaming, abusive guards who shoved them around and terrified them as personal enemies, they were a threat to her physical and emotional well-being and made clear that they loathed their captives. She hated the anonymous fliers who'd dropped the bombs on the innocent civilians in Singapore, leaving so many homeless and bereft. But she couldn't think in big enough terms to hate a whole country, and that now appeared to be a large part of how patriotism was measured in wartime. Funny that she'd never known that.

On the other hand, she was no crusader—like some of the missionaries who went about trying to get everybody to pray for the strength to love the enemy. All Hazel wanted, she decided, was to be allowed to ignore the enemy as much of the time as possible—and, with any luck at all, be ignored by them.

She wanted to talk to her mother about her insights, but knew it was hopeless. Peggy would understand, though.

    Chapter 13

Dear Jim,
    There is a constant miasma of news here. It's as hard to grasp and identify as a cloud. Nobody knows the source of any of it, but that doesn't stop most of us from tending to believe anything we hear. Now we hear the Philippines have fallen. This is sad indeed, if true. I felt if we could keep our military toehold there, we'd have a strong base from which to drive the Japs back. There must be a great mob of Americans trapped.
    Silly wishing it, but if I had to be imprisoned this way, I'd have rather been there with my own. There are Americans among us, but not many. The majority are British and Australian and don't much care for Americans. It's not that they actively dislike us, but rather that we hardly exist. When we are noticed, it's as those people whose fault this war is. Because we are in the minority, we're easy to blame.

After the meal they were put back on the boxcars. Dr. Millichope managed to convey in garbled Malay that shutting the doors in the heat would kill the children—she didn't mention the adults, knowing the Japanese didn't care what happened to them and would probably be thrilled if a few of them died. But the guards didn't want the children to come to harm, though they feared the women would escape if the doors were opened. After a long session of wrangling with a great deal of confusion on both sides, she convinced them to put one guard in each doorway to prevent this from happening. Hazel's car, luckily, was assigned Mickey, who sat happily, dangling his long legs outside and leaning his face into the wind like a dog riding in an automobile. Since no one had any intention of leaping from a moving train into the dense, inhospitable jungle, there were no incidents.

They arrived at another village at sunset, were put out bag and baggage, and once again were fed by clearly hostile natives.

"Why do they look at us that way?" Hazel asked her mother. "It's not as if we imposed ourselves on them deliberately. Can't they see we didn't choose to be here?"

"I imagine we're being fed their whole food supply. They don't care who ordered it, we're the ones gobbling it up."

But as Hazel looked around, she realized it was mainly the men of the village who were glaring at them. The women, especially the ones with young children, watched them with expressions of guarded sympathy.

When they'd finished eating, the guards lined them up and separated out the women with babies and very small children. They were ordered back onto the train, which pulled out, leaving about thirty of them behind. "Good heavens!" Beryl Stacton exclaimed. "They don't mean we're to stay here?"

"What's so particularly wrong with here?" Nancy Muir asked her.

Beryl looked at her as though she'd never seen her before. In a sense, she hadn't. Nancy almost never got into conversations with the others. "Well, it's so—so primitive."

"Yes, but there isn't any barbed wire," Nancy said reasonably.

"But—but," Beryl sputtered, "but we're prisoners! How can you pretend you like a place that is a jail to us?"

Nancy was sorry she'd started this. Better to have continued to keep aloof and silent. "I don't like it any more than you do. I was merely suggesting that it was the lesser of two evils," she said before abruptly walking away.

"Wimmens go there!" A guard came by, shouting and gesturing. He was pointing to a large, atap-roofed hut that was apparently the community gathering place. "Wimmens sleep."

For the first time since they'd been captured, they went to sleep without the sound of babies crying.

The next morning there was an insurrection of sorts led by, of all people, the four missionaries and three nuns in the group. After the captives were rudely awakened and dragged out to be counted, they were told, "We walk now. Wimmens walk!"

"Not yet," one of the missionaries said firmly. They all turned to look at her, wondering if she'd gone mad. "It is Sunday, the Lord's day, and we must have our religious services," she told the guards. "And furthermore, we must have food before we undertake a walking journey."

The guards—there were only three of them left behind, Mickey and two others—clearly didn't understand a word of this. They turned to Dr. Millichope, who did her best to interpret into Malay. Since neither she nor the one guard spoke the language well, it got garbled in the translation. Nancy, listening knowledgeably to the guards discuss it, was amused to discover that the appeal for a short, interdenominational church service had turned into some sort of faintly distasteful female mystery. The guards believed the women wanted to have some sort of "cleansing" ceremony. They had a fearful, superstitious respect for such a request and wanted to know nothing more about it except how long it would take.

"What are you smiling about, Miss Muir?" Hazel asked.

Nancy hadn't realized the girl was standing beside her and certainly didn't know she was being observed. "Nothing. Just enjoying the fresh air."

"Oh?" Hazel said suspiciously. She hadn't formulated what her suspicions added up to, but she was beginning to sense from the way Miss Muir observed things that she knew something—something the rest of them didn't. At first she'd thought it was an inflated sense of moral superiority, but she didn't preach or criticize. She just watched and listened and sometimes smiled oddly.

After a meager breakfast and short church service, they were organized to set out on the next leg of their journey, a journey with an unknown destination. Dr. Millichope had tried to find out where they were and where they were headed, but the guards wouldn't talk about it except to hint that it would be several days walk. They just shouted, "Hully up, wimmens! Walk now!"

Dr. Millichope did her best to prepare them for what might be a long trip. "Wear flat shoes if you have them, and stockings, or even better, wool or cotton socks. If you have extras, share them. I know it will be hot, but you'll get fewer blisters. Take everything you don't need out of your suitcases and wrap something soft around the handle so you don't blister your hands. Be sure you have on a hat that thoroughly shades your face and wear long sleeves no matter how uncomfortable—as protection against the sun and insects."

"We'll have heat strokes!" Roberta objected.

"Possibly," Dr. Millichope replied bluntly.

Peggy Bright took charge of other areas of preparation. "Put the children and the slowest walkers at the front of the line, to set the pace. Otherwise they'll fall behind and the guards will harass them. I'll walk with the doctor at first and we'll trade off turns guiding her. Hazel, see if you can get the natives to give us some of those bamboo poles to hang things on to carry. The children can take smaller items; it will make them feel useful."

"How wise," Roberta muttered sarcastically. Catching Hazel's surprised glance, she said softly. "I do wish you could find someone else to spend your time with than that woman."

"Why?"

"She's bossy and aggressive and a know-it-all. None of which are attractive assets. Lord knows I'm not old-fashioned, but a woman should act like a woman, not a drill sergeant."

"Mother, she's nothing of the kind. She's very nice and interesting."

"Just what an acolyte should say. Don't think I don't see you, sitting at her knee, soaking up all her little wisdoms."

Hazel was stunned. Her mother had always been able to turn a quick quip, but her sharpness was always surface, not genuinely nasty. This kind of talk was utterly unlike her. "Mother, I don't have a lot to do here, you know," she said as mildly as she could manage.

"You could spend your time with me, your mother, instead of that woman."

"But I don't play cards," Hazel said angrily.

"Then you should learn! Lord knows I've tried to interest you."

Audrey St. John was having problems. She'd managed all these weeks to hang on to all three of her heavily laden suitcases. Now she was going to have to carry them. She asked the nuns first, thinking that Christian charity would compel them to help her. In this, she was mistaken.

"No, Miss St. John," young Sister Maria said with surprising firmness, "I'm helping one of the mothers carry a sick child. And don't ask Sister Edith, she's got a bad heart and somebody else is carrying her things." The third nun either didn't speak English or pretended not to. The missionaries also refused with a variety of excuses.

Finally Audrey had to ask Sister Warbler. "Sorry, dearie," she answered with terrible sweetness Audrey suspected was sarcasm, "I'm carrying the medical supplies for Dr. Millichope."

Gloria overheard the exchange and approached. "I'll carry one of them for you, Miss St. John."

"You will?"

"Yes, one dress of my choice and one pair of those nice lacy knickers per suitcase per day."

"What!"

"Take it or leave it, as the Yanks say."

"That's robbery!"

"No, it's free enterprise. Supply and demand, you know."

They haggled for a while, Gloria insisting on payment in advance, and finally worked out a deal by which Gloria got a three-quarter-sleeved navy and yellow dress ("but not the belt— it didn't come with the dress") and a pair of pink silk panties in return for hauling Audrey's second heaviest suitcase ("I'll take the heaviest one if you'll throw in the bloody belt").

And so they set out.

At the front of the procession was the little wiry guard who thought he spoke English and Malay. Behind him there was a very heavy, elderly Englishwoman named Englethorpe with a beaten-down servant she called simply Evans. Evans carried the bags; Mrs. Englethorpe huffed along trying to carry her own extra weight, an effort that had her red-faced and sweat-soaked in the first mile. Behind them Peggy Bright walked with Dr. Millichope a little behind, her hand resting lightly on Peggy's shoulder for guidance. Caroline Warbler was with them, carrying the medical supplies and one of the young mothers' suitcases.

Immediately behind them were six children ranging from seven to about twelve years old; the youngest three were boys, the eldest three were girls. Fortunately, at the onset of the journey, they thought it was fun—much nicer than being cooped up in a dark old boxcar. They skipped, shouted, and had contests to see who could throw rocks farthest ahead while the five mothers with them tried to get them to conserve their energy.

Helping to keep an eye on the children and carrying the youngest child, a little girl of about six, was young Sister Maria. She had, many weeks before, given up her spare uniform to Caroline Warbler. Now she'd shed part of her headgear to make a sort of parasol to protect the child from the sun. The elderly nun with the bad heart and the French one who didn't speak English kept close to her and cast appalled glances at her incomplete habit.

Following them, and staying in a protective clump, were the Protestant missionaries. In addition to their own belongings, which were proudly minimal, they were in charge of the water supply—jugs and bottles and canteens they'd filled at the village water tap. Glugging and sloshing faintly, they walked four abreast and kept trying to urge the rest to sing some nice rousing hymns to help the time pass. No one was much inclined to join in, and so they sang by themselves for a few miles until the guard at the front of the column could stand no more and threatened them with his bayonet. Mickey, who'd been walking beside them and humming along tunelessly, looked disappointed.

Next in line were Nancy and Hazel. Each of them supported the front ends of bamboo poles on each shoulder. Two or three suitcases were strung on each pole, and Gloria and Roberta brought up the rear of these conveyances.

In an effort to stay away from the children, the missionaries, and those carrying the heaviest loads (who might actually expect her to help), Audrey St. John had ended up at the end of the group with Beryl Stacton—her very least likely choice of companions. For the first mile they utterly ignored each other. Audrey struggled along with her two remaining suitcases. After a while she felt they were literally pulling her arms out of their sockets. She traded arms, but that was even more painful, so she switched them back. The raised stitching on the handle of one expensive lizard case had been one of the points that drew her to it when she persuaded Dennis to buy it for her. Now it was a nightmare, like a tiny serrated knife that rubbed and rubbed and eventually caused her fingers to blister and throb.

She turned to the guard who was bringing up the rear and asked if she could get a scarf out to wrap around her hand. He didn't understand, but replied by shouting something at her and raising his hand threateningly. Gritting her teeth against the pain, she kept going another hundred yards before she tripped over a rock and fell heavily. He shouted at her again as she struggled back to her feet. She'd thrown her hands forward to break her fall. The blisters had broken as she smacked into the compacted dirt and now were oozing pinkly.

"Give me one of those," Beryl said brusquely. Without waiting for a reply, she snatched up the heavier case—the one she rightly suspected her husband had purchased for his mistress with her money—and strode ahead, walking hard on her heels.

Amazed, Audrey picked up the remaining suitcase and stumbled back into motion. After a while she figured out to imitate one of the mothers farther ahead and lifted the suitcase onto her head. That way she could walk and balance it with the hand that hurt the least. As she caught up and came alongside Beryl, she said, without looking at her, "Thanks ever so."

After a while the four carrying the suitcases on poles rotated positions. Hazel ended up walking beside Gloria. "I bet you didn't learn about this in nurses' training," Hazel said.

"Actually, I learned something very like it at home. We used to have to carry our water, and my sisters and I did it with buckets on poles. We were nothing to my old dad but pack animals. Not so strong as my mum, but trainable."

"You don't like your father, then."

"Not much. But it wasn't all his fault. That's what things are like in Australia. Men are men and women—women are nothing."

"What about your mother?"

"She's dead and she's probably happy to have done herself up a martyr. She was from a nice family in Perth, but she met my dad and put her brain, if she had one, in the cellar and went off to a sheep station with him. Had the six of us, four girls and two boys, bang, bang, bang, along with half a dozen miscarriages between times."

"It must have been a hard life for her," Hazel said, shifting the weight of the pole a bit.

"Hard? Hard isn't the half. No running water. No electricity. No neighbors. And Dad wouldn't lift a finger to help her. She did all the gardening, cleaning, cooking, even made all our clothes because he couldn't be bothered to take time to ride in to Perth and buy ready-made. And even if he had been willing to make anything easier for her, she wouldn't have said boo to him. She was a sufferer, was my mum. Loved it. Thought my sisters and I ought to suffer, too."

"Did any of them?"

"Not a one. My oldest sister left home at sixteen. Married a fine bloke and set up to winkle the rest of us away. As we got old enough and fed up enough, she'd take us in, send us to school. She put me through my nurses' training, bless her, and told me it would get me out of Australia. Thank God, it did. My mum died the year the youngest girl left home. Nobody to see her noble suffering anymore, I guess. I was on hols. I went home to bury her and see that Dad and the boys were all right. The old man already had some half-witted neighbor girl in, cooking and sleeping with all of them."

"Your father *and* your brothers?"

"They'd all gotten to be like the damned rams they were with all the time. Probably shared the sheep with the rams. That girl was no different to them. She was a woman—nothing but breasts and a vagina and a good strong back to carry water." She shuddered.

"Won't you ever go back? Certainly not everyone in Australia is like that."

"No, my brother-in-law is a good bloke. Some are all right. But it's too close to that damned station. Anywhere in Australia is too close."

"Wimmens walk more fast!" the lead guard kept urging all day, to no avail whatsoever.

The more time passed and the more shrill he became, the more slowly they moved. It wasn't entirely deliberate. Few of these women had ever done any more walking than was involved in a stroll through the Botanic Gardens. Even those like the sisters, both religious and medical, who were accustomed to being on their feet all day, had never been required to carry heavy loads for long distances.

So in spite of his determination to reach some destination at some specified time, they made very little progress. Several of the women and two of the children were having digestive upsets and had to keep going off into the bushes at the side of the road to relieve themselves. This drove the guards mad; they were desperately afraid it was a ploy to escape and needed to be closely guarded on such trips, but at the same time they had an enormous revulsion to any accidental intimacy with their captives. So the women were ordered to keep talking continuously while they were in the bushes so the guards knew they weren't sneaking off.

"Where do they think we would escape to?" Gloria asked anyone who might be listening. "Do any of us have the faintest idea where we are or where we'd go if we got free? Well? Do we?"

"Oh, Dinki, do shut up," Sister Warbler called back cheerfully. The child she was carrying thought this was funny and started giggling. Soon they were all laughing at the clear, sparkling child's laughter. The lead guard, whom they'd named Spike for his hairstyle, turned and screamed at them in Nippongo. The rest were startled at his fury. Only Nancy knew he was accusing them of laughing at him.

That evening he was nearly beside himself about their lack of progress. He let them put their burdens down in a small clearing next to the road. "So what now?" Roberta asked. "Do we get fed?"

"Probably. I imagine they'll send food along in trucks or something," Nancy said. She'd heard the guards discussing when the food was to come along.

Using their luggage as furniture, they sat down and assessed the damage. Nearly everyone had blisters on their feet, many having burst and glued their stockings in place. Dr. Millichope had a small supply of sulfa, which she distributed stingily for the worst cases. Some were near collapse from heat and dehydration. Everyone's clothes were soaked with sweat. They were allowed to drink the last of the water supply. There was nothing to be done for the many severe sunburns except to warn the victims to cover up better the next day. Nor was there any help for Hazel and the others who'd carried the bamboo poles and had swollen, bruised lumps on both shoulders from the weight.

As they rested, a native wagon pulled by a carabao, the native ox, came along the road. It belonged to a farmer and was laden with various fruits. Two of the mothers hastily unpacked some items they'd decided they'd rather do without than carry, and approached the wagon to trade them for food. The farmer traded some cabbage for a hand-embroidered linen pillowslip with some misgiving, but took a real fancy to a dictionary for some reason and gave the owner a nice bunch of bananas for it. She divided them up among all the children.

"Which is the greater mystery—why she had it with her or why he wanted it?" Peggy asked the others.

The rest of them sat down to contemplate their belongings with an eye toward discarding weight and bulk and possibly acquiring something more useful along the way. Hazel studied everything in her purse and suitcase and decided she really wanted to keep it all, regardless. Even the books, heavy as they were, had been a great comfort in the normally boring existence they'd been forced into. Even though she wanted to believe the rumor that the fighting had already started to free Sumatra, she still wanted to be prepared to endure a few more weeks, perhaps even months, of incarceration.

A young woman approached and sat down by Hazel. "Can't bear to part with it, can you? Neither can I. I don't believe we've really met. I'm Jane Kowolski." She was a plump but compact young woman with short reddish hair, blue eyes and freckled skin that was now beet red and badly blistered.

"I'm Hazel Hampton. You sound American."

"I am. New Hampshire originally, then New York for years."

"What are you doing out here?"

"Singing for my supper. A touring opera company."

"And you brought your daughter along?" Hazel asked, looking across the clearing at the little girl.

"Oh, no. I'm not even married and she's no relation to me, though she calls me Auntie Jane. We just ended up on the same lifeboat."

"What happened to her mother?"

"I have no idea. She wasn't on our boat. I keep begging the Japs to search through those endless records of theirs for her, but either they don't or won't understand me. So little Vivian and I are stuck with each other for the duration." She said it with a fond smile.

"I think Vivian's very lucky."

"And I think I am. Say, those are awful bruises on your

shoulders. Let me take turns with those suitcase poles of yours tomorrow.''

As Nancy had predicted, a truck came along the dusty road shortly with the ubiquitous kettle of cold, overcooked rice. ''Oh, rice for a change! How divine!'' Gloria exclaimed.

The guards had to run in front of the truck to stop it and were loudly berated for having made so little progress. ''I do love to see the little bastards get shouted at,'' Gloria observed.

''Oh?'' Peggy said grimly, ''And whom do you think they'll take it out on?''

Two of the guards were in particularly ill humor the next day, but Mickey was happily oblivious to the fact that he was in trouble. He seemed to be actually enjoying the walk. Halfway through the morning he spoke to Sister Maria, who was stumbling with fatigue from carrying the sick child. He gestured that the nun was to hand the child to him, which she did with great reluctance. The child's mother gave a little whimper of fear, but he ignored her. He draped the little girl over his shoulder and strode along, humming to her and patting her gently on the back. Pretty soon she started perking up, as though this were some form of powerful medicine.

When one of the little boys stubbed his toe badly on a rock in the road, Mickey scooped him up as well. By midday he was positively festooned with children. Those he wasn't carrying were hanging on him. And there was a constant babble of conversation and laughter. The fact that the children spoke English and he spoke Nippongo didn't seem to interfere in the least with the communication process.

''It's not right, letting those children associate with him,'' Roberta Hampton complained to her daughter.

''Nonsense. He's just a big child himself. If their mothers don't mind, I don't see why you should,'' Hazel snapped. She'd never realized just how tiresome her mother could be. After a few minutes she said, ''Mother, I'm sorry I was rude.''

Roberta's voice shook as she replied. ''No, you were quite right, Hazel. I'm turning into a harridan. This damned, damned war!''

On the third day of their walk, it rained. At first it was just a drizzle that turned the road to paste that accumulated on their feet. After a while, however, it turned into a real downpour that drenched them. They didn't just walk, they dragged their feet out of the sucking mud with every step. It was exhausting. Even the guards, laden as they were with their own heavy equipment, were bogged down. Except Mickey, who strode along as though he didn't notice. He kept throwing his head back to catch raindrops in his mouth.

That night they crowded together in the shelter of an abandoned godown. It was filthy, and they had to clear out several animal nests and a good many broken coconut shells, but it was at least slightly drier than the outdoors. The guards slept in a small tent they put up in front of the doorway. During the night the elderly lady gave a terrible cry and then made a horrible gurgling noise. Dr. Millichope crawled over to her and after a moment said, "She's dead, poor thing."

They woke the guards and told them. Mickey turned up two small shovels from someplace and held one out, offering it to whoever would help. "Miss Evans?" Dr. Millichope asked.

"With respect, mum, I don't work for her anymore," Evans said.

Hazel saw the look of relief on the servant's face and suddenly had a sense that poor Evans had just been freed from a kind of imprisonment. "I'm strong. I'll help," she volunteered. Someone laughed nastily and Hazel realized it was because she was being so damned wholesome again.

In the morning the rain had stopped, but the food truck apparently forgot them or got bogged down somewhere. They waited for a while, peering up and down the road for any sign of a vehicle. While they waited, they discussed the disposition of Mrs. Englethorpe's belongings. Naturally they couldn't waste anything. It was the consensus that Evans should have what she wanted and that Hazel, who had helped bury her, should have second choice. Hazel turned this right over to Gloria, who had the greater need.

When they'd sorted it all out to everyone's satisfaction and distributed the old woman's things, one of the children started crying. "I'm so hungry," she sobbed.

Finally Peggy, after consultation with the mothers, asked Dr. Millichope to put a proposal to the guards, who were bound to be as hungry as the women. The proposal was this: If the guards would allow the women to go into the jungle to find food and firewood, the women would leave the children behind as hostages and would furthermore prepare the food and share it with the guards.

It was a complex business, conveying the subjunctive in a language neither side really knew. Nancy Muir very nearly broke down and explained it in Nippongo, but finally with a lot of pantomime, the concept was gotten across and approved. The guard they called Spike and the little fat one who always brought up the rear of the column took the hostage part of it very seriously, however. They made the children sit in a circle on the ground and stood with their guns trained on them. This spectacle, which chilled them all, was made all the more peculiar when Mickey sat down in the midst of the children and started showing them some sort of elaborate game played with a handful of sticks. Soon, even those who'd been sobbing with fear forgot the guns pointed at them.

The women did fairly well in the jungle. Peggy and Jane Kowolski both found birds' eggs, three of which were unfertilized and fresh enough to feed to the children in tiny portions. There were a lot of bananas and other fruit. Gloria came back with an actual bird—a pigeon-size creature with violently colored feathers. "Dinki, we can't eat that," Sister Warbler said. "It was a sick bird or you couldn't have caught it."

There was a heated debate over this, and in the end it was agreed they shouldn't risk eating the bird. Gloria resentfully turned it over to Spike, who happily wrung its neck, plucked and gutted it, and popped it into a pot of boiling water Dr. Millichope had prepared. To their enormous disappointment, he suffered no ill effects whatsoever. They had just finished eating their makeshift meal when the food truck finally appeared. Unwilling to let the rice go to waste, even though they weren't hungry at the moment, they stuffed themselves and set out on full stomachs—a rare feeling.

On the fifth day of walking, they finally reached their destination. After a long uphill climb, they passed a long, rubber tree-lined drive, at the end of which sat a big white house of clearly European design. There was a blond woman holding a child standing on the veranda, watching them pass. They were too far away to read her expression.

"Who the hell is she?" Gloria demanded.

"Probably Dutch. Apparently they aren't locking the Dutch

up—yet," Peggy answered. "If her husband's cooperating with the Japs, they'll be left alone."

When they had passed beyond sight of the house, the guards let them stop and rest while they conferred over a map, then they ordered the women back to their feet and took them down a side road. This wound through a grove of rubber trees which were being tapped by a work crew of natives. Unlike the people in the villages they'd stayed in, these men looked at the dirty, bedraggled white women and children with neutrality, if not sympathy.

They took another turn and found themselves facing what had been the coolie quarters of the rubber plantation. It was a large, grim area and there were about a dozen stilted wooden buildings with a large, open-sided building in the center. And around it all there was a combination of stockade fencing and barbed wire. It was new, the sap still oozing from the boards and the sun glinting on the points of the barbed wire.

They stood silently contemplating the sight, unconsciously moving closer together, as if for protection, for a long moment.

"Home sweet home," Gloria said bitterly.

     Chapter 14

Dearest Jim,

It's been a while since I got an opportunity to continue this letter. We've been moved. A boat trip, a hideous train ride in boxcars, then a very long walk, just to reach—this!

We're in the coolie "village" of a Dutch rubber plantation. The coolies are gone, though they might well have made more amiable companions than some we have here. It's not that

*they're bad women—at least most of them probably were no
worse than average outside—but they're not accustomed to
either hardship or community living. They fight it every inch
of the way. Except the nuns, of course. But they are even less
equipped than the rest of us to be thrust suddenly into a situation where there are no "rules."*

*I believe that's what we need most: rules. Our own rules.
Not the rule of capricious brutality the guards are so happy
to enforce. The outside standards—which fork to use for the
salad—don't apply. We have neither forks nor salads. Oh,
Jim, I have such an itch to organize. . . .*

Peggy was writing by the light of a shaft of moonlight through
a crack in the sleeping hut. She was so engrossed in her thoughts
that she didn't hear Hazel come near and nearly cried out in
surprise when the younger woman touched her foot.

"Dear God! I thought I'd been caught," Peggy whispered,
folding the paper and sliding it into the slit in the lining of her
suitcase.

"I've got something. Look!" Hazel whispered. She held out
her hands.

Peggy stared in amazement. "Toothbrushes! There must be
fifty of them. How—?"

"The woman up at the big white house. I was going to the
wash hut and she hissed at me through the fence and gave me
these. She's Dutch, as we thought, but she speaks English. She
went to Palembang and bought all sorts of things she thought
we might need. She said she'd come back every night with bits
of it. Tomorrow is combs and then some sanitary pads."

"Hazel, put them away and we'll figure out tomorrow how
to distribute them equitably. The children first, of course—"

"—and divide up the rest between sleeping huts?"

"I don't know. Won't that just give everybody one more thing
to argue about? Better to have them all dissatisfied with the two
of us than with each other. There's already such an awful lot of
squabbling over trifles."

"What about a raffle? Buy tickets for chances and then we
could use the money to buy from the peddler for the children."

"Darlings, if you'd save your girlish secrets for daylight—?"
Audrey St. John hissed from her section of sleeping platform.

Hazel quickly hid the toothbrushes, but not well enough. . . .

The next morning, their fourth in the coolie quarters, they

were called out to *tenko* and made to stand a very long time waiting for something. They weren't told what. Hazel had learned to endure this forced boredom by picking out a specific problem to consider in detail. This morning she occupied herself by pondering the toothbrush problem.

How to fairly hand out forty-four toothbrushes (she'd counted them as she put them away) among a hundred and fifty people? Even the first step—giving them to the children—wasn't that easy. The seven babies in camp didn't need them yet. Should they get them now to be saved for later? And what exactly constituted childhood? They had girls of sixteen and seventeen who weren't quite children or adults. Of course, many of the internees, like Hazel herself, already had toothbrushes of their own, but Hazel had already begun to realize that wouldn't keep everyone from wanting their "fair share" of anything that came into camp.

Before she could come to any conclusion, her ruminations were interrupted by the arrival of three cars. The first two were very shiny black Japanese army staff cars. The third was a beat-up green Oldsmobile.

"Wimmens bow! All wimmens bow!" Spike shrieked.

The occupant of the first car was the officer who had addressed them once at the jail, the distinguished middle-aged man with the strange arm and the perfect English. His driver opened the door with a flourish and he stepped out and studied the captives with an utterly bland expression. Several officers of lesser rank, or at least less appearance of authority, scrambled out of the second car. The third had only the driver, a small, pock-marked soldier with a very yellow complexion and a bad limp.

Gloria reached out and grabbed Hazel's arm. "My God! It's the one from the beach. I'd know him anywhere, the bastard—" she said in a low, throbbing voice.

"The one who ordered the massacre? Dinki, don't do anything foolish."

"Yes, yes. Of course," Gloria muttered.

The important officer stepped onto the porch of the hut they were all facing. "I am Commandant Natsume," he said, his voice modulated perfectly to reach the back rows without sounding shrill in the front rows. An actor's voice. An actor's perfect sense of timing, too, Hazel thought. The speech was much the same one he'd given weeks earlier about how their countries had taken advantage of the peoples of Southeast Asia and made coolies of them and now the honorable and far-seeing Nipponese would reeducate the usurpers' women and children. But this time he had some more immediate and less theoretical remarks to add at the end.

"You will stay here for a very long time. Perhaps forever. Until now, the Nippon army and the people of Sumatra have taken care of you, but you must commence seeing to your own care. Beginning tomorrow, there will be deliveries of rice and other foodstuffs. But the preparation and serving are your responsibility. If you wish to augment your diet with fruit or vegetables, you must grow them. An area beside this camp is being fenced off if you wish to create gardens. Seeds and tools will be supplied to you at a reasonable cost."

"Reasonable cost?" Caroline Warbler muttered.

"As for your daily life," Natsume went on, "it is up to you to make it rich and fulfilling. If required to do so, the Nippon army will enforce order and discipline; it will be more pleasant for you, however, to manage this yourself rather than create the necessity. This is Officer Saburo Saigo. He will be responsible for discipline and the basic needs of this camp. Any questions you may have should be directed to him in future."

Saigo limped forward, glaring. Hazel could sense Gloria's tension and whispered, "Shhhh—"

Caroline Warbler, on Hazel's other side, cast a professional eye over him and sneered, "Bad liver and probably syphillis."

A woman in the front row stepped forward hesitantly. "Officer Saigo, may we be told where our husbands are?"

Saigo scowled at her. Natsume said, "Officer Saigo does not speak very much English."

A ripple of mixed amusement and anger went through the women's ranks. The same woman who'd spoken earlier said, "Are we to have an interpreter, then, to translate our questions and requests?"

"There is no need. You may learn Nippongo."

One of the doctors in camp, a large, severe woman who'd terrorized many a nurse and patient alike in her time, raised her hand and stepped forward confidently. "What about health care, Commandant? We are very short of medical supplies. I have prepared a list of what you must provide for us. According to the Geneva Convention—"

"A Nipponese army surgeon will call on each camp weekly to see selected cases and instruct you in treatment."

"I hardly think I need instruction from a Japanese army doctor!"

"Then you should think longer and harder on it," Natsume replied coldly. "You will have a good deal of time for your considerations."

While he'd been speaking to them, the men in the second staff car had disappeared. They had been searching the sleeping huts. Now one of them came forward to Saigo and handed him some papers. Natsume stood silent and seemingly disinterested as they conferred. Then Saigo held up the handful of papers and said, "Who is this papers?"

Jane Kowolski, standing in front of Hazel and to her left, stepped forward. "They are mine, Officer Saigo."

The other guard came over to her and jerked her forward. She stumbled, and he dragged her back upright.

Saigo addressed the group. "This papers hidden, but Nippon soldiers find!"

"Not hidden," Jane said. "Just put away. There's a diff—"

Saigo swung at her, a glancing blow to her temple. Jane reeled.

"Wimmens no write letter! No diary! No secret code!"

"It's not code, it's—"

This time she was knocked to the ground. The visiting soldier started to kick her, but Saigo pushed him away and delivered the kick himself. The toe of his boot made contact with her arm. Jane screamed and rolled into a ball. Saigo kicked her again, this time in the ribs. "No secrets! No codes! Nippon soldier punish!" he shouted, and glanced around to see if the other women were properly terrified.

They were.

Jane was pulled back up to her feet. She leaned sideways, whimpering and holding her side. She was the color of uncooked dough.

"You say sorry. You say never do again!" Saigo shouted.

Jane still hadn't realized that the truth counted for nothing. She said, "But it isn't anything secret—"

He struck her hard across the windpipe with the side of his hand.

Jane struggled to draw breath, clutching at her throat, then collapsed. Saigo drew back to kick her again.

Hazel couldn't stand it. She jumped forward, standing between Saigo and Jane's crumpled form. The little girl Vivian had run over and was huddled over "Auntie Jane," sobbing her heart out.

"It's music, Officer Saigo," Hazel said. "Sheet music. Look—" Propelled only by the adrenaline of terror, she snatched a sheet from him and pointed to the notes with jabbing motions, "See—music. Dah, dah, dah, dah-dah, dah-dum."

She sang horribly, her voice so frantic it hardly sounded human, but it was good enough to make the point.

He snatched the music back and gave Hazel such a sound slap that she nearly fainted. Then he turned and bowed to Natsume and spoke rapidly in Japanese. Natsume nodded curtly and descended from the porch. As he walked to his car, he noticed the gigantic guard. He'd slipped around the side of one of the huts and was standing with his hands over his ears and his eyes squeezed shut. "Take me back to headquarters," Natsume said to his driver.

As they left the compound, he spoke again. "Drive slowly. I wish to see the landscape." Actually, he wanted some time to think. But *not* about the redhead who'd intervened in the beating. He wouldn't think about her and the other woman she reminded him of so much.

What was he to do about Saburo Saigo? He'd disliked the man before meeting him, just from reading his record. The third son (as the name Saburo indicated) of an important village leader, he'd tried to take his honorable father's role in the village life when the parent died, but even though his elder brothers had both died in youth, the village elders had refused him. The reason wasn't in the record. It didn't need to be. The displacement itself was condemnation enough. A converted Christian, Saigo had then tried to become a priest, but the church rejected him as well. Natsume had never heard of the Catholic Church in Japan turning anyone away.

Saigo had then managed to join the army. Someone must have been "asleep at the switch" as the Americans said, to allow this. After two years service he had tried to join the Kempetai, the exalted Japanese secret police. Here the record went into much more detail as to the reason for his rejection. The Kempetai knew better than anyone that hatred and cruelty were fine arts to be practiced only by those with a natural grace and affinity for such things and after long instruction. Their work re-

quired that an agent be a world master of self-control and
dissembling. In the opinion of those who evaluated Saburo Saigo,
he had neither. His hatred for the white man (and possibly everyone else) was like a typhoon wind—wild, uncontrollable,
wreaking destruction to everything in his path. The men under
him didn't respect him; they were horrified by him. They lost
face by serving under him.

He was, in the opinion of the Kempetai, a madman.

After meeting him, Natsume agreed.

This report had kept him out of the Kempetai and away from
the war front, but had not dislodged him from the army.

So he had been swept into the collection of rejects and misfits
under Natsume's command. Such a command! Men like Saigo,
whom the Western women already knew for a fool; boys like
the soft-hearted, soft-headed giant; untrustworthy Formosans
and Korean conscripts. What a disgraceful way to end a long
and honorable career, Natsume thought, heartsick. And yet, he
told himself, if this was the way he could serve the emperor, so
be it. For he, too, was a misfit. A commander without a right
hand. If it weren't for his knowledge of English and his exem-
plary record from the last war, he'd have been left behind in
Japan with the women and children. He must keep that in mind.

But Saigo—the women might obey him out of fear, for they
would do well to fear him, but they would not learn to love and
respect the emperor and the Nipponese people from a man such
as him. Even the brash white women would soon see how utterly
stupid he was. They would laugh at him, and in doing so would
be contemptuous of all of Nippon. But Natsume couldn't get rid
of him by sending him down the ranks. This *was* the "bottom
of the ladder."

The car pulled up in front of the big white Dutch house that
had been taken over as a regional headquarters. In a way, it
reminded Natsume of the house in Sacramento, California,
where he'd grown up in the servants' quarters. That was part of
the reason he'd chosen it—to keep him constantly reminded why
the emperor's will must prevail over the proud white people.

He got out of the car and walked slowly around the house.
Just here, where his office window overlooked a part of the
lawn, there should be a garden. A proper Japanese garden, not
this lush, disorderly growth the Dutch had allowed. A graceful,
balanced garden with a winding path, perhaps a footbridge like
he and his wife had at home in Nagasaki—with a perfectly

branched plum tree in the background. Would plum trees grow in this foul climate? It might take many years. But then, he probably had many years here.

They carried Jane Kowolski into the hut being used as a hospital. The terrifying doctor, Letha Lange, looked her over. "She'll live," she said brusquely. "She's coming around now. She'll have a damned sore throat for a while, though."

"But will she be able to sing?" Hazel asked, holding Jane's hand and patting it.

"Sing? Good God, who cares about singing? She'll be able to talk after a bit, and that's what counts."

"Dr. Lange, you don't understand. She's a singer. An opera singer."

Lange waved this away as a minor consideration and went back to caring for another patient, a woman who had a badly infected arm, which was swollen to alarming proportions. Just then Peggy led Dr. Millichope into the hut. "Sorry, ladies," Dr. Lange said, "this isn't a social center. You can visit with your friend when I've let her out."

Dr. Millichope drew herself up. "I don't believe we've met. I'm Claudia Millichope. *Doctor* Claudia Millichope."

Dr. Lange glanced at her with barely disguised contempt. "Oh, very well. Do what you can for her."

"I'm not entirely blind, Doctor, and my mind is not the least impaired," Dr. Millichope replied.

"Certainly."

Leaving aside the question of professional authority for the time being, Dr. Millichope bent beside the hard wooden platform that served as a bed. She put both hands to Jane's throat. Her touch was as light as a pair of butterflies. As she moved her fingers, she closed her eyes, as if to see better in her mind what her fingertips were telling her. Then she leaned even closer and looked at the skin. "If only we had some ice, to keep the swelling down—" she said to herself. "Jane? Janie dear. Are you awake? Can you hear me, dear?"

Jane stirred, opened her eyes slightly. She tried to say something, but the effort was excruciatingly painful, and she gasped. That hurt even more, and she began to panic and fight for breath.

Dr. Millichope spoke quickly and firmly. "Don't be frightened. The airway is a little swollen and it feels like you can't breathe, but you can. Believe me, you can. Just take it very

slowly and don't try to say anything just yet. That's it. That's
right, dear. I'm just going to feel these ribs a little bit. Hmm.
Good. Fine. Nothing broken. Now, we're going to help you sit
up. That will make it much easier to get your breath, but you'll
probably have a terrible headache and feel dizzy for a moment,
but that will pass, too. Hazel, you lift her. Very slowly. That's
it—''

She went on talking as she continued to examine the patient.
"There's no damage to your spine, but I imagine you've pulled
this muscle. That hurts a bit, doesn't it? Yes, it would. But if
you don't turn your head, it will be much better in a few days.
Hazel, look at her fingernails. Is the nail bed bluish?''

"No, pink.''

"Excellent. That's excellent.''

Jane, white and shaking, kept trying to ask a question with
her eyes. Hazel asked it for her. "Will Jane be able to sing when
she heals, Doctor?''

Dr. Millichope looked surprised at such a foolish question.
"Why, of course. Why shouldn't she be able to? There won't
be any permanent damage, but she'll sound like a chicken for a
few weeks probably. All just temporary, though. No reason to
worry. Now, Jane, we're going to prop you up and make you
nice and comfortable so you can sleep. That's the best thing
now. Lots of rest. Sister Denk will be here in a minute to sit
with you, and Sister Maria is going to look after little Vivian,
so you're not to worry about anything.''

As they left the hut, Hazel put her hand under Dr. Millichope's bony elbow to help her down a step. "Was that true?
Will she sing again?''

Dr. Millichope shook her head sadly. "I have no idea of the
real extent of the damage. She might never even speak well, but
I do know that she can't recover her singing voice unless she
absolutely believes it's possible. In these circumstances we can
do so little for the physical state; we must concentrate on the
mental powers.''

Hazel glanced back and caught a glimpse of Dr. Lange. She
squeezed Dr. Millichope's arm and said, "Thank God we have
you.''

Gloria was sitting in the doorway. She was as pale as a bar of
soap. "He'll pay. By God, if it's the last thing I do, I'll personally see to it that he bloody well pays!''

Hazel went on.

* * *

"Peggy, you saw what happened. You heard him say *diaries*. You have to get rid of it," Hazel whispered hoarsely that evening. They'd taken their evening rice ration off to eat by themselves at Hazel's request.

Peggy looked off into the distance. "Hmm? Oh, yes. I expect you're right."

"Peggy, you're not listening to me. If they catch you with those papers you're writing, they might kill you."

Peggy forced herself to concentrate on what Hazel was saying. "That's probably true. I'll destroy them," she said.

No point in worrying Hazel with her real resolve. After the incident this morning and her visit with Jane Kowolski, Peggy had been terrified for her safety and had gone back to the hut with the intention of burning what she'd written. But she hadn't been able to get the time to do so in private. People kept coming and going from the hut. And as the day went on, Peggy had come to the conclusion that the diary, or long letter to her son Jim, or whatever it was, had become vitally important. The more dangerous it was, the more valuable it was. A record *had* to be made. She was a witness to history and she had to document it. As a scholar, as a woman, as an American caught in a war, in all those roles she had a moral obligation to write down what was happening to them as it happened—before memory and hindsight combined to alter the truth.

"Hazel, what happened to the toothbrushes?" she asked, to change the subject.

Hazel recognized the ploy for what it was, but decided to go along with it. She would nag Peggy more a little later. "The Japs stole them. After getting so close to Saigo, I wonder if it wasn't a good thing. His breath was foul."

"That was very brave of you this morning. You know you've got a black eye, don't you?"

"Yes and one tooth that hurts. But it wasn't brave. Bravery is something deliberate. I acted without even thinking. I just had to stop him before he killed her. I didn't know I was going to do it until I was doing it, and then I was sick with fear. I don't want to talk about it."

Peggy looked at her for a long moment, then said, "Very well. Let's talk about something else. I'd like to call a meeting tonight."

"A meeting? What about? With whom?"

"Everybody. About everything. Would you go around for me and ask everybody to assemble in—oh, say, an hour?"

"Gladly. What are you doing in the meantime?"

Peggy looked grim. "Inviting Officer Saigo to attend and praying he'll turn down the invitation. We don't dare assemble without his permission."

Saigo's office was outside the compound. After considerable wheedling, Peggy was taken to see him. She tried to adjust her own English to his level and hoped he wouldn't sense how condescending it was.

"Women must work. Women must be good women," she said slowly. "I tell them. Have meeting to tell them. You come, Officer Saigo? You listen to what I say? This is good?"

He looked at her suspiciously. "Who are you?" he snapped.

She bowed again and said, "I am teacher. Good teacher. I teach women to be good. Nippon like women be good."

He stood up and glared at her. "Honorable Nippon soldier have many important thing to do. No time listen women. You teach. You teach good."

She bowed very low and gave him her one Japanese phrase, *"Domo arigato, Saigo-san."* Thank you, honorable Saigo.

He looked almost pleased at her humble demeanor.

Peggy was suppressing a smile as she backed out of his office, bowing all the way.

The children had been put to bed and most of the adults were gathered in the central compound. A few were missing; some were in the hospital either as patients or caretakers, and a few like Audrey refused to attend the meeting just because they wanted to assert their independence. But the rest sat on the ground in groups. When she judged that everyone had arrived who was likely to, Peggy stood up. "I'm Peggy Bright, and although we don't all know one another yet, I'm sure we will before long. I've been a teacher and dorm mother at a number of schools and colleges." She didn't want to give her true credit, president of a college, for fear of seeming too important to the Japanese. "It's because of that experience that I've asked to speak to you. Commandant Natsume said something today that was quite true—"

There was a mumble of anger. "We certainly aren't going to

listen to one of our own berate and insult us," one woman said, getting up to leave.

"And I'd be the last person to do so. Please hear me out, and if you all disagree with me, you may reject my ideas. The remarks I refer to are the ones he made about governing ourselves and keeping busy."

"I should think we're busy enough, just trying to stay alive!" someone at the back said.

"That's quite true," Peggy said, overriding her before she could elaborate, "but we can do it more efficiently. Rather than lay out the entire plan I have in mind, I'd like to mention just two things, then make a suggestion. First, there are a great many children here who are forgetting everything they've learned at school at a phenomenal rate. If you haven't been a teacher, you have no idea just how much and how fast they forget. We should set up some classes and keep them brushed up on their basic skills so they aren't behind in school when we are freed. School hours also free the mothers a little bit."

There was a murmur of assent, loudest from the mothers.

"Secondly, there are things we must do. Natsume said starting tomorrow we must feed ourselves—"

"You didn't fall for that gardening business, did you?" a thin, discontented woman in front of Peggy asked. "To begin with, it's the duty of the Japanese to feed us. It would be downright unpatriotic to help them—to make it any easier for them. And besides, we aren't going to be here long enough to wait for some nasty foreign vegetable to grow up!"

Instead of replying in anger, which she longed desperately to do, Peggy said with a smile, "You'd be amazed at how fast a vegetable grows up in this climate."

There was a ripple of laughter, and on the tide of it, Peggy went on. "Actually, I was talking about cooking what they give us. If we have to find the firewood and cook the awful rice, we must have some sort of rotation system of those duties. I doubt very much that anybody's going to fight for the chance to stand over a hot kettle in this climate. Am I right?"

A chorus of grudging agreement.

"Very well. Here's my suggestion: I'd like to present a detailed plan to a committee made up of one woman elected from each hut—"

"Democracy in action—" someone drawled sarcastically.

"Not entirely. I plan to set myself up as absolute monarch

for the first week!'' Peggy said, then softened her tone. "But only for a week. Long enough to get things organized. After that I promise I'll back out and keep as silent as a tomb. If you like my ideas, you may implement them. If not, we'll go on just as we have been and I won't say another word.''

"You swear to that?'' Caroline Warbler asked with a smile.

"You may have to slap a bit of adhesive tape over my mouth, but yes, I swear to it,'' Peggy said. "I'll meet with the representatives after *tenko* in the main hut and just chat with myself if nobody else is there.''

It finished the meeting on a nice note. Everybody drifted away, some sneering at the whole business, but the majority speaking thoughtfully about the concept of getting organized. Beryl Stacton came over to Peggy and said. "I believe you're quite right, Miss Bright. Civilized society is utterly dependent on laws and standards. I've done quite a lot of club work in my time—military auxiliaries, garden clubs, charities, and so forth. If you can use me, I'll be only too happy to help run things.''

"Thank you so much, Mrs. Stacton. I'll certainly be calling on you,'' Peggy said graciously. As Beryl walked away, Peggy said quietly to Hazel, "Notice, please, she's willing to 'help run things,' not be one of the drudges who do the dirty work. Oh, Hazel, I think I've made a mistake.''

"Mistake? What do you mean? I thought it went very well.''

Peggy had been struck by a chilling realization halfway through her presentation. These weren't schoolgirls, young and docile, with parents who would add their own authority to Peggy's. These were grown women of strong and distinct personalities. The nuns and missionaries already had their own authority to answer to, and the mothers were like tigers, defending their own against the world—including Peggy, if they felt it necessary. As she herself had told Hazel earlier, many of them were in the Far East because they were the mavericks, the adventurous, independent ones, the well-educated, or the unusually courageous—or foolhardy. Was it possible to organize such people?

And do I have the strength to try? Peggy wondered.

Chapter 15

Dear Jim,
  *I have an almost physical craving to know what's going on
in the world. I'm a historian living through a vital period of
world history and yet I know nothing about it. Things are
happening. Important things. Someday grandchildren will ask
me, "What was the war like?" and I'll have to shrug and
say, "Hell if I know." Current news is that Clark Gable died
in a plane crash while selling war bonds. Where do people
get this information and why do they believe it? Dinki is
crushed.*

The cook hut was the large, partially open one in the center
of the compound. At the front there was a concrete area with
sunken troughs in which fires could be built. Behind this area
and open at both ends was an atap-roofed building filled with
rough wooden tables and benches. Ancient bare-bulb light fix-
tures hung at ten-foot intervals. The next morning, after *tenko*
and the last rice to be cooked for them by outsiders, Peggy stood
in the middle of the room, looking over the women who had
assembled.

She had a "full house" for her meeting. Not only had each
hut sent one representative, some had been unable to agree on
the selection and sent two. While this boded ill for their ability
to put the "miniature democracy" she had in mind to work, it
did indicate a high level of interest. Hazel's group had elected
Beryl Stacton and Peggy had asked Hazel to act as secretary, so
they actually had three people present.

"First, let me point out the obvious fact that we have no authority behind us," Peggy said when the group had assembled. "Let me suggest that we draw up a list of rules and appoint a committee to establish a rota of duties. Once the camp has agreed to our plans by majority vote—if they do agree—then anyone who refuses to cooperate will be denied as many as possible of the benefits of the group effort. I believe this may be the only way to force people to comply."

"What benefits have you in mind?" Beryl Stacton asked.

"Cooked food, for one thing. We cannot, of course, withhold anyone's allotment of supplies, but we can keep them from using the firewood we'll have to gather and those big cooking pots the guards hauled in this morning."

"But I can't really imagine that anyone will refuse to cooperate," a Frenchwoman with curly dark hair said.

Beryl and Peggy had both seen Audrey St. John walking past, intent on some errand of her own. They exchanged a glance.

"I hope you're right," Beryl said in a preoccupied manner.

"I've made a map," Peggy said, putting a sheet of paper on the rough-hewn table they were sitting around. It was one sheet of her precious stationery, and she'd regretted using it this way, but it was necessary. As a former teacher, she knew the value of making a plan visible. "This camp was originally twelve long sleeping huts for the coolies, six on each side, with this central building and the wash hut at the back by the stream. The Japs have fenced off two of the huts in one corner for their own use. That leaves us ten huts. One has already been taken over for a hospital of sorts, and we are dispersed among the remaining nine."

They all leaned forward, studying the hand-drawn map of the camp.

"What I propose is this: I think the hospital hut should be moved to the far end, by the gate, to keep anyone contagious as isolated from the rest of the huts and the cooking area as possible. Also, that's close to the Japs. If anybody is going to catch anything, it might as well be them. At the back end of the compound, I think the mothers with babies should all be put together in one of the huts next to the wash house. They have more washing to do. Then I believe we should empty the two huts on the other side of the wash hut for schools; one for the littlest children, one for the older girls."

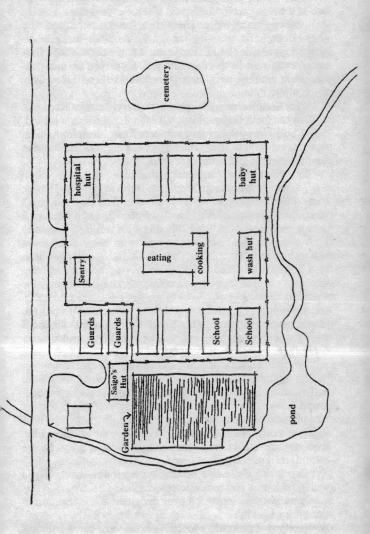

"But we'll be more crowded in the sleeping huts that way," one of the women objected.

"Not very much more. There are about a hundred and fifty of us. Using nine huts—leaving out the hospital—that's an average of sixteen per hut. Using seven, it's only twenty-one. They could actually hold about thirty, so we still won't be too crowded. And keep in mind, the children won't be in them all day. Only at night."

"I think all the religious people ought to be together," one woman said with obvious disgust.

"A holy hut?" Peggy said with a smile. "I understand your thought, but frankly, there's enough of a division as it is between the missionaries and some of the rest of us."

"Superior bitches," someone muttered.

"All the more reason to keep from isolating them and letting them get any chummier with one another than they are, don't you think?" Peggy asked. "Now, we need first of all to take a census. A census of skills, I suppose you'd call it. We need to know just what we have here to work with, what everyone is best qualified to contribute. Only those like the doctors who have a very specialized and vital skill should be excused from the nasty jobs like cooking and wood gathering and keeping the wash hut clean. Agreed? Let's make that our project for today and we'll pool our information tomorrow morning. I think we should have committees to handle the different areas of need. I myself would be qualified and willing to head up an education committee, to get the children started on lessons."

"Whom shall we make do the cooking?" Beryl asked.

"It's more than just cooking. We need a food chairman. Someone to organize the workers, determine portions to be allowed, make sure there is adequate firewood, collect serving utensils, and see to it that nothing's wasted."

The Frenchwoman spoke up. "There's a woman in my hut who says she and her husband ran a hotel in Brighton before they retired and moved out here."

"Excellent. We'll also need to set up rules—laws, if you will—and have a committee to enforce them."

A momentary silence fell over the group at the mention of this grim necessity.

"I believe that small women with the very black hair is a lawyer," Beryl finally said.

"Enforce the laws, though—enforce them how?" someone scoffed.

"By having a judicial committee that can take away privileges, I imagine."

"What privileges?" Hazel asked. Until now she'd kept silent, as befitted a good secretary.

"Well, I guess we'll have to create them," Peggy said.

Downcast at the prospect of a judicial committee and all the strife potential of it, they brightened at this remark. Peggy went on. "If there's anything we have too much of, it's free time. We'll need a committee to fill that time as enjoyably as possible under the circumstances. For instance, music can be a great joy to those who create it and those who listen to it. I've seen a number of people with musical instruments. The girl with the long blond ponytail has a flute—"

"She has two of them. Maybe she could teach someone to play the other one," one of the young mothers said. "I'd like to learn."

"—and a woman in my hut has a violin, but one string is broken," somebody else added.

"A lot of us like to sing," a third commented. "We could have a choral group."

"Bridge!" Hazel said. "My mother and some of the other ladies are always playing bridge. We could set up organized tournaments. Maybe they'd also teach those who don't already know how to play."

They talked a little longer about the various entertainments they could create, and all dispersed in high spirits. *Even if it doesn't work out,* Peggy thought, *at least it's given a few people an interesting morning, and that's worth something.*

Audrey St. John had an interesting morning as well, and not one that pleased her. She went to the hospital hut, determined to finally take care of her "little inconvenience," as she thought of it. Dr. Letha Lange was busy boiling some instruments in a makeshift sterilizer as Audrey approached her. "Doctor, could I have a word with you?"

Dr. Lange glanced up. "She's resting comfortably."

"I beg your pardon?"

"Aren't you one of the women from the singer's hut?"

"Singer? Oh, yes. Her. That's not what I came about."

Dr. Lange put a diabolical-looking instrument on a tray covered with a steaming cloth. "I've got an abscessed tooth to take care of. Are you ill or just wasting my time?"

"Not ill, exactly. But I assure you it won't be a waste of your time. I have this problem, you see. Terribly tedious, of course, but I'm pregnant and—"

"Oh, you're the woman the bossy one told me about?"

Audrey cocked a shapely eyebrow. "My dear, whatever can you mean?"

"I'm not your 'dear,' young woman, and what I mean is, you're the one who wants to terminate your pregnancy, aren't you?"

"Precisely so. I'm sure you can understand why—"

"I'm sure I do, and you can be equally sure I'll have nothing whatsoever to do with it. I'm a physician, not some back-street abortionist. Now, if you'll wait while I tend to this abscessed tooth, I'll examine you and see how far along you are."

"I don't need to be told how far along I am. I need to take care of the situation."

"Oh, the situation, as you call it, will take care of itself quite nicely."

Audrey was beginning to feel frantic. How could this be so difficult. She'd had a number of abortions before and never had a bit of trouble finding someone to do it. "Look, Doctor, I've got some money with me. I don't mean you should do this without cost."

Letha Lange folded the steaming towel over the instruments and looked at her. "Oh, I see. You'll pay me and then I'll just pocket the cash and run down to Robinsons to buy myself a nice new frock with it? Haven't you noticed where we are?"

"Of course I have. That's the whole problem. But believe me, money will still be useful to you."

"You fail to see my point. I don't want your money. I don't do abortions except when it is a dire medical necessity."

Audrey wrung her hands together. Perhaps if she tried that tack! "But Doctor, I can't possibly give birth to a healthy baby in these circumstances. The heat, the filth, the lack of proper nourishment. Why, I haven't had a piece of real meat for two months."

"No, it won't play," Dr. Lange answered curtly. "You're not even showing yet. We won't still be here when you're due, and even if we were, the one thing I know about the Japs is that they are quite gaga for babies. I've already prepared a list of the pregnant women in camp and I'll add your name before I turn it in. I'm certain they'll supply extra food for all of you. Maybe even some vitamins. As for the heat, well, millions of people in this part of the world have had babies in the heat. The filth, of course, is up to you to cope with. Regular washing and—''

"You don't understand! I can't have a baby! It will ruin everything! I don't want a baby!''

"Why? Because you're not married? Well, you're not the first and you won't be the last.''

"No, that's nothing to do with it. It will ruin my whole life to have a baby.''

"I'm sure you'll find out otherwise. Now, if you'll excuse me—''

She picked up the tray and started to walk away. Audrey grabbed her arm to hold her back and made her drop the tray. Dr. Lange turned on her furiously, and Audrey screamed, "Don't be so damned holy. I know you woman doctors. You're just jumped-up nurses. Old maids who couldn't get a man. You'll do it." She knew she was spoiling any chance she might have had, but she couldn't seem to stop herself. "It's just a question of money, isn't it? Well, I've got more than you know. I'll pay you really well. Better than you're paid on the outside.''

"Get out," Dr. Lange said in a voice so low and menacing that it made Audrey fall silent. "You've got yourself into this, and money won't buy you out.''

"Oh, yes, it will. You're not the only one here with the secret. If nobody else will take care of it, I'll do it myself. There are ways.''

"Yes, there are. And you'll kill yourself in the process. And that might be good riddance. Now, get out of here and let me take care of the people who need care.''

Audrey turned on her heel and sailed out. She was so furious that she was shaking and was soaked with sweat. How dare that old bitch! What was she going to do? She sat down in the shade of the stockade fence to get a grip on herself and think this out. What had happened before? She'd been put on an examining table. There had been instruments and some sort of chemical douche, as she recalled, a few hours of pain and rather nasty discharge, then a few lovely, self-indulgent days in bed with her maid bringing her meals on trays. That was all there was to it.

But what kind of instruments? What chemicals? How could she do it herself?

No, that wasn't necessary to worry about yet, she told herself. There were other people to talk to first. The blind old doctor was a washout. She'd already tried her and the old bat had dithered on about the sanctity of life. Dead bore. Just a cover for the fact that she probably couldn't see to do the job properly anyway. But there were nurses in the camp, in their own group. Nurses knew about these things and not everybody had the same high and mighty attitude as Dr. Lange. In Audrey's experience, practically nobody had.

She sat for a moment longer, getting her normal calm, slightly bored demeanor back under control, then she got up and went in search of Caroline Warbler.

Nancy Muir had once again assigned herself the job of creating toilet paper out of old newspapers. She took the stack that Mickey had brought her to a quiet spot behind one of the huts in the shade of the fence. As she read, she kept a close eye out that she wasn't being observed. Most of the papers were old, dating from before the evacuation of Singapore, but there were a few that were more recent, and she examined them carefully.

Even allowing for the patriotic exaggeration she'd expected and found in heavy measure, the Japanese newspapers told a terrible story. Singapore had fallen only two days after she and the others had joined the huge civilian evacuation in Keppel Harbour. The Japanese said they'd taken two hundred thousand British, Indian, and Australian prisoners. It was probably closer to a quarter or a third of that number in truth, but even that was a terrible defeat. The Nippon army had then taken Sumatra, Bali, Java, and had even destroyed a great many Allied aircraft on the ground at Broome, in Western Australia in early March. Could that be true? Were they actually attacking Australia? She searched for a more recent edition, but found none.

She continued cutting up little squares, depressed by what she'd learned. The other women kept nattering on about how it would be only days or weeks before they were freed, but they had no idea of the extent of the recent conquest. There probably wasn't an island for a thousand miles in any direction that was free of the Japanese invaders. And it would have to be won back mile by mile. Maybe inch by inch. It might be a long, long time. What a terrible thought. She must, in the meanwhile, find a way to get along with the women with whom she was imprisoned.

Nancy leaned back against the fence and closed her eyes.

Why was *she* in such a hurry to be freed anyway? The rest of them had husbands, families, or professions to get back to. Naturally they wanted to resume their lives. But her life had come to a dead end before she was captured. She had nothing to go back to and nothing to go forward to. Life here was hard and cruel, but would it be easy and kind to her outside? Not likely. But freedom is itself a reward, she realized.

"Oh, Miss Muir, I've been looking for you."

Nancy, caught half dozing, sat up suddenly and knocked over her tidy stack of newspaper squares as Hazel approached.

Hazel enjoyed a small twinge of pleasure at having disconcerted Miss Muir. "I'm taking a census of the people in our hut. A skill census, Miss Bright calls it. I need to know if there's something in particular that you're very good at."

Nancy, feeling low, almost said, "Stealing."

"What about teaching, Miss Muir. You're a missionary, aren't you?"

"No. My father was a missionary—medical, not teaching," Nancy said firmly. "I'm not good with children."

Hazel would have guessed as much. In her opinion, Miss Muir probably wasn't much good with anybody. "What about cooking?"

"I've never cooked anything in my life."

"Sewing?"

Nancy looked down at her disreputable, thoroughly unstylish clothing and back at Hazel.

"Do you know how to play a musical instrument? Speak a foreign language?"

"Neither."

She said it a little too firmly, and a long silence followed. Finally Hazel said, "Look, Miss Muir, I don't want to interrogate you, but everybody is going to be given jobs to do and I'm sure you'd rather do something you like than something that's just assigned to you."

"Yes. You're quite right. Actually, I had thought of a thing or two that might be useful," Nancy said, trying to make up for what she knew had been a churlish response to Miss Hampton's questions. "For one thing, a lot of people brought books in. I thought we might ask everybody to contribute them to a library of sorts so we may all read one another's. I'd be librarian if you'd like. I'm fairly adequate at keeping records."

"That's a good idea—" Hazel said hesitantly. It was a good

idea, one she wished she'd thought of, but hardly on a par with the kind of commitment she was hoping to get people to make.

"Also—" Nancy paused.

"Yes?"

"Perhaps it's silly, but I've been thinking about birthdays. My father didn't believe in celebrating them, so perhaps I have an exaggerated concept of their importance because of my own sense of deprivation—" Good Lord! What was she doing, pouring out this long-standing and intensely personal complaint?

"No, everybody thinks birthdays are important," Hazel said. For a moment she sensed how unlike Miss Muir it must be to admit to a longing. "Go on."

"If people would tell me their birthdays, I could keep a calendar and make sure other people knew when it came time and maybe—well, arrange for some kind of gift or special food or something."

"That's excellent. Excellent! How clever and imaginative you are, Miss Muir." Nancy could practically feel herself swelling up with pleasure. Nobody—ever!—had said such a thing to her. But Hazel's next words brought her down to earth a little. "How much time per week do you suppose these things would take?"

"The library? Perhaps two or three hours each week for checking in and checking out. Getting the books and arranging them somewhere would take more, but that's just at first. And the birthdays? Perhaps another two or three hours each week. Why?"

"Miss Bright suggests that we try to find at least fifteen hours a week work for everyone. Can I put you down for ten hours of general work detail? Latrines, cooking, wood gathering, that sort of thing?"

"I suppose so." What a long vista of drudgery. "Wait, Miss Hampton. Don't go yet. There is something else I'd like very much to do. Direct a singing group."

"We talked about having one, but I had thought Jane Kowolski would do that."

"But she's not well now. I could start it and I'd turn it over to her whenever she wanted."

Hazel couldn't picture Miss Muir in the role. "You don't think one of the missionaries might be better—?"

"Certainly, if you want nothing but religious music," Nancy said coldly.

It worked. "I'm sure we don't. Well, I guess—"

"I know I don't look musical, and to tell you the truth, I can't sing a note, but I have an excellent ear and my father had a large collection of records that I used to listen to all the time. I know a great many songs I could teach a group to sing. We could practice four hours a week and you could put me on any duty you want for the rest of the time."

"Done! That is, if the women vote to follow the plan Miss Bright has us making."

Roberta Hampton approved of organized bridge tournaments but disapproved of the overall plan. "My dear Hazel, I think it's fine for you and that Bright woman to think of all these things. It keeps you occupied and no doubt makes her feel very important and admirable, but you mustn't expect everyone to fall in with it."

"But Mother, we might be here a long time. We have to have a sense of community for our own good."

"Hazel, being here is bad enough without creating all the worst of the world outside that we're missing."

"The worst?"

"All those duties and pointless responsibilities. One does what one must under normal conditions, but this isn't normal and I think we may all be excused for letting our hair down a bit."

"But how do you define *a bit*, Mother? Where do you draw the line between letting down and anarchy?"

Roberta shuffled the cards and laid out another hand of solitaire. "I really don't know. It sounds the sort of question you ought to pose to your friend Miss Bright. She probably has the answer."

Hazel walked away, thinking it sounded like her mother was jealous of her friendship with Peggy. But that was clearly absurd. Wasn't it?

Late that afternoon they were summoned for *tenko*. As Saigo came into the compound and the women bowed, there was an atrociously loud farting noise. Nobody was quite sure where it came from or if it was real. The children—and a few of the women—started laughing. Saigo glared around the group but couldn't find anyone guilty-looking or embarrassed-looking enough to fasten his wrath to. He gave them a long, fierce lecture in Japanese, seemingly unaware that they didn't understand and there was no one to translate. When he turned to go and they bowed again, another juicy fart echoed around the compound. He whirled, studied them for a sign of the culprit, then finally strode off.

"You're going to get in trouble that way," Hazel said quietly to Gloria as they walked toward the cook hut to eat the evening rice ration.

"Me? What makes you think it was me?"

"I know it was."

"Just a touch of gas. Can't help it," Gloria said with a smirk.

"How's Jane?"

"Better this evening. I've been giving her water and tea to drink all day. By tomorrow we'll see if she can swallow a little rice."

"Can she talk?"

"Lord, no! We don't dare even let her try yet. She could damage her vocal cords even more by straining them now."

They waited in line for their rice, and when the gluey mass was dumped onto their plates, Gloria asked, "What in hell is this muck?"

A tall, toothy woman who was dishing up said, "This 'muck' is rice cooked by people who have never cooked in a huge pot over an open fire. Any other questions, Sister?"

"Yes, what are the stringy brown bits?"

"I haven't any idea, and if you find out, *please* don't tell me."

They went to a table at the back end of the hut. Roberta Hampton and Beryl Stacton were already there, poking through their food as if actually expecting to find something appealing in it somewhere. Just as Hazel and Gloria were climbing over the benches to take their places, Audrey St. John came storming into the cook hut.

"Mrs. Stacton, I would like to have a word with you!" she said furiously. "I'll thank you to mind your own business from now on!"

Hazel expected a like outburst from Mrs. Stacton, but was surprised when she merely looked up and said, "Oh?"

"I've been told that you've talked to practically everyone in camp about—about my condition. It's absolutely none of your business."

Beryl was still calm, though her face had lost its usual pinkness. "I'm afraid you're quite wrong, Miss St. John. It's my belief that you're carrying my husband's child."

"What if I am!"

"Then it's my duty as a wife to save my husband's child, and I intend to do so."

Audrey gaped. "Are you insane?"

"Quite the contrary. That baby belongs to my husband, and what belongs to him belongs to me. You see, we never had children, and now we're going to. I admit it's utterly selfish, but I expect selfishness is something you understand, isn't it?"

"I'm not going to have this child. I don't want it!"

"Ah, but I do," Beryl said.

"You're starkers! Starkers!" Audrey said, throwing her arms up in a gesture of furious frustration.

Beryl turned coolly to Roberta and said, "I think this rice would be greatly improved if it had a little salt and pepper, don't you? I wonder if we might get some if we asked."

"My God!" Audrey exclaimed dismally before turning and leaving the hut.

Nobody referred to the incident again. Nobody dared to, except Gloria, who would have spoken except that Hazel gouged her with her elbow the moment she started to open her mouth. As they left the dining areas, she said, "What a balls-up for La St. John. She must be chewing sticks."

"I'm amazed at Mrs. Stacton," Hazel said.

"You've sort of got to admire the old bitch, haven't you? Who'd have thought—?"

That night, lying in the darkness, Hazel mentally went over the list she'd compiled during the day. She had a mathematics teacher for the children, a choral director, a girl of twenty who was willing to be a "games mistress," whatever that was, and three women who knew about gardening and were willing to supervise a vegetable plot. She'd also located a woman whose family ran a perfume business and knew all about scents—a skill for which there appeared to be no practical application in these circumstances—and a painter who said airily if Hazel could get paints and canvases, she would give lessons. As if they might find these supplies!

On the whole, however, she was pleased with her day's work. The prospect of starting to create a life with specific things to do and places to be at specific times was comforting. On the other hand, the longer she thought about gardens and choirs and classes, the hotter the lump of homesickness in her chest grew.

She, like the rest of them, could hardly stand the thought of being here long enough to see the culmination of such projects. In the steaming, snoring darkness, Hazel suddenly understood those who refused to cooperate by saying they were going to be freed any day.

Hazel wanted to believe that, too.

     ## Chapter 16

August 1942

> *Dear Jim,*
> *I want a corned beef sandwich with greasy, grilled rye bread and gobs of salty, tooth-squeaking sauerkraut—or has it been renamed "liberty cabbage" like it was in the last war? I want to know!!!*

Roberta Hampton was the first to get seriously ill with malaria, and there was little that could be done for her. A number of women in the camp had brought in small supplies of quinine to hold off their own long-standing cases of the disease, but, naturally, wouldn't part with them. In addition, Dr. Lange had received some pills from the Japanese army doctor that were not only meager, but very, very old and of questionable strength. Still, they did help some, but within a week of Roberta's first attack, two other women came down with it. They were both young mothers responsible for small children. Lange felt the limited supplied of drugs should be used for them. Hazel agreed in theory, but only in theory.

It was hell watching her mother suffer and being unable to do anything for her. It was made worse by the fact that Hazel had felt irritation more often then affection for her mother since they'd been captured. Hazel sat for hours by her plank bed in the hospital hut, bathing her arms and legs when she had the sweats and bundling her up in all the warm clothing she could find when she shook violently with chills. When Roberta was in the grips of fever, she cried out constantly for her husband, Ronald, and even when she was relatively lucid, she talked about him constantly.

Hazel spent hours trying to reassure her. "He's fine, Mother. I'm sure of it. He probably got out and is back in Evanston right now taking care of things and waiting for us. You just have to rest and get well so we can all be together when it's over," she said over and over. But Hazel knew it wasn't true. If her father had survived the invasion of Penang, he was almost surely captured just as they were.

Dr. Lange was coldly realistic when Hazel managed to get her aside and ask about her mother's chances of survival. "Not very good," she said. "Not without medication." Hazel despised her for her unfeeling honesty.

Dr. Millichope said the same thing, but in a much more compassionate way. "You must prepare yourself to lose her, my dear. She's suffering horribly and you must consider her death as a blessed release. You can't save her, Hazel, and you must not feel guilty about that. She's very fortunate to have you with her. I know your comfort means the world to her even if she doesn't say so. She's resting nicely now. Why don't you go back and join the choral practice for a while. I'll sit with her."

"I couldn't leave her."

"No, you must. Hazel, you've been a good daughter all your life. You don't have to 'prove' it now. You must keep your own health intact in order to help her, and that means your mental health as well as the physical. You'll be a better daughter to her if you get out and refresh your mind for a while."

Hazel was grateful for the authorization to flee the dismal hospital hut. Until her mother became ill, Hazel had spent very little time there and had no idea what a horrible place it was. It was the most depressing area of the whole camp, not because people were ill, but because there was so little that could be done for them. Most of the medical complaints would have been minor outside but assumed terrible proportions here. An abscessed tooth, which would have been a painful but treatable affliction elsewhere, was a life-threatening problem when there were no painkillers and few other drugs. Even hemorrhoids, the most common complaint, became serious. One woman, suffering excruciating pain and bleeding, had become so obsessed with not having bowel movements that she refused to eat and had literally starved herself to death.

The nutritional defiency diseases were beginning to show up as well, albeit still to a minor extent. Many of the women had already stopped menstruating because of the stress and poorly balanced diet. Hazel was half sorry she wasn't among them. She'd used up her precious supply of sanitary napkins and was now using rags that were washed and reused. Others were beginning to suffer vitamin B deficiency, which caused pain and numbness in their hands and legs that was only slightly relieved by massage and exercise. Then there were the rashes and bites and scratches and infections. All in all, the hospital hut was the last place anybody wanted to spend any time, and Hazel had, somewhat against her will, come to forgive Dr. Lange her cold attitude. How else could she be, a doctor without the means to treat her patients?

Hazel walked out and stood for a moment on the tiny porch step, drawing a long breath of fresh air. The choral group was practicing by the front gate and Nancy Muir briefly signaled an invitation that was very nearly a command to join them, but Hazel didn't want to quite yet. More than anything, she wanted a few blissful minutes of peace and quiet—the rarest commodity in the camp. In the months since they had first arrived, it had become increasingly crowded. There were now nearly two hundred and fifty women and children, many of the newcomers Dutch citizens who had been allowed to live under house arrest at first, but were now incarcerated.

Gloria had just gotten off duty as Hazel was leaving the hospital hut. "Want to see if we can beg a cup of that foul brew the cooks call coffee?" she asked, hooking her arm through Hazel's.

"I imagine I could survive some. Does the noise ever get you down, Dinki?"

"What noise?"

"What noise? Children yelling and playing, the singers practicing, women talking and arguing and calling back and forth, the guards shouting at us and one another. And the jungle noise. Those birds forever shrieking."

Gloria glanced around. "I guess it is fairly noisy. I don't

usually notice unless I've just gotten some patient to sleep and that gang of bloody-minded little boys goes by playing soldiers. You're feeling low, aren't you? It'll soon be over."

Before coming here, Hazel would have regarded a person who comforted her by assuring her mother's imminent death as a good deal less than a friend, "Thanks, Dinki. I know."

They went into the cook hut and were just in time to be given a cup of something hot and brown that actually smelled a little bit like coffee. "You're in luck today," the woman on duty there said. "We got a little pot of honey smuggled in today. Taste!"

They sipped gingerly and expressed their genuine appreciation of the sweet taste. Sitting down at one of the tables and fanning herself, Gloria said, "Speaking of smuggling, what do you hear about your Dutch friend up at the big house?"

"Nothing for a while. You know, I never got to speak to her except a few words occasionally. She'd just leave the things hidden by the fence and I'd get them when I could slip over there. But there hasn't been anything for weeks and weeks. Not since we got those tins of tooth powder."

The tooth powder had been far too tasty to waste on teeth. Instead, it had been taken over by the cooking crew and sprinkled over rice to make an illusion of dessert.

"I wonder if they've put them in a camp somewhere," Gloria mused. "Most of the Dutch seem to have been. Of course, if the husband's still collaborating—"

"I don't think he ever was. The Japs just let the family stay in part of their own house. If it were me, I wouldn't insist on being locked up instead of staying home, and I hope nobody would call me a collaborator."

"Sorry. Didn't mean to ruffle your feathers. By the way, I've reserved the cook hut for a little knees-up the night after the concert."

"A knees-up?"

"A party. Don't you Yanks speak English? I've got a nice bit of booze that ought to be about ready. Been laid down in the family vaults since—oh, three weeks almost."

"Not that spoiled oatmeal stuff again!" Gloria's first attempt at making liquor had involved some corn meal mush, prunes, and fermented rice water. It had inspired the Birthday Observance Group (fondly known as the Boggies and long since given over to people more naturally festive than Nancy Muir) to move into the awards business and give Dinki a little paper certificate for "The Most Disgusting Recipe Yet Devised in Internment."

"No, this is elegant stuff," Gloria assured her. "Mostly coconut milk and a bit of pineapple juice. Bloody healthy, I should think. Say, your ladyship," she added sarcastically to Audrey St. John, who had just come into the cook hut, "you want to come to my knees-up day after tomorrow and taste my new booze?"

Audrey was enormously pregnant now in spite of all her best efforts to dislodge the baby. She'd tried everything, even jumping off the top of the wash hut several months before—a tragic but laughable effort that had given her a broken finger, but not the desired miscarriage. She waddled past, grimacing and holding one hand to the small of her back. "So kind of you to ask, darling," she drawled, "but I've got an appointment with my stockbroker that evening. Too boring."

"You just don't like my booze," Gloria said.

"Quite the contrary. I'm devastated that you didn't go into your little brewery business earlier, which might have helped me. That poison could have taken care of all my problems."

There was the distant sound of shouting and a woman screaming, and everyone in the compound fell suddenly silent and alert. Even Audrey straightened up and squinted into the distance.

"What's going on?" Hazel asked.

"Something in the garden—" Gloria said. They ran to the section of fence that had been removed to allow for expansion into a newly fenced garden. Everyone was crowded together. Gloria, too short to see over the crowd said, "What is it, Hazel?"

"I can't tell. That pig Spike is beating someone with the handle of a hoe. I can't see who it is."

Suddenly the crowd parted and four of the garden crew came through, carrying a fifth woman. She had blood running down the side of her face and there were red welts on her arms and legs, but she was smiling.

"My husband . . ." she whispered. "I saw my husband."

She was hurried to the hospital hut with Gloria leading the way. Hazel had become accustomed to many things, but this random brutality still sickened her. Pale and a little nauseated, she turned to Miss Evans, the woman who had been a servant to the obese Mrs. Englethorpe and was now a member of the garden crew. "Has she got a fever or something? Hallucinating?"

Evans smiled, a peculiar expression on her severe face. "No, Miss Hampton. She really did see her husband. You know that stretch of road you can see from the corner of the garden? We were working there, and three trucks came along the road. They were loaded with men. White men. They started yelling at us as they went by and we yelled back, and Mrs. Webber tried to climb the barbed wire fence. That's when Spike went after her."

"White men? Did you see them yourself?" Hazel asked, still not believing the story. They hadn't seen any of the captive men since their stop outside Palembang.

"Only briefly, but I think they were a work crew. They had long-handled tools. Rakes and shovels and such."

"So they must live in a camp somewhere around here?"

"They must."

Hazel was suddenly struck with how odd it was for her and Miss Evans to be so happy about the men. Miss Evans was a dedicated spinster of at least fifty and Hazel had a beloved fiancé, but they were nearly as pleased as Mrs. Webber. There was something magical and uplifting about simply knowing some of "their own" men were near.

When the firewood crew came back an hour later, they were also elated. They'd actually passed the men on the road. One truck had broken down and they'd been able to speak briefly to some of them. Their guard, Mickey, would have been willing to let them chat forever, but the men's guards shooed them away.

"We exchanged names as fast as we could talk," Beryl Stacton told Hazel over dinner. "There were at least three of our women's husbands there, not including the Dutch, of course."

"Did they say where their camp is, Mrs. Stacton?"

"About ten miles west was their guess. But they think they're being moved soon. Lots of official sorts of Nips looking things over and taking inventory."

"It might be closer to us."

"Or farther," Beryl said.

"How did they look? Besides wonderful and male?"

"The Dutch didn't look bad yet. But the British were thin. Tired. Worse than we look, on the whole. But as happy to see us as we were to see them."

"Speaking of tired-looking—you must be exhausted. You shouldn't have volunteered for such heavy work."

Beryl preened for a second over the attempted pampering, but then said, "I really had to. You know the guards had assigned That Woman to the crew and I couldn't let that happen."

The allusion was, of course, to Audrey St. John. Beryl almost never referred to her by name. As the container who was carrying Dennis Stacton's child, she had to be kept from any activity that might injure the child, but in Beryl's mind that certainly didn't mean she deserved an actual name. Besides, there was the question of what one would call her. "Audrey" would have been much too familiar and could be seen to smack of friendliness. "Miss St. John" would have seemed polite, possibly even respectful. No—That Woman she was and would remain.

At *tenko* that evening, they were given another long lecture delivered at the top of Officer Saigo's shrill voice. It was apparent without any attempt at translation that he was warning the women not to take any interest in the men.

"No mens! No white mens here!" he threw into his tirade at intervals.

"A proper grasp of English would help him immeasurably," Jane Kowolski said huskily as they were getting ready for lights-out. "For example, that informative little talk tonight—did he mean to say there are no white men here at the present? That we may not invite white men here? That white men are not coming here? Or was he trying to convince us we'd never seen them at all?"

In the hospital hut, too, they talked about the men until one by one they fell asleep. Hazel curled up on the floor next to her mother on a mat she'd improvised out of her clothing. She dreamed she was with the women who had met the men in the road. The men jumped from the trucks, taking women in their arms and dancing in the dust. There was music coming from someplace, but they didn't question it. Hazel kept looking for Frank among the men, but couldn't find him. Instead, a tall, blond Dutchman swept her into his strong arms and twirled her around. The other couples started drifting off into the jungle and making love. The moans of misery in the hospital hut turned into moans of ecstasy in the dream. Hazel was left alone with the Dutchman. He tilted her face up with his big, callused hand and gently stroked her cheek while murmuring endearments. Then he slipped his other hand up under her halter top and caressed her breast.

Hazel gave a little cry of pleasure, and in so doing, woke

herself up. She was sweating and trembling and felt ashamed. What awful, disloyal thing in her mind allowed her to imagine making love to a stranger? Checking quickly that her mother was sleeping comfortably, she crept out of the hospital hut, which stank of sickness and misery. She stood for a moment outside, her hands to her burning cheeks, remembering every detail of the dream in spite of her earnest resolve to forget it.

How could she—even in a dream—be so stimulated by a strange man? She'd had dreams like that before, but they were always about Frank. She'd walk a couple times around the hut. Maybe that would clear her mind. Think about something else. Anything else. As she rounded the back corner, she ran smack into someone coming the other way. "Jesus Christ!" Gloria snapped. "You nearly made me piss in my knickers, Hazel."

"What are you doing out here?" Hazel demanded in an angry whisper.

Gloria held out her hand, in which there were three little dark, gummy balls. "Opium. Spike and that fat guard with the scar are addicts."

"How did you get that stuff?"

"I stole it, of course."

"From the guards' hut? Are you crazy? How did you get out of the compound?"

Gloria shook her head at this naïveté. "There's a dozen places to get through the fence."

"Oh, Dinki, you'd have been killed if you were caught, and they'll punish all of us when they discover this stuff is missing."

"No, the two of them blame each other. Haven't you seen them fighting?"

"You mean you've done this before?"

"Several times."

Hazel took her shoulders. "Dinki, you can't go around risking your life just to make the guards mad at each other. Throw that stuff away before you're caught with it."

"Throw it away! Hell, no! Hazel, don't you know how valuable this is?"

"To an addict, very valuable, I imagine."

"No, to us. Opium is wonderful for stopping diarrhea. I didn't steal this stuff just for the fun of it, but," she added, "it is great fun."

* * *

The first performance of the choral group was to take place following dinner and before the evening *tenko*. Any break in the dreary routine, especially a pleasurable break, brought everybody's spirits up—everybody but the choral members themselves in this case. Nancy Muir had been a hard taskmaster. In the months they'd been practicing, there had been tears, arguments, attempted mutinies, a few near-hysterical outbursts, and a good deal of flouncing around and muttering dark threats against her. Nancy had taken the job partly in the hope that it might make her a member of the group, and thereby make her liked. In that she had failed utterly. The choral group, while respecting her obvious abilities, had come to universally despise her for her perfectionism.

They had one last practice before the performance. While the others were lining up to eat, Nancy ran them through the most difficult parts of three of their songs. In one, Jane Kowolski had a small solo. Her recovery from the injury to her throat had been remarkable and due solely to a determination that was frighteningly intense. She still spoke in a voice that was husky when she grew tired, but she had practiced singing several hours every day from the moment Dr. Lange authorized her to try. As she rehearsed her solo piece, the others listened in awe, and when she finished, she had tears in her eyes.

"Yes, I know," one of the other women said, patting her shoulder. "It's amazing. You sound wonderful, just wonderful."

She was surprised when Jane turned to her angrily. "It's *not* wonderful! I've lost half an octave at each end of my scale."

Finally released from the last practice, the women ran for the wash hut rather than the cook hut. This one night it was more important to be clean and attractive than it was to eat. Nancy went looking for Hazel and found her sitting by her mother in the hospital hut. "Are you joining us tonight?" she asked quietly.

"I'm sorry, Miss Muir, but I just can't leave Mother to sing with the group. She's worse today."

"I do understand, but we really need you."

Gloria was putting a new dressing on a leg ulcer next to Roberta. "Go on, Hazel. I'll sit right by your mother the whole time."

"Thanks, Dinki, but I've missed most of the practices the last two weeks. They'll all sound better without me."

"I don't want you to sing. I just need you standing in the

second row, moving your lips," Nancy Muir said bluntly. "Otherwise I'll have a hole in the lineup."

After a few more equally honest but unflattering pleas, Hazel was finally prevailed on to take part. "Mother, I'm going to join the singing tonight," she said to the unresponsive woman on the plank bed. "I'll be singing just for you."

Later, standing on the improvised riser, Hazel was surprised at the warm feeling she had as she looked over the assembled group before them. Everybody had dressed up for the occasion—as much as they were able. Carefully hoarded lipstick had been used. Hair had been washed and even curled. The children had been cleaned up and bribed or threatened into best behavior. Even the guards, standing at the gates behind the women, stood a little straighter as if anticipating a special treat.

Nancy stepped to the front and addressed the audience. Her voice was shaking with nervousness. "While our travel plans of late have been unfortunately curtailed"—there was a chorus of hoots—"we'd like to take you on a little tour tonight." She turned to the singers and said, "Ladies, are you ready?" Raising her thin arms, she led them into the first notes of "Stars Fell on Alabama," and then a rousing version of "Deep in the Heart of Texas."

Moving her lips as instructed, Hazel watched the audience watching them. One woman from Texas was crying, but everybody else was smiling broadly and swaying in time to the music. Hazel's heart contracted at the sight of Mickey. He'd put down his gun and was grinning and hugging himself with simple happiness. He didn't understand a word, but obviously grasped the good cheer in the music.

After the applause for this number, they began a complex arrangement of "The Last Time I Saw Paris," and following it, a truly haunting rendition of "Over the Rainbow." Jane did her solo piece, and if she was disappointed in her range, no one else was. To those whose senses had been starved for beauty, the sound of her voice was like a feast. There was a long round of clapping and cheering at the conclusion.

The next song was "It's a Big, Wide, Wonderful World." As they sang, Hazel glanced toward the hospital hut and saw Gloria in the doorway. Her arms were crossed and her head bowed. She's supposed to be with Mother, Hazel thought angrily, and then realized the truth. Dinki wasn't with Roberta because there was no longer any need. Roberta was dead.

The song was over.

Nancy faced the audience again and said, "And now, a very special piece, written especially for us."

After a dramatic pause, the group began to sing, "I Got Plenty o' Nothin'." The first few bars were drowned out by the laughter of the audience. This time Hazel tried to join in the singing, but her throat kept clogging up.

When it was done, Nancy said, "If you will stand and join us—?"

She led them in "God Save the King," the handful of Americans singing their own "My Country Tis of Thee," to the same melody.

As the last notes echoed away, and tears were blotted, the women in the audience surged forward. There were kisses, hugs, and congratulations all around. The choral program had been a grand success. Nancy Muir was suddenly and disconcertingly the most popular person in camp. She was dizzy with praise. Her sallow complexion was flushed an attractive pink and her face already ached with smiling.

Hazel stepped down and edged her way slowly through the crowd. Smiling and responding mechanically to the compliments directed at her, she kept moving toward the hospital hut.

Gloria stepped down from the small porch and came forward. She put her arms around Hazel. "I'm so sorry," she said softly.

"Hazel, you're going to get Mickey in trouble, persuading him to let you come up here every day," Peggy said one afternoon a week later. Hazel was standing at the foot of her mother's grave on the slight rise outside the camp.

"I feel like I have to visit her," Hazel said.

"Yes, but this isn't where she is. She's with you. My mother's with me—here and here," Peggy said, putting her hand on her own heart and then on her forehead.

Hazel balled her fists and looked at the ground. "I shouldn't say this, I guess, but I don't feel sad. Just angry."

"With your mother?" Peggy asked matter-of-factly.

Hazel crossed her arms, as if she were cold. "Yes, with her. At first. She wouldn't have died if we hadn't been here, and we wouldn't have been here if she hadn't been so horribly stubborn. It was stupid to wait for my father. He either could or couldn't have gotten out, and having us sit there in Singapore until the last was no damned help to him.''

"That's all quite true, but if you're anything like me—and I think you are—you'd have been angry anyway. When my mother died, I was furious with her. She was my *mother*, for heaven's sake. Didn't she know mothers are supposed to always be there? I was thirty-nine years old, but she was still my mommy. I felt abandoned and betrayed. That was eleven years ago, and I still feel it more often than I like. I wonder if that's not what people mean when they say they miss someone?''

Hazel nodded. "Maybe so. I'm pretty disgusted with myself, too. She was so miserable and scared, and I was often irritated with her. I shouldn't have been.''

"Why? She was an irritating woman.''

"Peggy!''

"Sorry, my dear, but she was. Here, at least. You've got to realize that dying doesn't make people saints. They are what they are, and death doesn't erase anything. We're all frightened and hungry and lonely here, Hazel. Everybody reacts to it differently. I organize and pontificate and boss people around. I wonder that someone hasn't strangled me yet. Your mother reacted a different way. She played cards to obsession, she found fault with you. She seemed to change and that frightened and annoyed you. But that's how it was. The facts are the facts. Trying to change them in retrospect is a terribly useless drain of energy. Come back to camp, dear. Mickey is half frantic.''

Hazel turned with a watery smile. "Thank you, Peggy. I thought—I thought all of this was just something horribly wrong with me.''

They started down the hill toward camp. "I'll tell you something else, Hazel. Maybe you're starting to realize it already. It's a feeling of being bottled up to overflowing with things you want to say to her. And to ask her.''

"I do know! I've been thinking since yesterday about a family rumor about something scandalous in my mother's sister Corny's past. Nobody seems to know exactly what it is, but I always thought I'd ask my mother right out when the time was right. I woke up last night, nearly frantic with frustration because now I can't ever ask her.''

Peggy grabbed Hazel's elbow as she slipped on a wet leaf. "Do you know what I think heaven really is? I think it's a state of having all the answers.''

Hazel laughed.

"I mean it. I believe if I live a good life, I'll find out everything I ever wondered: who Jack the Ripper was, where I lost
my Phi Beta Kappa key, what really happened to the little princes
in the Tower, why I can't grow clematis, what became of Amelia
Earhart. Everything."

"I hope you're right."

"I'm sure I am. Come to think of it," she added cheerfully,
"that's what people dislike about me."

 *Chapter 17*

Dear Jim,
      *There must be a radio in the men's camp nearest us.
How in the world do they keep it running and concealed and
why can't the news make any sense after it's been through the
native grapevine? We hear, tantalizingly, that the Allies are
attacking Guadalcanal, New Guinea, and the Solomons, but
we get no hint of whether it's successful or not. I wonder if
no news at all might be better than these unsubstantiated hints.*

"Ladies! Come to order please!"

The regular weekly meeting of the hut leaders and committee
chairs was beginning. Mrs. Valentina Smith, a British woman
in her sixties who was the recently and somewhat reluctantly
elected camp leader, presided. Banging a tin cup on the tabletop, she called for order again. Peggy Bright had been persuaded
to serve for many months beyond the week she had promised,
but had finally insisted that they elect a replacement. Only Ha-

zel, who knew why Peggy wished to avoid the Japanese limelight, understood why she had stepped down.

Mrs. Smith, the forceful and imposing wife of the owner of an enormous rubber plantation in Malaya, had been elected in her place. A woman with thin gray hair, an imposing bosom, and a penetrating voice, she was the former mistress of a large household, and as such was felt to be supremely qualified for the position. While flattered by this assessment, which she considered quite accurate, she wasn't entirely pleased. In spite of missing the luxury of her former life, she'd been rather enjoying the cessation of her many duties and responsibilities. In a sense, internment camp represented a kind of freedom she hadn't known for years. Working twenty hours a week in the cook hut and having the rest of her time available for bridge and gossip had suited her very well. Still, when duty called—

Once it got quiet, Mrs. Smith said, "At Dr. Lange's request, I have scheduled her first on the agenda, so that she may get back to her patients. Doctor?"

Letha Lange curtly reported on the admissions and discharges from the hospital, including those who were discharged by Higher Authority. Since Roberta Hampton's death just over a week before, a newborn infant had died and the mother was still hanging on to life by a thread. "As you know, two of the four babies born here have died at birth. We have only one more pregnancy, however, that of Miss St. John, who is due any day now."

"There's a rumor that you received Red Cross parcels," one of the hut leaders interrupted. "I don't suppose that could be true."

"Yes, it is—"

A babble of conversation broke out which Mrs. Smith suppressed brutally. "*Ladies!* Dr. Lange has the floor!"

"It is true, but they are practically antiques. They appear to be parcels the Americans sent to Japan on the occasion of the 1923 earthquake. I'm afraid they're of very little value. The foodstuffs are hopeless; the bandages are about as useful as cobwebs, and most of the medicines have solidified in their bottles. I'm saving those that may have some potency remaining."

When Dr. Lange had completed her brief report, Mrs. Smith addressed a question to her. "I saw Sister Maria wearing a skirt and blouse today and have been told that you know something about what happened to her habit?"

Dr. Lange drew herself up and looked like an offended eagle.

"Isolated as I am, I do hear the gossip, and contrary to public opinion, I did *not* demand she give me her habit to tear into bandages. She volunteered it and, in fact, delivered it to me in neat strips before asking my opinion."

One of the Catholic Canadian women was distressed about this. "Has she no other to wear?"

"No," Dr. Lange replied, "she said she gave her other one to Caroline Warbler some time ago. Sister Warbler has also given that one up for the same purpose. Now that she's lost so much weight, she's able to wear Mrs. Hampton's clothing, which Hazel gave to Sister Warbler and Sister Denk."

The Dutch woman couldn't let it go. "It's just not right. She's a religious. She should wear her habit."

Mrs. Smith had a bridge tournament she wanted to get to. "You're entitled to your opinion, of course, but it's hardly a matter for us to consider. It's clear no one has broken any camp rules. Judicial committee, will you make your report?"

It had been an orderly week. A small boy had stolen one of the Dutch women's hairbrushes, but his mother, furious and mortified, had promised that she would administer justice herself and it was felt that her retribution would be stronger than any the committee might dish out. One of the young mothers had refused to take latrine duty and had been sentenced to three-quarter rations until she changed her mind. She had done so the next day. These matters resolved, the committee chair brought up the matter of the mysterious jars of grape jam. Four of them, fresh and newly bottled, with American labels, had been discovered two days earlier by the cooking crew when they came to work.

"They've obviously come from American Red Cross packages. Probably the same ones the guards got those new shoes they're wearing from. The question is, who stole them from the guards and put them in the cook hut?" the judicial chair asked.

Mrs. Smith had little patience with this sort of thing. Her view of justice was less theoretical than practical. "May I remind you that our rules are set up to protect us, not the Nips. Their losses are just that—theirs. I would also like you to reflect on how very much the children enjoyed the jam—which was rightly ours to begin with!"

The chair persisted. "We all know perfectly well that Sister Denk is responsible!"

"There is no positive proof of that," Mrs. Smith said, "and even if there were—"

"I don't care about proof—"

"I *beg* your pardon?" Mrs. Smith said.

The woman cringed a little, but couldn't be silenced. "She'll get us all in trouble again if she isn't stopped. None of us have forgotten that long *tenko* the other day—all because she put some kind of nettle juice in Saigo's underwear when it was hanging on the line. She played her silly trick and we all suffered."

Mrs. Smith sighed. "I know there are many who feel as you do, but there are an equal number who thoroughly enjoyed the sight—" She broke off, stifling an undignified giggle that was welling up at the memory of Saigo hopping around, scratching his crotch, and screaming. It was almost worth the long *tenko*. She made a noise that was something between a cough and a laugh and continued sternly. "Until and unless you have a legitimate case of Sister Denk actually violating a specific rule, I don't wish to have her name brought before this body again. Entertainment committee? Your report?"

Jane Kowolski was teaching Vivian to knit. "That's right, honey, now purl three. No, from the back. That's it. Hello, Hazel. You look sad."

Hazel made herself smile as she glanced approvingly at Vivian's work. The yarn was from her own red knit suit. She'd worn it, her best outfit, to bury her mother on the hill behind the camp. On the way back she'd gotten snagged in a thorny branch and torn a great hole in it. Jane, a world-class knitter, as she proclaimed herself—"One has to do something with one's hands to fill all those boring hours in rehearsal"—had declared it unfixable, but suggested that it be unraveled and reused. "There must be a good three thousand yards of yarn in it. At least twenty-five hundred. It could be turned into a number of things—"

Hazel, suspecting that Jane needed a project more than they needed "a number of things" agreed to sacrifice her suit to the common good. "You're doing a nice job, Vivian," Hazel said, wondering how the knotted mess strung on Jane's best ivory knitting needles would ever become a recognizable object.

"Viv, do you want a rest from this?" Jane offered. "I want to talk to Miss Hampton." When the girl had gone, Jane cleared her throat with obvious discomfort and said, "What's up?"

Hazel reached into the pocket of her skirt and slipped Jane

two pairs of khaki socks. "Dinki stole them from the guards' hut last night."

"And nobody dares to wear them," Jane said, nodding.

"Right. I thought you might want to unravel them as well."

"The khaki will make a nice contrast to the red. Not the same weight, but perhaps doubled—? I can teach Vivian about stripes later on. Dinki can't get anything white, can she?"

"I'll ask. Also, do you know where Mrs. Webber is? A native slipped me a note this morning. I think it's from her husband."

"That's wonderful. I think she's on latrine duty today. I knew it was only a matter of time before somebody managed to open a direct line of communication."

"The native said it was from the hospital down the road. At least, I think that's what he meant. His English is awful and I don't understand Malay."

"A hospital down the road? Do you mean to say we've got people dying in our wretched little hut and there's a real hospital nearby?"

"I'm not sure, but if it's true—"

She didn't finish the sentence. There was no need to tell Jane she was thinking that her mother might have been saved.

Mrs. Webber was thrilled with the tiny scrap of paper from her husband. She told her friends the good news and they told others. The excitement spread, took hold of the other women, and was inevitably noticed by the guards. Usually they patrolled outside the compound and entered only for the morning and evening *tenko*. That afternoon, however, Saigo, sensing something in the air, had them patrolling inside. They poked and pried and barged into the middle of things. While Mickey spent most of the day in the school hut with the children, the others were nuisances. The one they called Spike was the worst. He flipped over boxes to see if anything was hidden under them, poked his bayonet into makeshift pillows, riffled through books, and dumped out suitcases.

Hazel and Peggy were in their sleeping hut trying to figure out a way to fashion sunshade hats out of fresh palm leaves, when he came in. He thrashed through the hut while they stood at respectful attention. After barking something abusive, he stormed out. When he'd gone, Hazel glanced at Peggy and noticed the rivulets of sweat running down the sides of her face.

"Lucky for you he didn't find it," she said softly.

"Find what?" Peggy picked the palm leaf back up and studied it.

"The diary. You're still keeping it, aren't you?"

"No, I told you I wasn't."

"You're lying."

Peggy stared at her defiantly. "Hazel, this is history. This!" She made a sweeping gesture. "The living history of Oriental philosophy run amok. I used to think that only what's happening in the rest of the world was significant, but what's happening to us is vital. Not just to us, but to everyone. To history. It *has* to be recorded as it happens."

Hazel sat down heavily. "I don't want you to risk your life. You're so important to me. I've lost my mother, I couldn't stand to lose you, too. Look what they did to Jane Kowolski just for writing sheet music. If they found that you're writing a diary—"

"The same could be said of you, Hazel. Taking that note to Mrs. Webber."

"But it was from her husband. I *had* to give it to her!"

"Exactly, And I have to do what I have to do."

"But if they find out—"

"They won't—unless you keep talking about it!"

Saigo himself sat up in the little observation tower that had been constructed by the front gate. By nightfall the women's excitement had turned to nervousness. Saigo's wariness had made them more wary. Tempers began to flare; things that were better left unsaid were shouted; the children got cranky; two of the missionaries, whose antagonism had seethed gently for months, got into a flaming row.

That night the guards prowled the compound and entered the sleeping huts repeatedly to shine their flashlights in people's faces and count them. Saigo fancied that the earlier exuberance had to do with an escape plan and had threatened them with dire consequences should any of the women disappear. At about two in the morning they were all hauled out for a *tenko*. At first it was assumed Dinki had played yet another trick they were all being punished for, but Saigo's ranting soon convinced them otherwise.

"If they're so worried about an escape, that must mean it's possible," Hazel said speculatively the next morning as she sat bleary-eyed over her morning cup of pseudo coffee with Jane.

"Not necessarily," Jane said, laboriously unpicking a row of Vivian's knitting. "It could mean they're edgy for some other reason. Something to do with the war that we don't know but they do. If the Allies had retaken Singapore or—"

"The Allies have retaken Singapore?" a woman at the other end of the table said. "That's wonderful."

Jane hastened to correct her. "No, I just said *if*—"

But it was too late. The woman had run out of the hut, calling for her friend Mabel to tell her the good news.

"How enlightening," Hazel said. "I've always wondered how the wild rumors we're always hearing started. I didn't think it was done maliciously—now I know. But what about escape, Jane?"

Jane knew Hazel wasn't seriously considering it but was doing as they all did so often—offering the internees' favorite conversational gambit, like discussing what books you'd take along to the North Pole. She fixed a couple more stitches and said, "We'd have to change our appearance. We could dye our hair and probably our skin with that berry juice they put in the coffee to make it look real."

"And we'd have to learn Malay first."

"Yes. I'm taking lessons, you know. From Mrs. Smith. Unfortunately, all she knows to say are orders you'd give to servants. I now know how to tell a Malay to lay the table for sixteen and polish the coffee urn before throwing away the faded flowers in the sun porch. Not terribly useful in the jungle, of course." They elaborated on the theme, laughing at the image. As Gloria sat down to join them, Jane stopped her giggling and said, "It's a shame nobody can speak Nip. That's what would be really useful to learn."

Gloria slammed her cup down. "Bite your tongue!"

Hazel and Jane looked at her with surprise. "About what?"

"About learning Jap chat. It would be the worst thing we could do."

"Why?" the other women asked in unison.

"It would just be wrong; it would be adapting to their ways. Knuckling under to their rule."

"Admitting we had to accept their language," Hazel mused. "I don't think I agree, but I guess I see your point. But think, Dinki, if you could understand what they're jabbering to each other about and they didn't know you knew."

Gloria smiled. "Well, that does have pleasant possibilities."

* * *

The one person of whom this was true wouldn't have agreed.

Nancy Muir had drawn garden duty that week and was working as closely as she dared to the guards' wash hut. What she'd overheard this morning was deeply troubling, and she was trying to figure out what to do with the information. Saigo had told his men he was going to another part of the island. He had been vague—deliberately so, Nancy thought—about whether he was being reassigned or merely sent on an errand. But it was clear he would be gone at least a week or more because he had given orders about how to handle the following Friday's rice allotment.

The guards were as delighted to hear this as the women in the camp would have been. But that was what worried Nancy. While Saigo himself was an ogre, he liked to keep that power to himself. Sometimes it was he who kept the guards from acting with even more cruelty than they did. It wasn't nice of him, it was because he wanted all the pleasure of inflicting pain and humiliation on the prisoners to himself. Still, when he wasn't there to order and control them, what would happen? The women had learned to spot and avoid Saigo. How could they avoid all of them?

As she carried buckets of water back and forth all morning to soak the sweet potato cuttings, she argued with herself. She should warn the others, she felt, but what good would it really do? There wasn't any way they could prepare themselves for whatever might happen to them without Saigo around—unless it was to tie that damned Sister Denk up someplace to keep her from starting needless trouble.

Perhaps she was wrong to worry. These were, above all else, essentially lazy men. It was possible that they'd just lie about drinking and smoking and talking all the time when Saigo wasn't around to make them work. It might turn out to be a lovely holiday for everybody. Besides, if she did tell them, how would she account for knowing Saigo's plans? She had managed to convey some information to the others in the past by careful phrasing. "I think, just from watching the way they're acting, that there might be a search tonight, don't you? They're certainly up to something," she would say when she knew full well there was going to be a thorough turnout.

Nobody had ever questioned her "instinct," except for Hazel Hampton, who always looked at her very oddly. Well, let Miss

Hampton be suspicious. Just so long as she didn't actually know that the stoic Miss Muir understood every word the enemy said.

As she brought another bucket back and started tipping out water onto the cuttings, she overheard Spike and Mickey talking about the wood Mickey was to pick up on Spike's orders. That must mean Spike would be in charge, Nancy thought with a sinking heart. Mickey wasn't looking happy with the idea either. There was some talk about nails and hammers. They were too far away for Nancy to catch all of it, but the gist was that something was going to be built as soon as Saigo left. They moved away and Nancy was left to comfort herself with the thought that whatever they were up to couldn't be too horrible, simply because Commandant Natsume was still using the plantation house as a headquarters and they wouldn't dare try anything too outrageous right under his nose.

Would they?

In the end, Nancy kept quiet. The next morning Saigo got into his disreputable-looking green Oldsmobile and chugged away. "I don't imagine he knows anything about spark plugs," Hazel muttered at the sound of a distant backfire. His absence didn't interest the women; he was often gone for a few hours. And nobody but Nancy noticed that Mickey drove off in one of the captured Dutch transport trucks shortly after Saigo's departure. When he returned that evening, the truck was fill of weathered planks of wood.

At *tenko* Spike said, "Tomollow strong womens work for soldiers. Six strong womens. No womens work, no food." Accordingly, six of the younger women were lined up at the gate in the morning. They were put to work unloading the building materials from the truck. Then they were given tools and an incomprehensible hand-drawn plan for a small building.

"Are we supposed to build something?" one of them asked.

"I don't even know which end of a nail you hit," another said.

But they figured it out as the day went on.

"What do you think it is?" they were asked that evening when they returned.

They had no idea, but the guesses were plentiful. Some thought it was a new barracks for additional guards. But it was too small. Perhaps a new latrine since they'd probably fouled their other one so thoroughly. No, it wasn't near any pipes or water. The most acceptable explanation was that it might be some sort of a communications hut. It was near the road and there might be a telegraph line strung from someplace. Whatever it was to be, the work continued without much mishap. There were a few mashed fingers from ill-timed hammer blows and a lot of splinters to be removed. The women also acquired a number of bruises from the slaps and shoves they received whenever they seemed to be doing something wrong, or worse yet, enjoying themselves as they worked.

After three days it was done. The women were excused and Mickey was given a paintbrush and bucket to complete it. "Apparently we can't be trusted with the decorating," one of the building crew said with an ironic smirk.

That night when the light went out Gloria said to the hut at large, "Say, have you noticed Officer Shitface hasn't been around for a while?"

Beryl Stacton turned over in her threadbare covers with an audible flounce. "Really, Sister Denk, such language!"

The next morning at *tenko*, Spike said, "Womens, listen! Tonight you send six womens. Six little womens. Pretty womens. Wash and be pretty."

The women stood as though paralyzed while the implication of this order sunk in.

They had built a brothel and were now supposed to staff it with their daughters.

Chapter 18

Dear Jim,
When we were first captured, we were terrified of being
raped. Helpless women in the hands of the enemy. And we'd
all heard, of course, of the atrocities the Japs had committed
in China. But, apparently, so had the world and I believe
Nippon lost face terribly in its own eyes. It appeared, after a
while, that this army is under the strictest possible prohibition
about forced sex with Western women. Not out of respect,
mind you, but just the opposite. Out of contempt. We have
become complacent, forgetting that these little yellow fiends
are, after all, men, and now . . ."

They held an emergency meeting in the cook hut. The hut leaders and committee chairs crowded around one of the tables while
everyone else who could fit in hung over their shoulders. Valentina
Smith rose to the occasion. "First, the young girls must all be
confined to the school building. We must keep them safe and out
of sight. Let's say all the girls between ten and twenty. Let's take
care of that first." The mothers immediately left the meeting to
bustle their girls into a prison within a prison. Some of the younger
girls didn't understand what it was all about and there were a
number of hushed, hasty, and shockingly blunt lectures on the
facts of life which left both mothers and daughters shaken.

All the women were infected with a new feeling of horror.
Until now they had regarded the guards as nonsexual beings—
enemies, foreigners, oppressors, sometimes buffoons, but not
really men. And they had assumed the guards had no sexual

216

interest in them either. "They think white women are repul-
sive," several women had said with an air of sure knowledge.

"But why would they want to do this?" one of the hut leaders
said now. "They hate us!"

"I think that's part of the reason," Mrs. Smith said. "It's one
more means of humiliating and degrading us."

"I would sooner die than permit this!" Beryl Stacton said.
And for once, she spoke for all of them.

"It's imperative that we remain calm and show that we're
completely united. We will keep the girls hidden in the school
and simply refuse to obey the order," Mrs. Smith said.

"They'll kill us," someone said.

"There are more than two hundred of us and only—what?—
eight of them? They can't kill us all."

Gloria sat rubbing the still-tender bullet wound on her thigh.
"Yes, they can," she said softly, but no one heard her.

"I think we could overpower them," somebody at the back
of the room said. "Even if a few of us were hurt, or even killed,
the rest might get free."

"Free? And then what?" another woman replied. "Run out
into the jungle and make friends with the tigers and snakes and
poisonous insects—not to mention the hostile natives?"

"Not all the natives are hostile. There are some who bring
us food," the woman at the back of the room said.

"Not exactly out of the goodness of their hearts," a woman
who'd traded a valuable silver spoon for a sweet potato the day
before said bitterly. "Besides, there's nowhere to go! We don't
even know where we *are*!"

"What about the men's camp? Could we get word to them?"

"And what could they do? They're prisoners, too."

The meeting was disintegrating into dozens of separate, desperate conversations. Mrs. Smith banged her tin cup. "Ladies!
We must remain calm and united. We must simply refuse them,
but in a way that does not inflame them any further than we have
to."

Old Dr. Millichope raised her hand and Mrs. Smith gave her
the floor. "Our camp leader is quite right," she said. "If we
act hysterical and try to insult them in return, they'll lose face
and the consequences could be deadly. We have to convey with
dignity that this is an unacceptable demand and that we are
prepared to stand firmly on our rejection of it."

"But the filthy little yellow bastards—" one hut leader with a fifteen-year-old daughter began, but she dissolved into tears before finishing the sentence.

Several other women started crying from sheer anger and frustration at the terrifying injustice of the situation. Sometimes lately they were able to maintain a busy daily round of duties and lessons and gossip and almost forget for days at a time that they were prisoners. But this had brought them crashing down to the stark reality.

"Ladies, we mustn't let them see how frightened and upset we are," Mrs. Smith insisted in a bossy, bracing tone. "Now, I suggest we stay as much as possible to our own huts today. No school, of course, or other classes. Keep out of their sight. We shall prevail—one way or another."

"I think a prayer would be in order," one of the missionaries said.

"Oh, very well," Mrs. Smith replied grudgingly.

That evening at *tenko*, the guards sensed immediately that there were people missing. "Where others womens?" Spike shouted.

Mrs. Smith stepped forward. "Six are in the hospital and twenty-one are in the school." Knowing in advance that this sort of higher mathematics would defeat them, she'd drawn a little map of the camp on a title page she'd torn from one of the library books and had put the proper number of hatch marks in the squares for those two huts. She handed this to him. He studied it for a moment with perplexity and shook his head. "All womens *tenko*!"

"No," Mrs. Smith said impassively.

He slapped her. Hard. She reeled back for a moment, but she stood her ground. "No," she repeated with stunning calm.

Spike stared at her with furious amazement, then turned and barked an order at two of the other guards. They started toward the school hut, and as they did so, over two hundred women broke ranks and ran for the building. Before the guards reached it, it was surrounded by a living wall of women. Silently, they stood shoulder to shoulder. The only sound was that of some of the girls inside crying.

Spike's face was purple, and he was sputtering in Japanese. He and the two other guards lunged at the women, slapping and punching them. But they didn't give way; bending forward, covering their heads with their arms, they held their position. Spike

screamed an order, and he and the other two stood back and
aimed their rifles at the crowd around the doorway. There was
a throbbing silence, punctuated only by the calls of a flock of
birds in a tree just outside the compound. *This is the end of it
all,* Hazel thought with hypnotized calm. One of the guns was
pointed directly at her.

They stood that way for what seemed like hours, the prisoners
frozen with fear and determination and the guards waiting for
Spike's order to fire. He had now gone white with fury, but it
was obvious he was thinking hard.

How could he explain all our bodies to Saigo? Nancy Muir
thought, unknowingly echoing his own question to himself.

Finally he screamed another order at the other guards. "Little
womens come out or no food for all womens!"

The guards left the compound, glancing over their shoulders
and occasionally turning and making threatening gestures. Released from their immediate fear, the women sagged with sick
relief. Two ran gagging toward the wash hut. One didn't make
it. Several, including Hazel, sat down abruptly on the ground.
The nuns prayed silently, the missionaries out loud. Most of the
mothers crowded into the school hut to comfort their daughters.

As darkness fell, they set up a rotation for guarding the hut.
Twenty women at a time would take three-hour turns. When
Hazel got to her sleeping hut, the others were buzzing with
conversation. "It's the mothers I feel sorriest for," Beryl Stacton said. "Danger to yourself is awful, but danger to your daughter must be—"

"Save your pity. The stupid cows don't deserve it," Audrey
sneered. She was climbing awkwardly onto her section of sleeping platform and laid down with a groan. "If they were good
mothers—"

"Good mothers? Good mothers! What would you, of all people, know of that?" Beryl snapped. "You've been trying to kill
your child for months."

Audrey wasn't the least intimidated. Punching up the wad of
clothing she used as a pillow, she drawled, "I know that if I did
care for someone—someone young and defenseless—I'd have
gotten her to safety before the Nips attacked. Everybody knew
it was coming. We were all asses to be caught, but it shows
criminal neglect on the mothers' part that these girls are even in
this camp."

This remark caused the whole hut to fall absolutely silent,

not because it was so offensive, but because it was something nearly all of them had thought at one time or another. While everyone joined in the effort to protect the children, there was often the most subtle undertone of resentment toward the mothers who had allowed this to happen to their offspring. But no one had come right out and said it and they were sorry that Audrey had done so now. To have her confirm their own critical judgment was most uncomfortable.

When the light went out earlier than usual, Audrey was relieved. In the darkness she didn't feel so ugly and bloated and unkempt. On the other hand, she was always so much more aware of how dirty she smelled in the dark. The baby gave a great kick and she winced, thinking, *Oh, God, do let me be rid of this damned thing!* The rest of the women probably wouldn't speak to her for days for what she'd said, but she didn't care. It was the bloody truth and they knew it as well as she. Mothers ought to take care of their daughters. Little girls deserved that. She knew better than most what could happen when mothers let down their daughters and the lifelong loathing and resentment a daughter could feel for the mother who didn't protect her.

But she wouldn't think about her own childhood. She'd put it out of her mind years before, and there it would stay. And yet it was impossible not to be reminded of it here. The hunger, the stench of unwashed bodies and sickness and fear. The sound of children crying in the night. And the bleeding God-gabblers, forever going on about the good Lord delivering them from this terrible place. Well, God just didn't give a damn and asking him for help never got anybody out of anywhere. People did that for themselves, just as Audrey had done for herself. Asking God to do it for you was spineless and useless.

If she had anything to talk to God about, it was to demand an accounting of why the almighty son of a bitch did this to her. She had made the life she wanted for herself and it had cost her plenty, but she'd been well on her way to accomplishing all her goals. She had thousands of pounds tucked away in banks in England, all earning lovely untouched interest. Adding in the jewels and securities, she was ahead of her schedule. And it was a good thing! She'd always figured her beauty would begin to go by forty or forty-five and she'd need to have her fortune made by then. She wasn't going to turn into one of those raddled old whores that practically had to pay a man for a bit of slap and tickle. No, the day she could afford to get men out of her life, she was going to have one lovely, unpaid affair with a handsome young man, just as a bit of a treat, then put the bastards out of her life entirely.

Now, in this wretched place and with this damned baby wrecking her figure, she was afraid she was aging at a terrible rate. She'd had between ten and fifteen years to go. Perhaps now it was only eight to ten. Would this war make the interest rates go up or down? That was the news she'd like to get from outside.

She fell asleep toting up numbers in her head.

In the morning *tenko* Spike repeated his demand that the girls be sent that evening to what he was now calling an "officer crub." The potential prostitutes were still shut up in the school-room, weeping, sweating, and getting into fights with one another. The guards didn't even bother to try to count the women. This, in an odd way, alarmed Nancy Muir. It was an unspoken acknowledgment that they'd lost a measure of control, and in the Japanese, this was a very dangerous thing. An elaborate network of rules which everyone knew and everyone obeyed was the glue that held the culture together. The guards were barely able to cope with the fact that the Western women wouldn't follow the rules, but when they themselves started to let them slip, chaos was bound to follow.

She kept reminding herself that these men, the dregs of a highly rigid society, didn't know how to think for themselves. They had no training in it; it was not a virtue to the Japanese. To live within the rules and obey the wishes of one's superiors was the ultimate virtue—and it was now one that was apparently starting to crumble around the edges. Not counting the women at *tenko* was a dangerous sign. She found herself longing for Saigo to return. He was a threat, too, but he was a single threat and he was the authority these men recognized even if they hated him as much as the prisoners did.

"You send little womens?" Spike was demanding of Mrs. Smith again.

And again she said, "No."

This time he didn't strike her, he just smiled grimly and said, "Then no foods for all womens." He signaled to Mickey to pick up the morning *soempit*s, the large burlap bags of rice and mixed vegetables that had already been dumped in front of the cooking hut. With an air of profound apology Mickey lifted the heavy bags to his shoulders and carried them out of the compound. There was a rebellious stir among the women. Nancy took a deep breath and stepped forward. "It is said by all civilized nations that the Japanese people love children and are good to them. You will not let the children go hungry, will you? How shall they eat?"

Spike said, "Womens makes children hungry, not Nippon."

It was the longest day yet. By midmorning they were sick with hunger and snapping at each other. In the confusion of the night before, the big cooking pots hadn't been cleaned, so the mothers added some water to them to dislodge the bits of food stuck to the sides. To this someone contributed three eggs that she'd bought through the fence from a native the day before. Each child got a cup of this water in which a few forlorn grains of rice and shreds of egg floated. The women got nothing but water.

As the day went on, the girls in the school hut became hungrier, hotter, and restless. The women wouldn't even let them go to the wash hut without an adult to accompany them. The smaller children, especially the gang of little boys that always hung out together, became horrors. Cranky and not really understanding why they weren't being fed or paid attention to, they whined and nagged until their mothers nearly went mad.

Strange conversations sprung up. "I hear they have tiny little you-know-whats."

"What?"

"The Nips. The men. You know. Organs."

"Would that make a difference?"

"Of course not."

"Not true anyway. I saw them bathing in the stream one day while I was working in the garden and that Mickey one—well, my dear, I've never seen anything so enormous! Quite terrifying."

"I don't believe he'd know what to do with it."

"Men *all* know what to do with it."

In the afternoon they tried again to get some nourishment for the children from the cooking pots, but all they could manage was water with a scum on top that tasted slightly metallic and salty. There was a movement to put some grass from the edges of the compound into it for taste and vitamins, but the fear that it might be poisonous prevailed. The little boys were put to work throwing stones at birds in the hopes that they might accidentally bring one down, but they failed to do so.

In an impromptu meeting, Hazel's hut examined the alternatives. "We have to do something. We can't let the children starve," Beryl Stacton said—rather pointlessly, Hazel thought.

"We can starve or we can give them the girls," she said. "Neither choice is acceptable."

Peggy was sitting in the doorway and turned around to say, "No, those can't be the only choices. There must be alternatives we haven't thought of. Certainly two hundred and fifty women can outthink a handful of Nip soldiers."

"You'd think so," Hazel said. "Have any suggestions?"

"Well, Dinki could sneak out tonight and burn the damned brothel hut down."

Gloria perked up for a moment, then said, "Nothing I'd love more, but I don't think it would make a bit of difference. Now that they've got ants in their pants, the hut won't matter."

"I'm afraid you're right."

"I've been thinking—" Nancy Muir said slowly. They all stopped chatting to listen, simply because her participation in a discussion was such a novelty. "They're under orders not to sexually molest us."

"How do you know that?" Hazel asked.

She knew because she'd heard the orders given—repeatedly. But she replied, "It only makes sense. If they weren't, this sort of thing would have happened from the very beginning. But it didn't happen until Saigo went away."

"How does that help us?"

"I'm not sure. But if we could find out where Saigo's gone and try to get the information to him—"

There were several groans. "Somewhere in Sumatra, probably," Audrey said sarcastically. She'd just come back from washing her long blond hair and was sitting on the platform trying to drag a comb through the tangles.

Peggy waved a hand to shush her. "But maybe he's close by. The natives might know. We could try."

"The natives know we're in trouble," Gloria said. "Even the ones who will normally take the risk of slipping us things for the money haven't been anywhere near us today."

"Wouldn't a steak and kidney pie be bliss?" Audrey suddenly said.

"You bloody bitch!" Gloria replied.

Miss Evans, the former maid, had been sitting in the corner mending a dress. She said, "In purely practical terms, the girls might eventually have to be sacrificed in order to save the rest." There was a furor of objection, but Miss Evans was unmoved. "I'm not recommending it, mind. Just saying the truth the way I see it."

"I don't believe talk about 'sacrificing' anyone will do us a bit of good," Peggy said firmly. "You surprise me, Miss Evans."

Miss Evans didn't answer. She was staring out the doorway as if deep in some private thought. Putting aside her mending, she got up and walked out.

The next morning when they were summoned for *tenko*, the same question was asked, the same answer given, and another day without food passed. That afternoon everyone expected it to be a perfunctory repetition of the same. They lined up as usual and Spike approached Mrs. Smith.

"You send womens?" he demanded.

"Yes," she replied.

There was a silence as stunning as a thunderclap.

Mrs. Smith, Miss Evans, Miss Muir, the old nun Sister Edith, and Dr. Millichope stepped forward in a group. They were, together, the plainest, oldest, least attractive women in the entire camp.

Caroline Warbler reached out and grabbed Gloria's arm. "Oh, the dear old trouts!" she said, hovering between tears and laughter.

Gloria was touched, too, but rather than admit it, she whispered back, "It would probably do them a world of good."

"No, no, no!" Spike was screaming. "No ugly womens! No old womens!" He turned and stormed out of the compound. The other guards trailed along. Hazel, watching Mickey, thought she saw a smile on his wide, simple face.

The old ladies who had volunteered their "virtue" were surrounded by an appreciative crowd.

But a single voice said, "We've not only refused them, we've humiliated them. It's just worse now. They'll kill us all for this!"

Hazel went to take her turn guarding the huts where the young girls were still being kept. She sat in the doorway watching the evening shadows grow long and tried to think about anything but her stomach. Like the rest of them, she'd been drinking a great deal of water, just to have something inside, but it didn't allay hunger; it only made her feel "sloshy" and slightly nauseated. Think about Frank, she told herself. But she couldn't quite picture him. She could get his hair and his chin and his eyebrows, but his face wouldn't quite come together. Not here. Not when she was so hot and hungry and sick. Evanston and Frank and freedom were too distant to conjure up.

And yet—something about Frank, and her, was nagging at her mind and could not be ignored. Her virtue. Her damned virtue. They'd never made love. Not quite all the way. She'd almost gone along with his constant urging to consummate their love before the family came out to Singapore. She was as eager as he, if truth be told, but she was terrified of the threat of pregnancy. If she'd slept with Frank and then come clear out here only to discover she was pregnant, it could have been awful. Admitting such a thing to her parents would have been bad enough, but having to wait to marry until their return would have resulted in a baby only a scant few months after the wedding. Everybody would have known she hadn't been a "nice girl." At the time, that had seemed the greatest humiliation possible. Now, of course, she knew the real meaning of humiliation.

It was too late to change things. For her. But what of Frank? What was Frank doing without her? He was a handsome man anyway and in a uniform? The girls must be falling all over him someplace. Would his love of her keep him celibate? Was it possible for a vigorous young man in his prime? What if he'd found someone else? Not just for sex, but for love. If only she'd slept with him before coming here. She'd at least have that. She'd be rid of the now-hateful virtue she'd preserved. And if she came out of this a dried-up old maid, she'd have the memory of consummated love.

This is maudlin and foolish! she told herself as she sat against the door frame, half listening to the girls inside while watching the women move restlessly and nervously around the compound. At the far end, Mickey and another guard were standing by the gate talking to each other. Just inside the gate, Nancy Muir was squatting on the ground fixing a broken toy for one of the little boys. Odd that she didn't look more awkward sitting that way. Most women did. But Miss Muir looked entirely comfortable. The child got bored with watching her and wandered off while Nancy continued to try to fix the wooden axle into the truck's painted wheel.

As Hazel watched, Nancy slowly put down the truck and cocked her head ever so slightly, as if listening to something. But what? There were none but the usual sounds in the camp, and of course from where Nancy was seated, the voices of the guards.

The voices of the guards—

Hazel sat up straighter, squinting at Nancy to bring her into sharper focus.

A few minutes later Caroline Warbler wandered by and Hazel asked her to take her place for a few minutes. She went to where Nancy was still working on the toy truck. "Wouldn't you be able to see better in the cook hut, where there's a light, Miss Muir?"

"Oh, this is fine. I'm almost done."

"So are they," Hazel said, glancing toward the guards. Mickey was leaning against the gate, yawning hugely, and the other guard had ground out his cigarette in the dirt and was walking away.

Nancy glanced around as if noticing them for the first time, then went back to her project.

"Did they have anything interesting to say?" Hazel asked.

"I beg your pardon?"

"You know what I mean, Miss Muir."

Nancy looked up at her for a long moment. She knew sooner or later Hazel's suspicions of her would congeal into knowledge. She'd hoped it would take longer. "What do you want of me?"

"Information. How well do you understand them?"

Nancy sighed. "Perfectly. I speak better Nippongo than they do."

"Why didn't you tell us?"

"Because a secret ceases to be a secret as soon as two people know. If the women know, so will they before long." She looked over her shoulder at Mickey, who was nearly asleep standing up.

"You're wrong. I can keep a secret. And I will—but only if you tell me what they were talking about that interested you so much."

Nancy didn't answer at first. Three women were walking by. When they were out of earshot, Nancy spoke in an undertone. "We're going to lose this fight. Saigo is gone. Somewhere else on the island. Even the guards don't know where. The rest of them, except for Mickey, are prepared to kill us if we don't go along with their demands.''

''Are you saying there's nothing we can do but become the guard's whores?''

''Well—Commandant Natsume is headquartered at the house—the plantation house.''

''Yes, I know. The Dutch woman, Mrs. de Groot, told me, but the last time I saw her, several weeks ago, she said he'd packed up and gone away.''

''Yes, but the guards think he's come back.''

Hazel sat back on the ground. ''I see. Even if we don't know where Saigo is, we might know where to find Natsume, and he might put a stop to this.''

''Just what I was thinking.''

''But how do we get word to him?''

Nancy was looking out across the compound. ''Well—''

Hazel followed her gaze. It was almost dark now, and Gloria Denk was just helping guide Dr. Millichope back to their sleeping hut from the wash hut. ''Yes. She comes and goes as if there weren't fences around us. But she can't just go find him and say, 'Commandant, terrible things are going on in the prison camp,' can she? She'd probably be shot before she got the first words out.''

''True, but she could leave a message. He speaks perfect English, so I imagine he reads it as well. Would she do it? Could she?''

''I think so. The only problem is explaining to her how I know what I do. I've already mentioned to her that Mrs. de Groot said he'd left. I don't want to give you away.''

Nancy gave the toy wheel a final twist and stood up. ''I don't know, Hazel. But it's up to you.''

''How do you know this?''

''I'm sorry, Dinki, but I can't tell you.''

''You expect me to believe something this important and act on it besides and you *can't* tell me how you know it? You haven't been messing around with that ouija board those silly cows in hut four made, have you?''

''No, it's a little more reliable than that. But only a little.''

''But I'm supposed to risk my life, sneaking all over the bleeding jungle in search of Natsume? Why should I?''

"Because it's our only chance, Dinki. They won't mind a bit starving us all."

"We could wait and see what happens," Gloria said without conviction. "Maybe Natsume will come visit under his own steam and see what's going on."

"As hungry as we are, imagine how the children feel. How long can we wait?"

"Most people don't realize that a healthy human can go for weeks without food."

"How many healthy humans do you see around here? Besides, it's entirely possible they'll kill us before we get around to starving to death."

"I don't know, Hazel. Slipping out for a few minutes is one thing, but this—? There are all sorts of dangerous things out there, not the least of which are a bunch of sex-starved Nips. We don't know the terrain, or exactly where the house is, much less whether or not Natsume's really there. And even if nothing eats or rapes me, I'll be as good as dead if they have a *tenko* and realize I'm gone. I'll have to think about it."

"Good enough."

When Gloria found Hazel an hour later sitting in the dark on the step outside the wash hut, she said, "I'll do it on one condition."

"Name it."

"Well, there's something about me I haven't wanted anyone to know. I have no sense of direction. None. I can get lost in a room with one door. On the whole march here, I kept thinking we were going back and forth the same stretch every day. If I go, I've got to make sure I can get back before I'm missed."

Hazel was so hungry she felt faint and getting irritable. "What do you want me to do? Tie a long string to your hand?"

"No, I want you to go with me."

"Dinki, if I have to go *along*, I might as well go *alone*. Just tell me how you sneak out." She didn't mean it; the very thought of creeping around the jungle in the middle of the night made her shrunken stomach turn over and cold beads of sweat pop out all over her body.

"No. I'd worry about you on your own. You haven't—well, you just haven't the knack for this kind of thing."

"You bet I haven't!"

"Well, like it or not, that's my offer. I'll help you get out if you'll help me get back."

"I don't like it, but yes. I'll do it. When do we start?"

📰 *Chapter 19*

Dear Jim,

    I don't think I ever thought of God as going in for this sort of overdone irony. Those of us like myself, older, experienced, possibly able to control our revulsion long enough to sacrifice ourselves to save the girls—we're not what they want. Wouldn't have us served up on a silver platter with watercress all around, as Wodehouse would say. But the girls—I despair for these girls. Provided they survive, what will they think of men? These are formative years for many of them. Will they think men are like this, stupid, dirty, murderous?

It was a clear night and there was a full moon. That made it easier to see where they were going, but also easier to be seen. The guards had been turning the electricity off shortly after sunset as part of the punishment, and everybody went to bed early. There was nothing to do, and sleep was the only way to avoid the full knowledge of hunger. As soon as everyone was sleeping, albeit fitfully, Gloria and Hazel crept out of the hut wearing dark clothing, their heads covered with squares of black cloth Gloria had found someplace.

Based on Nancy's recollection of which direction the big house had been plus her own conversations with Mrs. de Groot, Hazel had mapped out a plan. They'd go over the hill behind the camp where the cemetery was, then follow the stream just past

it to the road. Keeping close to the road, but not on it where
they might run into soldiers, they ought to be able to see the
house from a distance. Gloria's escape route began with a section of fence where the barbed wire met the stockade. Cautiously propping up a section of the wire with a branch, they
crawled under, flat on their stomachs, then ran stealthily for the
dense jungle beyond. Stopping to get her breath, Hazel felt in
her trouser pocket for the note she'd written. It said:

> *Commandant Natsume, sir. While Office Saigo is away, the
> women in the internment camp are being starved to death
> because they will not give up their young girls for the guards'
> sexual use. We believe you are an honorable soldier who will
> not allow this to continue. We beg your help.*

She'd been glad she hadn't had to have a camp vote on the
honorable soldier part. Of course, if she'd told the others what
she was doing, they'd have never been able to agree on a word
of it. Pray God he could read English.

"To the left?" Gloria whispered, tugging on her sleeve.

"No, up the hill."

Etsu Natsume laid aside the report he'd been reading and
rubbed his eyes. He was getting more and more far-sighted and
needed better reading glasses, but who could guess how long it
would be before he could get them? Part of the problem was his
sheer weariness. After weeks of traveling around central Sumatra, familiarizing himself with all the camps under his command, he was exhausted. And he had to go out again next week.
The job needed a younger man; but the healthy young men were
all at the front, fighting for the Emperor. And his hand was
hurting again—his right hand, the one he'd lost in the first war.
At first it had terrified him to have such pain in a missing limb,
but over the years he'd come to expect it whenever he got tired.
The doctors couldn't explain it, but his wife always said it was
a reminder of his bravery and the pain should be welcomed. He
tried to believe that.

He turned off the green-shaded desk lamp and went to the
window to gaze at the moon-bathed landscape. The yard was
even more ragged and disorderly now that it had been a few
months before. To neglect a cleared section of jungle for a few
days was to give it back to the jungle. Such voracious growth.

Perhaps he'd get some prisoners from the closest men's camp brought in to work on making a decent garden for his contemplation. He'd do it from memory, like the garden his father had made in San Francisco.

Etsu Natsume's parents had both been from wealthy, influential samurai families, but his father had wanted to be a scholar and had gone to America to study. Unfortunately, America wasn't at all what he'd expected. No sooner had they gotten off the boat, than their money had been stolen, and instead of honor as befitted his rank, he'd had to take a job as a gardener to a wealthy family and his elegant wife had become a cook. It was a terrible loss of face, and they should have committed seppuku, but because she was large with child and because he couldn't bear to die so far from home, they'd gone on with life. This in itself was further dishonor. There was no going back.

As a small boy, Etsu Natsume hadn't been aware of their real status. He was treated as a child of the large, wealthy household, playing on the grounds with the American son, being given presents and sweets by the mother of that boy, having free run of the house and learning English faster and better than he learned his own language. He adored his quiet, learned father who dispensed Oriental wisdom and family history as he weeded the azaleas.

There had been an awful, inevitable time, however, when he was ten years old and realized that this wasn't his home and that his parents were servants. *Servants!* It had been a crushing blow, one that could still make his heart pound with outrage. The boy he'd grown up with was having a birthday party. His friends—the same children Etsu played tag with when they came to the house one by one—were all invited. When Etsu told the boy he hoped there would be chocolate cake to eat, the boy said, surprised, "But Etsu, you aren't invited. You aren't one of us. You're just a Jap."

That was when he first discovered that the master and mistress of the house didn't consider him another son, but a novelty, like a bright pet. He despised his parents for throwing away his heritage, for allowing themselves to be so degraded and dishonored. Samurais as servants to foreigners. Unthinkable! He himself would commit seppuku as they should have. But he couldn't do it. The Oriental acceptance of karma and belief in death before dishonor had been overlaid by American ambition.

By the time he was twelve and had started to outgrow his

crushing disillusionment, Etsu began to feel sympathy for his father. He, too, had been fooled by the white devils. Etsu vowed that he would become the scholar his father meant to be and take his parents back to Japan with all the honor they deserved. He studied hard and eventually was within months of receiving a master's degree in history from the University of Southern California when he met the girl. Her name was Elizabeth and she was a student of his. A shy, soft-spoken redhead, Elizabeth ignited in him a contemptible Western emotion he'd believed himself immune to: romantic love. The ramrod-spined, rigidly self-controlled Japanese scholar became a stuttering American boy. To his astonishment, his approaches weren't rebuffed, and in time she admitted she loved him as much as he loved her.

She took him home to meet her family.

They were outraged.

Her father called him a dirty Chink and threw him out of the house. Actually laid hands on him and physically flung him out the door. Humiliated, he went back to school like a beaten dog. Elizabeth never returned. Not that he blamed her for not defying her father. Quite the opposite. To revere the wishes of a parent, even when the parent is dreadfully wrong—*especially* when the parent is wrong—is a virtue. He admired her only the more for sacrificing her own happiness to obedience.

But within twenty-four hours he'd decided that Elizabeth's father wasn't wrong to forbid them to marry. He was right, but for the wrong reason. The wisdom and superiority of Nippon should not dilute and degrade itself by congress with the foreign devils, even one so gentle and attractive as Elizabeth. His hatred of her father spilled over and made him loathe everything Western in himself. Suddenly all the slights and insults and bigoted remarks he'd heard and managed to ignore during his lifetime swelled up in his breast, nearly choking him with the dishonor.

He left school without receiving his degree. The American stamp of approval on his education meant nothing to him anymore. Less than nothing. What mattered was what he'd learned about the Americans—the enemy, as they now were in his mind. And to know them was to have the key to their destruction. He went to his parents and told them they were all going back to Japan. Their spirits beaten down by a generation of servitude, they obeyed him.

Natsume didn't often allow himself to think of his past, but tonight, gazing out at the garden that might someday look like the garden his father had labored over most of his adult life, his mind was drawn back into that welter of pain and confusion of youth. As much as he loathed the position he was in now, responsible for the lives of thousands of dishonorable captives, there was a sort of justice in it that appealed to him. Just as he, a proud samurai, had been mocked and degraded, these once-proud white devils were being humiliated. If ever they could be forced to accept that as their karma, a few of them might be able to eventually learn the true superiority of the Nipponese ways.

His thoughts were suddenly interrupted by a sense of movement in the darkness. He moved back into the shade of the curtains and peered closely. Yes, just there. Two figures. Dark. Slight and graceful. Women? Why would any women be slipping about in the night? They were approaching the house. Best wait and see what they were up to before raising an alarm. He eased back farther into the shadow and laid his left hand lightly on his sidearm.

"Where are we to leave the note?" Gloria asked.

"We have to find out which room is the commandant's office and put it there."

"How do we find that out?"

"We look in the windows, you dolt!"

"Shhhh!"

"Here, I think this is it," Hazel whispered, peering over the top of a high sill.

"I'll climb in."

"You're too short. Just give me a boost."

Gloria made a stirrup with her hands and Hazel crawled through the window. Her heart was pounding like a steam engine, and she stood inside the room for a second with her eyes closed, trying to get control over her breathing. As she laid the paper in the center of the desk, there was a tiny click that sounded like a gunshot to her highly strung nerves, and at that same instant the room was flooded with light.

Natsume was standing across the desk from her.

They stared at each other for a long, shocked moment. Hazel's first impulse was to shriek or scramble for the open window, but she managed to suppress it. Bowing low, she said, "Commandant Natsume, sir."

"What are you doing here?"

His calm dignity washed over her. At least he wasn't going

to shoot her immediately. "I'm bringing a message, sir." Another bow.

He studied her. Not really so much like Elizabeth up close. Not in actual appearance. Only in coloring and manner. He picked up the note, opened it, and read impassively, then laid it back down. He expected her to burst into speech. These Western women never seemed to be able to keep their mouths shut. But to his surprise, she said nothing.

"You are going back to the camp," he said.

She wasn't sure if it was a question or an order. "Yes, Commandant, sir," Hazel said, getting her tongue unstuck from the roof of her mouth with considerable effort.

"You can find your way?"

"Yes, Commandant, sir."

He gestured her dismissal and she walked shakily to the window and half climbed, half fell out into Gloria's arms. "My God," she whispered.

"What happened? I thought you were dead for sure!"

They bent down and scurried back into the shadows of the jungle. The light in the office had been turned back off.

"Why didn't he kill you? Or even call his guards to drag us back?" Gloria asked. Even though she'd heard every word of the brief conversation, she kept believing there was some secret to the commandant's mysterious behavior that eluded her but which Hazel understood.

"*Will* you keep your voice down and stop asking me that! I don't know. I don't know! Dinki, not that way. Over here." They crouched down in a ditch next to the road as a jeep full of drunk soldiers rattled by.

"What did he look like when he read the note?"

"Like nothing. Utterly blank. I don't even know if he actually read it. I don't know if he *can* read English."

"Do you think he'll do anything about it?"

"How in hell would I know? Dinki, please shut up. I just want to get back into the camp and go to bed and forget all this. I was so scared I thought I was having a heart attack."

Just at dawn Audrey woke them all with a terrified scream. "Something's happened!" she cried.

Her water had broken and she was rushed off to the hospital hut by Beryl Stacton. "Do pipe down, you common thing! You're making a great fool of yourself," Beryl said, dragging her out into the faint pinkish light.

"I'm going to die! I know I'm going to die!" Audrey sobbed.

"I don't hold out much hope for it," Gloria muttered. "God hasn't been that good to us lately." She turned over and went back to sleep. But no one else in the hut did. Some had already been awake out of hunger and fear. There was a lot of quiet, terrified talk and a lot of whispered speculation.

When they were summoned to *tenko* a half hour later, some of them started crying with fear. Peggy took a firm line. "We must go out there, for whatever is going to happen. If we're to die, let us at least do so with dignity."

But as they assembled, they discovered that there was a visitor. Natsume stood by his shiny staff car, watching as they fell into line. The guards looked sullen and Spike had a red mark across the side of his face. When the women were in place and had bowed, Natsume walked slowly to the front. He looked at them for a long while in silence. His gaze met Hazel's for only a fraction of a second longer than the others. For an instant she feared he might be playing some devious emotional game with her. Had she been let go last night only to be punished now? Was she to be pulled out of line and beaten or shot?

He cleared his throat. "Because I have recently seen evidence that one among you is honorable"—again his eyes swept the group and lingered momentarily on Hazel—"I have decided to rescind the previous order given you."

So it had been a test, a contest for which she hadn't been told the rules or forfeits. Had she and Dinki not returned, he'd have allowed the others to starve to death. The bastard.

Audrey St. John gave birth to Jonathan Stacton that evening. He was a remarkably healthy baby. They had no scale in the camp, but Dr. Millichope held him for a moment and declared him an eight-pound three-ounce baby. Beryl Stacton took him to Audrey every two hours so that she could nurse him, but the rest of the time Beryl kept him with her. "My son, Jonathan," she called him.

Audrey lay alone and ignored in the hospital hut. She was exhausted and sick with depression. She kept putting her hands to her abdomen. It had a hideous, spongy, crepey texture that absolutely revolted her. Like a huge rotten peach. And her breasts—her beautiful, shapely, silky-skinned breasts!—were

huge and streaked with stretch marks and oozed repulsively. She
wished she *had* died. She wept all the first night after the birth.
It was the first time she'd cried since she was a girl and it hurt
all over.

A week later there were more new arrivals. Saigo returned
and a few hours behind him, a rickety bus dropped off a clutch
of disheveled geishas. Travel-worn and nearly swooning with
the heat, they did a great deal of bowing and then minced along
the road a few feet and were shown into the brothel hut. Their
traditional robes were stained and getting ragged at the bottom
hem and they had dead white skin and sad eyes.

"Prissy little trollops, aren't they?" Gloria said, peering
through a section of the fence at them.

"Poor things," Caroline Warbler said. "I feel sorry for them.
They can't like having to do—what they have to do with those
filthy ghouls."

"I don't know. I imagine it's like us when we have to assist
at a bowel resection. Not as much fun as a nice dinner and
dance, but part of the job."

"You didn't see it that way when it was us they wanted."

"No, but that was *us*."

"Look at Mickey. He's sneaking away. See, he just slipped
behind that tree."

"Maybe he's a pansy."

The geishas—or whatever the proper term for them was—
remained only two days. The women in the camp were left alone
while their captors indulged in a great deal of drinking, singing,
and sex. Then the Japanese girls were packed up on another
passing bus with a guard to accompany them to the next camp.

That same afternoon some new prisoners arrived. When they
came, Hazel was sitting on the edge of her sleeping platform
engaged in one of their favorite pastimes. "My turn? Okay,
when I get home I'm going to have a dinner party and serve"—
she glanced at Gloria—"cherry brandy," and at Caroline—"fried
potatoes with onions," Nancy Muir—"real coffee with three
spoons of sugar," Sister Maria—"lemon pie with meringue,
and—let's see—asparagus with lots of hollandaise sauce!"

"Hazel?" Dr. Millichope said from the doorway. "Are you
in here? They say that Dutch woman from the plantation house
and her daughters have been brought in. I thought you'd want to
know."

"That's too bad, but I guess it was bound to happen sooner or later."

There was a heap of suitcases and boxes just inside the gate and a crowd standing next to them. Hazel eased her way in. Poor Mrs. de Groot. She was such a timid thing, so terrified of the Japanese and yet compelled to help the rest of them by slipping food and other necessities in to the camp. It was a shame—

Hazel was stunned at the sight of Hannah de Groot. She was clutching a small child in her arms as though afraid someone was going to take it away from her. She was a plump, pretty blonde in a white silk day dress, but the front of it was soaked with blood. Her face was the color of the dress. "What's happened to her?" Hazel asked the others as Dr. Lange led her away to the hospital hut.

"She said they shot her husband about an hour ago. Right in front of her and the little girls," Caroline Warbler said.

"Girls?"

"Yes, the one she's carrying and—where's she gone? Oh, my God!"

A leggy, dark-haired girl of about twelve had run for the gate and was trying to climb over it. Hazel and Caroline ran for her and pulled her back before the guards noticed. "No, they'll shoot you!" Hazel said.

She struggled with a strength born of sheer terror. Suddenly she collapsed against Hazel and gave a long, shrill cry. "There, there," Hazel said. "It's all right. I'm not going to hurt you. Are you Mrs. de Groot's daughter?"

Her face buried in Hazel's bosom, the girl nodded.

"Come here to the cook hut with me and we'll sit in the shade, then we'll take you back to your mother after the doctor has looked her over. Do you understand English?"

The girl hiccuped and nodded again.

"What's your name?"

She struggled for control and finally whispered, "Elise de Groot."

"Well, come along, Elise. Sit down right here and I'll get you a cup of tea. Well, what we call tea. It's just brown water, but we pretend. That's right. Here's a handkerchief."

When Hazel got back to her, she was sitting bolt upright, but her eyes were nearly swollen shut with crying.

"I'm Hazel Hampton, Elise. I'm sorry about your father."

This was like opening the floodgates. "Daddy wasn't doing

anything wrong! Natsume had gone away someplace and Daddy was just changing one of the parlor chairs for one in the office Natsume used. They said he was stealing papers. But he didn't—he wouldn't—he said we had to be very nice to them so we wouldn't have to come here. But they killed him. They k-k-killed my daddy!''

Hazel sat with the girl for a long time, sometimes talking to her, sometimes just letting her cry. Finally, when Elise had grown a little calmer, she said, ''Shall we take you to your mother now? She'll be worried about what's become of you.''

''No, she won't. All she thinks about is Annie.''

''I'm sure that's not true.''

''What do you know!''

Hazel could remember thinking the same about her mother and Barbara, and when it had been her own martyrdom, the last thing she wanted to hear was a contradiction. ''I guess Annie is your baby sister.''

''Yes, and she's sickly. She always has been. Stupid baby!''

How hard it must have been on her, Hazel thought, to be the pampered only child for ten or eleven years and then to have a rival that took all her mother's attention. ''You speak English very well. So does your mother.''

Elise blew her nose on Hazel's handkerchief and gave her a suspicious look, surprised that she hadn't chided her for speaking meanly about Annie. Mother and Daddy were always shocked and angry when she said things like that.

''Thank you. My grandmother was British. My mother's mother. She lived with us until she died last year, and we had to speak English to her because she wouldn't learn Dutch.''

''Hazel, do you know where—'' Gloria came into the cook hut. ''Oh, you must be Elise de Groot. I told your mother I'd look for you. I hear the sodding Japs killed your father.''

''Dinki!'' Hazel exclaimed. ''Will you watch your language!''

Elise looked surprised. ''Is that a bad word? Sodding?''

''That's what bad words are for—bad people. Come with me now?''

''Oh, yes,'' Elise said admiringly.

It was the beginning of a friendship that was to have profound repercussions.

Chapter 20

December 1942

Dear Jim,
    The grapevine now says the British are massing troops in India and preparing to invade Burma. The same grapevine says President Roosevelt is divorcing Eleanor, and that can't possibly be true.
    How I miss your father. More now than when he first died. We need men in our lives here. Not just men, our men. White men. Not for the overt sexual reasons, but for subtle ones I never particularly noticed. I want to see big white American teeth and hear deep voices. How fine a real Texas cowboy would sound!
    We wonder all the time about the men's camps. How they're faring. Worse than us, I'm certain. I know their physical treatment is worse than ours. We are allowed and encouraged to die of neglect. The guards threaten to shoot us all the time, but so far haven't done so even though they probably would, given half an excuse. But the men are actively tortured and killed. Sometime recently two men at the nearby men's camp escaped and twenty, picked at random, were lined up and shot.

It was raining again, a roaring tropical torrent that beat on the roof and almost drowned out the sound of the choral group practicing for the Christmas program. The singers were gathered at the back end of the cook hut. Peggy was sitting at a table at the front looking out over the drenched compound. It had rained most of every day for a week now. The ground was a muck into which the feet sunk to the ankles. There'd been a heated dispute in the meeting of the grounds committee the night before about the mud. A large contingent wanted to tear down a lean-to at the back of the compound and use the planks for walkways. Both the wood crew and the cooking committee opposed this vehemently. They'd both been keeping the unused lean-to in mind as a potential supply of wood to burn for cooking. The wood crew was having to go farther every day to gather dead branches and the cooks were already complaining about how much of it was green and smoky. They capped their arguments with the theory that the planks would just sink into the mud and be lost in a few days anyway.

The grounds committee countered this by saying if the planks did sink, they could be dug back up when the rain stopped and could still be dried out and used for burning. They carried the motion. And now four women, soaked to the skin, were putting the planks down in a line from the cook hut to the front gate with a branch to the hospital hut. Peggy had her elbows on the rough table and her chin cupped in her hands, watching them with her eyes but not her mind. She didn't notice Hazel approach until the younger woman touched her shoulder. "Peggy, you must be a thousand miles away."

"I wish I were."

Hazel sat down across from her, then realized she was under a small leak in the roof, and moved over a foot. "You're missing the canasta tournament in hut three."

"Valentina Smith will win. She always does."

"I know, but I thought you liked to watch. Peggy, what's wrong with you today?"

Hazel counted on her to be efficient and matter-of-fact. Normally Peggy found Hazel's dependence—and everyone else's—flattering. Today it was just one more burden she'd run out of strength to carry. "Do you know what today is, Hazel?"

"Tuesday. Or is it Wednesday? I lose track."

"It's December eighth. The war started a year ago today."

"Oh!" Hazel said, slumping a little.

The sirens at four in the morning. The sound of the bombs. Johnny Leighton buzzing over in his little car to tell them it was all a mistake. Nothing to worry about. Standing on the balcony with Mother watching the flashes of light and wondering where Daddy was. "Oh, yes. A whole year—"

"I didn't really think we'd be here this long," Peggy said.

"We should be encouraged," Hazel said with determined optimism. "The longer it's gone on, the closer we are to the end. Isn't that right? Isn't that what you always say?"

"Yes, of course. But I can't help but wonder just what it really is we're learning from this."

Hazel didn't realize it wasn't a question that was meant to be answered. Instead, she considered it very seriously for a long moment. "I've learned some things, I think. I've learned that I'm a grown-up. That I can get from day to day without my parents telling me what to do. Or Frank. I think what I'd really planned to do before all this happened was to go from being Ronald and Roberta's child to being Frank's wife without any just plain Hazel-by-herself in between."

Peggy looked at her with some surprise. "You've thought about this a lot, haven't you? Is this better, though? Will you be better at being Frank's wife when we get out than you would have been?"

"I don't know. That scares me sometimes. Frank's so—so sure of himself. So sure of what to do and why and how. I'm not certain he'll like me as well now that I've gotten so—so grown-up."

Peggy sensed she'd taken Hazel by the hand and led her into dangerous territory, something she hadn't meant to do. "Don't worry," she said briskly. "If your Frank is half the man you've always said, he'll love you all the more for your independence."

Hazel clutched at this like a life raft. "Of course, you're right. What about your husband, Peggy? Would he have minded if you changed?"

"Harry? Oh, he wouldn't have minded my bossiness. I've always been that way. You see, he was the oldest child of his family and had four little sisters and a wishy-washy mother. He was sick to death of soft, clinging women when we met. Harry was one of those rare men who actually admired Eleanor Roosevelt for all her tearing about and interfering. He said she reminded him of me. I'm glad in a way that he didn't live to know this happened to me. He'd have worried to death about me. Of course, I wouldn't be here if Harry hadn't had that stroke and died."

"And your son? What's he like? You never say much about him."

"I'm afraid to even think about Jim. He'd just finished college and gone to England to join in the fray when I came over here.

That's one of the reasons I came. I thought I'd worry less about him if I were busy in some other part of the world. One of my worst decisions. He felt strongly that America ought to be getting into the war and standing behind our heritage nations—Jim's a historian like his father and me and sometimes talks like that then looks embarrassed about it.'' She smiled for the first time since they'd been talking. ''Anyway, he finished his master's and went to England to sign up. I have no idea where—'' She couldn't finish the sentence.

Hazel was shaken. Peggy was always her island of calm common sense in a sea of confusion and fear. To see her near tears was terrifying.

''Do you know what Dinki told me the other day?'' Hazel said with nearly hysterical cheerfulness. ''We were working in the garden and the guards sent her to fetch them some drinking water from the stream. As she came back—she was wearing a dress, you see, that baggy green one of Mrs. Englethorpe's— she stopped and sat down to talk to me for a minute. I heard this funny trickling sound and realized she was squatting over the water can and peeing it it. She said she always does that when she brings them water.''

Peggy blotted the corner of her eye with her sleeve and grinned shakily. ''Don't they notice it tastes funny? Salty, I would think.''

''Apparently not.''

Hazel got up and moved around to Peggy's side of the table to watch the walkway crew work. They had the main section nearly done. Suddenly Gloria Denk and Elise de Groot ran out of the hospital hut with tattered rain ponchos over their heads and skipped the length of it, which elicited screams of outrage from the builders. ''It's not done yet. Get off there!''

They ran into the cook hut, grinning at each other. ''Hiya, pardners. No grub yet?'' Gloria asked in an awful imitation American accent.

''Where did you steal those ponchos?'' Peggy asked. ''They look like Nip army issue.''

Dinki and Elise looked at her innocently before Dinki said, ''We found them in the wash hut. They must have crawled in there by themselves.'' Having delivered this piece of nonsense, the two of them ran back out into the rain.

''As much as I love Dinki, I wish that stupid Hannah de Groot would keep Elise away from her,'' Peggy said. ''She's the worst possible influence on the girl. And they're thick as thieves.''

"Hannah's too worried about Annie to pay attention to Elise," Hazel said, wondering as she spoke why she was defending her. She was enormously resentful of Hannah's neglect of Elise. "Dr. Millichope doesn't think the baby will survive. Something to do with her lungs because she was premature. And now she has an infection."

"Hannah can't do anything to help Annie, but Elise needs her supervision," Peggy said. "I hope Elise didn't have anything to do with Saigo's gun." Gloria had managed to fill the barrel of Saigo's handgun with excrement and since he fired it so seldom, he didn't know about it until the material had dried and solidified. Three days earlier, when he tried to bring down a monkey from a rubber tree, the gun blew up in his hand. He'd been rushed off somewhere, screaming with pain, and hadn't returned yet. The incident had divided the camp down the middle. To half of the population, Gloria was a heroine for having cleverly inflicted this damage on the enemy. The others were angry and frightened about what sort of punishment would be dished out to all of them as a result.

"They can't prove we had anything to do with it," the pro-Dinkis said.

"They don't have to *prove* anything!" the anti-Dinkis replied.

"Can't Elise be forced to get involved with the girls her age?" Hazel asked.

"I tried to get her to sit still and let Vivian show her how to knit, but they took an instant dislike to each other. Gloria's a powerful attraction to a girl that age—older, but immature and adventurous and irreverent. I'd have a crush on her myself if I were Elise."

"A crush—? You don't think—?" Hazel wouldn't have even known to wonder about the real nature of a crush before coming to the camp, but in a world that lived on gossip she'd learned a lot, much of which she'd been much happier not knowing about.

"No, I don't think that. It's probably perfectly innocent. But still unwise for a lot of reasons—"

The wind driving the rain grew stronger as the afternoon went on. "Do you think it's a typhoon?" everyone kept asking. A section of roofing on the hut Hazel and her friends were in was threatening to blow loose. "I ought to patch it before it flies away," Gloria said.

"How are you going to do that? You don't know anything about building," Caroline asked.

"I do know how to climb, and that's essential to the job."

"Come look at what's happened!" Elise said from the doorway. She looked half drowned, but happy. "The guards' hut blew down or blew up or something."

They all dashed out, heedless of the driving rain. The one-time brothel had only one wall. The other three were flat on the ground. The best part of it was the guards' consternation. They were running around in the rain screaming at one another and making wild motions with their arms.

"Dinki, that was a good one. How'd you do it?" Hazel asked as they hurried back into their relatively dry building.

"Me? I didn't do it. Wish I had."

Old Sister Edith, sitting in the corner, said grumpily, "What's she done now that will get us in trouble?" Sister Edith had retreated almost completely into her own private world of prayer, emerging only occasionally to complain—usually about Gloria or young Sister Maria, who didn't look like a nun anymore.

"She made the brothel fall down, Sister Edith."

"I didn't!"

Jane Kowolski came in and shook her soaking hair like a dog. "It looks like she pulled out most of the nails so the whole thing was hanging together by a thread. Then the wind did the rest. Good one, Sister Denk."

"I didn't *do* it!"

"Come on!" Hazel said, "It's got your fingerprints all over it."

"For Christ's sake! When my friends don't even believe me! And while I'm at it, I didn't steal those ponchos either. I found them in the wash hut like I said."

"Sure you did."

Gloria went back to trying to mend little Vivian's only pair of shoes, muttering to herself about false accusations. The rest of the women also picked up their abandoned projects. The camp had decided they must do what they could to make a real Christmas for the children and everybody had things to do. Hazel had cut up her beige slip to make the bodies of a number of small dolls. Peggy had tapped a rubber tree in the compound for the glue to stick on the hair, which was made of shreds from a black taffeta dinner dress hem. Miss Evans was making shorts and halter tops for the dolls from a large paisley-printed silk scarf she'd "inherited" from Mrs. Englethorpe.

Jane was making checker pieces for the four most obnoxious little boys in the camp with the fond hope that playing checkers might keep them out of trouble for a while. She'd found a long, straight branch two weeks earlier and borrowed a rusty handsaw from the guards to cut it into disks. Using a leaf from the surrounding jungle that had a rough back like emery paper, she'd sanded them down, then soaked the different sets in dyes she'd made from berry and bark infusions. One set was a deep maroon, another a bright crimson, a third was a warm yellowish-brown, and the last was a light purple-blue. The board itself was two shingles, hinged with strips of rubber from an inner tube and painted with squares of white and blue—oddly enough, the same colors the brothel had been painted. Nobody asked her how she came by the paint. The children had been let out of school for a few weeks—a far more appreciated present than any of the others being made—and the gifts were being stored in the school hut with the sure knowledge that they wouldn't be discovered.

The storm abated during the night, and in the morning, when Saigo came back, was only a drizzle. There were women assigned each week as "lookouts." Their job was to loiter as much of the time as possible by the section of barbed wire that gave the best view of the guards' quarters. That morning they reported that the guard had returned with only a light gauze dressing on his hand. Apparently the injury from the gun explosion was minor, but the women were still nervous and became a great deal more so when they were called to *tenko* in the middle of the day.

They expected to be blamed for the gun, but apparently he didn't know why it had blown up. Instead of punishing them, he gave a long tirade which Spike translated into Malay, and Dr. Millichope in turn tried to translate into English. It had to do with the benefits of the Greater East Asia Co-Prosperity Sphere. Old stuff that they'd heard dozens of times before. He then added a few minutes of propaganda about how the war was nearly over and the Japanese were assured of victory. Hazel kept glancing at Nancy Muir to see what her reaction was, but her face was as blank as everyone else's. Finally, they were ordered to go to their huts and remain there. This was different. And alarming.

A guard came to each hut with a paper carton. "Womens give all pictures. Now! Womens obey!"

"Pictures?" Gloria asked. "What pictures?"

He went to the wooden shelf over Jane Kowolski's section of the sleeping platform and swept all her belongings off. From the heap he extracted a photograph of her parents. "This pictures!"

Hazel glanced at Peggy and saw horror in her eyes. The diaries! Of course. They hadn't had a search for weeks, and she'd probably gotten careless about hiding them. Dear Lord, they would kill her if they found them. Not only was Peggy in danger, but she herself had something to hide. She'd worn the scarf with her mother's jewelry in it around her waist almost the whole time since the day they were captured. But just last week, when she'd started getting a funguslike rash around her waist from the constant dampness, she'd hidden it under the sleeping platform. They might well find that as well.

She stepped up to the guard and bowed. "I talk to women. Okay?"

"Okay. Speedo, speedo."

"Yes, I talk speedo," she said, then turned to the others and spoke very quickly indeed, partly to placate him, partly to keep him from understanding. "Look, he's going to take the pictures whether we give them to him or not, but if we don't do it willingly, he'll tear up everything and probably break all the children's Christmas presents, so let's just hand them over." She guessed from the quick agreement most of them expressed that some of the others had things hidden as well. They went through their belongings and handed over every photograph they had. Hazel took her only photo of Frank out of her wallet with terrible reluctance and took one long, and presumably last look at it before dropping it into the guard's paper carton. The guard, satisfied, left without any more searching.

"Do you know what the worst thing about this place is?" Sister Maria said.

At least once a day someone asked the same rhetorical question, and the statement that followed was always different.

"The worst," she went on, "is that we never know why they do anything. Like this! Why take your pictures? You've had them all this time, they've seen them every time they searched, and suddenly today they take them away. It doesn't make sense. I want something to make sense! Does it make sense to them? Do they have a reason?" She suddenly stopped, looked shocked at the shrillness in her voice, and crossed herself as though to ward off any more unnunlike outbursts.

"She's right," Caroline said. "Last week when we unloaded their sweet potatoes from the delivery truck for them I stole one that fell out of my pocket when I came back. Spike saw it happen and just laughed. But yesterday when I tried to steal one, he nearly broke my arm."

"And then he slapped me and I wasn't doing anything wrong!" Miss Evans added angrily.

Caroline jumped back in. "And remember when he walked into the camp one day last week, went straight over to that woman in hut two, and knocked her down? There wasn't any reason for that, either. Did he come in looking for her specifically or did the hateful hoodlum just say to himself, I think I'll go smack the first woman I see wearing a green skirt?" She suddenly ran out of steam and tears filled her eyes. "Oh, damn them! Damn them all!"

They were planning their Christmas concert for Christmas Eve. The morning of that day, Nancy Muir went to invite the guards to be their guests. They'd learned that this made it far less likely that they'd be forbidden to gather and sing. Besides, the concerts usually made the guards feel as mellow and happy as they did the women, and life was always easier for a few days after each one.

Hazel was on her way to the school hut to finish sorting the children's presents when she saw Nancy come in the front gate and head in the same direction. Carrying a bulgy *soempit*, she was running. Running! The plain, leggy spinster looked like an especially awkward giraffe. Hazel hurried to meet her. "Miss Muir, what is it? Did you see Saigo? What's in the bag?"

"Come in here. The children can't see. Oh, Hazel, it's too wonderful!"

They closed the door and Nancy handed her the *soempit*. "Saigo said this is from the 'white mens' for the children. Just look!"

Hazel opened the bag and began removing toys. All were handmade, mostly carved wood. There were dozens of little animals, a veritable zoo of elaborately carved and painted animals. Pigs, dogs, elephants, birds, tigers, lions, cows, horses, ducks, and cats. And there were fanciful ones, too. Dragons and griffins and others she couldn't put names to. And on each one the man who made it had managed to put his initials.

"Oh, Miss Muir," Hazel said, her voice thick with emotion. "We might be able to give some of them toys made by their own daddies. I never thought—as much as the children sometimes drive us mad, think how awful it must be for their fathers to be without them. What a lot of time and love went into this, and they must have turned it all over to the Japs without any idea whether it would be given to us or thrown away. I wish there were a way to tell them."

"We must find out what all our children's fathers names are and try to match them up."

"Let's ask Peggy to ask around and make a list so the mothers won't associate the question with what we're doing. So they can be surprised, too."

Nancy hesitated. "For some it won't be a good surprise."

"Yes, I see what you mean. But it will mean only that their husbands aren't in the camp that made these."

Natsume and a visiting Japanese bigwig loaded down with medals and ribbons attended the concert. They stood at the back of the audience and watched with the utter impassivity that had always characterized Natsume.

Hazel performed with only half her mind on the familiar Christmas songs. She found her eyes and her mind wandering over the people listening to the concert. A year of war. Ten months of captivity. Some had changed a great deal; others very little. Peggy Bright was looking older—much more so in just the last month. As if she'd come to the end of both her energy and the intellectual detachment that had been so valuable to all of them in setting up this bizarre society they were forced to live in.

Dinki was the same as ever. Wiry, tomboyish, a good deal more tanned and younger-looking than when they first came here. Having a well-defined enemy to play her tricks on suited her.

Beryl Stacton was another one who'd improved. The matronly fat had started to melt away and the condescending severity she'd started with had evaporated when baby Jonathan was born. She was as bubbly and proud as any new mother. Almost likable in her happy obsession with him. Except when it came to Audrey St. John. Beryl still referred to her as That Woman and while taking fanatic interest in her physical health, made no secret of her dislike for the biological mother of "her" baby.

Audrey was, as always, impervious to Beryl's opinion. She faithfully nursed the baby when he was handed to her, but other than that, she paid no attention whatsoever to him or to Beryl. Since the birth, her appearance had improved and she spent almost all her free time attending to it, washing and brushing and curling her long hair, filing her nails, taking exercises to keep her thighs and hips shapely. She couldn't return to her fully glamorous state here, but she did her best. Like the other nursing mothers, she was among the best fed in the camp. When eggs or fruit or the occasional piece of real meat found their way in, the nursing mothers and children got first chance at it and the others divided up the minuscule portions that remained.

The most stunning change in appearance was Caroline Warbler's. She must have lost nearly a hundred pounds. "She's sweated and shit away a whole person's worth," as Dinki put it. Tall and big-boned, she was still a large woman, but she had a sort of serene stateliness that was both impressive and beautiful and rather rare in such a young woman.

Others hadn't fared so well. Old Sister Edith had disintegrated badly. Both her mental and physical health were poor and her disposition was abominable. Jane Kowolski had aged a great deal, too. She practiced her singing rigorously, but was always dissatisfied with her progress and the lines of unhappiness in her face were becoming deeper. But she always made an effort to be pleasant and cheerful to the others and was well liked for it.

Poor Hannah de Groot had deteriorated the worst. Just since her arrival in the camp a few weeks earlier, she had gone to pieces. She had to be brutally evicted from the hospital hut at intervals to eat and bathe. She'd never willingly leave her sick baby alone. She wouldn't hear of taking on any camp duties, and nobody had the heart to insist that she do so. "Leave her be," Dr. Millichope advised. "Annie's desperately ill. It'll be over before much longer, and then we'll work on shaping her up."

Dear Dr. Millichope, Hazel thought fondly. The hideously efficient Dr. Lange still treated her like a nobody and refused to give her any real duties at the hospital hut, but it was to Claudia Millichope that most of them took their problems first. She might not have any greater medical knowledge than Dr. Lange, but she had an enormous heart that dispensed comfort and assurance and sometimes sad, blunt truths.

Hazel suddenly felt a sharp elbow in her ribs. She'd missed her cue. She stepped forward to sing her solo piece, but even as she was doing so, she was thinking, *As well as I know them all and love a few of them, I'd give anything to be home for Christmas.*

 Chapter 21

Dear Jim,
We are happy most of the time. Isn't that amazing? We work very hard at it, of course. We've invented a world here, created things to look forward to, and convinced ourselves they're important. A performance by our chorus becomes as exciting as sitting in the front row to hear a big-city philharmonic. An impending appearance before the judicial committee is as unnerving as going before the Supreme Court. Winning the weekly drawing or one of Miss Evans's special concoctions is as exciting as anything could be.
But there are cycles of discontent that are so strong they're almost mystic. Days and sometimes weeks when we're all frantically edgy and claustrophobic. Nancy Muir claims the barometric pressure is responsible. I think it's hormones. Even though most of the women don't menstruate anymore and joke bitterly about not having hormones, we do. God knows what would happen if one of the guards' spells of unusual cruelty coincides with our communal madness—

Three days after Christmas, Nancy Muir came around to the sleeping huts and said Saigo had given orders that all the members of the choral group were to assemble by the gate the next morning and be ready for a truck to come. "Oh, dear. We aren't *that* bad," Hazel said.

"I don't think we're being taken away to be shot for our singing," Nancy said. "He told us to 'be pretty womens' for the occasion."

"Uh-oh," Caroline said. "That sounds like the brothel business."

"I don't think so," Nancy said. "There didn't seem to be anything leering about the order. More like children being told to dress up and mind manners when rich Uncle Edwin comes to dinner."

"Where do you suppose they're taking us?" Hazel asked.

"Probably to entertain some Nip troops someplace. That old boy with Natsume the other day seemed to like us."

"How could you tell?"

"Well, he didn't kill anybody," Nancy said. "Help me pass the word and don't forget the 'pretty womens' part."

In spite of the efforts of Gloria Denk and a few others to suddenly join the choral group just to get out of the camp, the original twenty-seven singers and their director were standing at the main gate to the camp early the next morning. They were washed and spruced up and wearing their best—or somebody else's best, in many cases. A few were wearing lip rogue in the hopes they might pass a men's camp. A troop transport rolled up shortly and they climbed in, eager for the adventure, whatever it might be.

By noon the others started watching for them to return. "I think they were just driven to the de Groot's house and other Jap officials were invited to come hear them," Mrs. Smith opined. "They ought to be back any minute now."

A larger crowd was by the gate by midafternoon. "Maybe they're being taken around some of the villages nearby," Miss Evans suggested.

"No, the Nips don't care if the villagers are entertained. I think they're being taken around to other camps like ours," Caroline Warbler said.

By early evening fully a half of the adults in camp were standing or sitting around the gate, waiting. "Shhh! Hush!" Gloria exclaimed. "I think I hear a rumble like a lorry. Listen!"

They fell silent and, sure enough, heard a backfire somewhere down the road. They were all craning their necks as the transport came over the hill. "Christ on a crutch! What the hell have they got on?" a voice at the front asked.

The singers were waving and calling to their friends as Mickey swung the gate open and the transport turned into the camp. Every one of them was wearing a long seersucker nightgown over her other clothes. In clean, fresh pastel colors, the nightgowns were a feast to the eyes, but looked so silly that some of the observers laughed so hard they choked and had to be pounded on the back. The back flap of the truck was let down and the singers spilled off. Each one of them was carrying some food item: tins of bully beef, chocolate bars, fresh fruit, packages of cheese, even a loaf of bread—the first real bread they'd seen in the camp.

"Oh, God! We don't have to give *all* of it to the children, do we?" someone cried, echoing the thoughts of many.

Nancy, still standing at the back of the truck, raised her voice and said, "We decided to turn it over to Mrs. Smith to appoint a committee to disperse it fairly."

"I'll head the committee!" someone volunteered.

"And I'll guard it in the meanwhile!" another woman countered with a greedy laugh.

"What happened? Where did you go? How did you get all this?" Gloria asked, grabbing Hazel's elbow as she headed for the cook hut carrying a dozen oranges in the skirt of her nightgown.

"We went to two small camps like ours, all women, then to a big camp that has men and women. Probably eight or nine hundred prisoners—"

"Together! Men and women together!"

"Not exactly. They're in different camps, but they all surround a big open place like a playing field. Anyway, the Nips gave us these 'dresses' as they called them, from some Red Cross parcels in a godown near the big camp. There must have been a couple hundred parcels stacked up in there. Then we were driven to a place in the big camp that looked like a school or convent and it had an auditorium kind of room. In the front, in chairs, were dozens of Jap officers and down the middle of the room behind them were about a hundred nuns. The men were on one side of the nuns and the women on the other. They were all standing. Anyway, we sang everything we know and a couple of things they liked and asked us to sing again."

"But did you get to talk to the other prisoners?"

"Not officially. They watched us carefully to keep us from mingling, but of course we made all the contact we could. Nancy Muir actually talked to a man. A little clerkish man she seemed to know, but she got caught and hauled away from him."

"Forget about her—where did you get the food?"

"When we started back, they stopped at the godown again and gave it to us."

"For good behavior," Gloria said.

Hazel was surprised and offended at the sneering tone. "For good singing."

"For being nice, well-behaved prisoners. For jumping to their tune like a bunch of bloody marionettes."

"That's just sour grapes, and you know it! If Miss Muir had let you join the choral group yesterday, you wouldn't be saying such ugly things."

"I would, too. I've been thinking about it ever since you left and it was the wrong thing to do. It was collaborating."

"Gloria Denk! How dare you say that? Look at all the food we brought back and the nightgowns."

"They were ours anyway. Now, if you'd stolen them—"

"Is that all you can think of? The sneaky, underhanded way of doing things? Stolen or given makes no difference. Having the food's what matters."

"That's exactly how collaborators justify themselves."

"Gloria, we didn't sleep with the bastards or give them military secrets or—or turn you in for your tricks. We just sang a few Christmas songs! And a lot of our own people got the pleasure of hearing them."

Peggy Bright, seeing their belligerent postures and flushed faces, hurried over and took Hazel's arm. "Come on, get those oranges over here to be counted."

"Just a minute, Peggy—"

"Now, Hazel. Dinki, I think Dr. Lange needs you in the hospital hut."

"That's fine with me," Gloria said haughtily. "I've said everything I have to say."

Hazel watched her go. Her hands were trembling. "That bitch! That absolute bloody bitch!"

"Now, you don't mean that. Whatever she said to you, it was only because she was eaten up with envy because of the wonderful day the rest of you had. You know how childish she can be."

Hazel wasn't mollified. "She'd be even more jealous if she knew how grand it was to see those men. Oh, Peggy, they were thin and ragged, but it was a feast to just look at them—so tall and fair compared to our guards. You know, I think if I'd gotten near enough to one of them and guards weren't looking I'd have—I'd have done anything."

Peggy smiled. "I'm not sure I understand what you mean."

"I think you know exactly what I mean. You know, before I came here I really believed being a 'nice girl' was the most important thing in the world. Going down the aisle a virgin, behaving with decorum and modesty, talking quietly, knowing all the delicate social arts."

"And you don't believe in any of that anymore?"

"I don't know. It certainly doesn't seem to mean much here, does it?"

Peggy didn't answer. *Don't pontificate*, she told herself. *The girl is figuring life out quite well by herself.* "Let me borrow one of your oranges. I won't eat it, I just want to rub it in my hands and smell it."

Nancy kept going over and over in her mind the brief encounter with Herbert Dreyer. "I'm glad to see you," he'd said during a brief interval when the men managed to mingle with the visiting singers. "Do you remember me? Herbert Dreyer?"

"Of course!"

"I think about you a lot."

"And I, you," she said without shyness. They both sensed their time was too short to waste on cupidity. "Are you married?" Not another Ivan. She wouldn't let herself be that much of a fool again.

"Widowed. No children," he answered briefly. "You?"

"I'm an old maid."

"A maid, for sure. But not old," he said with a grin that seemed to make his round face light up. "Can you get out of your camp?"

That surprised her. "Out? No, of course not. Well, some do, I think."

"Would you meet me sometime?"

"I'd love to, but it's too dangerous."

"Everything is dangerous here."

A guard noticed them talking and shoved them apart. Nancy stumbled backward. "Yes. Yes," she said. "I will."

* * *

Very late that night Hazel was awakened by whispering. She sat up and said quietly, "Who is it? What's happening?"

"Just me," Gloria said. "I was telling Caroline Dr. Lange wants her to take an extra shift in the hospital so she can give her whole attention to little Annie."

"Is she worse? Annie?"

"Much. It's only a matter of minutes, and Hannah's nearly out of control."

"Can I help?"

"You can try."

Hazel hastily threw on her clothes and followed Gloria into the darkened compound. Just before they reached the hospital hut, Gloria stopped and said, "Hazel, I meant what I said earlier and I can't take it back, but—but I'm sorry I said it to you. I spoiled your happiness."

"I guess that's an Aussie apology, isn't it," Hazel said coldly.

"I can't help what I think. Hazel, you didn't see those women and babies in the surf. Helpless. Murdered for no reason. I can't forget that. Nor can any of us overlook what he did to Jane. I never will."

"And how are they vindicated when you make the rest of us miserable? Have you brought so much as one of them back to life by insulting me? Is Jane's voice better because of it?"

"No, I said I was sorry. Please stay my friend."

"I will, Dinki, but please, let's don't talk about it anymore tonight."

But Hazel knew she was lying a little. She'd stay friends with Gloria because she had to, but she'd never feel quite the same about her again. The friendship had been wounded, betrayed. In more than a year she'd only had a single day that she was happy all day long and Gloria had spoiled it at the end. A happy day was too precious a commodity to have taken away without lasting regret. That scar, like the one on Gloria's leg, would never fade completely.

They buried Annie the next morning on the rise behind the camp. Hannah picked a low spot between two small trees. Except for the babies who'd died at birth, this was the first death of a child in the camp, and it saddened everyone. Elise, too, had a strong element of genuine sorrow mixed with her resentment. In spite of her jealousy, she'd loved baby Annie, who, even in death, took her mother's whole attention.

When the burial detail came back, they found that the guards had dumped an enormous boxful of photographs on one of the tables in the dining hut. It was the pictures they'd confiscated weeks before. Each one now had official-looking stamps in vile black ink all over it, mostly on the faces. Still, they were glad to have them back and spent hours sorting through the mutilated pictures, cursing the Japanese, and trying to get the photos back to their proper owners.

It rained all afternoon and evening. The dark day and the baby's funeral cast a deep gloom over the camp. Nobody wanted to talk to anyone. Most of the women had learned various means of achieving a degree of privacy in the crowded camp and employed those means. Hazel reread one of her novels, Gloria polished and cleaned their meager supply of medical implements, Peggy pretended to sleep, Audrey used the last of her nail enamel on her fingers and toes, Jane went to the wash house and went through her parts in the three entire operatic scores she had in her head, Miss Evans made a tam out of some of the yarn from Hazel's crimson dress, Nancy recatalogued the library. The rain poured down all night.

In the morning Hazel came to Peggy in the wash hut and said, "Please come with me!"

"What's wrong," Peggy said, wrapping a tattered bit of toweling around her freshly washed hair.

"I'm not sure. I was over by the gate and Mickey came running in all upset and babbling. He seems to want me to go someplace with him. I told him to wait."

"Mickey? I thought he took Hannah to the grave with those flowers."

"Did he? Well, he hasn't got her now."

They dashed back across the compound and followed the guard's long-legged stride along the road a few yards and up the rise to the graveyard. Hannah was slumped forward on the ground. As they rushed forward to her, Hazel saw what she was holding and felt her stomach lurch. The rain had flooded the new grave and Annie's body had come back up to the surface of the loose soil. During the night dogs had torn chunks from it. One leg was badly mangled and one little arm was gone. Hannah was clutching the remains of the baby.

"Oh, God—!" Peggy said, retching.

Hazel turned away and vomited in the grass.

Mickey was leaning his forehead on a tree, gasping through his big, crooked teeth and crying.

Peggy was the first to come to her senses. "We have to do—something. Oh, God. Hannah. Hannah! Put Annie down. Lay her down on the grass. We'll take care of her for you. Just put her down. Mickey, shovel. Get shovel. Dig! Do you understand? Mickey!" she went to him, shook him fiercely, and finally reached up and slapped him. He kept crying. "Mickey, get shovel!"

He stumbled off, saying, "I get. I get."

"Hazel, climb down there to the creek and bring the biggest rocks you can carry. We'll make a new grave and put them on top."

Hannah had obeyed Peggy. Having put the baby's body down, she was now wandering off into the jungle. Peggy ran after her. By the time she got her back, Mickey was coming back up the rise with a shovel and had Nancy Muir with him. Peggy rushed forward, pushing Hannah, unresisting, in front of her. "Nancy, thank God he brought you. Don't look over there. Just take Hannah back to camp. She's had an awful shock. We all have."

With much gagging and crying, Hazel, Peggy, and Mickey got Annie reburied and then went down to the creek and washed as thoroughly as they could. Then they just sat down on the bank, not yet able to go back to the camp. Mickey had tears running down his face.

Peggy moved a little closer to him and patted his big, nail-bitten hand. "Poor old Mickey, you don't understand this any better than we do, do you?"

Mickey looked at her and nodded, not understanding the words, but grasping some of the sad sympathy of her words.

"Poor Mickey," Peggy repeated. "Poor Annie. Poor Peggy. Poor world."

Hannah's mental state after that day was unpredictable. Most days she did absolutely nothing; just sat on her section of sleeping platform without speaking, without reacting to what was said to her. She was as agreeable as a vegetable. The women would take her by the elbow and guide her to the cook hut, put a dish of food in front of her, and hand her a spoon. With enough reminders she would eat. Sometimes she even wet herself because she didn't think to get up and walk to the wash hut.

Occasionally, she came back to reality, but it was an eerie old reality, before Annie was even born, and on those days she drove Elise nearly wild. She thought she was still in her big white house on the hill, and that the other women were the household servants. She had been a considerate, gracious mistress then and still was, only shaking her head sadly when the orders she gave weren't carried out. On those days she wanted to keep Elise, whom she seemed to think was still five or six years old, at her side every moment.

Poor Elise, her own safe childhood jerked out from under her, was terrified of Hannah, contemptuous of her mental breakdown as only the young can be, and deeply hurt that her mother wanted to love her now only because Annie was gone.

"Mummy, don't tell Miss Bright to do the laundry. She's not a servant," Elise would say, blushing with embarrassment. "We're not at home anymore; we're in a camp. A prison camp."

"Your father is almost out of clean shirts. He'll be very cross if there aren't any folded in his drawer."

"Daddy's dead, Mummy! Don't pretend you don't remember!"

"I'd better darn some of his socks, too. I must get down to Palembang and do some shopping soon. I do hate the trip, though. So hot and jolting."

Elise turned more and more to Gloria, and on the majority of days when her mother was silently mad, they were inseparable.

"She has to have someone act as mother to her!" Hazel said furiously the morning after the bamboo bomb scare. Gloria had discovered that a fresh green section of bamboo, buried in the embers of a fire, would build up steam as it grew hot and eventually explode with a wonderful noise. She and Elise had sneaked out and managed to play this stunt on the guards the evening before to their own enormous satisfaction and the terror of the rest of the camp. "Dinki is a terrible influence on her, and Elise brings out the worst in Dinki."

Peggy was tired. "I know that, Hazel, but there's nothing we can do. She has a mother, at least some of the time. We can't just take her away from Hannah. The poor thing has lost everyone else in her family already. And even if we could, who has the energy to cope with the child? I certainly don't."

"I've tried, but she won't have anything to do with me. I'm

too young. An older woman with more authority needs to take charge of her.''

"Don't look at me that way. I never raised a daughter, and I'm too old to start now.''

"Peggy, this isn't like you.''

"Nothing's like me anymore. Hazel, please leave me in peace to take a nap.''

In the end, it was little Vivian who brought the crisis to a head. One day, several weeks after Annie's death, Vivian was sitting on the tiny porch of the hospital hut waiting for Jane, who was having a splinter removed from her foot. Elise approached her and said, "Give me some of that red yarn you're always fooling with, Vivian. Dinki and I need it for something.''

"It's for knitting,'' Vivian said.

"But there's lots of it and we want only a little bit.''

"No. It's for knitting,'' Vivian repeated singlemindedly.

"I'll have Dinki get it from you, then.''

"I don't care. I'm not afraid of her even if she is a lesbunyan.''

"A lesbunyan? What's that?''

"A bad thing. A real, real bad thing.''

"You made that up.''

"Did not. I heard Mrs. Smith say Sister Denk was a lesbunyan and shouldn't be around young girls, and if your mother wasn't crazy, you wouldn't be allowed to have anything to do with her.''

"Mrs. Smith is the one who's crazy. That's not even a word,'' Elise said, tossing her head and walking away. Vivian, afraid she was on her way to steal the rest of the red yarn, chased after her.

Neither of the girls had seen Gloria standing just inside the doorway.

"Sister Denk, have those dressings been boiled?'' Dr. Lange called.

"I—I think so. I've got to go—someplace. I'll be right back, Doctor,'' Gloria said breathlessly.

"What's the matter with you? You're not coming down with something, are you?''

"No—yes, I am a bit rocky. Excuse me!''

There was no privacy in this place. She ran to the wash hut, praying that no one was there. But somebody was bent over one of the rusted basins, washing her face. Frantic, Gloria ran around the side of the hut and collapsed against the wall. Curling into a ball, she wrapped her arms around her legs and pressed her burning face to her knees. She felt that she was about to explode like the bamboo bomb, but with anger and mortification and a horrible inside horror of herself. A sob escaped and then another and another.

Suddenly she felt a hand on her shoulder. She jerked away. "Leave me alone. Just leave me bloody well alone!"

"Are you sure that's what you want?" Dr. Millichope asked softly. She had been in the wash hut and had heard Gloria crying outside.

"Oh, Doctor, I could die!"

"No, you won't. You're much too tough to die."

"I just felt sorry for the poor girl. Her father murdered in front of her and her sister dead and her mother gone crazy. I just thought she deserved a little bit of a good time. She's just a child, and it's all so awful here."

"You mean Elise, I imagine."

Gloria looked up at the old woman with a tear-ravaged face. "And now they're saying I'm a lesbian. They're all talking about me behind my back, the bitches, and saying I'm a lesbian!"

"Are you?" Dr. Millichope asked gently.

Gloria stared at her for a long moment, then sobbed, "I don't know! I don't know. Maybe I am! I don't like men much."

"Oh, Gloria, I hear you talk all the time about your dates before the war."

"Yes, but I didn't—didn't *do* anything with them. It's all just talk."

Dr. Millichope knew better than she'd have admitted what Gloria was going though. When she was young, she was too obsessed with getting a medical degree to pay much attention to men. That was the only way a woman *could* get a degree. But later, as she approached thirty and all her friends were married and mothers, she'd heard the whispers about herself. There were women who'd been friends who heard them, too, and avoided her. She knew the pain it caused. More crucial, she knew the self-doubt it created. *Maybe I am what they think,* she had agonized. As the lonely years went by, she realized she wasn't homosexual, but she always knew the stigma.

She wrapped her thin old arms around Gloria. "You poor child. You're a nurse, you know what awful tricks poor diet and stress can play on people's minds and their hormones. It's worse for you young ones. Answer me this: do you find yourself wanting to touch or kiss Elise?''

"God, no! Never! I'd sooner die than kiss anybody in this place!'' But she was terrified that she was lying, to Dr. Millichope and to herself.

"Then there's no cause to worry—about yourself. But you should think about this gossip.''

"That's all it is. Gossip. Filthy gossip.'' Gloria mopped furiously at her eyes with her skirt.

"You're quite right, but you have to live here in the midst of it. You can't leave. None of us can leave.''

"You think I should stay away from Elise, too?''

"It might be best for you—and for her.''

"I just wanted to give her a little fun.''

"I know. But she should be having fun with girls her own age. Fun that can't get her in trouble. Sister Denk, it's one thing for you to risk your life on the games and tricks you play. You're an adult and entitled to live your life any way you want, but she's a child. You shouldn't be subjecting her to risks, no matter how much fun it is. You can see that, can't you?''

"I guess so. But the things I do aren't just to have a good time. They're to demoralize the Nips.''

"That's for adults to fight out. Not the children. We must protect them. All of them.''

Gloria wiped her face again with her skirt and said, "Do you know why I like Elise? Because she likes me. She thinks I'm funny and clever and she doesn't tell me what I've done wrong like all the rest of them are always doing.''

"I know, dear. Now, come along and wash up and get back to work before Dr. Lange comes looking for you with a net.''

Gloria laughed shakily.

"Dinki, I've got some of that yarn.''

"If you stole it, you better give it back. We don't need it anymore.''

"But you said—''

"I know what I said, but I'm very busy, Elise. I don't have time for games right now. Why don't you see if Vivian will teach you how to knit?''

"Knitting is stupid. You said so yourself. Besides, Vivian is a dumb sissy.''

Vivian's a very nice little girl. You ought to get to know her better. And Cynthia Webber. And Dorothy Bush.''

"Dorothy Bush! Dorothy Bush picks her nose!"

"Then tell her not to. Go away, Elise. I've got work to do.''

"Dinki? What's wrong? Don't you like me anymore?"

Gloria fussed with getting a dressing hung neatly on the drying line. "Of course I do. Don't be daft. It's just that I have things I'm supposed to be doing and so do you. Now, run along, that's a good girl.''

Chapter 22

Dear Jim,

 In the outside world charm and money mean everything, but the measures of worth here are endurance, restraint, and primitive skills—cooking, storytelling, healing.

Elise knew she'd been dropped, though she had no idea why. But she knew she couldn't just accept it. She'd lost her security— her father, her baby sister, her home and, to all practical purposes, her mother. She wasn't going to lose Dinki's friendship as well. She couldn't afford to. Not without a fight. She had one trump card up her sleeve, and she waited impatiently for the right time to use it. The opportunity arose in March.

She was sitting at the end of the table and listening to Dinki talk to Hazel. "Poor old things. They're miserable. It's scurvy. If we only had some ascorbic acid, we could hold it off.''

"Where does it come from? Ascorbic acid?"

"A decent diet has plenty—oranges, tomatoes, limes, that sort of thing, but some ordinary ascorbic acid tablets would do it."

Hazel finished eating and got up. Elise moved a little closer to Gloria and said under her breath, "I know where there are three bottles of ascorbic acid and vitamin pills."

"What!"

"Shhh! When we thought the Japs would come, Mummy and Daddy bought a kit of things in case we had to go into hiding."

"Where is it?"

"Hidden."

Gloria looked at her suspiciously, only half believing it. "Hidden where?" She glanced around and noted that two women at the other end of the hut were watching them and whispering behind their hands. Gloria felt her face flush with anger and embarrassment.

"Buried in our yard. I'll show you if we sneak out."

"No, I can't do that. It's too dangerous. Just give me directions. A map or something."

Elise got up. "You have to take me along or I won't tell you."

Gloria watched her walk away, then went to Hannah. "Hannah . . . Mrs. de Groot? Are you listening to me?" she asked her. "Did you hide some medical supplies?"

Hannah turned a blank gaze on her. "Hide?"

"Yes, did you dig a hole someplace and hide things in your yard?"

"Hide? Yes, I always hide Horst's Christmas presents. He's just like a child about holidays."

"No, not presents. Medicine. Ascorbic acid tablets. Where did you hide the ascorbic acid tablets?"

"This year I'm getting him a backgammon game. He likes backgammon so much. I think it's boring, but we often sit around in the evenings and—"

"Hannah! Listen to me! Where did you hide the medicine?"

"—play chess and cards and backgammon."

Gloria kept at her for a while longer, but couldn't jar her into the more recent past. When Nancy Muir came into the hut complaining bitterly that someone had stolen her only sewing needle, Gloria gave up on Hannah.

She went looking for Elise. "What else is in this kit?"

"I'm not sure. Some yeast tablets, I think. And bandages and scissors. Maybe some alcohol. I didn't really pay much attention. I was with Mummy in Palembang when she bought it, but I was getting new shoes and—"

"Why didn't your mother tell us about this before?"

"Mummy's been crazy since we got here. She probably just forgot or thought there wasn't any way of getting to it."

"Elise, do you swear this is the truth? That there is a medical kit and you know exactly where it's hidden?"

"I swear."

"Then you must tell me where it is. You're old enough to understand how important these things could be to the women and children who are sick."

"I know, Dinki. I want to give it to them, but you have to take me along."

"Elise, I *can't* do that!"

"But you can't do it yourself. You know you'd get lost."

"And you wouldn't?"

"Dinki, this is my home. I've lived here all my life. I know every inch of the plantation," Elise said, crossing her fingers behind her back. Well, it was almost true. "I'm the best person to take, and you know it. And you have to take me."

Gloria brooded over the situation for the rest of the day and finally gave in that night. "Elise, I'll take you with me, but if you're lying, I'll do something so utterly horrible to you that you'll never forget it."

"What?"

"I don't know yet, but you know I'll think of something phenomenally awful. Now, are you sure you want to stick with this story about the hidden medicine? I won't be angry if you tell me the truth now."

"It's there. I know exactly where."

It turned out to be remarkably easy. Elise crept through the night jungle like a seasoned sneak. "I used to come down here and look at the coolies when Mummy was taking a nap and wouldn't miss me," she whispered. "I thought they were very interesting. Mummy said it was dangerous and unhealthy to get near them. I don't think she'd ever seen the coolie quarters—and now she's living there."

She led Gloria directly and silently to the house. Natsume was presumably gone because there wasn't any staff car around, and there were no lights on in the house. There were only two guards in evidence, both of whom were sound asleep and snoring loudly on the porch. There was one bad moment, when they got close to the house and Elise suddenly stopped.

"That's where they killed my daddy," she said tearfully as she pointed to the little screened summerhouse. "They took us all out there to ask some questions, they said, but then they started screaming at him and they shot him. There was blood everywhere—"

"Don't think about it, Elise. Where is the medicine buried?"

"Just behind it. Come on."

The soil was still loose enough to claw through with their hands. Dinki pulled out a tin strongbox about the size of a shoe-box. It wasn't locked. She took a quick look inside, then tucked it under her arm. "Let's get back."

They didn't have any problems returning, either. A village dog barked for a while, but too far away to be any threat. They crawled back under the fence and Gloria whispered, "Go back to bed. I'll just sneak this into the hospital."

"See? I wasn't lying, was I?"

"No, you weren't. Thanks. Now get to bed."

The mysterious appearance of a few meager medical supplies was a great wonder. The ascorbic acid tablets were carefully cut in two and stingily dispensed to those in greatest need of them. The other vitamins were given to the children. No one "blamed" Gloria. A few thanked her.

The next evening Elise sidled up to Gloria and said, "There's some tinned milk, too."

Gloria's mouth dropped open. "You little dope! Why didn't you tell me sooner?"

"I forgot. But we can go back for it. It was easy, Dinki."

Gloria didn't have to agonize for so long this time. It had been easy, and going by Elise's shortcut, it didn't take any time at all. There was almost no chance any of the other women would miss them, and even if they were to notice, who would complain when they brought back something so valuable? She should go by herself, of course, but she knew she still couldn't have found her way on her own and was certain that Elise wouldn't tell her where the canned milk was hidden. Just this one more time, she told herself.

It was a night of patchy clouds that kept drifting across the moon and blotting out the light, but even when there was no light at all, Elise guided Gloria through the jungle as if by in-tuition. This time they didn't see the guards, but they could hear the sound of snoring from inside an open window.

"Where's the tinned milk?" Gloria snapped.

"In back of the kitchen. By that bunch of bushes," Elise whispered.

This was harder to remove from the ground. The cans had been in a paper box which had disintegrated. They gathered up as many as they could carry and started creeping away.

There was a sudden sound. A door opening. Both froze for a second. Gloria dropped a can, which hit her big toe, nearly making her scream with pain.

A harsh male voice shouted in Japanese.

"Forget the milk. Run!" Gloria said.

There was a flash of light and a gunshot rang out.

Gloria dropped the rest of the cans and grabbed Elise's hand.

"No! Dinki! Not that way. This way!" Elise said as they ran for their lives.

Gloria kept running, and Elise kept pulling the other way, finally breaking Gloria's grip on her hand. "Follow me, Dinki!"

The guard was pursuing them, still screaming at them.

Gloria tripped, scrambled to her feet, and kept running. Where had Elise gone? Leaping over rocks and logs and dodging trees, she peered into the darkness. Where in hell was the girl? She kept running, afraid to call out for fear Elise would answer and alert the guards to her location as well.

Suddenly Gloria ran out of ground. She'd fallen down a steep creekbank. Her knee twisted agonizingly and she thought she heard her wrist snap as she struck the shallow, muddy water. The darkness got darker. She was fainting. Breathing deeply, she sat still for a minute, waiting for the pain to ebb and her wits to recover. In a moment the ringing in her ears stopped and she realized the only other sound was some dogs barking in the distance. No pounding footsteps, no shouting, no gunfire.

Dear God, where was she? What had happened to Elise?

She crawled up the bank of the creek and took a few steps before tripping again. This time it was a little wooden cross she'd fallen over. She was in the cemetery. Only a short way from the camp. She could see the lights in the guards' huts. Even she could find her way back from here. But *where was Elise*?

She waited for a long time, rubbing her ankle and wrist, neither of which appeared to be broken, and wondering what in the world she should do. Elise had probably already gotten back to camp. After all, she knew her way. But it was possible she was out here someplace looking for her. Or worse yet, caught by the Nip guard. No, that wasn't apt to be true. Elise had been well ahead when Gloria tripped and lost sight of her.

After sitting and worrying herself sick to no avail for about an hour, Gloria finally gave up and limped back to camp. As she crawled under the barbed wire and started back to the sleeping hut to look for Elise, someone in the darkness said, "Dinki? Is that you?"

"Hazel!"

"Where have you been? Where's Elise?"

"Oh, God! You mean she's *not* here?"

"Of course she's not, or I wouldn't ask. Where is she?"

"Oh, bloody hell, Hazel, I don't know—"

She poured out the story of what had happened. "I know it was a stupid thing to do. You don't have to tell me. But it was so easy the first time and everybody was so happy to have the medicine and I thought—"

"Never mind what you thought. The question is, what do we do now?"

Dr. Millichope, her hearing sharper as her eyesight grew dimmer, had heard their whispered conversation and had crept out of the sleeping hut. They told her the situation. "We've got to make her mother tell us where she might have hidden," the old doctor said.

"We can't tell Hannah!" Gloria groaned. "Please don't tell her that I've lost her other child."

"We have to. There might be someplace Elise would hide and Hazel or somebody could go to get her back."

"But she won't understand what we're talking about. You know how she is," Gloria objected. "And if she did understand, she'd probably scream the place down."

"That's true."

"There's one other thing we could do—" Hazel said hesitantly. "We could tell the guards."

"Are you mad? *Tell* the guards?" Gloria exclaimed.

"Shhh! If we tell them she walked in her sleep—"

"Walked in her sleep?" Gloria repeated doubtfully.

"They might believe that," Dr. Millichope said. "Children often do. They could go look for her and nobody would be in trouble."

"And we'd save her from the tigers and snakes and dogs and everything else out there," Hazel said.

"Unless the guards at the house already have her," Gloria said.

"If that's the case, nothing will help," Dr. Millichope pointed out bluntly.

"Should we tell Hannah?" Hazel asked.

Dr. Millichope considered. "No, not yet. I think we should tell Mrs. Smith, however. She's the camp leader and will have to deal with whatever happens."

"Not Mrs. Smith! She hates me!" Gloria said.

Claudia Millichope normally had a great deal of sympathy for Gloria, but not at the moment. "My dear, that isn't even a consideration. The girl's life is at stake."

"Yes. You're right. And it is all my fault. Let's tell Mrs. Smith."

Everyone was awakened by the hubbub. The camp was divided in opinion and no one seemed the least reluctant to share her own view of the matter. Half were furious that the women had taken upon themselves to alert the guards to Elise's absence. The others were in accord that it was the only possible action to take for the child's own safety. Most were ready to lynch Dinki, all except the mothers who would have welcomed the milk for their children and the women who had received the ascorbic acid tablets the day before.

Nancy Muir was frantically worried about what the women might have inadvertently conveyed to the Japanese about the reason Elise was missing in the jungle. They were naively content they'd convinced Saigo that a child had walked in her sleep and accidentally wandered outside the compound. Who could guess what Saigo actually understood them to be saying?

Hannah de Groot suddenly and tragically came to her senses. "You've sent the guards to hunt down my Elise?" she asked, weeping. "How could you? How *could* you?"

"She's out there by herself, Hannah," Dr. Millichope tried to explain to the distraught woman. "There are wild animals and hostile natives. It was her own safety we were concerned about. Mrs. Smith told Saigo she walked in her sleep. She won't be in any trouble. It's not as though she was trying to escape."

"But Elise never walked in her sleep in her life."

"No, that's just what we told them."

"But what *was* she doing out?"

"We're not sure," Claudia Millichope said diplomatically.

No point in having Hannah going after Gloria with murder in her eye just at the moment. Plenty of time for that when—and if—Elise was safely back.

Jeeps came and went, rattling and honking. Lights flared up here and there in the surrounding jungle. The guards shouted back and forth at one another. A group of natives, pressed into joining the search, were taken past the compound gates. The women inside paced and talked; cried and prayed. As dawn came, the cook crew started their fires from the embers carefully banked the night before. Only Spike was left to guard the camp, and he couldn't leave to accompany the wood gatherers, so they had to use up some of their carefully hoarded planks from the one-time shed.

Gloria had aged ten years in one night. Haggard and exhausted, she paced back and forth along the fence at the front of the compound. Her body might be locked inside, but her mind and spirit were out in the jungle, desperately searching for Elise. A few people spoke to her; whether to comfort or to deride made no difference. She didn't hear them.

Finally, Saigo's green Oldsmobile came down the road with Saigo himself at the wheel. He jolted to a stop and the fat Formosan guard got out of the back, dragging Elise behind.

"Thank God! Elise!" Hannah cried, flinging herself against the gate.

The girl was as pale as rice flour and her eyes were huge with terror. There was a long scratch across her cheek and her knees were scraped and bleeding.

"Elise! I'm sorry!" Gloria cried.

They expected that she would be tossed back into the camp, but to their horror, Saigo gave an order and the guard started to drag her toward the hut Saigo used as an office.

"No, no. Please. Mummy! Help me, Mummy!" Elise screamed.

"Give me back my daughter!" Hannah shrieked in reply.

Nancy Muir had pushed several of the women aside to gain a place at the front. In a carrying voice, and in Japanese, she called out, "Officer Saigo, may I have the humble honor of speaking for the child?"

Saigo whirled and stared at her. So did the other women.

"She speaks Nip?" several whispered.

"Thank God!" Hazel said.

Nancy went on, still in Japanese: "She is but an ignorant

child who has no idea of the trouble she has caused the Nippon army. Her mother is ill in her mind and cannot care for her. I beg you: let me speak for her.''

Saigo gave a curt order and Nancy was let out to join them.

The women fell silent. Some went back to the necessary work of the camp, stoking the fires, picking the weevils out of the rice, scraping the dirt off the cucumbers that would be served with it. They were silent and nervous. Mothers hushed their children. Sister Edith and Sister Maria knelt on one side of the gate and began going through their rosaries. The missionaries gathered in another clump and prayed together. Hannah and Gloria, unaware of each other, clung to the fence.

The interview went on for an hour. They could hear Saigo's shrill voice, accusatory and furious. Occasionally he paused, presumably so Nancy could talk, but they couldn't hear her. Often, after one of these brief silences, there would be the resounding noise of a slap or the sound of a body being thrown against the wall and a muffled scream.

Eventually, the door was opened and Nancy was flung out like a sack of rice. She picked herself up and started walking slowly toward the gate of the compound. As she did, the Formosan guard dragged Elise out and shoved her into a jeep. Elise was sobbing and trying to get away. The jeep's engine coughed to life and it lurched off. The women surged forward, pushing against the gate.

"Oh, my God! My God! My God!" Hannah cried.

Many of the others, the mothers especially, were sobbing. Angry voices were raised. A rock was thrown over the fence. Saigo stepped out and shouted orders. The guards lounging in their hut raced out, half undressed, dragging their rifles, which they trained on the women. Gloria shrieked and ran at the fence. Spike, taken by surprise, whirled and fired at her. And missed. But the gunshot had stunned them all into a realization of their situation. They were animals in a cage. Nothing they could do would bring Elise back and it might get them killed. A sticky, thrumming silence fell over the women. One by one they drooped and retreated.

Nancy had reached the gate, which Mickey opened for her when the women reluctantly moved back. Her face was bruised and swollen. There was blood trickling out of one side of her mouth. "I'm sorry," she mumbled to Hannah.

"They're going to kill her. My Elise!" Hannah tried to climb the gate. When two of the missionaries pulled her back, she gave a long scream and fainted. They carried her to the hospital hut.

"What happened?" Gloria asked Nancy.

"They didn't believe the sleepwalking story. They said she was a wicked child because we were wicked women who sent her out to steal from the Nippon army."

"Sent her? They didn't know I took her along with me? I'll tell them—"

Nancy grabbed her arm. "It won't help anything. They wouldn't believe you, and even if they did, they'd just have two to punish instead of one."

"But what are they doing to her? Where have they taken her?"

"I don't know. They said they were taking her to another camp."

"Did they mean that?"

"I have no idea."

"They could be taking her somewhere to rape or kill her, couldn't they?"

Nancy nodded, wincing at the pain in her jaw.

Peggy and Hazel had been standing by, listening to this conversation. Peggy said, "You need some attention, too. Did Saigo do this to you?"

"Yes, he'd lost face, having all those talks with me in his pathetic English when all the time I understood his language. He was furious to begin with and then every time I tried to defend Elise—and us—he got angrier."

"Nancy, you did your best," Hazel said. "We're all grateful."

"My best was worth exactly nothing, and I've given away the most valuable thing I had to help everyone with. A waste!"

Nancy Muir went back three times in the next week to inquire about Elise. Each time she was beaten for her efforts and learned nothing. Hannah sank back into her mindless cocoon of memories of happier times. Now she lived her life as a bride, before Elise was born. She spoke endlessly about her wedding trip to Antwerp. Gloria went into her own cocoon—one of guilt and anger at both herself and the enemy. She was so preoccupied that Dr. Lange temporarily dismissed her from her duty shifts at the hospital. Gloria signed up as a rice picker, one of the least

desirable jobs in camp, involving hours of tediously sorting the
dirt and insects out of the rice allotment before it was cooked.

Of those in Hazel's hut, the only ones who seemed immune
to the depression cast by Elise's plight were Beryl and Audrey.
Audrey, of course, was insensitive to anyone's difficulties but
her own, which at the moment involved a swollen, inflamed
gland in her right breast. She was disturbed about the pain and
possible disfigurement of one of her most precious assets. Beryl
was frantic that it might dry up her milk supply and deprive little
Jonathan. Dr. Lange said the breast had to be lanced and the
infection drained. Audrey would not even consider such makeshift surgery.

Jane Kowolski stepped in. "Miss St. John, would you taste
this and tell me what you think?" she said one morning.

"Another of the booze recipes? Why not? Probably quite
foul."

"What do you think? It's made from those little soya beans
they bring us. Miss Evans has been experimenting with them.
Take a bigger gulp. You have to drink a bit before you really can
judge."

"Gruesome!"

"Then what about this one? It has some banana pulp mixed
in and it seems to kill the bitterness."

Before long, Audrey was drunk enough that they could haul
her to the hospital hut and tie her down to operate.

The next morning they were summoned to a noonday *tenko*.
Apparently the near loss of control in the women when Elise
was taken had alarmed Saigo as much as it alarmed the women
themselves. He had all the guards in place, rifles trained on the
women. He had Nancy Muir brought to the front to translate.
He spoke for a long time, then stood back and waited for her to
take her turn. "He says half of us are to leave tomorrow morning. We are to have all our things waiting by the gate. He says
we may take anything we can carry, but no—no pianos or refri-
gerators. That's what he said, ladies." She spoke very sternly,
trying to prevent anyone from laughing at the ridiculous order.
It almost worked.

"Dr. Lange and the sick are to stay here, as are the women
and children in the huts on the south side of the compound. He
does not say where we are going. He says it is not up to us to
question the wisdom of the Nippon army." She caught Beryl's

panicked look and addressed Saigo in his own language. "One of our ill is nursing another woman's baby. May the mother stay behind with them?"

He agreed curtly and Nancy said, "Mrs. Stacton may stay behind with Miss St. John. Officer Saigo also said we must carry most of our own food. He doesn't say how long a journey. That is all."

She turned and bowed to him. The rest of the women bowed and he walked off, leaving them to speculate on what it all meant.

"It could be someplace better," Miss Evans said.

"Or much, much worse!" Sister Edith grumbled.

"Now, Sister, nothing can be worse than this," Sister Maria said.

"They're just taking us off to kill us," one of the missionaries said. "And I for one will be glad to meet my Maker."

"If they were going to kill us, they wouldn't tell us to bring along food, would they?" Jane said snappishly.

"Well, I'm happy to get away from this place," Caroline Warbler commented. "No matter where we end up. How about you, Dinki?"

"What? Oh, I don't care."

"What are you doing, Hazel?" Peggy asked.

"I'm making a map so I can come back someday to my mother's grave. I'd hate not knowing where it is. I want to tell my father and sister when the war is over."

"When the war is over—" Dr. Millichope said softly.

"Hannah, you must get your things packed," Hazel said. "We're leaving in the morning."

"Leaving? I can't leave."

"You have to. We've been given orders."

"But I must be here when Elise comes back."

"No, Elise is in another camp now. You must come with us, and when the war is over you will both come back here."

"Hazel, I can't leave here. Horst will worry if I go away."

"No, we've already sent a message to him, Hannah. He knows. He sends his love and says to be careful on the journey. Now, let me help you put your things together."

They were getting lined up in the morning when Dr. Lange came out of the hospital hut on the warpath. "Ladies, I want those surgical scissors back. They're the only decent pair left and I need them more than any of you might. Now, turn them over, whoever has them.''

There was shuffling, cranky muttering and a chorus of denials.

"Come now, this won't do!" Dr. Lange insisted, growing angrier. "If I have to, I'll ask the Japs to search you. I won't mind a bit who gets in trouble, just so long as I get those scissors back.''

Jane looked around at the group. "Where's Hannah?"

A momentary silence fell. "Here are her things," someone said, pointing to a suitcase and bundle.

"I brought those out for her," Hazel said. "I thought she was in the wash hut.''

"I haven't seen her this morning," Jane said. "I just came from the wash hut.''

They found Hannah de Groot wedged into a narrow space between the back of the wash hut and the stockade fencing. She had cut her wrists, but apparently death had not come quickly enough and she had stabbed herself in the jugular. The scissors were still protruding from her throat.

 Chapter 23

Dear Jim,
    Something has happened in the Bismarck Sea. An important battle. Disastrous to the Japanese, we hear. Can't get any details!

This time they walked for four days and on half of the third they rode a truck for a few miles. The trip was much easier than the last time they moved. They were all tougher now; the weak among them had not survived. And they carried fewer belongings. Not only had they used up or traded away much of what they'd had earlier, but on the first morning a truck driven by Spike and commanded by Saigo caught up with them and they were ordered to put all their extra things into it. This threw the women into a quandary. On the one hand, it would make the journey immeasurably easier if they didn't have to carry everything; on the other hand, they had no idea if they'd ever see their belongings again.

Peggy was especially distressed. Saigo pointed out her battered suitcase as the example of what should go on the truck, and she could hardly refuse without making him suspicious. But the suitcase lining was stuffed full of the hundreds of little bits of paper that made up her diary. Every time they heard a vehicle approaching on the road, Peggy grew pale, certain someone had searched the suitcase and was coming for her.

"And what are you writing?" she asked on the fourth day when she found Hazel bent over, scribbling with a shard of charcoal on a scrap of paper.

"A map. I know where we are—sort of. The last three months I've borrowed Nancy's watch and sat every Friday afternoon in a certain spot in the compound where you can see the sun set. It set at exactly the same time all three months. So we must be right on the equator. And since Sumatra is a long, skinny country, there isn't a great deal of it on the equator. It's mostly above or below. Added to that, I've been on this road before. When they took us out for the Christmas singing. I remembered that village we went through this morning because of the strange color of the roofs. The big camp they took us to is a mile or so off to the right about ten miles farther."

"And what good does it do, knowing all this?"

Hazel stuffed her map in her pocket and looked at Peggy with surprise and disappointment. "Well, we don't know yet, do we? But it might be useful. Knowledge for knowledge's sake, maybe."

"You know you'll be in trouble if they catch you with a map."

"Oh, but I will be sooner or later whether I do anything wrong or not. I might as well have something to show for it."

Jane Kowolski approached them. "Come on, ladies. Mickey says speedo."

They gathered up the few things they still had to carry and

set out. One of the women was carrying Mickey's gun so he had his hands free to carry two of the smaller children. After a while, Hazel said, "I've been wondering—about Hannah. Why she did it. There's still a chance that Elise is okay someplace. Why did she give up? I know it had been horror upon horror for her, but she's not the only one."

"But she'd lost everything—or so she believed."

"Haven't a lot of us? Haven't I? My mother's dead. My father's probably dead. For all I know Frank is buried on some battlefield in Europe or drowned at sea. I don't know for sure, but it might be that I'm as much alone as she is."

"But you're young. That makes some difference. And none of those you've lost or might have lost are your children. We all care for our parents and our husbands, but there's a special kind of responsibility you feel for a child of your own. Fate—God— whatever you might call it took her Annie away and the Japs took her husband, but I think she must have sensed she gave Elise away. She should have been taking care of the girl instead of indulging her own grief. At least I'd feel that way. Even with my Jim, a grown man, if something happens to him in this dreadful war, I'll believe I should have stopped him from going."

"Could you have? Stopped him?"

"No. But the birth process instills some sort of automatic guilt."

Jane Kowolski had been walking just in front of them and she fell back alongside. "Giving birth has nothing to do with it. I feel the same about Vivian and she's not even mine. Who's Jim?"

"My son."

"Then you're not really Miss Bright, the spinster. I never believed you were. Spinsters usually have a sort of 'hungry' look that's a tip-off. Like Nancy Muir. Like me, for that matter."

"I'm a widow," Peggy said. She knew Jane well enough now to trust her with information. "My name's Sutherland," she added, then wondered at why she'd done so. It was the first time in over a year that she'd succumbed to the urge to reassume her own identity.

Hazel was deep in thoughts of her own. "Why do you think they're doing this?" she asked. "Moving us around."

"You aren't falling for the theory that we're being marched

all over to be murdered, are you?'' Jane asked. "Vivian! Put that down. It's dirty.''

"No, why didn't they just kill us all to begin with? We're no use to them.''

"Maybe we are,'' Peggy said. "We haven't any idea what kind of propaganda they're making of us. Remember last month when that little soldier with the terrible teeth came and took photographs of the garden crew working? They've probably sent copies off to Washington and London with a caption saying, 'Happy Western women voluntarily gardening under the benevolent enlightenment of the Nippon army' or some such rot. Nobody would fall for it, but they don't know that.''

"But what do they think is going to happen when the war is over? With us? They must think they'll win this war and what do they think they'll do with thousands of Western women and children and civilian men? Can they believe we'll ever knuckle under and turn into good little pseudo-Asians?''

Jane gestured toward the woman who had Mickey's gun slung over her shoulder. "Why shouldn't they? Would any of us have done that a year ago? There must be about fifty of us in this group and one guard. Even without the gun we could overpower him. She could be shooting him right now, but she won't. He knows it, she knows it, and we know it.''

"But that's because it's Mickey. If it were Saigo or that little rat Spike, we'd be fighting for the chance to pull the trigger,'' Hazel said.

"Oh, I doubt that. We'd all know we can't get off the island and safely back to our own people. And where would fifty of us find to hide? *One* white woman couldn't hide in this country without danger of betrayal.''

Jane made an exaggerated sad face. "You mean that every single native in Sumatra hates us?''

Peggy laughed at her. "No, maybe not even most of them. But telling which is which is the trick. And when the Allies win the war, the question will still exist.''

When the Allies win, Hazel thought. *That's the one single thing we all agree on, that the Allies will win. I've never heard anyone say "if" we win. But aside from the sheer, desperate need to believe it, why should we? What do we know of what's going on in the world? Only that we have some natural superiority that must prevail? Isn't that why Singapore fell while we all went on believing in Western superiority in the face of daily proof to the contrary? Are we so superior? To the individual guards, certainly. But these men were the rejects, the dregs, the bottom rung of the Nippon army. What do any of us, except Nancy Muir, really know of the military leaders or the Japanese people?*

"Hazel? You're daydreaming," Peggy said, shaking her arm. "We're coming to another road that looks like a major one. Don't forget to put it on your map."

Miss Evans was now alongside, having fallen back to try to adjust her sun hat, which kept slipping off. "Here, let me hold your bag while you fix that," Hazel said.

"No need," Miss Evans said, continuing to struggle while her handbag knocked her in the face.

"I don't mind," Hazel said, taking it away from her. To her surprise, it was extremely heavy. "What in the world have you got in here?"

"Odds and ends," Miss Evans said with an expression that was very nearly a smirk. "A few nails that might come in handy for something."

"Nails? Where did you get nails?"

Miss Evans didn't answer, and as they continued along the road, Hazel had a sudden vision of the guards' brothel laying flat on the ground and somebody saying that it looked like someone had stolen all the nails. "Miss Evans . . . ! You?" The older lady now had her sun hat firmly in place and took her purse back. Hazel was chuckling. "All the time everybody was blaming Dinki and it was you! The rain ponchos—? Did you steal those, too?"

"It's always a great mistake to judge people by appearances," Miss Evans said primly.

Their next home was a small village built on and around a barrow-shaped hill. Encircling the hill itself were eight small Western-style bungalows with wide porches and three or four tiny rooms each. The top of the hill was fairly level and had been cleared for gardens and three latrines with open drains. The drains converged, ran south, and joined with drains from the latrines serving the three houses across the road and then finished up in a low garbage area beyond. Behind the three southern houses was a large, semi-open building that would be perfect for cooking and storage and eating.

At one end of the road on the south side was a bathhouse

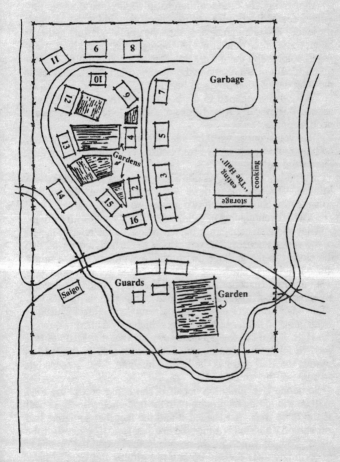

built around a well, and at the other end another well and a cluster of small buildings that had been shops and were now to belong to the guards. The truck with their belongings was parked in front of this area. Just inside the gates at the north was another house which they judged to be Saigo's own, as his dreaded green Oldsmobile was parked next to it.

After living for fourteen months in coolie quarters, the tiny village seemed very pleasant in spite of the evidence of Saigo's presence. It was much cleaner than the coolie quarters had ever been; some of the bungalows had been painted recently in pretty pastel colors, and there were flower gardens, the simple domestic prettiness of which made the women catch their breath after the long deprivation of visual beauty.

"But what happened to the people who lived here?" Hazel asked. "They can't have been gone long. The gardens barely need weeding."

"Do you suppose we'll have it all to ourselves?" Peggy said. "That would be about five to a house. What heavenly privacy that would be!"

"Afraid not," Nancy said. She'd hung back, chatting with Mickey. "He says many more women are coming. We are first so we get to choose which two houses we want."

"Two? Twenty-some of us in each?" Peggy said with a groan.

They spent an hour exploring and assessing the relative merits of the various houses. The one closest to the bathhouse was also the closest to the garbage dump, and a southerly breeze might make it hideous. The house farthest from the guards would have been desirable except that it was in the worst condition, having an extremely bad roof and evidence of massive rat infestation. "I'd rather be closer to the guards, actually," Hazel said later as they met in the largest building, which they'd already dubbed the Hall. "You can keep a better eye on what they're up to that way. Besides, that first house on the south side of the road is nearest the Hall and has the best latrine and it has screens left on some of the windows."

Someone else spoke on behalf of the house across the road to the north, citing its proximity to the first-choice house as well as the three trees that shaded it and the fact that someone had left behind a bedstead (minus the mattress) and a large wardrobe chest, both of which might be handy for something or other. Accordingly, they divided up into two groups and went to stake out their individual spaces in the houses. Hazel stood at the westernmost window of their house and gazed down at the guards' area. "Say, Dinki, did you notice the fences?"

"New and ugly," Gloria said, dragging a metal chaise lounge frame into the room. "Look what I got for us."

"No, look where the fences are. All around us. Dinki, the guards are *inside* the fences with us."

Gloria dropped the frame and came to the window, then laughed. "Why the buggers *are* locked up with us! Sheer bliss, as La St. John would say!"

For the next two weeks other groups of women came into the camp nearly every day. Though rumors were plentiful, no one knew why the shuffling of camps was going on. As each group came in, they were lined up, weighed, and asked all the same questions they'd been asked many times before. Forms were consulted, filled in, and filed away somewhere. Aside from the twice-daily *tenko*, there was little organized activity. A few volunteers grudgingly served as cooks, but many of the new women had been in camps previously where the food supply had been divided and prepared in small groups, and they continued to do so once they arrived.

"That's a terrible waste of food, effort, and wood. All those wretched, smoky little fires all over the place make the air unbreathable besides," Peggy complained.

"Then why don't you do something about it?" Hazel asked. "You got the other camp organized. You should do the same here." It was getting harder to like and admire Peggy as much as she once did and that made her feel irritable and guilty.

"I'm too old and tired."

"Somebody has to do something. This is anarchy. It's a terrible shame Mrs. Smith had malaria and had to be left behind. She might have been able to pull things together." They were sitting on the front veranda of their house, watching some new women being processed. Nancy Muir was sweeping the steps with a handmade broom. "You're the best qualified, Peggy," she said.

Peggy shifted on the rickety chair they'd repaired with Miss Evans's stolen nails. "I don't care," she said angrily. "I've retired. I'm entitled to."

Nancy went on sweeping as she said grimly, "Why are you more entitled than the rest of us? What makes you so special that you're allowed to hoard your natural talents and deprive the

rest of us of them? Should Dr. Millichope and Dinki refuse to
help the sick just because they're tired of it and don't have the
proper medicines? Should Jane abandon Vivian because it's a
strain to try to raise a stranger's child in a prison camp?''

"That's not fair!" Peggy said, getting up.

Hazel's inclination was to intervene, to try to make peace,
but she decided this time she wouldn't. Maybe what Nancy was
telling Peggy had to be said.

"Oh, it's fair," Nancy said. "You just don't like to hear it.
You'd rather feel sorry for yourself. Maybe you can get to be as
pitiful and self-absorbed as Hannah de Groot was. I never figured you, of all people, as a shirker. It's a great disappointment,
Peggy."

"I didn't come here to try to get your approval, Miss Muir,
and I don't give a damn for it!" Peggy said furiously, brushing
past her and storming off to the bath hut.

Nancy came up on the porch and sat down in the chair she'd
abandoned. "Are you angry with me, too, Hazel?"

"No, not with you. With life. Dear God, how I hate . . ."
Her voice trailed off.

"What is it?" Nancy asked.

"Look over there at the new women coming in. See the guard
weighing somebody? Wait until he moves aside—"

Nancy squinted. "Oh, my God, it's Elise, isn't it?"

They ran down the steps and hurried over just as Elise's "processing" was completed. "Miss Hampton! Miss Muir!" the girl
said as she spotted them. "You're here! I didn't think I'd ever
see anybody I knew again!"

Hazel gave her a hug and held her back to study. "Are you
all right? They didn't—do anything to you?"

"Nothing much. They took me and dumped me in another
camp with these other women and told them I was an evil child."

"You're no such thing. We'll take you back," Hazel said.

"Are you all here? Dinki, Miss Bright, and everybody?
Where's Mummy?"

Hazel and Nancy exchanged glances.

Suddenly Elise's brightness faded. "What's wrong. Where's
my mother? Take me to my mother!"

Nancy took her elbow firmly. "Elise, come sit down over
here. I need to talk to you."

* * *

The adults had a house meeting that evening to talk about Elise. Hazel had taken the girl for a tour of the camp so they could discuss her. "Someone has to take charge of her," Jane said. "I'd do it gladly, but she and Vivian are like oil and water. They'd slaughter each other."

"It has to be somebody with a strong personality. She's run wild for a long time," Peggy said. "What about you, Dr. Millichope?"

"I could supervise her only while I could keep her literally within hand's reach. I couldn't see what she's up to. Why not you, Peggy?"

"No, not me," Peggy said firmly. "Maybe Caroline Warbler?"

"I'd like to be her mum, but I've got my nursing duties. Who would look after her then? How about Hazel?" Caroline suggested.

Jane said, "Not Hazel. She's not old enough or bossy enough. It needs to be someone terrorizingly firm."

"Nancy Muir," Peggy and Dr. Millichope said in unison.

The next day they were summoned to an early morning *tenko*. Saburo Saigo made his first official appearance since they had begun arriving. Nancy was dragged forward to stand beside him and translate. "Officer Saigo says I am to tell you that the war is nearly over," she said in a carefully uninflected voice. "That the brave Nippon forces have nearly driven the evil white influence from the entire Southeast Asia Co-Prosperity Sphere. The American navy has been sunk to the last ship."

He spoke again, and she went on in her bland voice, "The imperialist British dogs have crept home with their tails between their legs, and the Germans have invaded and conquered Britain. The western coast of America is being bombed daily. The ports of San Diego, Los Angeles, Denver, and Seattle have been destroyed. There is great loss of life, and the American government is now drawing up their surrender documents."

She'd barely finished speaking when Saigo burst into another spate of speech and arm waving. "Officer Saigo says furthermore we have been bad women. We must recognize the superior wisdom and social structure of the Nippon people. He says we are stupid and willful and arrogant in spite of the Nippon army's benevolent efforts to educate us in our true roles as women. We are, he says, the women of fourth-class nations now. We are

fourth-class women and must learn to live modestly and pro-
ductively and—''

This time he cut in before she was finished. He raved for a
while and finished up with some sort of inquiry. Nancy bowed
to him again and translated. ''Officer Saigo says that we have
lived on the bounty given us by the Nippon army long enough.
Now we must contribute to the victors and earn our own way.
He says we shall now go to work at a factory nearby. If fifty
women work six days a week, they will be given a modest payment and the camp will be provided with food. If they do not
work well, there will be no pay, and no food will be brought to
us. He asks if we have a camp leader who will see to it that fifty
women work.''

The camp was silent. Several dozen pairs of eyes focused on
Peggy.

Saigo barked an order. ''We must have a leader or Officer
Saigo will have the guards decide everything for us. He is in a
hurry, ladies!''

Peggy straightened her back and stepped forward. She said
quietly, bitterly: ''I will do it. I will organize the camp.''

There was an audible sigh of relief from those who knew her
and had been waiting for her to volunteer. Order would be restored now. There were also a few moans. They were dismissed,
and as they walked back to their house, Hazel laughed and said
to Nancy Muir, ''You know, I've been to Denver twice and I'll
be damned if I noticed their port. I never even saw an ocean.''

Nancy smiled. ''I sometimes have the mad thought that the
Allies have undercover men who are sneaking into his house
and actually writing his speeches, just to cheer us up.''

''Have you talked to Elise yet? To tell her you're in charge of
her?''

''Not yet. I'm still thinking what to say. I'll take care of it
today.''

Jane Kowolski caught up with them and said, ''Hazel, Miss
Muir, wait a moment. I need some advice. It's about Vivian.
You know she was in a lifeboat with me. One of only two from
our ship that made it to land. There was no sign of her mother.
I assumed she was dead and took responsibility for her, but I
still keep asking about her every time we meet someone new.
Well, I just found a woman who thinks she was in a camp with
her for a few days at the very start.''

''She survived the shipwreck?''

"If this woman is right about it being Vivian's mother, she did. But she was desperately ill. Sunstroke, dehydration, internal injuries from the bomb concussions. When they were moved out, that woman and the others who were terribly sick were left behind. Should I tell Vivian?"

"I don't think so," Nancy said. "Look how distressed this has you. There's no need to do the same to her. Her mother, if it was her mother, probably died if she was that ill. You know how many did at first."

"Thanks. That's what I needed to hear. She grieved so horribly for her mommy, but now she's pretty much over it at last. I'd hate to set her up for the same sorrow over again."

"Excuse me, but I've got to go find Elise," Nancy said. "I have to give her what I imagine she'll see as very bad news."

Hazel hung back with Jane, and they walked slowly to the bathhouse together. "If that was what you wanted to hear, why do you still look so sad, Jane?"

The other woman didn't answer at first and finally said, "At the beginning I was desperate to find her mother or even someone who knew her mother so that I'd be free of the responsibility. But today's the first time in a year that I've actually thought about what'll happen when this is over. Whether her mother's alive or not, some of her people are, and I'll have to give her back to them someday. I know she isn't mine, but in my heart she's as much my own daughter as if I'd given birth to her. I can't imagine just handing her over to strangers. Especially if they're people who don't know and understand what we've all been through."

"Don't worry, Jane. She'll be happy to be back with her family."

Jane smiled. "I guess that's part of what I'm afraid of, Hazel."

Chapter 24

June 1943

> *Dear Jim,*
>   *Why are we more cheerful than the guards? They are the oppressors. Are the oppressed always happier because they make themselves so? Because they have so little to lose?*

"What time is it, Maria?" Hazel asked.

Maria looked down at the serviceable watch that had once been concealed in the folds of her nun's habit and now was fastened to the shoulder strap of her ragged halter top. "Almost five." She was among the very few who still had a clock that functioned, and she was constantly asked the time.

"Does today seem like it's lasted for weeks?" Hazel said, taking a break to stretch.

They were working their shift in the factory that made rope. Every morning bundles of hemp fiber, which came from the leaf stalk of a bananalike plant, were dumped at the front of the big converted godown a mile from the village camp. Most of the walls had been removed, leaving only the posts that supported the roof. Around the inside perimeter of the building there were spikes in the posts about six feet up. The women came in every morning, paired up, and were each told the diameter and length of rope they were to work on that day. They would hang the first hemp bundle on the nail, then each took half of it and started twisting counterclockwise so that the two halves twisted together. As the ends of the individual fibers of the bundle played out, new fibers from the next bundle were fed in. Usually they made half-inch-diameter rope, which two women could manage. Occasionally, however, they were ordered to make much bigger ropes, hawsers for ships and such. This took as many as a dozen women to twist and feed in the bundles of fiber and another three or four to hold the completed section taut and get it coiled and ready for shipment.

It was relatively easy work, discounting the terrible damage the coarse, splintery fibers did to the hands and the perpetual ache in the arms and shoulders caused by keeping an even tension on the rope. But it was mindless, and at first it was nearly impossible to make up pairs of women who wouldn't bicker constantly out of sheer boredom and irritation. Peggy Bright had solved the problem, however, with what they now referred to jokingly as "internment university." Each workday two extra women came along with the workers. They didn't make rope. They lectured, one in the morning, one in the afternoon—on practically anything.

A woman from house three who had grown up in Russia and Poland lectured frequently on the culture and social customs of those countries. A nun who was a first-class electrician lectured on the principles of electrical conduction. A native New Zealander talked about the history of her country. A rubber plantation owner's wife described the various steps of growing the trees, harvesting the latex, and processing it. Missionaries often told Bible stories or recounted trips they had taken to the Holy Land, though their lectures were not always well received. "Education is one thing; trying to convert is quite a different matter!" people would often complain to Peggy when one of the missionaries strayed from the strictly instructive.

Women taught one another about astronomy, French Impressionism, the influence of the Black Plague, Madame Pompadour, Greek mythology, medieval architecture, physics, the causes and treatment of leprosy, the American Civil War, points to consider when buying a pedigreed bloodhound, astrological signs, the English Civil War, the life of Beethoven, embroidery art of Lapland, pearl diving, proper dress and terminology for fox hunting, Egyptian scarabs, famous pirates, how to grow roses, how to repair a hole in a plaster wall, the rise of Italian merchant bankers, the stories of O. Henry, the proper feeding and care of canaries, Christmas customs around the world, how the combustion engine works (Hazel's speciality), the instruments in a symphony orchestra, Paul Revere, what the different blood types mean, plants and insects of the rainforest, the causes of the Industrial Revolution, and anything else that anyone had a smidgin of knowledge about.

The information wasn't always correct and was occasionally so downright erroneous that it caused heated disputes, but it was welcome anyway. They soon discovered that some women could make the most interesting subject sound dull, while others had a gift for adding vitality to the driest topic. Oddly enough, the nun who lectured on electrical wiring was among the favorites, and so was an old character actress from house seven who, like Jane Kowolski, had gotten stranded while on tour and now gave frequent lectures on her life on the stage. Her talks contained such juicy, scurrilous gossip about the famous and near famous that women asked to be put on the factory shift that would be working when she spoke.

The all-time favorite lecturer was a shy English bird-watcher who nervously gave her first lecture, "Tits I Have Known." Her description of the great tit and the blue tit were met with gales of laughter, but when she got to the bearded tit, the whole factory crew became hysterical and work came to a halt. She burst into tears of humiliation, but once she was calmed down and the double-entendre possibilities of the subject were explained to her, she rewrote her speech to make the best of them. Every time she gave her talk she improved on it a bit. After a while everyone who worked in the rope factory could repeat most of it along with her.

Sometimes a speaker would renege and the factory workers would have to provide their own entertainment. Usually this was a round-robin mystery story that they made up in turn as they went along. Sometimes they would just sing together, but the guards posted to supervise them didn't approve of this. Organized concerts like Nancy Muir produced were acceptable, even encouraged, but casual singing together to pass the time seemed too frivolous and happy to suit their ideas of how women should behave when they were working for the glory and victory of Japan.

Despite the efforts to make life as interesting and bearable as possible, everyone was subject to days of deep depression occasionally. Sometimes it affected most of them at once—Valentine's Day, a few months before, which marked the second anniversary of the day most of them were captured, was terribly difficult. So were Christmas and Armistice Day. Individuals had private bad times—their own birthdays and those of their husbands or children from whom they were separated.

And sometimes, for no reason at all, they would find themselves in a perfect frenzy of distress. Hazel woke one morning loathing the color of Jane Kowolski's hair—hating it so much she seriously wondered if she was justified in tearing it all out so she'd never have to look at it again. "What's wrong with you?" Peggy asked, seeing her glaring at Jane.

Hazel started trembling. "I've gone mad. I've gone utterly mad."

But when she explained it, Peggy smiled understandingly. "One day last week I heard Caroline Warbler talking to someone in that sweet, soft voice of hers and I had the urge to strangle her so she couldn't talk anymore. Then I figured it out. It wasn't the voice I hated, it was this place, the war, the food, all the things I can't do anything about. It'll pass, Hazel."

And it had passed. But it shook Hazel and made her wonder if everyone was subject to like fits of irrationality. As she got another bundle of fibers, she asked Maria, "Have you ever thought about breaking your watch so that people would stop asking you the time?"

Maria laughed. "Not until now, but it might not be a bad idea. After all, it doesn't really matter if it's five or ten of. We can't quit until the guards say so. But then, it's all I have left of my habit, so I think I'll keep it ticking along."

"How do you stay so cheerful?" Hazel asked. The question was composed of equal parts of admiration and resentment.

"Oh, praying helps. But you see, I went into the convent when I was sixteen—seven years before we came here. Nuns must learn acceptance of community living and giving up material things. I don't suppose I'll ever be entirely easy about either one of those, but I did have a head start over you lot."

"Do you know what I want to do when I get home? My mother's mother has a farm in southern Illinois. You can walk out into the fields and not see anything but the fields. No people, no trees. Nothing. I'm going to go out in the middle of the field and sit down and stay until I'm so filled up with the silence that there isn't room in my memory for the sights and sounds and smells of this part of my life."

"That's what I meant about praying," Maria said. "That's what it does for me here—usually."

"You're lucky."

"I am fortunate—to have found God and to have had this experience."

"This? Lucky to be *here*? How can this be good for anyone?"

"I've learned how a great deal of the world's people live. You see, we think we're being terribly mistreated, but, Hazel, thousands if not millions of the world's people, women especially, never in their lives have life any better than we are now. In much of India and Africa and Asia, our life here would be considered the norm. I keep telling myself that knowing this firsthand will make me a better nun. But I'm pretty tired of the lesson. I'm eager to move on, to put the knowledge to better use than making miles and miles of rope."

"Five o'crok! Five o'crok!" a guard shouted, coming into the factory godown. "Womens get on trucks!"

"Whoopee! Friday night!" the woman working next to Hazel said. "Believe I'll have a shampoo and set and have a late supper at the Savoy with Princess Elizabeth. Poor darling has been asking forever. Will you join me, Hazel?"

"So sorry, but I promised Franklin and Eleanor I'd drop in at the White House for drinks and sandwiches tonight. I adore the way Eleanor trims the crusts off."

The woman laughed. "I do wish she'd remember to send them over to us if she hasn't any use for them."

Mickey was driving one of the trucks that took them back to the camp every evening. "Herrow, Hazer Hammon," he said as she climbed on.

"*Komban-wa, Mickey san,*" Hazel said, trying out the Japanese Nancy Muir was teaching her. "*Tabako arimas'ka?*"

Mickey pulled a battered cigarette tin out of his shirt pocket and shook out the crumbs to show it was empty. "*Arimasen, Hazer.*"

"*Arigato gozaimas.*"

"What was that all about?" Maria asked when Mickey went to start up the truck.

"Oh, he likes those foul cigarettes we make with the home-grown leaves wrapped in Bible pages better than he likes the real ones. We sometimes trade. I wonder what's wrong with the truck?"

Mickey was opening the hood. Hazel went to join him as he peered into the engine. She didn't know how to ask what was wrong so she asked him what he was doing. *"Nani, sh'te imas-ka,* Mickey?"

He shrugged helplessly and stared at the engine in complete dismay. Obviously he had no idea how it worked or what was wrong. Hazel leaned over. "Mickey, it's nothing. Just a loose distributor cap," she said a moment later. "Now start it."

The truck started right up and Hazel wouldn't have thought any more about the incident had she not been summoned to Saigo's office the next morning. Nancy Muir went with her. "Officer Saigo wants to know what you did to the truck yesterday."

"I didn't do any—oh, yes." She explained and Nancy struggled to translate the unfamiliar term.

"Officer Saigo wishes to know how do you know about such unwomanly things."

"My father taught me."

He asked a few more questions, then dismissed them. Later in the day she was summoned again, this time to examine a sick jeep. "It needs new spark plugs," Hazel said.

Nancy was unable to translate this to Saigo's satisfaction. "He says we are to go with Mickey someplace to learn words for engines."

"Where?"

"I suppose we'll find out when we get there."

"There" turned out to be the big godown near the large camp—the godown the singers' nightgowns had come from. They were taken to the place where there were bins and shelves laden with engine parts. Saigo had given Nancy a tiny notepad and they took a linguistic inventory. "What do you call these, Hazel?"

"Gears."

The Japanese supply officer said, *"Giya."*

"And these?"

"Taillights."

"Teruraito."

In an hour Nancy had compiled a fairly thorough dictionary of terms. They were rushed out. They did their best to take a surreptitious inventory of the rest of the contents of the godown, but the supply officer was intent on preventing them from doing so and they came away with a hazy idea of what else was stored there. They did, however, have their pockets stuffed with every tiny item they'd been able to steal: a bar of soap, two combs, a bottle of vitamins, a tiny bag of bouillon powder, several pencil stubs, and a cigarette lighter.

On the way back to camp Hazel made mental notes of the route to add to her knowledge of the area. Though the roads were hilly and winding, she had a fairly good grasp of the "neighborhood." The big camp by the godown, their own village camp, and the Dutch hospital where their severely ill were sometimes taken formed an elongated triangle with the hospital at the northern point. Somewhere about halfway between their camp and the hospital there was another men's camp. Those men, mostly British and Dutch civilians, often worked as a road crew, repairing and leveling the roads after the monsoon rains. Just past the hospital there was another women's camp. Hazel had learned about it when she accompanied a woman with appendicitis to the hospital and met some of the women from that camp while she was waiting to be taken back.

When they got back. Dinki was at the gate, waiting. "Where have you been? We thought they'd taken you both off to another camp. Come see the banquet Miss Evans has made and tell us all about it."

Miss Evans was in charge of the cook house and had made it her mission to do inventive and interesting things with the meager foodstuffs they were given. She experimented on their house, and when the experiments were a success tried them on a larger scale for the whole camp. Tonight's menu was based on her latest efforts to make soya beans palatable.

"I cracked the beans in that coffee grinder we brought from the last camp," she explained as she poured a coconut shell full of something that looked like milk. "Then I soaked them overnight, poured that water off, pounded them to paste, added more water, and cooked them awhile in that pressure cooker we found in the storeroom. This is what I poured off."

They passed the cup around and took sips. "Not too bad," Dinki pronounced.

"But that's only the beginning," Miss Evans said proudly. "If you leave this stuff for a couple days, it turns sour and congeals. I put the gooey stage in a napkin, tied up the corners, and let it hang up to dry out a bit for two more days and got—this!" She unwrapped a napkin and they stared at the result.

"It looks just like cheese," Hazel said.

"Taste!"

"It's wonderful, Miss Evans!" Nancy exclaimed. "Almost like real food."

They finished off the pseudo-cheese and complimented her a bit more before wandering off to their various pursuits. "I'd like all those things better if she weren't so damned set on telling us how she makes them," Dinki said. "Remember that anchovy paste stuff? It tasted fine until she went into the whole story of how she roasted old fish heads and pounded them up. So, where did you and Nancy go?"

Hazel told her about the trip to the godown. "We saw some Red Cross parcels, but not so very many. They didn't want us to see what else was in there. Mostly it seemed to be Japanese stuff. Engine parts and weapons and uniforms. There were also some big *soempits* that looked like they had mail in them. Packages and things."

"Ours or theirs?"

"I couldn't see any of the writing. I don't know."

"All in all, a good place to steal from, though?"

"No. Heavily guarded. It's right by that big mixed camp. Besides, it's too long a way to go on foot without being missed, so don't even think about it."

Hazel was called on frequently after that to give advice about ailing motor vehicles. After Saigo's Oldsmobile broke down twice on the road and she had to be taken to the scene, Saigo started making her accompany him on his jaunts around the countryside. At first she sat in the front seat with the driver. But after a shift in personnel that left them one guard short, she was pressed into service to drive him herself. "I don't see how you bear it, Miss Hampton," Elise said as they sat over a dinner of water-lily roots which had been boiled and sliced then fried in red palm oil. "He smells so awful. Those shirts of his—!" She shuddered.

Saigo had only two shirts, which he alternated weekly, the sweat rings under the arms identifying their age like the rings on a tree. "It's not too bad while we're moving. He's in the back with the windows open. It's only when we stop for a while that it gets awful." She didn't want to add that it was a small price for the heady illusion of freedom that driving around the jungle gave her. "Where's Nancy?"

"Copying out some lyrics for the choral group. I offered to help, but she said she was almost done."

Elise had, after an initial period of rebellion against Nancy's assigned authority, settled in nicely. Afraid she was going to be "mothered," she soon learned that Nancy had no intention of trying to act maternal. She was, instead, a fairly benevolent dictator. She told the girl briskly that she hadn't wanted to look after her any more than Elise had wanted it. Elise was both insulted and relieved by this. Further, Nancy told her, if she wanted the privileges of being an adult (which was just fine with her), she would have to take the responsibilities and signed her up for all the worst jobs in the camp: rice picking, drain cleaning, fire building, and foot rubbing. This last was considered the most boring, tedious job in the whole camp. One of the frequent results of beriberi was that the nerves to the feet started going and resulted in a sensation like electric shocks. The victim had to keep moving constantly, and the only way she could get any sleep at all was to have people take shifts constantly massaging the afflicted feet. Elise had stuck it out for over a month, doing all these hateful jobs, but had then swallowed her pride and asked Nancy if she could go back to school with the rest of the children.

Since then, an understanding and even a bond of affection had started to draw them together. Nancy's severity was bracing to a girl at an age and in circumstances to feel sorry for herself. The rare signs of affection—a smile, a pat on the shoulder, a quick hug—were all the more significant and welcome because they were so rare.

Nancy's power and influence over the child were helped along by the fact that since the move to the village camp, Gloria had studiously avoided her. This was partly Gloria's choice, partly Peggy's management. When Peggy reluctantly took over the organization of the camp, she mapped out Gloria's life as brutally and efficiently as she did everything else. "I could send you to the hospital," she told her, "but you're the least trustworthy one to let out of camp. You'd be getting us in trouble all the time. I understand they have plenty of nurses there already from other camps. Have you any other skills? Other than making trouble, I mean?"

Gloria stomped off, insulted.

Peggy left her alone for a day or two, then caught up with her in the bathhouse and said, "Hazel tells me you sometimes talk about wanting to be a doctor someday. Is that true?"

"You're going to send me to bloody medical school?" Gloria asked, rubbing a threadbare scrap of towel over her short hair.

"Yes, I thought I would. Dr. Millichope's poor old head is stuffed with the knowledge of a lifetime and there's no way to put it to good use. They won't use her at the hospital because of her eyesight, and we've got that other doctor to run our little infirmary. She has nothing to do and her talents are being utterly wasted. I've talked to her about teaching you—and Caroline Warbler, too, if she's interested."

Gloria was quiet for a long moment and kept rubbing at her hair until Peggy thought it might start falling out. Finally she said, "Well, if it would give poor old Dr. Millichope a feeling of usefulness, I suppose I could."

But Peggy knew her too well by then to fail to hear the suppressed note of enthusiasm in her voice. And in the fourteen months they'd been at this camp, Gloria had undergone at least a partial change. Although Caroline Warbler dropped out of the lessons after a few weeks ("I don't really want to be a doctor, I want to get out and marry some rich bloke before I put my weight back on") Gloria fell into being a "medical student" with eagerness and intelligence. It didn't stop her silent war of sabotage she constantly waged on Saigo and the other guards, but it did slow her down and keep her out of trouble.

Now, as Hazel and Elise sat in the Hall, gnawing their fried-water-lily-root dinner, Gloria came in to join them and there was no discomfort, but neither was there any particular friendship, between her and Elise.

"What's the latest rumor?" Hazel asked Gloria.

"How in hell should I know cooped up with Claudia learning chemistry? Oh, I did hear that the Aussies have taken Java and are about to take Banka Island."

Hazel nodded. "We hear that one at least once a month. Don't you have anything better than that?"

"I'm not out in the social whirl like you are," Gloria said.

"Yes, riding around with Saigo is quite a whirl, I must say."

"If it were me driving, I'd run the car off a cliff and kill the son of a bitch."

"And yourself with him. Have you thought of that?"

Gloria grinned. "Say, speaking of his car, I've been—"

"Hazel? Saigo wants to see you," Nancy Muir said, coming into the Hall and giving Elise a handful of old yellowed papers. "Give these to the choral group and tell them they better have them memorized by tomorrow. First rehearsal. Come on, Hazel.''

''Doesn't anybody want to hear what I'm doing to Saigo?'' Gloria said pitifully.

''You can tell me later, Dinki,'' Elise said as the other women left to see what Saigo wanted. ''I've got to get this music passed out.''

Chapter 25

October 1943

> *Dear Jim,*
> *Nancy tells me the word* inkyo *means a state of formal retirement from active life. Not just job, but everything. An honored state to the Japanese. Yesterday when a guard ordered me to help dig a new latrine pit, I drew myself up and shook my head, saying, ''Inkyo. Me inkyo.'' He knocked me down. Apparently this isn't a concept they wish to export to fourth-class women.*

''A pig? I'm to go pick up a pig?'' Hazel asked Nancy.

''A pig or pigs. He wasn't clear. Nippongo doesn't have singulars and plurals like English.''

''Pigs?'' Had the heat cooked her brain?

''You'd better stop repeating that and get on with it. He says you may take someone trustworthy along. He specifically excluded Dinki and Sister Warbler.''

''Dinki I can understand, but Sister Warbler—?''

Nancy shrugged. ''I guess he especially dislikes her for some reason. And don't look at me. I don't go on pig errands. And neither does Elise.''

Hazel went looking for Jane Kowolski. "Are you saying that Saigo is actually letting us drive off in his car by ourselves without a guard?''

"I guess he's finally realized that we know there's no way to escape and he doesn't want to ride around with a car full of piglets. Will you come?''

"Are you kidding? Of course I'll come. I've got drain-cleaning duty today. Little pigs are kinda cute. At least in photos they are. We'll see about the real things.''

They set out briskly, Saigo's note authorizing them to be on the roads by themselves safely in the glove compartment. "Wouldn't it be fun to just drive around a bit first?'' Jane said. "Back in the States, my mother used to like to be taken for rides in the country on Sunday afternoons. I hated it. I had to take the subway to Brooklyn and borrow my brother's car and go clear back into the city to pick her up, then reverse the whole process at the end of the day. I was always so concerned about not hurting my brother's precious car that I was nervous the whole time. Now I'd love nothing better than to ride around aimlessly,'' Jane said wistfully.

"I don't think we dare. The note may be specific about where we're allowed to be. It's in Nip; I can't read it.''

"Still—drive slowly. Let's enjoy this as long as we can.''

Hazel didn't have to consult the little map Saigo had drawn. She knew the moment she first looked at it what village he meant and just where it was. They dawdled as long as they dared. Eventually they pulled into the kampong that was a cluster of native huts surrounding a large building with the characteristic Sumatran saddle-shaped roof. A native woman was sitting in front of it. On the ground next to her was a vast heap of grayish-pink flesh. She was keeping company with the most enormous sow either of them had ever laid eyes on.

"Oh, my God—'' Jane said, awed. "That thing's the size of Rhode Island.''

"It must be the mother of the piglets we're supposed to take back,'' Hazel said, hope draining away as she looked around for some sign of little pigs. She stopped the Oldsmobile, pulled on the hand brake, and got out. Approaching the woman, she repeated the Malay phrase Nancy had told her to say. It meant "Where is Saigo's pig?''

The native woman smiled and nodded and pointed to the gigantic sow.

"Oh, my God—" Jane repeated.

"Stop saying that and help me figure out what to do!" Hazel snapped.

Jane started giggling. "We could harness it up and ride it back. Or we could let it pull the car."

"Jane!"

"All right. All right. Let's see—why don't we tie a rope around its neck and let it walk along behind the car."

"It's a long way and uphill. The damned thing would probably have a heat stroke and we'd be in trouble for killing it."

"Do you mean we have to actually put it *in* the car?"

"I don't see what else we *can* do."

"But there isn't room. Not unless we walk and let it drive."

"Then we'll have to make room," Hazel said grimly. "If we fail at this errand, he'll never let me out again."

It took the whole morning. First Hazel got out the tool kit Saigo kept in the trunk and took off the back door and pulled out the backseat. Then some natives helped her build a ramp to run the sow up. The whole kampong got into the spirit of the thing, crowding around, laughing, talking, and getting in the way.

When it got to be the pig's turn to participate, however, they had a problem. The pig didn't like the idea of a ramp. Not one little bit. As soon as she was led forward and saw what she was meant to do, she sat down. Hard. The native woman prodded at her with a sharp stick and she let loose with a deafening shriek that made all the children go into gales of laughter. It took eight men, dragging, kicking, and screaming at the sow to get her back on all four trotters and onto the base of the ramp. Jane sat down on the ground a little ways off and laughed until she was hiccuping. Hazel wrung her hands and wondered if she'd get more satisfaction from killing Saigo or his goddamned pig—or maybe Jane.

The sow was finally shoved all the way into the Oldsmobile, and Hazel hastily set about putting the door back on its hinges. The pig kept thrashing around, squealing hideously the whole time. "Jane, get in, quick! Let's go before she tears the car up."

They were halfway back to camp before they remembered they'd left the backseat at the kampong and would have to go back for it. The whole car rocked wildly from the sow's efforts to escape, and they were nearly deafened by the noise she was making. As they pulled into camp, Hazel said, "Oh, Jesus! What's that smell?"

Jane stuck her head out the window for fresh air. "I think Madame Pig has done something extremely rude to us."

This time Hazel had to take the other door off the hinges because they didn't think they could make the sow back out. The creature kept trying to bite her the whole time she worked. The women and children of the camp gathered around, just as entertained and annoying as the villagers had been. Jane stood by, smacking the pig's snout with a switch every time it lunged for Hazel and screaming, "Stop it, you great big stupid bitch!"

When the sow finally lurched out of the backseat, she took off at a terrific clip. Jane and Hazel sat down on the ground, watching impassively as Saigo screamed at the guards to chase her.

"I never knew it was possible to have such personal hatred for an animal," Hazel said dully.

"Let's hose the shit out and go back for the seat, shall we?" Jane said. "There's one saving aspect of this. It gives us the excuse for another jaunt through the countryside."

Saigo didn't appear even to notice the lingering aura of pig and apparently was pleased with Hazel's work. When the sow delivered a half dozen piglets a week later, he actually gave one to House One as a reward for her efforts. This turned out to be a mixed blessing and not half as generous as it first appeared. The piglet, which was clearly the runt of the litter, should have been nursing, but they had to share their precious food supply with it and try to keep it alive on Miss Evans's soya bean concoctions while Saigo's piglets thrived on the extra mother's milk. House One's piglet survived only three weeks, and when they cooked up the little carcass, there was barely a bite of pork apiece.

But Hazel didn't much care. There was another benefit; Saigo now trusted her to run his errands. Every few days he'd send her off to one place or another, usually in a jeep, sometimes in the camp's big truck, and rarely in his precious car. Most often she was sent back and forth to the big camp with messages and mysterious parcels. She was also pressed into service delivering the seriously ill from the camp to the Dutch hospital and bringing back the few who actually got well. These were her favorite trips because she got to sit around and talk to people from other camps while she waited. This hospital was central to a number of men's and women's camps and was always full of new faces and new rumors.

Unfortunately, her relative freedom didn't sit well with many of the others. It was plain jealousy and she knew it, but it was still hard to be snubbed and criticized. The accusation of collaboration was tossed around pretty freely and it hurt her deeply. "My running a few errands isn't going to influence the war in the least!" she defended herself.

"Still, we have a duty to make every aspect of their lives as difficult as we can. Helping them is helping them, whether it's with big things or little things," one of her most vociferous critics claimed.

"You work in the rope factory, don't you?" Hazel came back. "That's helping them a lot more than my driving our own people to the hospital."

"Of course, but I have no choice. They make us work there."

"And they make me drive around. The only difference is that you hate the factory and I like the driving."

In spite of her conviction that she wasn't collaborating, Hazel was unhappy being involved in these disputes. She loathed confrontations. It was that unhappiness that caused her to make a decision she was later to regret. The next time she was sent to the godown by the big camp to pick up a part for the jeep, she sought out Mrs. Webber. "Your husband is in the big camp, isn't he? I'm supposed to take someone along to help carry things. Would you like to come with me? You might at least get a quick look at him."

Mrs. Webber was thrilled. She distributed her children among her friends in moments and rode along, babbling about how kind it was of Hazel to give her this opportunity. By sheer luck her husband was working in a garden behind the godown, and while Hazel dragged out the process of selecting the parts she needed, Mrs. Webber managed a few stolen words and kisses with her husband, to whom she'd not spoken for over two years. She cried all the way back to their camp and spent the next few days telling everybody who would listen what a wonderful person Hazel was.

It worked—too well. Hazel was soon being beseeched by women who'd never had the time to speak to her before. "I've heard that my husband is in the hospital. Please take me along next time you go."

"My fiancé might be in the big camp. If you'd just let me go along once, I promise I won't ask again."

"I got separated from my daughter and her baby at the very beginning. I just want to ask if anyone else has met her—"

And then there were her friends. "You took Jane for no reason. I want out of here for a few hours, too," Miss Evans said.

"I want to see if we can't trade some books with another camp. Everybody's read everything we have over and over again," Nancy Muir argued.

Hazel starting keeping lists in her head of all the promises and half promises she'd made.

On one memorable day in October, Gloria's turn came up. Hazel had hoped it never would. She didn't trust Gloria an inch, but had put her on the list out of secret gratitude for her not having started any fights about collaborating. Gloria had asked, on her own and Dr. Millichope's behalf, to go along on a hospital run in order to see if there were any organic chemistry books there they might borrow. An admirable reason and one that was confirmed by the doctor.

"I'm supposed to take Spike to the hospital this morning," she told Dinki with reluctance.

"Oh, good. I guess it's too much to hope the little bastard's dying—?"

"He's just got the squitters."

"Too bad. Could be the beginning of cholera or dysentery, though. I'll be ready in a shake."

"Now, Dinki, no tricks. Understand? We'll have a guard along, and I don't want to get in any trouble. Promise?"

"Cross my heart."

They set out in the jeep. Spike was in the back, bent over double and moaning every time they hit a pothole—which Hazel did as frequently as she could manage. They'd gone barely a mile when Spike made an especially pathetic noise and gestured to her to stop. *"Benjo! Benjo!"* he wailed. She pulled off to the side of the road, and he leapt out and ran frantically into the jungle to empty his agonized bowels.

"I don't know if he's contagious or what, but I feel a bit bad myself," Hazel said.

"He'll be a while. You can go on off the other side of the road," Gloria suggested.

"I think I will." Hazel climbed out, picked her way down the embankment, and stalked off into the dense jungle to find a private spot. It took her a few minutes to find a tree to lean against and some leaves that would serve as toilet paper. When she returned, she heard Spike long before she saw him. He was screaming at the top of his lungs.

As she came up the embankment, she saw all too well what had upset him so. The jeep was sitting right where she'd left it, but Gloria was no longer in it—and the tires were no longer on it. Somebody had stolen all four of them. As she reached the road, she heard Gloria thrashing along behind her. "What the hell is the matter with him?" she asked as she emerged from the jungle. "Oh, my God. How bloody grand!"

"It's not bloody grand. Why didn't you stay with the jeep?"

"I had to go, too."

Hazel looked at her suspiciously, but Gloria looked as innocent as a newborn baby—if a great deal more amused.

They had to walk back to the camp. Spike dashed off into the jungle every few hundred yards and came back pale and shaking. When he reported to Saigo, he apparently got the full blame for the incident.

"How come he didn't manage to pin it on us?" Gloria wondered out loud that evening as they were getting ready for lights out.

"I guess he just didn't have the energy left," Hazel said.

"Oh, Miss Evans. There you are," Gloria said as the older woman came into the house. "I've got something for you." She fished in her halter top and pulled out a sweat-soaked wad of bills. "Here, buy some eggs from the peddlers for the children, will you?"

Hazel sat for a long moment with her mouth open, then leapt at Gloria. "Where did you get that money!"

Gloria grinned at her. "I sold the tires, of course. As soon as you left, a carload of natives came along. They worked like those guys at the speed races. I've never seen anything like it. Zip, zip, zip and they were gone. Tires and all. Then I plunged into the undergrowth and circled around behind you."

"Oh, hell! I knew I shouldn't have let you come along."

"Why not? It was the most profitable trip you ever made. Wasn't it?"

A week later Hazel was sent to the hospital again. This time she refused to even consider taking Gloria. She didn't want to take anybody but the ill woman, but as soon as the word got out that she was going somewhere, she was surrounded. Agreeing, reluctantly, to take along a girl named Dotty Quentin, she reported to Saigo to get the keys to the jeep. But the jeep was still missing a tire and he ordered her to take the Oldsmobile.

The pig smell might not have bothered him, but the women, especially the sick one, were nearly overwhelmed with it. "Oh, God, this stinks!" Dotty said, opening the door.

"You don't have to come along," Hazel remarked caustically.

"Sorry. I won't say anything more about it," Dotty replied, breathing through her mouth.

"Where's Hazel?" Gloria asked Elise.

Elise was cleaning the porch of their house with a rag and a tin pan of water. "She took Mrs. Humber to the hospital."

"Then she must not have left yet. The jeep's sitting in front of Saigo's house."

"No, they went in his car. Don't walk on the part I've just done, Dinki."

"They took his car? Oh, damn!"

Elise put down the rag and looked up. "What have you done to his car?"

Gloria sat down on the step and put her head in her hands. "I've been putting pebbles in the gas tank for two weeks so he'd run out of gas."

"Dinki!"

"Well, he almost never lets Hazel drive it! How was I to know?"

They delivered Mrs. Humber without incident. As they started back Dotty said, "Hazel, you know where that camp is just off this road?"

"I think so," Hazel said warily.

"Could we go near there? Just so I could look for a minute."

"Afraid not, Dotty."

"Hazel, please. You don't even need to get close. Just near enough so I could sneak up and look for a minute. Leslie—that's my fiancé—is in that camp. We've been paying natives to take notes back and forth, but I haven't heard from him in two months and I'm afraid he's ill."

"But you couldn't learn anything just from looking at the camp."

"I might. If I saw him there, I'd know he was well. Maybe he just ran out of money to pay the natives. Oh, Hazel, it would make all the difference in my life."

"Dotty, I really can't—"

"Oh, Hazel." She started to cry. "You're engaged to a boy back home, aren't you? Imagine if he were here, just a few miles away, and you didn't know if he was alive or dead."

It brought Hazel up with a start. Frank. She hadn't even thought about Frank for days.

"Even if I don't get any word of him, I could get word *to* him. Maybe my notes aren't getting to him and he's worried about me. Hazel, I've sold everything of any value that I brought in. This is my last chance to contact him. It means so much."

"Oh, all right! All right!" Hazel said, hating herself for giving in but knowing she'd hate herself more if she didn't. She turned off on the side road that led to the men's camp. When she thought she was almost to it, she pulled off into the jungle, where the car would be concealed from passing traffic, should there be any. "Which way do I go?" Dotty asked.

"I'll show you," Hazel said. She wasn't about to turn Dotty loose to come back whenever the fancy took her. She had a bad feeling about all this—she felt both frightened and put upon.

They struggled through the undergrowth for a few hundred yards until they came within sight of the camp. "There he is!" Dotty said in a suppressed shriek as a man with his arm bound in a sling walked through the center of the compound.

"Be quiet! Now, let's go."

"That's why he hasn't written. Poor Leslie—"

"Come on!" Hazel dragged her away, hushing and rushing her. They hopped in the car and Hazel pulled back onto the packed earth track. Hazel was sweating and felt sick. As they neared the intersection with the main road between the hospital and their own camp, the Oldsmobile started chugging and lurching.

"What's the matter with the car?" Dotty asked, still in a haze of happiness over having found her fiancé alive and almost well.

"I don't know," Hazel said, hunching forward and willing the car to keep going.

It sputtered up a slight rise and stopped at the top. Hazel slammed the gearshift into neutral and turned the ignition key. A feeble attempt to turn over, then nothing.

"What's the matter with it?" Dotty repeated. She was alarmed now, too.

"It's acting like it's out of gas, but the gauge reads full," Hazel said, her voice shaking. "That's odd, though. We've gone miles. Why would it still read full? Dear God, there must be something wrong with the gauge. Get out, Dotty, we've got to push it to the main road. It's bad enough being broken down, but we can't be caught here!"

Dotty suddenly realized what a bad position they were in and did as she was told.

"I'll steer as I push," Hazel said, positioning herself at the open driver's door with one hand on the frame and the other on the steering wheel. "We have to get up as much speed as we can or we won't make it up that next hill. Dotty, push for all you're worth or we're dead."

Fear gave them the necessary strength. The Oldsmobile went creeping, then rolling, then charging down the hill. As soon as it started losing momentum on the way up the next rise, the two young women pushed until they thought their hearts would burst. The car just crested the top. Hazel pulled on the hand brake and they collapsed, gasping and sweating. They'd rested only a few seconds, however, when Dotty said, "Oh, God! There's a lorry coming!"

Hazel leapt to her feet, her mind churning. Completely apart from the problem of being somewhere they weren't authorized to be, if they were found pushing the car, they'd look like they'd stolen it. There was nothing to do but try to brazen it out. She ran to the front of the car, lifted the hood, and leaned over the motor. Dotty followed suit and asked frantically, "What are you doing?"

She received no answer. The truck approached and slowed to a stop. A Japanese soldier got out of the passenger side, came around, and started shouting questions at them while he waved a handgun around.

Hazel turned around and bowed to him. He shrieked some more questions and she answered him in halting Japanese accompanied by a lot of helpless shrugs. He stared at her for a long moment before he and the driver burst into laughter. Without another word he got in the truck and they roared off, still laughing.

"What did you say to him?" Dotty asked.

"I—I don't know. I was trying to say a wire had come apart

in the car I was driving for Saigo. That's obviously not how it translated. God only knows what I actually said. Let's push it again.''

They got the Oldsmobile to the main road and had the good fortune that a transport truck came along a few minutes later with Mickey in it. With his help, they hitched the Olds to the back and towed it back to camp. Dotty rode in the transport with Mickey, Hazel in the car itself.

She kept saying to herself, ''Never again! Never, never, never again.''

Gloria was on her way to the bathhouse when Elise found her. ''Hazel's back. She ran out of gas and had to be towed.''

''Did you tell her?'' Gloria asked.

''No, I think you should.''

''I can't. I just can't. You tell her. Then, later, when she's not so mad, I'll talk to her.''

''But Dinki, that's not right—''

''I don't care what's bloody right! I'm sick of everybody always nattering on about right and wrong. 'Cause it's always me that's wrong. I said I'll talk to her later and I will.''

Gloria managed to avoid Hazel until darkness fell and she tried to sneak back into House One. Rather than having a quiet moment to explain herself, she found herself facing the whole population of the house having a meeting. ''Come in. We've just been talking about you, Dinki,'' Peggy said to her.

''I can imagine,'' Gloria said.

''Actually, that's not quite true,'' Hazel said coldly. ''I mentioned you only in passing, but I want you to hear the rest of what I have to say. Sit down.''

Gloria was astonished. This wasn't the old Hazel. She sat down as she was told.

''I want you all to understand something,'' Hazel went on. ''I'm through taking people along when I'm sent places. Never again! If other people want to risk their lives, I don't care, but they're not dragging me into it. Because of Dinki's trick with the gas tank and my own soft heart in taking Dotty to the men's camp, I nearly got in terrible trouble. By sheer luck the Japs who found us chose to laugh at us instead of shooting us. But it was just luck.''

''Hazel, I—''

"Shut up, Dinki. I'm not through. Everybody's been taking advantage of me and I let them. I went along with things that I knew better than to do because I didn't want people to dislike me, but I realized today that I want to stay alive more than I want to be liked. Far more. And I'm going to do everything I can to survive this. You can call me any names you want and it's not going to make the least bit of difference. I'll drive the people I'm ordered to drive. When I have to take somebody along of my own choice, it's going to be Nancy Muir because she speaks Nip. That's it!" She sat down abruptly, her face flushed and her breath coming quickly. She refused to meet anybody's eye.

Peggy, sitting cross-legged on the floor, got up. She glanced at Hazel briefly with a faint smile and then addressed the group. "We have other business to conduct before we can adjourn. As you know, my term as House One representative to the camp council expires this week. As depressing and—we all hope—unnecessary it is to elect someone for the next six-month term—"

There was a chorus of groans and mutterings.

"—we need to get on with our election. I'll take nominations from the floor."

"I wonder if the parliamentarian who thought of the phrase 'from the floor' had in mind a bunch of women literally sitting around on the floor?" Jane Kowolski said. "I nominate Hazel Hampton."

"I second!" Gloria said.

"Are there other nominations?" Peggy asked. "No? Then Hazel will be house leader and camp council representative."

Hazel was stunned. As soon as the meeting broke up, she wandered outside to puzzle on it. Peggy followed her. "Congratulations, Hazel."

"I don't understand, Peggy. House leaders were always chosen for age, experience, and strength of personality. People like you and Mrs. Smith and Dr. Millichope. Why me?"

"Don't you really know? I think it's because you grew up before our very eyes tonight."

"I didn't 'grow up.' I just got fed up."

Peggy took her hand and patted it. "Sometimes that's what growing up means, Hazel."

Chapter 26

September 1944

My dearest Jim,

I wonder why I bother with this letter. This endless, whining letter you'll probably never see. I risk my life and possibly the lives of my friends to keep it going. I tell myself there is a noble cause here. "That they should remember" and all that sort of high-flown philosophy. The truth is far more selfish. I write this to keep reminding myself who I am—or who I was. To the enemy and the natives who sometimes gawk at us, I'm just another scrawny, tired, cranky, frightened, half-sick old woman. I'm dirty about ten cells down. I think it would take a week's soak in lye soap to get me clean again. My hair looks like it's been styled with a pair of hedgeclippers. The dress I wear most of the time (as opposed to my "good" one, which I wear on Sundays and special occasions. Oh, yes, we do have special occasions. We invent them!) has more patch than original.

I was once healthy, well-groomed, serene, and intelligent. A woman who was sure of herself. Proud of herself. Was that just a surface thing that's been worn away, perhaps never to return? Or was it something essential, something the dirt and weariness have merely covered up temporarily? Only when I write to you am I assured of feeling like that woman I once was. And so, I keep on writing and trying to convince myself it's for the good of mankind.

And I keep on thinking of getting free. Though it's getting harden to believe in. Two years and nine months! God! It

*makes my empty stomach heave and hurt to write the words.
The odd thing isn't that we've adjusted. It's how well we've
adjusted. I used to wonder about people who came as foreigners to our country and remained steadfastly uninfluenced
by it. The Germantowns and Chinatowns of America seemed
peculiar to me. Almost insulting. I wondered why people
wished to maintain their old culture to such an extent, and
how they did so. But we've done the same. We've recreated
our own Western culture in the jungle.*

*We have schools—good ones, you'd be impressed—and just
had a high school graduation of five girls I'd put up against
my American students any day. We have our clubs and committees and social rankings—never mind the committees deal
with things like shoveling out the open sewage drains or cart-
ing the corpses of our friends to the cemetery and digging the
graves ourselves. We've adapted all the social and moral
principles of the church rummage sale to the distribution of
vegetable scraps to those suffering beriberi. Sometimes I'm
agog with self-admiration about this. Sometimes it makes me
want to weep.*

*We, like the people in the pockets of foreign culture in
America, have done this for survival and because it's the one
way we know how to conduct our lives. Except for the bowing
and the occasional tedious, translated lecture on the superiority of all things Nippon, the enemy has made remarkably
little effort to impose their culture on us. I suppose you'd have
to say they're simply neglecting us to death. I think nothing
would please them more than some effective little plague that
eliminated us without putting them to any trouble. . . .*

Hazel found Nancy Muir giving an impromptu lecture to a
few of their housemates. "The difference between us is primar-
ily the difference between guilt and shame."

"Pretty much the same thing, if you ask me," Gloria said.

"Not at all. Guilt makes us do what we believe right whether
anyone else knows about it or not. Our obligation as Westerners
is to our conscience. But shame has entirely to do with others.
The whole of Japanese culture depends on everybody knowing
all the rules and appearing to follow them. If you are seen to
break the rules, you are shamed before others."

"I still don't get it," Gloria said.

"Suppose the Americans are making a movie and so are the

Japanese. Same story beginning. Young lovers who want to marry in spite of their parents' objections. The 'right' ending for a Western audience is the young lovers breaking with convention, taking their happiness at all costs. Right? But the Japanese would be appalled at such an ending. To them, the 'right' ending is for the young lovers to give each other up out of obedience to their families. That is how they show honor and virtue.''

"Well, I think—''

Nancy didn't even listen to Gloria's opinion. "Are you looking for me, Hazel?''

"I'm taking a parcel to the main camp. Will you come with me?'' Hazel asked Nancy.

"Could you give me a minute to pick up some books to trade with their library?'' Nancy asked.

She asked the same question every time Hazel requested her to come along and she was prepared for it. "I can only wait a minute. Saigo's in a hurry to have this box taken over.''

A few moments later they were on the road. Nancy was bracing herself against the dashboard with one hand and trying to keep the now-tattered books from sliding off her lap with the other. Hazel was driving in zigzags to avoid the holes in the road. "It gets worse every week. They have the men out working on it more often than they used to, but it doesn't seem to help. I wonder if that's a sign of anything. Sorry,'' she added as they bounced violently.

"The war can't be going well for them or it wouldn't have gone on so long,'' Nancy said.

"More than two and a half years,'' Hazel said, slowing down a little for a particularly rough patch of road. "Who would have thought? I suppose it's a good thing we didn't suspect how long it would be when we were first captured. Although—sometimes I think that's the worst thing about all of this. Not knowing how much longer it will be. Most awful things have a time limit—like having to take college physics. No matter how terrible the first week is, you say to yourself, 'In eight months and three weeks this will be over.' Then a month later you get to say, 'Now it's only seven months and three weeks.' But with this, we don't know. Even if it were going to be years and years yet, I think I'd rather know how many so that I can start looking forward to the end of it with a specific goal in mind.''

They jolted along another half mile before Nancy said, "I

suppose that ties in with what I think is the worst—what I hate is how we've accepted it. Not even knowingly most of the time, but in little ways.'' She held up a book as an example. ''I lend books back and forth to the other camps for several months at a time. That's my inadvertent acceptance of the fact that we'll still be here then. In fact, when you were elected as house leader, I found myself thinking that maybe I'd put my name forward next time. Then I realized to my horror that next time is six months from now.''

Hazel nodded. ''You're right. To think consciously of being here that much longer is devastating, and yet we do it unconsciously all the time. But I'm not sure that's a bad thing. Remember that first camp, the one in the jail? We were awful then. We wasted what we had because we had no idea we'd be here long enough to need it. We were rude to people we thought we'd never have to see again instead of realizing we'd live with them for years.''

''You weren't rude,'' Nancy corrected her. ''You were a peacemaker. You still are—most of the time. But I was very rude to you. I do regret that.''

''There's no need,'' Hazel said, and yet she was gratified that after all this time Nancy Muir had finally unbent enough to offer an apology. Even after years of enforced community living, Nancy was reserved and private, almost secretive. Except around Elise. Around Elise she was quite human.

They rode in silence a little longer and then Hazel asked, ''What will you do when we're liberated?''

The question took Nancy by surprise. It was something she didn't often let herself think about. She knew Hazel was asking about the long term, but she said, ''I'll have to find Elise's people first thing.''

''But what about you. What will you do? You didn't leave any family behind in Japan?''

''There was only my father and me, and he died before the war started. I have cousins in California, but I've never met them. I don't know what I can do. I have no valuable skills, and I certainly haven't acquired any here.''

''Maybe you could work for the government. With your knowledge of Japanese and all the international 'sorting out' that will go on, I bet you'd be useful.''

''Perhaps. I'd never thought about that—'' Nancy said, preoccupied. Actually, there was another scenario that she lived with. Lived for. But while she and Hazel had grown closer lately, they weren't close enough to share it. She was afraid Hazel would laugh at her.

They pulled up to the main gate of the big camp compound. Beyond the gates there were five different camps; one for British soldiers, one for Dutch soldiers, one for nuns, one for civilian men, and one for women and children. All were partitioned from each other so there was the least possible mingling. Nancy and Hazel had come often enough that guards didn't challenge them much nowadays. The gates were opened and they were waved in. "Did you notice the doors on that big godown were open?" Hazel said to Nancy in an undertone. "It looked half empty. Do you suppose they're moving things somewhere else or are they just running out?"

"I hope they're not running out, because you know who will be the most deprived. Us."

They went to the block of buildings that served as the Japanese administrative center for the camp complex. The camp commandant ordered them to sit down while he opened Saigo's parcel. It was full of paperwork. He glanced through, then told them they would have to wait. Nancy spoke to him briefly and he nodded, scowling fiercely. "He needs to fill those papers in, and we are to wait," Nancy explained to Hazel. "He says I may go to the gate of the civilian men's camp if I come right back. You're to come with me."

She actually sounds disappointed, Hazel thought. *But surely I'm imagining things. Why wouldn't she want me along?*

They walked through the central open area which had once resembled a grassy playing field and was now merely packed earth with occasional patches of mud. Hazel was surprised that Nancy seemed to know exactly where she was going and commented on it.

"I've come here before when you were getting parts for the vehicles," Nancy said. They reached the main gate, where a remarkably old Japanese soldier stood guard. Several men inside the camp had seen their approach and clustered around. Nancy spoke to the guard. He shrugged with an expression between disgust and indifference. Nancy then spoke to one of the men, a boy of about twenty wearing almost indecently tattered shorts. "I'm Miss Muir. Will you tell Mr. Dreyer I've come with books to trade?"

"Herb Dreyer? Let me see if I can find him," the man she'd

addressed said. While he was speaking to Nancy, he didn't take his eyes off Hazel. She was embarrassed and vaguely flattered.

They waited, not speaking. In fact, Nancy was not speaking in a noticeable manner, ostentatiously looking around as though intensely interested in her surroundings. Too interested to spare words. Hazel had an odd feeling there was something going on with her, but hadn't a clue to what it might be.

"Where you ladies from?" one of the men inside the fence asked. Hazel struck up a conversation with him, but the guard found this unacceptable and ran him off. Hazel was left to study the men in the compound. Most of her errands took her to the big godown or to the administrative headquarters. She seldom saw much of the camps themselves. It was a depressing sight. The men were even more dirty, tattered, and thinner than the women. There also seemed to be a greater number of them with injuries, presumably from harder forced work and more severe punishments.

After about ten minutes a clerkish-looking man of about forty came hurrying across the center of the camp compound. He held a dozen books in his thin arms. He had a round face, a broad smile, and glasses that had one lens shattered but still in place. One earpiece was attached with a bent piece of wire. "Miss Muir! Have you got—? Oh," he added when he spotted Hazel.

"Mr. Herbert Dreyer, this is Hazel Hampton."

"Hello, Miss Hampton. Miss Muir's told me all about you. Pleased to meet you," he said.

"How do you do, Mr. Dreyer."

The wizened guard barked on order and jabbed at Herbert with his fist. Herbert got busy shoving books between the strands of barbed wire to Nancy, then she did the same. Hazel watched closely. It was obviously a familiar routine, just as they were obviously familiar to each other. When the trade was completed, Nancy and Herbert stood staring at each other for a long moment.

"Nancy, we better get back to the commandant's office," Hazel said.

"Yes, yes. Of course. I'm—I'm so glad you managed to locate that Edna Ferber for us, Mr. Dreyer. I've had a lot of people ask for it."

The guard took another swipe at Mr. Dreyer, who dodged it and backed away. "See you again, Miss Muir. Soon, I hope," he said. Nancy smiled and waved self-consciously, almost dropping all the books in the process.

When they were on their way back along the main road, Hazel said, "Mr. Dreyer seems to be a nice man."

"Very nice," Nancy said.

Hazel glanced at her. Was she blushing? "You know him well?"

"We—we were on the ship together leaving Singapore, and I've run across him several times here. Lately, of course, we've been trading books."

"You like him, don't you?" Hazel asked bluntly.

Nancy was growing more and more disconcerted by the conversation. "He's—he's a nice person."

"Are you in love with him?"

"Hazel! Really!" She looked like she might jump out of the jeep in a moment to avoid Hazel's questions.

"What's wrong with that? Aside from the fact that it's none of my business," she added with a smile. "You are, aren't you?" Hazel had always thought of Miss Muir as a confirmed spinster. Suddenly Hazel felt that she was the older, wiser one and Miss Muir was a green girl.

"What could anybody know about being in love in this place? In these circumstances?" Nancy said defensively.

"As much as they could know anyplace else, I think. There's nothing wrong with it, you know. In fact, it's quite nice. I'm glad for you. That is—he's not married, or anything, is he?"

"He's a widower. His wife died two years before we were captured."

"What did she die of?" Hazel asked, testing a theory.

"Peritonitis. Her appendix burst."

"I see. No children?"

"No. One miscarriage."

Hazel nodded. She'd been right in guessing that Nancy knew her Herbert very well indeed. How had they managed to get that well acquainted? Not in the process of shoving books through the wire under the watchful, impatient eye of a guard. Hazel was so engrossed in her thoughts that she failed to see a hole, and the right tires hit it so hard there was a grinding metallic sound. "Hell! I hope that didn't break anything," she said, stopping to look. As she examined the vehicle, she kept talking. "The first time I met Dinki was when she was stuck along the side of the road with a truck that had a ruptured gas tank. She was bringing wounded soldiers down from upcountry and one got sick all over me. At the time, I thought that was the worst thing that could happen to a person. But since then I've learned—"

She kept on chattering, and Nancy used the opportunity to surreptitiously flip through the pages of the Ferber novel. Toward the end, and jammed into the crack between two pages, there was a flimsy scrap of paper. "Road crew Tues. Meet in same place. Love, H." Nancy rolled the tiny paper into a hard little pellet and flung it into the jungle as she got out to see what Hazel was doing.

"Don't think anything's broken. What are you smiling about, Nancy?"

There were furious goings-on when they got back to camp. A crowd of House One residents were on the porch. "What's wrong?" Hazel asked.

"When the rice ration came today it was cut by a quarter," Jane Kowolski explained, her face creased with worry as she watched Vivian and her friends scratching out a hopscotch pattern in the road. "Miss Evans thought it was a mistake and went to tell Saigo about it. He got furious and told her it was all our fault because we weren't obedient women and all that crap. Then he told her the worst. Instead of giving a fourth of our vegetables we grow to the guards, we have to give them half. Half! We hardly have enough as it is."

"The sodding bastards have been trying to starve us to death for nearly three years and now they're going to do it with a vengeance!" Gloria said.

Peggy was sitting on the steps with her head tilted forward so that Miss Evans could trim the back of her hair with their one dull pair of nail scissors. "I keep telling you there's a bright side to this if you'll only look. They aren't 'trying' to starve us." Her voice was muffled, but they all listened. "They don't *mind* if that happens, but they're not *trying*. It means they're in deep trouble. And if they're in trouble, it could mean we're very close to winning the war."

They all fell silent for a moment, and then Jane asked, "What'll happen to us? When it's over?"

"We'll all go home, you dope!" Gloria said.

"Will we?" Jane asked in a very quiet voice. "Will they let us?"

No one answered her.

* * *

Hazel climbed up in the rafters that night and brought down the silk scarf in which all her mother's jewelry had been sewn so long ago. The scarf, once white, had been around her waist for most of the first year and a half of their imprisonment and had turned a filthy grayish-yellow. When Hazel got a fungus infection around her waist, she gave up wearing the scarf and had found a spot in the rafters of the house to hide it. Now she dragged it down, unfolded it, and looked at what she had.

There was a cameo brooch she suspected was valuable but had never liked. Might the natives like it well enough to trade her food for it? There were several rings: her own engagement ring with the tiny chip of diamond, her mother's engagement ring with the enormous diamond, and the matching wedding band. Those she'd die before she'd trade away. There was a square-cut amethyst in a silver setting that had belonged to her great-grandmother on her father's side. It was probably very valuable for both its intrinsic and its antique value. It wouldn't be right to trade away something like that for a basket of sweet potatoes or a bucket of shriveled cucumbers. Another ring was one she remembered from childhood, a dinner ring with a big topaz surrounded by pearls. Her mother had worn it sometimes with a brownish-gold silk dress Hazel loved. It looked like an enormous daisy and Mother had said Hazel could have it when she grew up.

"Well, now I'm grown-up," Hazel said out loud, her eyes filling with tears.

She sniffed and pulled herself together. What about the gaudy silver and turquoise ring and matching thunderbird pin her mother had bought on a trip to New Mexico? That would be a good set to dispose of. Flashy and of more apparent value that real worth. No important memories associated with it. At least, none of her own. She'd never know now what it might have meant to her mother. That was only one of the millions of things she wished she'd had the opportunity to ask Roberta.

She glanced over the rest of the jewelry. A tarnished silver bracelet with tiny garnets in each link. That had been her tenth birthday present. She liked it, but not enough to starve to death to keep it. A very valuable string of pearls, a "keeper." A rhinestone choker. A woven gold chain necklace. Funny, she couldn't remember if that had been hers or her mother's. Her own Kappa pin. She smiled at that. Sorority girl. How different that society of women had been from the one that was her life now. Their greatest concern then had been whether they'd have a date by Friday night; now she lived with women who worried whether they'd still be alive by Friday night. She pulled the silver and turquoise ring and pin loose, tucked them into her halter top, and wrapped the rest back up to put away.

Elise came into House One late Tuesday afternoon. She was pale and clutching a wad of fabric in her hand. "Miss Muir, could I talk to you, please."

Nancy was making a pair of shorts out of her allotment of black fabric that had been a nun's habit until the sister died the day before. She glanced up and noticed how pale the girl was. "Of course, dear."

"Outside, please."

They walked to a relatively private spot between their house and the Hall. A road crew was working outside the front of the camp, and most of the women who were not at work in the factory were by the fence, filling their senses with the sight of men. Nancy never went to watch. She couldn't bear it when the men were abused and berated in front of an audience. Sitting down in the shade of a small bush, Elise said, "I think—well, I don't know, but—I just went to the latrine and—"

She unfolded the fabric. It was one of her three pairs of dingy, ragged panties. There was a dark stain on the crotch.

"Oh, my dear Elise," Nancy said matter-of-factly. "You mustn't be upset. You've started to menstruate."

"I thought that was it, but I hear the grown-ups say they've all stopped. And I wondered—"

"I imagine your hormones are just at a higher pitch than the rest of us. Most of us still have the occasional period, and I wouldn't expect you'll get regular as long as we're here."

"Does this mean I'm a woman now?"

Nancy smiled. "I think just being here has made you more of a woman than anything your body might do. Elise, do you know—uh, do you know what this is all really about? Periods? Sex?"

"I think so. I mean, I hear things and—"

"But your mother never told you? No, of course not. There was no need then. All right." She drew a deep breath. God! She never expected to have to explain this to anyone. In a louder voice than she intended, she said, "Do you know what a man's penis is?"

A woman walking by with a shovel stopped, then went on, covering her smile with a fake cough.

Elise blushed furiously. "It's one of those things between their legs, isn't it? I've seen the guards when they're bathing and the little boys here have tiny ones."

Oh, dear! Nancy thought. Gathering her wits for a moment, she proceeded with a very clinical explanation of the biology of reproduction. When she finally paused to draw breath, Elise said, "That sounds awful! You have to do all that every time you want to have a baby?"

"My dear, I've explained badly. It's not awful at all, and people do it for pleasure, not just to have babies. I mean, married people who love and trust each other."

"No!"

"Yes. You see, that's one of the things that makes marriage very special: that something that sounds so awkward and silly and even distasteful becomes a joy and a blessing. It's a miracle of sorts, I think. When you're grown and meet a man you really love, who loves you, you'll understand."

"Miss Muir, you weren't ever married. How do you know all this?"

Nancy smiled and put her arm around the girl. "I listen to the grown-ups talk, too, Elise."

"Do you think—well, I know we're not really related, but Vivian calls Miss Kowolski Aunt Jane and I wondered if I might call you Aunt Nancy?"

"My dear child, I would love that beyond anything else."

It was an overcast night with a light drizzle. Nancy was afraid she'd get lost, but nothing would stop her. Herbert would be waiting. She crept out of the house and around behind the guards' quarters to avoid passing beneath the light in front of Saigo's house. Under the barbed wire, then along the road. She heard a vehicle coming and leapt into the ditch along the side, praying there weren't leeches in the stagnant water. Of all the nasty things she'd gotten used to, she still went nearly berserk over leeches. The truck passed and she came back onto the road, glad she couldn't see her feet. If she'd picked up a leech she was better off not knowing about it. Ahead, there was a tall, gnarled tree just off to the side of the road. She crossed and picked her way gingerly, silently, through the undergrowth. "Herbert?" she whispered.

"Here, Nancy," a voice came back.

A moment later she was in his arms.

They were thin, dirty, hungry, and lying on spongy ground in the rain, but none of it mattered. "I didn't think I could still do it," Herbert said with some wonder as he rolled onto his side and put his hand to her breast.

Nancy turned to meet him. Their lips brushed. "It wouldn't have mattered."

"No, it really wouldn't, would it? Nancy, how can you risk your life this way for the likes of me?"

"For the love of you," she said softly. "Oh, Herbert, I want this war to be over. I want to make love with you in a bed with clean sheets. I want to come to you with freshly washed hair and fresh breath."

"You will. Someday. Come on, sit up, Nancy. You have to go back. So do I."

She felt around on the ground for her clothes.

"They say the Allies have taken Paris back," Herbert said, pulling on his shorts.

"Paris is a long way from here."

"The Americans are supposed to have taken part of New Guinea and are bombing Iwo Jima."

"Where's Iwo Jima?" Nancy asked, finally getting up the courage to feel her feet for leeches. There weren't any.

"I have no idea. I didn't risk asking. If the natives tell us they've taken it, I'll inquire."

"Do you think any of these rumors are true?" Nancy said, standing up.

Herbert put his arms around her. "I hope so. I think there must be something in them. I don't think the natives know anything more than we do about places like Iwo Jima. They must be hearing it on a radio someplace."

"The women believe—or like to try to believe—that some of our own men are in the jungle."

"We hear that, too. Fellows do occasionally make a break for it. They're usually dragged back and—" He stopped, not having meant to talk about the ones who didn't get away with it.

"And what?" Nancy asked.

"Tortured to death. With everybody having to stand at attention and watch it."

"Which is what would happen to you if we were caught here."

"And you."

"No, I'd be strung up to a post for a day or two as an example, then shot if I were still alive. They did that to one woman who tried to get away. Poor thing was mad to even try it."

"As you are mad."

She heard a new note in his voice, a note of determination that chilled her.

"Nancy, I've been thinking about us."

"I think of nothing else."

"But you do. You think of Elise. But you should think more of her and of yourself."

"Herbert, no. Don't say anything more—"

"Nancy, I have to. If we survive this, we have our whole lives ahead of us. But we won't survive taking these chances. We've been lucky, but that kind of luck is in short supply around here. I have an awful premonition that we've used it up."

"Herbert, don't—"

"We can't meet again."

"I'd die without seeing you."

"Shhh. You're in more danger of dying from seeing me. You're not a frivolous girl, Nancy. You know the risk we've taken these last few months. And it's not just a risk to us. Elise needs you. She's lost her whole family. She can't lose you. And neither can I."

"Herbert, we've been careful, if we go on—"

"The rumors are flying. The food's been cut back. The Japs are nervous, and you know when they get nervous they start those middle-of-the-night *tenko*s. Your camp might be having one right now. No amount of care can protect us."

Nancy was shaking with frustration. "You're right. I know you're right. Dammit it all! But what if—"

"If we die without meeting again?" he asked bluntly. "Then we have to remember what extraordinarily good luck it was that we ever met. That we've been able to see each other occasionally over these last months. And we'll still meet at the camp when you come with Hazel."

"But not to touch—?"

"To remember touch, Nancy. I'll walk to the road with you now."

Chapter 27

Dear Jim,
We hear the Allies are taking France back from Hitler. But what of us? What about Southeast Asia? Are we forgotten?

Hazel came to breakfast with a chicken under her arm.

"A friend of yours?" Peggy asked her.

Hazel held the chicken up for inspection. It was a scrawny thing with a bald patch on its side. "A laying hen. I traded some jewelry for her. But my official story is that she wandered in through the wire and I adopted her."

"So you succumbed to the chicken mania," Gloria said. "This place is starting to look and sound like a barnyard."

"The string on her leg's a leash? What are you going to feed her?" Sister Maria asked, putting a protective hand over the top of her bowl of rice.

"Feed her? She's a wild animal—more or less. She'll go around and eat whatever chickens eat."

"What a farm girl you'd make!" Peggy said with a laugh. "Chickens are domesticated. That means they eat what people feed them. And she certainly can't forage for herself on a three-foot leash."

"Hell! Do you mean I've got to share my food with the beast? Well, I suppose for an egg a day it's worth it—" Hazel said doubtfully. She tied the chicken to the leg of the bench and gave it a dollop of her rice. Looking sadly at what was left, she wondered how she'd find the energy to get through most of a day on that. But tomorrow the hen would lay an egg and she would boil it and eat that with her rice. Maybe scrambled. Or poached. And she'd smash up the shell and add it to her soya milk for the calcium. Gritty but healthy. She was having a hard time remembering what an egg actually tasted like. It had been years since she had more than a tiny shred of egg. As she ate her rice, a grain at a time to make it last, she thought about some of the eggs she'd eaten before she was incarcerated.

From spring through fall there was a farmer who came to Evanston and called on the Hamptons and a number of other families along the lakefront. He always had fresh brown eggs with the fruit and vegetables. Mother bought a lot of eggs from him. In the summer she'd boil them up late at night to keep from making the house hot. Then they'd have them sliced with mayonnaise in sandwiches, cut into quarters in potato salad, and sometimes cooked in a sauce and poured over fresh asparagus. Oh, God, that was good! Often, too, she and Barbara would eat them as snacks out of hand with just a sprinkle of salt and pepper.

"So who do you think did it?" Gloria asked. "Hazel?"

"I'm sorry. I wasn't listening. I was thinking about eggs."

"Then think about the piano."

"The piano?" Hazel looked over toward the corner at the beat-up, ancient piano that they'd found in the storeroom and restored. At least they'd tried to restore it. It was old and abused to begin with and had suffered greatly from the climate. "What's wrong with it?"

"That's what we've been talking about, if you'd pay attention. It's a first-class mystery," Sister Maria explained patiently. "The night before last Nancy Muir used it for practice with the choral group and it was working. Yesterday nobody had time for it, and this morning most of the straps holding the hammers are cut."

"Who would do that?"

"Oh, Hazel! That's the point," Gloria said. "Who, indeed. We're all trying to be Agatha Christie. I think it was the damned Japs who did it just for the hell of it. To keep us from having anything to enjoy."

"Dinki, they wouldn't bother," Maria said. "They're too stupid anyway to figure out how to sabotage it. If they'd done it, they'd have hauled it into the middle of the compound and smashed it up in front of us to make the point. This is much too subtle for them."

The chicken had finished its rice and was now pecking at Hazel's toenails. Hazel glared at it, pulled her feet up, and sat cross-legged. The chicken sat down and clucked contentedly. Hazel said, "I think Maria's right. Who are the other suspects?"

"My theory is that the cooking crew did it," Peggy said. "They're the ones who have to hear it all the time. If I had to listen day in and day out to children being taught to play a piano, I'd kill the piano. Even if it sounded decent, which this one didn't."

Hazel smiled. "This is fun. I've got a suspect. You know those two missionaries in House Eight who are always complaining about how we sing secular music instead of hymns as we should be singing—"

"Oh, that's good," Gloria said, rubbing her hands. Then her smile faded. "No go. They were on duty at the factory with me yesterday."

"That doesn't matter. Whoever did it didn't risk doing it in broad daylight when the cooking crew was in and out. It was a sneaky, middle-of-the-night deal, or they would have been seen," Peggy said. "The House Eight missionaries are still in the running."

"I think it was the piano teacher herself," Miss Evans said. She'd been passing by, heard the discussion, and sat down to join in.

"That's pretty good, Miss Evans," Maria said. "If I had to listen to all those children mangling music all day, I'd sign up for drain-cleaning duty instead."

"Well, speaking of drains," Gloria said, rising, "it's my job today, and I want to get it done before the heat. They really get ripe when the sun gets to them. Let's interrogate the suspects, find out if they have alibis and such, and meet again tonight to see if we can narrow it down. I'll take the House Eight missionaries."

"No, you won't. You give them the screaming meemies every time you get near them," Peggy said.

"Nonsense. They're batty for me. They think if they can convert me, they'll get into heaven without having to do a thing the rest of their lives. I count for at least twenty ignorant heathens."

Everyone wandered off to various jobs, and Hazel tucked her squawking chicken under her arm and walked up the hill to the gardens. "Keep that thing away from my seedlings!" a woman working there said as soon as Hazel appeared.

"It won't hurt anything. I just want it to find some worms."

"You're the fourth one this week with a chicken," the woman said. "And let me tell you something. They are fiends from hell. The creatures would far rather eat our tender new plants than worms. We need the worms anyway, to work the soil for us. Keep that chicken away from the gardens."

"But what am I to feed her?"

"That's your problem. You should have thought about it sooner."

Yes, I certainly should have, Hazel thought, feeling both stupid and put upon, a depressing combination. She went back down the hill and spent the rest of the day supervising the chicken as it pecked around the perimeter of the camp. With so many people in such a small area, there was hardly any ground that wasn't either trampled to the texture of concrete or under extremely watchful cultivation. After a while she figured out that she could slip the chicken through the barbed wire and it could peck around outside, but she was worried about the string coming loose. Toward noon it started to rain and Hazel spent most of the day sitting in the mud holding the string with one hand and trying to keep a sheet of oilcloth over her own head with the other.

That evening they were no further with the piano mystery. None of the suspects had adequate alibis. A few acted guilty in the view of their interrogators. Others simply went into hysterical laughter when the "crime" was outlined. "You don't seem interested, Hazel. What's wrong?" Peggy asked.

"I *hate* that chicken."

"Good. Let's kill it and eat it," Gloria said.

"I can't do that. I paid too much for it. I have to keep it alive for the eggs. It was a long-term investment."

"If it's really long-term, you shouldn't eat the eggs. You should get a rooster and raise chicks. Then you'll have lots of eggs."

"They have to grow up first," Hazel said sullenly. "I'd murder them before then. Have you ever noticed how stupid chickens are? And how horrible they smell when it rains? It rained most of the afternoon."

"Still, think how nice your egg for breakfast is going to be," Maria said cheerfully.

* * *

"Where's the egg?" Hazel asked the next morning. She'd made a nest of her clothes next to her bed and was rummaging furiously through it.

"Maybe she didn't lay one," Gloria said, stretching.

"She *has* to lay one. That's what she's for!"

"Did anybody tell her that?"

"Damn!"

The chicken lasted a week. It never laid an egg. Hazel traded it to the cooking crew for a week's worth of double rice ration and one medium-size sweet potato. They stewed the chicken with rice and morning glory leaves.

An elderly Australian woman in House Four confessed to cutting the piano straps. She said the devil was sneaking in at night and playing music so loudly it kept her awake and that God had told her to stop it to save all their souls. She confessed in the afternoon and that night she went to Saigo's hut and told him she was tired of being incarcerated and was going home now. He had no idea what she was saying but knew madness when it appeared in front of him. He had her taken away. The women never knew where. Nor did they ever find out if she really ruined the piano or just liked the idea of confessing to something.

In November the choral group was again taken around to the nearby camps to perform. This time they returned empty-handed. No food, no clothing from the Japanese storehouses. "They should never have given us anything for performing; then we wouldn't have missed it so," Hazel said as she sat down beside Nancy Muir on the floor of the jolting transport truck. "Did you get to see Mr. Dreyer?"

Nancy didn't say anything. She didn't ever appear to hear. Hazel repeated the question. "No," she answered finally. "He's not there anymore."

"What? How do you know that?"

"A friend of his found me and told me. They took him away along with about a dozen others last week."

"Where were they taken?"

Nancy looked at her contemptuously. "Do they ever tell us?"

"Now, Nancy, I know you're thinking the worst. We always do at first, but consider it. They don't take people away to do

awful things to them. They do it in front of everybody as a
'lesson.' They probably just transferred him to another camp.
We'll find him. You'll see.''

"I'll never see him again.''

"Of course you will. I promise.''

"*You* promise? You can't promise a damned thing!''

Hazel looked away. "I know.''

Two days later she was standing at a remote section of the
barbed wire talking to a native. She handed him her Kappa pin
and a slip of paper. "This is the man's name. You keep pin.
Find man. This man. Herbert Dreyer. Understand?'' The native
turned the pin over, studying the catch. Hazel held out the silver
bracelet with the garnets. Too bad it was so overcast and cloudy
today. The garnets would be more appealing if they sparkled in
the sun. "You bring message from this man and I give you this,
too. Do you understand?''

The native reached for the bracelet. Hazel held it out of his
reach. "No. You get this when you bring paper back from this
man. Please! Do you know what I'm saying?'' He looked once
more at the bracelet and shrugged before disappearing into the
jungle.

Hazel walked back to her house, brooding over what she'd
done. She had no idea whether he grasped a word of what she'd
been saying or—if he understood—whether he had any intention
of helping her. Why should he? She'd given him a piece of
jewelry for nothing. He could go back to his kampong and keep
it, or trade it without doing a thing. He seemed to like the pin
better than the bracelet. She should have done it the opposite
way. Given him the bracelet and promised the pin if he returned
with a message from Mr. Dreyer. If only she could have dealt
with a woman. A woman might have understood how important
it was. A woman would have cared.

"You, too?'' Jane Kowolski said from the porch as Hazel
came up the steps. "Come in out of the rain.''

Jane hadn't even noticed it had started to rain. During monsoon it was the norm. "Me, too, what?''

"Broody, moody, depressed. Dr. Millichope says it's the barometer.''

"What in the world are you talking about?''

"The air pressure is dropping. Dr. Millichope says that's
what's wrong with all of us. Haven't your ears popped?''

Hazel stepped onto the porch and sat down by Jane. She watched the women in the street in front of their house. Always busy in the morning, today the street traffic did seem strange. Everyone seemed to be moving a little slower, a little more quietly than usual. There was something strange and still in the air, and everybody seemed to be listening or waiting for something. Hazel scooted backward and leaned against the front wall of the house. "I'm tired, Jane. Very, very tired of this. I feel terribly old and sad today."

"It's the barometer."

Hazel closed her eyes. "If you say so."

She fell asleep and woke only when Jane shook her. "Hazel, you dummy! Have you been out here all this time? Wake up. You're soaking wet." She'd slid sideways and had a crick in her neck and a terrible headache. Reluctantly opening her eyes, she thought at first that it was night. But she quickly realized it was only the rain. It was coming down in sheets—waves of rain that lashed sideways, drenching everything, including her.

"Good God! I've never seen it like this," she said, getting to her feet and swaying in the wind.

"We think it's a typhoon coming."

"A typhoon? Is that like a tornado?"

"Yes, but bigger. We're trying to stuff rags in the shutters to keep the rain out of the house. We need help." The rags they used were their clothes, and they were useless against the storm. Fortunately, one thing they had in abundant supply was rope. Many of the mothers now brought bundles of hemp back to camp so they could work and stay with their children. The women used the finer rope to tie the shutters closed. It grew dark very early. There was no dinner that night, nor was there any sign of the guards.

At what would have been dusk, they heard screams from outside. Hazel opened the door, which let in a blast of rain so strong it nearly knocked her over. "Let us in!" a voice called. Hazel couldn't make out a person to go with it. Several of the women poured out of the house and dragged in a group of sodden women carrying small children. "The roof of our house is about to blow off," one of them explained over the terrified shrieking of her child. "We were afraid only part of it would go and the rest would fall in on us. You have the best roof. Please let us stay here."

"Of course," Peggy said, instinctively taking charge.

One of the women had been smacked in the face with a branch that had torn loose. "You need stitches in that forehead, dear, but there isn't light enough to do it tonight," Dr. Millichope said. The feeble electrical system of the camp, never reliable, had given up hours earlier. They had a single lamp that burned red palm oil, and even it was flickering violently with the wind that blew through the cracks in the house.

They got the children settled in the middle of the house, as far from the windows as possible. The women huddled around them. As they feared, the shutters were soon ripped off and the wind drove the rain in on them like needles.

"Oh, shit! I hate this!" Gloria screamed above the noise.

"At least it'll wash away the garbage dump!" someone else shouted. Those who could hear her laughed nervously, but their laughter was dissolved in the roar of the wind.

It kept on for hours and hours, growing stronger and stronger. The walls of the house shook under the blasts. Then suddenly there was a loud *crack* and they all looked up into the darkness. There was no ceiling in the house, only the open raftered roof.

"Dear God! The roof is going!" Jane shouted.

"We've got to hold it down!" Peggy screamed back.

"How!"

"With ropes. It's all we've got. You younger girls help each other sling them over the rafters—"

Groping in the fierce, howling darkness, using each other for ladders, they managed to get ropes over most of the rafters, then hung on to them for dear life. Hazel and Elise shared a rope. The roof shuddered. Something hit the west wall with a terrible crashing, thrashing sound. Their one glass-paned window shattered, spraying glass on the women closest.

"I think we've gone to hell!" Nancy Muir said. "It can't be worse than this."

Hazel was trembling violently, frigid with exhaustion and fear. She'd never suspected how awesome and horrible the forces of nature could be. It was as if the wind could and would rip them off the face of the earth.

There was a sudden explosive sound just outside which turned into a gigantic ripping, tearing noise and then an enormous thud that made the floor of the house shake. The big tree outside had fallen. Hazel felt faint. It could just as well have fallen in on them, crushing them all.

She wasn't sure if she finally slept or just fainted away. But when she woke, the howling wind had abated a little and there was a faint hint of light at the open windows. She could hardly get her hands loose from the rope she'd clung to all night. Her arms and fingers were numb and had stiffened and locked into position. Looking at her palms, she could see dark blood, but felt nothing. "Lie down, Hazel," Dr. Millichope said from behind her. "It's going to be over soon. Rest." She pulled on Hazel's shoulders and Hazel dropped over across the old woman's lap.

When she woke again, it was much lighter and people were moving around lethargically. Hazel stood up, suddenly aware of pain in her arms, shoulders, back, and hands. The door opened and two sopping wet women came in. One of them was Jane Kowolski, the other was Sister Maria. Jane pushed her wet hair back from her face and said grimly, "We couldn't get up the hill. There's too much water still pouring down in rivers. There are two roofs missing up there that we could see, but I don't know about the women inside them."

"The roof of the Hall has collapsed," Maria added, "and there's a body out by the latrine behind us, but we couldn't get to it. When the rain slows more—"

Hazel suddenly realized she was the house leader and was expected and obligated to take charge. "You shouldn't have gone out yet. No one else is to step foot outside until I say you may. Now, let's clean up in here. Gloria, take care of that glass on the floor. If anybody has any food stashed away, you must give it to the children. They haven't had anything to eat since yesterday morning. Maria, you coil up the ropes and throw them out on the porch out of our way—"

There was enormous damage.

The stream that flowed through one corner of the camp had overflowed, ripped out the bridge and a section of the road, and washed away Saigo's house—but unfortunately he'd not gone with it. Two roofs had blown away. One roofless house was empty because the women had already taken refuge in House One, but in the other, three heavy beams had fallen in on the women. Two of them had died outright. The other had been pinned down and died of shock hours later. A fourth had her legs crushed and was unlikely to live another day.

The open cement drains had indeed been washed clean by the downpour, but sections of them had been torn loose.

Branches and trees were down everywhere. Two of the latrine huts had blown over. One had blown away entirely. The worst damage to the camp itself was to the gardens. They'd been washed away. Hardly a plant survived. Great muddy gullies cut through where cucumbers, eggplants, cabbages, and sweet potatoes had been growing the day before. "My God! We really will starve now," Jane said, surveying the ruin with Hazel.

"But at least we're alive now," Hazel said.

Many weren't. The body by the latrine behind House One was that of Sister Edith, the cranky nun who was perpetually complaining about Sister Maria. "I don't know when she left," Maria said, her eyes reddened with tears. "I should have kept an eye on her."

"Poor vain old thing," Gloria said. "Couldn't just piss in a bucket like the rest of us. Had to go out in a damned typhoon. She could have just wet herself and nobody would have ever known. We were all sopping wet all night long anyway."

"She'd have known," Sister Maria said softly. "She thought her habit was—well, sort of holy. That's why she was always so mad at me for giving mine up for bandages."

Caroline Warbler had slogged through the mud to check on the farthest houses. She returned with mud nearly to her waist and sad news to report. "Two of the missionaries went out into the storm early on and never came back. An old woman in House Nine had a heart attack and died and that Steele girl, the one with the short dark hair, had hysterics, went into some sort of convulsion, and apparently choked to death."

"Where are we going to bury them all?" Hazel asked, coming directly to the practical for fear they might all just drown in their emotions if they let them go.

"I don't know. You can't dig a hole anyplace. The mud would just pour into it as fast as you could dig," Caroline said.

"Maybe by tonight at the top of the hill," Hazel said. "It should be drained off by then."

"What about the guards? I suppose it's too much to hope any of them got killed?" Gloria asked.

"No, I've seen them all," Hazel said. "Mickey has his wrist splinted and Saigo had a bandage on his leg, but the rest are fine."

"They would be!" Gloria said bitterly. "The bastards."

"Come on, Dinki, you can't blame this on the Japs," Elise said.

"If you believe that, you greatly underestimate me," Gloria said haughtily, then turned on her heel and walked out.

Hazel smiled weakly. "I'm going to sit down and think about Evanston for five minutes, then I'm going to work," she said to the others.

"Maybe we could pray together," Maria said softly.

"Thinking about Evanston *is* praying," Hazel replied, closing her eyes and folding her hands.

 Chapter 28

December 1944

> *Dear Jim,*
>   *We have eaten many inedible things: plants we can't identify, fried green banana skins, tapioca roots, insects (on purpose, they're full of vitamins), and snakes. But there is one thing we never eat—monkeys. Early on, one of the little boys brought one down with a rock and it was skinned in preparation for cooking. Only then did we realize it looked exactly like a human fetus. In our worst hunger, we do not consider monkeys.*

This year there were no Christmas presents. All the prisoners' energy, time, and resources went into trying to rebuild the camp to minimal living standards. The nun who had entertained them with lectures about electricity drafted a few apt students, and with their help rewired the camp system. To everyone's astonishment, no one was electrocuted. Men from the main camp were brought to rebuild Saigo's hut and the roof of one of the houses. The women cared less about the roof than the sight of the men so close to them. The other roofless hut was left to be reclaimed by the jungle, but before the wood borers, vines, humidity, and fungus could take it back, the women dismantled it, using the wood for other repairs and cooking fires. They were excused from duty at the rope factory for several weeks and were given a dozen *chunkal*s, heavy hoes, with which to work on the gardens. It was clearly as vital to the guards as to the prisoners to get the gardens back into production as soon as possible, and every able-bodied woman and child was pressed into duty. *Soempit*s of precious seeds were delivered to camp, and the guards watched closely that they were all planted, not eaten.

They had a lethargic Christmas Eve. The only sign that it was a holiday was a concert given by the choral group. "I'll either be dead or home by next Christmas," Peggy declared as they got ready for bed that night. "I can't survive this much longer." No one argued with her. They all felt the same way. In spite of the hundreds of encouraging rumors they'd heard during their long stay, they were rapidly approaching their third anniversary of internment. For the first time Christmas didn't bring joy; it was merely another tragic milestone.

On Christmas Day they were told at *tenko* they had a week to make the camp nice for visitors. "Make it nice? Nice would take an act of God!" Gloria complained.

A few brooms and rakes and even some paint were delivered that day. Though their energy was low and their enthusiasm to impress Japanese officials nonexistent, the lure was irresistible. For their own sake, they tidied and painted and raked. Hazel and Gloria were the unlucky pair who happened to be passing the gate when another new object arrived. A lawn mower. Saigo shouted to them, gave orders to Mickey, and sent them off to mow the lawn in front of the guards' part of the camp.

Gloria made a great show of being fearful of the rusty little machine. "What is that?" she cried, cringing.

"No afraid. I show. Look," Mickey said. He gave it a great shove and went off along the side of the road, then turned and came back, cutting two neat strips. "See? Easy. You do."

Gloria edged up to the lawn mower and gave it a gingerly little push, then shrieked and jumped back. Hazel had to turn away to conceal her smile.

"No. Easy. See?" Mickey took another dash down and back. Gloria tried again. This time she went very slowly and the blades just swished lethargically over the tall grass. "No work. Machine no work," she said.

"Go fast. See. Like this," Mickey said, tearing off on his fifth and sixth strips. He was sweating heavily when he returned.

"You're pushing your luck," Hazel hissed to Gloria.

"I see," Gloria said, and set off on her own. She came back looking very proud of herself. Contented that she had the hang of it, Mickey went off. Gloria bent down and fiddled with the machine, then said to Hazel, "Oh, dear. It's broken. Let's rest in the shade until Mickey gets back."

It took him a half hour to return and another half hour to fix it, then he did another four strips just to make sure it worked. By that time it took only two more passes to finish the lawn they were supposed to mow. When Mickey returned again, Gloria said in an exhausted voice, "Work hard, Mickey. You like?"

He admired the lawn he'd mowed most of and gave them a pack of relatively fresh Lucky Strikes for doing such a nice job.

On the morning before the visit was to take place, a truck pulled into the compound and delivered several large, mysterious crates. Saigo gave one of his longer harangues, and at the end of *tenko* ordered the house leaders to stay behind when the others were dismissed. They gathered around the crates, eager and curious. Through Nancy Muir he explained. "We are to make ourselves clean and pretty for the visitors and to that end the Imperial Nippon Army is making us a loan—heavy emphasis on the loan part, ladies—of some clothing to wear instead of our usual rags," Nancy explained.

"We won't wear kimonos," the House Three leader said angrily.

Nancy smiled fiercely. "We will if he tells us to, Mrs. Haver, and if you don't stop scowling this instant, I'll bring charges against you to the judicial committee." The House Three people were a very superior lot, seeing themselves as the moral and ethical standard to which the rest of the women sadly did not measure up. They were despised by the rest of the camp, and this only confirmed their sense of outraged martyrdom. Mrs. Haver was their representative.

Nancy bowed and thanked Saigo for the loan, and the moment he was gone, they fell on the crates, which turned out to be full of Western dresses. "My God! Where did they get this stuff?'' Hazel said, pulling out a hopelessly crumpled magenta velvet dinner dress.

Mrs. Haver said, "They must have emptied every white woman's closet in Sumatra.''

"And it must have been ages ago," Nancy added. "It's all falling to bits and reeks of mildew. If they'd even folded the clothes neatly—still, look at this! It must have been beautiful.'' She held up an ivory silk slip with rotting ecru lace trim at hem and bodice.

The other women were drifting back and Hazel sensed they were in danger of a riot of looting any second. "Close the crates quickly," she said. "We'll take it all to our house and distribute it.''

There weren't nearly enough dresses, even counting slips and fancy nightgowns, for everyone, but each house leader got an equal number of garments and had to promise to be responsible for returning everything she was issued. Those who didn't get clothes were given the bits of jewelry and makeup they found in among the clothing. The lipsticks had all melted in their tubes and hardened.

"Don't forget. You must return everything!" Nancy said as the house leaders prepared to take away their dresses.

"They can't have made any sort of detailed inventory of this," Hazel argued. "It was obviously all just scooped out of closets and dressing tables and hastily shoved into crates. As long as they get back roughly the same amount and don't see any of us drifting around camp in a formal ball gown, they'll never know if we keep small things." The others agreed, and it was the enthusiastic consensus of opinion that there was no need to return everything.

That afternoon there was a long line at the bathhouse to bathe and wash hair. They'd discovered a tree bark that when pounded and cooked down to a paste made a halfway decent soap, even though it smelled disgusting. Miss Evans was dispensing stingy little globs of it to each woman. Hazel washed her hair and went dripping back to House One. She borrowed Jane Kowolski's hand-carved comb and started the long, agonizing process of getting the knots out. "Why do you keep all that hair?" Jane asked, watching as she winced at a gigantic snarl.

"I don't know. Yes, I do. Frank likes my hair long."

"Well, I don't see your Frank around here to admire it," Jane said bluntly. "Why don't you cut it off like most of the rest of us have. It would be cooler and easier to comb and keep clean. Believe me, it'll make you feel like a new person. Tomorrow is a new year. A perfect time.''

''I don't know—'' Hazel waffled. Nearly all the women had their hair short now, but she'd resisted. She kept telling herself it was for Frank's sake, but Jane's comment about not seeing Frank around had struck home. For the first time since the war started, Hazel felt a twinge of disloyal, unreasonable resentment toward Frank. It was as though a traitorous whisper in the back of her mind were saying, ''He's home safe and sound. How dare Frank demand you keep long hair? What does he know about your life here, your constant struggle to keep clean.'' As quickly as the thought sprung up, she squashed it. But the notion of short hair had taken hold. ''Yes. I'll do it. Quick, find the nail scissors before I change my mind!''

Hazel was lying on her stomach, trying to read by the flickering light of their one bulb in their house. She felt Peggy's eyes on her. ''What's wrong?'' she asked, looking up.

''Just admiring your new 'do.' You look so young and pretty with that mop of hair gone,'' Peggy said, folding a little slip of paper.

''I feel literally light-headed. You haven't put my haircut in your diary, have you?'' Hazel said with a smile. She'd long since given up warning Peggy about the diary. The danger was no less, but they all had a different view of danger now.

''Just a mention,'' Peggy said. She rolled the little folded paper into a tiny tube and slipped it into the mouth of a battered canteen which she slid under the narrow wooden platform she slept on. She'd stuffed all the diary pages she could into the lining of her suitcase and had started filling the canteen a few months earlier.

''How are you going to ever get those out and sorted into order?'' Hazel asked closing her book.

''I date them. Sorting won't be a problem, and I suppose some judicious surgery with metal shears will liberate them. I'm not sure, though, that I ever want to read them again. It's hard enough to live through this without going back and reliving it. Maybe I'll just put the canteen in the suitcase and ship it to my publishers with a note to do whatever they want with it.''

''You know you won't do that,'' Hazel said as the light went out.

"No, but it makes a nice, pathetic thing to say," Peggy answered with a laugh.

"Don't we look a perfect treat!" Sister Maria said, surveying the housemates. She was wearing a backless blue sundress with navy overstitching and a matching wide-brimmed hat.

"Like a boatload of Marseilles whores going to the circus!" Gloria said happily. She'd been issued a pink, full-skirted day dress. One side panel of the skirt had rotted out, but she'd looped over the adjoining panels to create an interesting and rather exotic style.

They actually assembled for *tenko* before summoned so that they could look each other over. There was a great deal of oohing and aahing and ironic compliments. "Oh, so sorry, darling. I mistook you for Joan Crawford."

"Is that dress the latest rage from Paris?"

"Innertube sandals with chiffon, what will they think of next?"

"I love your hair—the braided look is so terribly chic this season."

"No, dear, it's not sweat stains, it's a new patterned fabric. Have you no sense of style?"

"That scent! It's Eau de Mildew, isn't it? Too divine!"

They were all in a state of high hilarity by the time Saigo started screaming at them to line up. They'd barely gotten into line before the first of the official cavalcade pulled in the gates. "My God, every high muckety-muck on the island," Gloria whispered as four vehicles started unloading Japanese officials. A half-dozen uniformed, beribboned officers got out. The only one they recognized was Commandant Natsume. He'd been to the camp briefly the day after the typhoon to inspect the damage, and now he glanced around, his usually impassive face registering slight surprise at the improvements.

They were made to stand for over an hour. The officer who seemed to be of the highest rank ("the most muckety-muck of all," Gloria dubbed him) gave a long, rattling tirade, which his beleaguered-looking translator endeavored to convey to the women in its entirety. But he couldn't keep up with the staccato speech, and every now and then got behind and skipped whole portions or just frantically threw out the nouns and verbs. It didn't matter anyway; they'd heard it all before. Honorable Nippon giving benefits of ancient and wise culture to Greater East

Asia. White oppressors getting what they'd long deserved. British navy sunk to the last ship. Americans begging the wicked Roosevelt to give in to superior Nippon culture. War nearly over. The same old rhetoric.

When the speech was done, the official photographer got busy. Women stand in small groups as if at tea party. Smile. Good. Now, sitting on porch in relaxation. Look like happy talking. Good. Ladies with sundresses kneeling in garden. Smile. Smile! Lady at piano, other ladies dancing. More smiling. Much smiling. Children in happy circle with guard playing game. No, that lady not in pictures. No skinny ladies in pictures.

"No skinny ladies? Where in hell do they think they'll find a fat one?" Gloria hooted.

Finally the women were sent to their houses so that a house-by-house inspection could be conducted. House One was first. They were sent ahead to be standing by their beds in obedient ranks when the officials arrived. Hazel shifted gingerly from one foot to the other while waiting. She had on actual shoes for the first time in many months, and they'd made blisters on the backs of her heels. She had just decided to take them off when Natsume, the most muckety-muck, and the translator came in. The official questioned some of the women. Where were they from? What was their age? Were they married? As the women answered, the translator gabbled the replies. The official then walked around, poking and prodding at their belongings. He leaned past Peggy to look at an old, faded magazine picture of a child and a puppy she'd stuck on the wall. As he stepped forward to look, his foot struck something. There was a metallic sound, and he bent down to see what it was.

He stood back up, holding her canteen.

Hazel felt a wave of cold horror wash over her. If he shook it, he'd hear the tiny bits of paper rattling around inside. Naturally, he'd be curious as to what she kept in the canteen. She exchanged a quick, terrified look with Peggy, who was standing as if frozen. There were only seconds to think.

Hazel lunged at the muckety-muck and snatched the canteen from him before throwing herself at Peggy. "You bitch! You lying, stealing bitch!" she screamed. "That belonged to my father and you know how much it meant to me and you even pretended to help me look for it. And all along you had it yourself. That's the most despicable, dirty trick a person could play

on someone. And to think I called you a friend.'' She was
vaguely aware of the translator chattering away at the officer.

The officer barked an order. Hazel went on raving. The translator hesitated a moment, then grabbed her arm and shouted,
''Stop now! Be quiet!''

''Some friend!'' Hazel shook him off and went on, shoving
at Peggy. ''With friends like you, nobody needs enemies—''

The muckety-muck shouted something else, then suddenly
swung on her, knocking her to the floor. Hazel landed heavily,
scrabbled backward as if to get away, and shoved the canteen
under her bed as she made a great show of struggling back to
her feet. She threw herself at Peggy again, still screaming abuse.
This time the officer knocked her against the wall.

The room was in chaos. The guards outside, hearing the commotion, had rushed in, shoving the other women aside. The
sudden upheaval and violence had rattled everyone. Several
women were crying, and somewhere a child was screaming.
Spike, apparently in an effort to impress his superiors, ran at
Hazel and rammed his fist into her stomach. She crumpled to
the floor in agony. But even as she was fighting to get her breath
and keep from vomiting, and blackness was creeping in around
the edges of her vision, she could see across the floor where the
canteen lay well under her bed out of sight. It was worth it.
They'd forgotten about the canteen.

She ruined the official visit.

They dragged her out, unconscious, and tied her to the punishment post in the central area of the camp. Hazel half woke
several times, but was in so much pain she didn't care where
she was. As they tightened the ropes, she sagged, her only hope
was that she would die and get away from all of it. Peggy tried
to approach her, but Mickey dragged her away. As the sun beat
down, the waves of pain gradually diminished, to be replaced
by an all-engulfing nausea. She fought it as long as she could,
then finally gave in. Leaning forward as much as possible, she
gave herself to the wrenching convulsions. It devoured the last
of her strength. She felt her knees go and slumped unconscious,
oblivious.

When she came to, someone was talking. The sun had mercifully been replaced with light clouds and drizzling rain. ''Hazel. Wake up. Hazel. Can you hear me?''

She raised her head slowly. It felt like it weighed tons. "Peggy? Are you all right?"

"Of course I'm all right. You're the brave, stupid one."

She made her eyes open and forced herself to take a deep breath. The pain seemed to be localized now. One side of her rib cage, her feet, and her head. "Have they gone?" she asked, her voice croaking.

"Not yet. They're all around the other side of the hill. Hazel—"

"The canteen. They didn't find the canteen, did they?"

"No. Hazel, I owe you my life."

"It was the only thing—kill you—only punish me."

"Hazel—"

"Look out, Peggy!" Elise said from somewhere behind Hazel. "They're coming back. If you're caught talking to her, it'll be even worse for her. Quick!"

Hazel was relieved that they'd left her alone. She put her head back, opened her mouth, and caught enough rain to make one decent swallow. It was amazingly refreshing. She rested for a moment, then worked on straightening up and shifting some of her cramped muscles. Mickey must have tied her up. He had a reputation of being merciful and leaving plenty of slack in the rope when someone was tied to the punishment pole. She had room to ease her arms around enough that they were nearly at her sides instead of twisted painfully behind her back. She worked for some time at getting the loathsome shoes off, shoving at the heel of one with the toe of the other. Ahhh, that was a relief. By the time she'd gotten more comfortable, she was exhausted again.

She'd closed her eyes and almost managed to fall into a light doze when she heard voices approaching again. It was the official visitors coming back around the hill after their tour. She tensed her muscles, standing up straight. She wouldn't let them see how horrible she felt. They approached her as though she were an exhibit in a zoo. She gazed over their heads, pretending to be oblivious to them. They talked among themselves for a long time.

Hazel tried to blot out the drone of their voices.

Something was buzzing in her head. Or around her head. A fly. A mosquito. It seemed to be getting louder. Or maybe it was just something inside her throbbing head.

As she gazed out over the camp, however, she noticed others falling silent, too. Listening.

The drone was louder.

She looked up, squinting at the gray eastern sky. Suddenly she saw a speck. A formation of specks.

The Japanese were talking in low voices again, but now there was an element of alarm in their tone.

"Planes!" one of the women said.

They were much closer now. Big planes. Not the little Japanese "island hoppers" with the poached eggs on the wings like they occasionally saw at a distance. Big, beautiful, new, silver-skinned bombers. Five of them in formation came closer and closer and suddenly shot overhead, the deafening noise of their engines drowning out speech, scaring the birds in the surrounding jungle into a flapping, shrieking panic. As the sound died out, no one spoke but the guards, two of whom were dashing for Saigo's house, where the communication equipment was. The rest were screaming at the women, waving their rifles, frantically trying to herd them back to their houses.

But the women ignored them.

Like a tawdry, wet, emaciated Greek chorus they stood facing west. Two hundred pairs of eyes on the sky.

Suddenly, from a distance, they heard a string of long, muffled concussions.

"Bombs!" somebody cried out exultantly.

Hazel sagged again. "Thank you, God!" she whispered. "Oh, thank you, thank you, thank you."

Chapter 29

Dear Jim,
    The Philippines! They say we've taken back the Philip-
pines! American bombers came over us. We are going to be
rescued. This nightmare will end. Thank God!

In the confusion following the bombing, someone cut the
Hampton woman down and took her away. Natsume noticed,
but said nothing. That was for Saburo Saigo to deal with, if it
came to his attention. Unfortunate that it had all come out as it
did; Natsume had wanted to question her. But of course there
were more important things to consider now than the unex-
pected behavior of a single woman prisoner. Still, it had been a
most peculiar manner of acting, especially for her. Since their
astonishing meeting at the de Groot house, Natsume had main-
tained a cool interest in her. She'd proved valuable and more
obedient than some, though he suspected it was a surface obedience, not a genuine cultural conversion. And yet, her attack
on the other woman was out of character, as the Americans
would put it. There was something highly suspicious about it.

His car sped back to the main camp and he watched the jungle
flash by. He dreaded returning to the big compound. As hysterical and disordered as the smaller woman's camp had been, the
big camp would undoubtedly be on the brink of chaos. The
men, especially the military men, were so much more difficult
than the women. They'd never adjusted, never accepted their
fate. Their arrogant Western pride and sense of manliness—
unsuitable to men so dishonorable as to be allowed to be taken

prisoner—had prevented them from achieving any sort of tranquility or inner peace. They ate up their energy in hatred. Such a wasteful emotion. So Western.

But the women—they'd been a revelation to Natsume. For the most part, they had quickly turned their backs on their guards; turned inward and toward each other. While the men tried to ignore and deny their dishonor, the women seemed utterly unaware of it. In the women's camps, even Saigo's, there was laughter. That never ceased to surprise him. Unfortunately, the laughter was sometimes at the expense of the Nippon guards, but not always. That must help account for the fact that they were still alive. He'd expected them all to wilt and die, those soft, pampered, immodest Western women. But they'd shown a surprising strength of will.

His driver turned and spoke. "There is a delay, Commandant. A jeep disabled on the bridge ahead."

"Do not disturb yourself. We shall wait," Natsume said, then sank back into the seat and into his reverie.

The bombers might well signal the beginning of the end. The news all over the South Pacific was bad for Nippon. The early victories had not held. Island by island and beach by beach they were being threatened. His Oriental fatalism allowed him to accept without rancor that Nippon might be defeated—this time. Karma. In another cycle of history, who could tell? His people's destiny was to rule, but perhaps not yet. He was saddened, however, that he would not see his family again. Or his own country. Tonight he would meditate on the tranquility of his garden at home. Perhaps he would start thinking about his death poem. It must be perfection.

But before he could spare time for his private concerns, he must think about his duty to the Emperor. If Nippon lost the war, he and the other soldiers would naturally commit seppuku when their duties were completed, but what of the prisoners? They, too, would have to die, and it was too much to hope that they would avail themselves of the opportunity to take their own lives.

There was, however, a slight chance that the Emperor would order their release in the event of Allied victory. Natsume shuddered at the thought of all the arrogant whites going back to their people with ugly stories of their treatment. Stories no one would be present to dispute or explain or put in perspective. He particularly hated the idea of the women in Saigo's camp going home to their people and speaking of Saburo Saigo as though he represented Nippon. Saigo was a syphilitic madman, a disgrace to his army and his people. No, Saigo's women must be taken away someplace so remote that they would never be found if the Emperor allowed them to live.

No one slept that night. They stayed up, talking, laughing, crying, making plans. "We'll be on our way home in a week. Just think!" some said.

"That soon? Do you really think so?" others asked.

"Of course. It's all over but the shouting."

But some, like Peggy, were more realistic. "The Japanese are all over the island. It could take months of fighting to overcome them. They won't give up just because a few bombers go over."

"Don't be such a spoil sport, Peggy!" Jane Kowolski said.

"I'm not. I just hate to see everybody get their hopes too far up just to have them dashed. We've endured this long. We can endure a little longer now that the end is in sight."

"Don't you want to go home?" Sister Maria asked her.

"More than anything. I just don't want to court disappointment about when it's going to happen."

They were exhausted, but happy, when morning came and the bell for *tenko* started clanging. They straggled into line half asleep. Saigo, just as tired as they, was fired by fury. He strode along the lines, slapping, shoving, screaming at them. When Caroline Warbler accidentally hiccuped, he went after her viciously, beating her nearly unconscious. Then, as suddenly as the attack had commenced, he abandoned her, walked to the front of the assembled women, and said, through a shaken Nancy Muir, that they were to wait for gifts from the Nippon army.

"I'll kill the hateful sod before this is over," Gloria said between gritted teeth. She was so pale with anger that her freckles stood out like they'd been painted on her face.

"Be quiet or he'll kill you. He's crazy," Hazel warned in an undertone.

They stood for another half hour. Caroline recovered enough to stand back up, although she had blood running from a cut on her chin and a red eye that would be black in a few hours. Finally, Mickey arrived in a jeep and handed Saigo a canvas bag with a red cross on it. There was a stir of excitement. Saigo glared at them, then contemptuously upended the bag. Forty or fifty envelopes spilled out.

"Mail! It's mail from the Red Cross!" Miss Evans exclaimed.

Saigo flung away the bag, then stepped onto the pile of letters and ground his heel on them before walking away.

"Stop!" Nancy Muir screamed before anyone could lunge at the letters. "Stay where you are! I'll call out the names. House leaders come to the front and see that everyone stays back."

Peggy turned and started back to the house. "Where are you going?" Hazel asked.

"Dr. Margaret Sutherland died at sea. She's not on any lists. There won't be anything for her," Peggy said.

"Oh—of course. I'm sorry."

"Barbara Hope," Nancy Muir called out. There was a happy shriek as Barbara Hope rushed forward and clutched the precious letter.

"Estelle Haver. Mrs. Robert Warren. Mrs. John Englethorpe—Miss Evans, you take this one. Dorothy Bissell. Sister Gloria Denk. Wanda Charles. Mrs. Harold Smith. Bunny Webber. Charlotte Nicholson. Jane Kowolski—"

Everyone was edging forward. As the lucky women received their letters, they clutched them and disappeared as if afraid they might be snatched back.

Say my name. Please say my name! Hazel thought.

"—Susan Wiggans. Mrs. William Bailey. Marsha Hillerman—"

So few letters for so many desperate women.

"—Lois Mendez. Sally Welsh. Doris Edsall. Irene Hutchinson—who was a friend of hers?"

The pile of letters was diminishing quickly. Too quickly.

"—Iris Kaganoff. Mary Helen McLaurin. Millicent Woods—"

Hazel had to forcibly repress the impulse to rush forward, snatch the letters out of Nancy's hands and find one with her name on it.

"—Mrs. Maxwell Townsend. Isabel Winters. Anne Van de Heuvel. Dr. Claudia Millichope—pass this back to the doctor, please—"

People were pushing against Hazel, as if getting closer increased the chances of hearing their names called. Finally Nancy was down to the last two letters.

"—Lucy Riggs. Evelyn Fayette. I'm sorry, ladies. That's all."

There was a collective sigh of disappointment. Several women started crying. Hazel started to walk away feeling stiff and old and unloved. Someone touched her arm. "Hazel? Would you read this for me?" Dr. Millichope said, holding out her letter.

"Of course I will," Hazel said, trying not to feel sorry for herself. She carefully tore open the flimsy envelope.

"Who is it from?" Dr. Millichope said.

Hazel glanced down to the end of the letter. "Betty Hart."

"Betty Hart? Who is that?"

"She put in a snapshot. A girl about twelve. The letter says: 'Dear Dr. Claudia Millichope, my teacher had names of ladies who are prisoners of war and told us we could write to you and the Red Cross would take our letters. I picked your name because you're a doctor and my sister's name is Claudia, too. I hope you're not hungry or sick or anything. My daddy is in the war. He is in France we think. My mother and my sister and I pray for him every night. We will pray for you, too. When the war is over, will you come see us? We live in Olathe, Kansas. That's near Kansas City. You can take the train. It stops three blocks from our house. Please write to me if the Japs let you. Love, Betty Hart.' "

"How dear of her," Dr. Millichope said in a quavering voice. "To think. A stranger. A little girl in Kansas, wherever that is. Thank you, Hazel. Maybe later you'll read it to me again so I can memorize it."

"I'd be glad to."

"I'm sorry you didn't get a letter, Hazel, but you must realize it doesn't mean anything. They must have tons and tons of them they aren't giving out. Your sister and your fiancé have probably written you dozens."

"I know you're right, but—"

"No buts—you'll be going home before long now and can take up your life where you left off. Or nearly so. That's what you should be thinking about."

"Of course."

After leaving Dr. Millichope talking to another woman about her letter from Kansas, Hazel walked slowly back to the house. Gloria came running down the walk to meet her. "My sister wrote to me. My younger sister. She got married and has a baby. They named it for me! Imagine doing a barmy thing like that. And she said Matron Eagleton has written to her several times promising she'll bring 'her girls' out safe and sound when the

war is over. Just think about somebody calling any of us 'girls.'
I've got to find Caroline and tell her. Have you seen her?''

"The Hall, I think.''

Gloria tore off, telling everyone along the way about her
namesake niece.

Jane Kowolski was sitting at the end of the porch, dangling
her legs over the edge. "Jane, who was your letter from?'' Hazel
asked.

Jane looked up, her eyes red. "My brother. He says my
mother is dead. She broke her hip and got pneumonia in the
hospital and died. The letter is more than a year old.''

"Oh, Jane. I'm so sorry.''

"My mother's been gone for more than a year. It seems so
strange that I didn't just *know* somehow. I've been storing up so
much to tell her and now I'll never be able to.'' There was
nothing to say. Hazel patted her shoulder and went away thinking perhaps it wasn't such a terrible thing to have not gotten a
letter.

They watched all day for more Allied bombers, but there
were none. The next morning, however, there was another
pleasant surprise. Nancy Muir found Hazel eating her morning
rice in the Hall. She took her aside and said quietly, "Saigo says
you and I are to take the transport truck to the big godown. You
can drive it, can't you?''

"Badly, but we'll survive. Are we leaving it there or what?''

"He didn't say.''

"Do you think there's any chance we're picking something
up?''

"I'm almost afraid to hope so.''

When they arrived at the godown, flushed with heat and anticipation, two sullen Japanese soldiers pointed to a big pile of
Red Cross boxes. They barked some orders to Nancy, who
bowed respectfully and said to Hazel. "Those are for us. *For
our camp*. We have to load them ourselves.''

Hazel could hardly keep from dancing with excitement.
"That's one job I don't mind. Oh, Nancy, let's hurry.''

They threw themselves into the work, counting as they went
and speculating on what was in the parcels. "I've never seen a
Red Cross box before,'' Hazel said. "Fifteen. Sixteen. Do they
all have the same things in them? Seventeen.''

"Eighteen. I think there are different kinds. Invalid boxes.

Medical boxes. Nineteen. Men's. Women's. Twenty. Food boxes. Clothing. Twenty-one. These are marked in Dutch or Afrikaans or something, but they feel heavy. They must be food. Twenty-two.''

"Have you noticed how angry those guards are about this?" Hazel said, pointedly not looking at them.

Nancy did the same. "I don't think they're at all happy with their orders to hand this over to us. I believe we better get out of here the second we're done loading, or they might just decide not to obey orders.''

It took the camp committee half a day to figure out what was in the boxes and how to distribute them fairly. An almost violent dispute arose early on concerning the origin of the boxes. Mrs. Haver, a loyal, patriotic Canadian from Toronto pointed out that most of the boxes were from the Canadian and American Red Cross and promulgated the theory that they ought to belong, therefore, to the Canadian and American prisoners. "You can't be sincere in that, Mrs. Haver," Peggy said. "There are only eleven Canadians and seventeen Americans here. Almost everybody else is British, Dutch, or Australian. Suppose they'd all come from Brazil; would you advocate giving all of them to Mrs. Mendez?''

"They didn't come from Brazil. Theoretical questions don't interest me, Miss Bright. I think it's only right to consider the fact that your country and mine supplied the parcels and intended them for us, their own citizens. I would be sorry if the others couldn't understand that, of course, and would endeavor to make them see the justice of it.''

"What about the South African ones. We don't have anybody from South Africa in this camp," Nancy Muir said.

"Then the others may share those.''

"Mrs. Haver, you are a nasty, selfish pig!" Gloria said from outside the doorway.

"Sister Denk, you are not a member of the committee and I'll thank you to take yourself elsewhere!" Peggy said.

"There's no rule that I can't listen in.''

"There is now! Get lost.''

In the end they had to take a vote and Mrs. Haver was easily overruled, but she made clear she thought they were all immoral, unethical reprobates and that she would share that opinion with everyone she could. Hazel thought it unfortunate that someone didn't just strangle her and be done with it.

They had enough food boxes for each house to receive six with the ten remaining to be given to Miss Evans to use in the communal cooking. The box containing sports equipment was to be given to the entertainment committee to take care of. The rest of the boxes, the general women's supplies, were given four to each house to be divided in any way the house residents decided. Hazel and Peggy carried their boxes home. Everybody was waiting outside and rushed to meet them. "Quick! Quick! Dump them out and let us see what we have!" Gloria said, reaching for Hazel's boxes.

"No, please! Make it last as long as possible," Caroline Warbler said.

Hazel sat down on the porch and lifted a corner of one box. "No peeking now. Ta-da!" She pulled out a flimsy tin of shoe polish.

There was a moment of silence, then a wave of laughter.

"Shoe polish!" Caroline said. "Who has shoes *to* polish?"

Hazel reached into the box and pulled out a pair of shiny new oxfords. "Shoes! Only one pair in each box. We'll see whose feet fit them and have a drawing among those women. Now look at *this*." She pulled out a roll of toilet tissue.

"Loo paper!" Gloria breathed. "Honest-to-God loo paper! We can spread it out across the street and cut it into even lengths for each. Oh, imagine—!"

"One of these is for Peggy," Hazel said, holding up a pencil.

She went on, item by item. A toothbrush, a cardboard container of Squibb's powder, Pond's cold cream, two bars of face soap and a small cardboard box of laundry soap, a real comb, a box of Tampax, a sewing kit, a pair of wool socks, a bottle of multiple vitamins.

"If we take enough of the vitamins, maybe somebody will need the Tampax," Caroline said. "Oh, look! A bath towel."

Hazel had gotten down to the fabric goods. She pulled out two pairs of rayon panties and a huge pink bra.

"Will you look at that!" Peggy said. "It looks like a pair of hammocks. What size is it?"

Hazel read the tag and sputtered, "Forty!"

Caroline reached for the bra and held it up in front of herself, giggling. "I used to wear a bigger one than this. My God! Now I could get both halves in one cup with room left over."

There was a striped cotton playsuit with a matching skirt, two pairs of khaki shorts, and a white blouse. Hazel laid them all out on the porch and they gathered around, staring. "How will we divide it all up fairly?"

"The things like the toilet paper and vitamins can be shared," Nancy said, "but the rest all ought to be numbered, then we'll draw lots."

"But I want shoes!" Gloria said. "I haven't had shoes since we were captured. It would be my luck to get the Tampax or the bloody great brassiere."

"Knowing you, you'd make a pair of hats from the brassiere and smoke the Tampax," Sister Maria said, collapsing in laughter at her own wit.

"If everybody gets something by random drawing, then we can trade until everybody is happy," Hazel said. "Don't forget, we've still got the food boxes to look at."

"Food—" Miss Evans sighed.

Hazel opened one box and started taking out the contents like a magician. There was an efficient little can opener in a brown paper wrapper, bouillon powder in a bag, a tiny bag of sugar, a pound of dried prunes, ground coffee, a twelve-ounce tin of corned beef, a half-pound package of cheese, a tin of evaporated milk, another of salmon and a jar of grape jam, and ten assorted cigarette packages. "Now, there are six of these boxes for the house and four of the others. I think we ought to divide them up as Nancy suggested. Does anyone object?"

"Of course not!" Gloria said. "Just hurry up with it!"

In spite of Gloria's nagging, it took an hour to get all the items laid out, counted, and numbered. Then they got into an argument over the order in which they were to draw their numbers.

"By age, from youngest to oldest!"

"No, from oldest to youngest!"

"By nationality—Aussies first," Gloria said, and was hooted down.

"We'll do it alphabetically!" Hazel declared firmly.

The next morning, attired in their new finery and feeling fairly well fed, they were told to get into a single line formation down the middle of the road. A visiting Japanese officer and his assistant set up a table at the head of the line and laid out boxes of serum bottles and hypodermics.

"What's this?" Gloria asked.

"It looks like some kind of inoculation," Hazel answered.

"This is some time to start worrying about our health. The bastards!"

When everybody had received their shot, whatever it was, Saigo ordered an extra *tenko* for an announcement. As always, Nancy stood beside him listening impassively as he talked. When he was done, he walked away and Nancy said, "Saigo says we are to leave here tomorrow."

"Leave? To go where?" Mrs. Haver demanded.

"He didn't say. We are to pack up our things and be ready at dawn."

"But the gardens—we did all that work on the gardens!" someone cried.

"They're taking us away to kill us all!" another sobbed.

"Don't be a nincompoop!" Nancy said. "They wouldn't have wasted medicine on us if they were going to kill us."

They went back to their houses, speculating like mad on what this all meant. "At least we won't have to go back to work in the damned rope factory," Peggy said.

"Do you know what I think? Well, maybe just what I hope—" Hazel said. "Maybe they're giving us up. Taking us to the coast and letting our people pick us up. A sort of late repatriation. Is it possible?"

"It would account for the food and clothes and shots," Dr. Millichope said. "Trying to get us in decent shape so we won't be believed when we say how badly we've been treated."

"I think Hazel's got something!" Sister Maria said.

They not only talked themselves into believing it; by morning the speculation had taken on an aura of fact and spread throughout the camp. The women, loaded down with their pitiful old belongings and wonderful new ones, lined up cheerfully, and most were smiling as they set out. Only a few paused to look back at the barbed-wire-enclosed kampong that had been their home for so long. Hazel had only one misgiving; the native she'd given her jewelry to had never come back with word of Herbert Dreyer. Now, if he did, she and Nancy wouldn't be there. Still, the war was nearly over. They'd find Mr. Dreyer somehow.

Chapter 30

April 22, 1945

Dear Jim,

 If we aren't rescued soon, we will all surely die. The Red Cross parcels of physical and emotional nourishment we were given in January were too little and too late in the face of what has happened to us since. As I was making my last entry, we were assembled to be told we must move the next morning. I thought it might be my last entry.

 You see, when we started this journey, which is certainly our last because we couldn't survive another, we believed we were being released. Even I, your old mother who never allows herself to believe the best, really thought we were on our way home. But instead of going east toward the coast as we anticipated, we were driven like cattle to the West. Up out of the swampy lowland. Up the mountains. Even then we told ourselves they were taking us to the other side of the mountain range and we'd be shipped off to India or Ceylon. But then we started going north. And going and going and going.

 Nearly a fifth of our women died on that journey. We left a trail of hasty, indecent graves. Fortunately, none of my closest friends were among the losses, but we lost Miss Evans and miss her more than we ever imagined we might. She just sat down in the middle of the road one day and said she was through, never walking another step. The guard Spike slapped and beat her and she took it like a Buddha. Serene. As though she didn't even feel it. She passed out eventually and died an hour later. The worst of it all was, when we buried her and muttered our prayers, we realized we didn't know her first name. All those years—all those hundreds of meals she tried to make palatable for us out of the most extraordinary garbage—and we didn't know her name.

Every morning, before we began, we had "ulcer call." Dinki came around with a sharpened spoon to slice and scrape the stinking black flesh out of the tropical ulcers many of us have. When a person is severely malnourished, the smallest scratch can turn into one of these obscenities. A week later, it can be a gaping five-inch hole exposing muscle and tendon; even bones show through. If there's a cure, other than food or the medicine we don't have, we haven't discovered it. But some do get better. I had one on my shin that's finally curing. You keep the dead flesh scraped off down to live tissue and when it starts looking granulated instead of smooth, you know you have a chance of surviving. Of course, more often it just eats up a leg or arm until amputation is required and under these conditions, amputation is a death sentence.

Every morning, after this ghastly ritual, we trudged on. Dying at increasing intervals. Digging shallower and shallower graves because we had less and less strength to dig. Finally we were just laying them out, poor dears, and covering them with leaves and branches. This is so wrong to die so near the end. It must be over soon. It must! We hear bombing along our way often, but always at a great distance.

Caroline Warbler became dreadfully ill on the way though, amazingly, she seems to be recovering very slowly. We made a litter to carry her. When she was shipwrecked she weighed nearly three hundred pounds. The last time we were weighed, she was down to a hundred and twelve pounds. Even at that, we could hardly last twenty minutes at a time with four of us carrying her weight. Saigo, who rode in a jeep most of the way, kept ordering us to leave her behind, but we wouldn't and he seems to have developed an intensely personal hatred of her. He's mad, of course. The nurses and Dr. Millichope say it's his syphilis, but I think he's just a man who lives to hate. Our old Mickey was sick, too, but Saigo reluctantly let him ride in the jeep. We couldn't have carried him.

We got here the third week in February. It's another plantation, long abandoned now by the former Dutch proprietors. Luckily, it hadn't been used as an internment camp until we and two other groups arrived. That means the ground wasn't *yet packed down to rock hardness and the trees weren't stripped of leaves and bark and dead wood yet. It means the million roaches and mosquitoes that are now finding us weren't here waiting.*

Except for being a million miles from anything, the site of this camp is an improvement over the others in geographical terms. It's high country. Cooler at night and less humid and oppressive. Although even that has another side to the coin. We have no warm clothing. What little we came in with, we'd cut up, used up, and worn to shreds. The villagers, unlike those in the more populated areas, are very wary of us. You see, we are fearsome. Several hundred sick, discontented, skin-and-bone white women. We must look to them like evil spirits. I'm afraid of us. And afraid for us.

One of the most remarkable things we found here was a pair we'd all forgotten about: Beryl Stacton and Audrey St. John. We left them behind at the first camp because Audrey was ill and Beryl got permission to stay behind with her and the baby. I didn't recognize them when we got here, and even when they were identified to me I didn't believe it. Audrey, the glamorous one, is a wreck. She lost several of her front teeth as a result of a beating. She also suffers badly from pellegra, a niacin defiency, and the lesions have ruined her once-lovely skin. Beryl merely looks lean and tough. But the child is a wonder. He's the most healthy-looking individual in the camp because he's got two adults seeing to his welfare.

A woman who's been in their camp all this time told me Audrey has never shown the least interest in or affection for the child. But she's ruined herself seeing to his welfare. About a year ago she started trading off all her belongings to buy food for him. When that was gone, she started writing checks. Yes, writing checks. You wouldn't think all this distance from a bank that they'd be any good, but you'd be surprised how many have been written. The recipients of them, knowing they may not live to cash them, always ask for an amount at least twice what the cash value of whatever they're trading might be. Sometimes a great deal more. I saw a woman write a twenty-dollar check for an egg at this camp. At any rate, things here are so wretched now that no one will accept Audrey's checks. So she's turned her last asset to cash. Her body. She is, to be frank, the camp prostitute. The guards give her pitiful scraps of food for her "favors." Sometimes

*they farm her out to a native, thereby adding "pimp" to the
list of names we are justified in calling them, although the
natives have understandably little interest in the scaly, dirty
white woman. If she were doing it for herself, I suppose we'd
call her a collaborator. As she's doing it for the child, we just
dislike her as we always did. No more. No less.*

*So Audrey and Beryl jog along like a miserably married
couple; unwillingly linked by a child whom Beryl cares for
and raises and Audrey goes out and supports. And all the
while, they go right on loathing each other. . . .*

"Peggy, put that away and come look at what Saigo's done
now," Hazel said from the doorway.

Peggy hid the paper and pencil and followed Hazel. In front
of the guards' hut there was a small, barred cage. Inside, one
of the guards' chickens paced about frantically, batting itself
against the bars. There was a sign, written in Japanese, hanging
on one side of the cage. "What does the sign say?" Peggy
asked.

"Nancy translated it. It says the chicken is in jail for destroying property of the Emperor."

"What in the world—?"

"It pecked its own eggs. Dr. Millichope says it's suffering a
calcium deficiency just like we are."

A small group was gathered around the chicken jail. They
were laughing among themselves, but Peggy wasn't amused.
She'd felt a sudden wave of horror. Saigo had gone quite mad.
Didn't any of them realize what an increased danger he now
represented? A man who would build a jail to punish a chicken!
She shivered and walked away.

They were provided with further evidence of his mental state
that afternoon when six women were summoned to be made an
example of. The six, who had no particular connection with
each other, were told they must stand in the middle of the dusty
compound until they apologized. "Apologize for what?" Caroline Warbler, one of those selected, asked.

Nancy Muir, her eyes wide with fear, put the question to
Saigo, received his reply, and said, "Saigo says you know what
for. You will stand there until you die unless you apologize for
whatever he thinks you've done."

Nancy understands now, Peggy thought, watching her perplexed and frightened expression.

The six stood for nearly two hours, determined that they would not apologize for unknown crimes. To apologize was to admit having done something, and that very admission might prove deadly. Finally, however, when three of them, including Caroline Warbler, had fainted, the remaining three decided to give in. They did so, and were released without ever finding out what it had all been about.

In May, Hazel once again looked over her dwindling jewelry supply. She'd traded the cameo brooch for six tiny, suspicious-smelling eggs along the way to this camp. The amethyst ring had been traded for a small *soempit* of sweet potatoes farther along. The rhinestone choker had given best value; it had become a fat duck that she'd stewed and shared with Dinki, Nancy, Sister Maria, Peggy, Elsie, and Caroline in return for favors they'd done her. The little silver bracelet with the garnets had only been worth a single, large cabbage head. Now there was a native outside the fence at the back of the camp with a bag of peanuts that he'd give her for a price. Hazel looked over what remained of her jewelry. She wouldn't give up her mother's wedding and engagement rings, nor her own. Perhaps the topaz and pearl dinner ring.

She no longer was struck so overwhelmingly at the disparity between the value of the jewels in the outside world and their value here. "Here" was all there was. Surviving was all that mattered. Unless she supplemented the bland, inadequate rice diet they were given, there would never be an outside world for her. She slipped the ring into her halter top and went to get the peanuts.

In mid-June, Saigo decided they were plotting to escape and instituted random middle-of-the-night *tenkos*. Even those who were ill had to be carried out into the middle of the compound to be counted. On one such night Hazel helped Caroline wobble out. She'd developed "wet" beriberi. Her flesh was swelling with edema and her craving for salt was driving her and her friends insane. "At least I'm putting back some weight." She laughed feebly as she staggered against Hazel. Her skin felt as squashy as a feather pillow with a taut cover.

The floodlight in the center of the compound was turned on, and they assembled, too exhausted for anger, their eyes shaded against the glare of the light, to be counted. Saigo strutted back and forth, mumbling to himself. Every time he passed Caroline, he slapped her. When the guards finally reached a number they could agree on, Saigo came back to Caroline. He held out his hand in front of her and shouted something. Hazel, standing next to her, could see the tablespoon or so of grains of salt on his palm. Caroline gulped back a mouthful of saliva and bowed to him. When she stood back up, desperate pleading in her eyes, he raised his hand and flung the salt into the air.

There was a long moment of horrified silence.

Then Saigo started laughing. A high, shrill laugh that made the hair stand up on the back of their necks. A second later there was another sound. Caroline began to scream in a weak, keening, inhuman voice. She'd thrown her head back, like a wolf howling at the moon, and was slowly raising her arms.

"Caroline, stop—" Hazel said, reaching out for her.

But as she spoke, Caroline's arms fell and she lunged at Saigo.

She was nearly a foot taller than he, and he collapsed under her weight. The laughter stopped suddenly, but Caroline's wailing went on. They struggled and thrashed together in the dust, Saigo lashing out viciously. Suddenly he got free of her, and staggered to his feet. She, too, dragged herself up and went for him again. He shouted at her, backing up as she threw herself at him. He jerked his pistol out of its holster and fired at her.

Her chest exploded in blood and she made one last, gasping cry as she toppled forward.

Hazel was suddenly overcome with an insane rage. She flung herself forward to attack him, unaware that a dozen other women had also done so. The breaking point had been reached. Like a single huge, wounded animal, the women fell on Saigo, flailing their arms, striking him, one another, and themselves. Hazel suddenly felt her breath being crushed from her body. Gasping, she gagged on the stench of Saigo's revolting body.

The guards, fearing they would accidentally shoot Saigo himself, were afraid to fire into the pile of thrashing bodies. Instead, two of them starting kicking at the women on the ground while dragging them away. The rest of the guards crouched with their guns aimed at the rest of the women, who stood in transfixed horror.

Hazel thought she was dead. Her vision turned red, then black, and she was aware in an impersonal way of a pain in her leg. As consciousness faded, her last thought was, *I hope I hurt the son of a bitch.*

When she came to, she was lying on her back with Peggy looking down at her. "Are you alive?"

"I don't know." She sat up gingerly, noticing that she'd wet herself, and realized Caroline was still sprawled lifelessly beside her. She crawled over to her, half crying, half retching. "What happened?"

"You don't remember?"

Hazel took Caroline's hand. Dinki sat across from her, cross-legged, her forehead on the dirt, weeping. "I mean Saigo. Did we kill Saigo?"

"No. But you scared the daylights out of him."

They'd scared the daylights out of themselves as well.

They buried her first thing in the morning. Gloria, rigid and white and silent in her outrage, had cleaned Caroline's body, combed her hair, and lovingly dressed her in Sister Cassini's uniform. Then she'd put on her own uniform, which she hadn't worn since her capture. "She's army," Gloria said to the others. "She deserves a military funeral."

They all put on their pitiful best, some of them, like Gloria, wearing clothes they'd saved the entire time to wear when they came out of imprisonment. As six of the women carried Caroline's body through the camp to the burial ground just outside the gates, the others lined up on both sides of the route and saluted as she was borne past. Even the guards (less Saigo, who had disappeared during the night) were impressed by the solemnity of the occasion and saluted smartly.

The camp was quiet all afternoon. Everyone was afraid to even try to express the horror and contempt they felt, but could think of nothing else to talk about. Hazel's horror was of herself. Attacking Saigo was the only time in her whole life that she'd utterly lost control of herself. Her own mindless savagery terrified her. Yet, in a peculiar way, she was gratified to learn she could still feel emotion at all. They had endured so much that was so utterly unspeakable, and had learned the only way to cope was to not feel anything. At least she knew she was capable of feeling murderous rage—

At dusk Saigo returned, dirtier and more rumpled than ever. He had a black eye and some scratches on his face. Of one accord, they all silently returned to their huts because they couldn't stand to look at him. There was no *tenko* that night.

* * *

Saigo's deterioration seemed to go in cycles. Astonishingly, there was no punishment for the near riot and the attack on himself. Perhaps he was as terrified their emotions might go out of control again as they were. Or perhaps there would have been some complex loss of face involved in acknowledging what had happened. For the rest of the week, he was—for him—quite normal. Then one morning, when their pitiful food ration was brought in, he ordered that it be dumped in the middle of the compound, the rice first, then the vegetables on top. He wouldn't let them touch it. As the scalding tropical sun rose, the vegetables quickly rotted and burst. Flies buzzed frantically over the pile of garbage, laying clumps of eggs. At dusk he drove the jeep over the whole mess, backing up several times to smash everything thoroughly. Then, he said, they could have the food.

Stomachs heaving with hunger and anger, they shoveled it up and dumped it at the most remote corner of the camp.

They feared this was the beginning of something more awful than ever, but fortunately, the Japanese army accidentally intervened in his descent into madness. The next afternoon a convoy of three transport trucks wheezed up the long, steep road and stopped at the gates.

Peggy was taking a nap in their hut when Hazel dashed in. "Oh, Peggy, come see what's arrived!" Hazel said.

Blinking in the sunlight, Peggy was at first alarmed. The first two trucks were disgorging a small army of Japanese soldiers. They, unlike the ragged, filthy guards the women had become so used to, were tidy and fresh, with neat haircuts and dressed all alike in clean uniforms. Her first thought was that they were a gigantic firing squad come to eradicate them in one big bloodbath. They were handing cases out of the back of the third truck. "Guns?" she said quietly.

Hazel looked at her with surprise. "Guns? No, Peggy. Instruments. Musical instruments. See, that's a tuba case. They're a band! A real band!"

The women huddled in groups, watching with fascination as the newcomers unloaded chairs and set them up in a semicircle in the middle of the compound. Then they arranged shiny music stands and fussed around unloading their instruments. Finally, they were ready to play, and the women and children came forward to sit on the ground in front of them.

From the first note they were transported. Hazel almost gasped out loud at the sheer physical pleasure of horns and woodwinds and strings instead of jungle noises and the shrill sound of women's voices. Audrey St. John was seated behind her. "Bliss. What utter bliss!" she said softly.

The band played familiar Western music, mostly German waltzes. There was a bit of Beethoven, some Bach, quite a lot of Strauss, and even some Handel. As the beloved music washed over them, Hazel looked at the players. The band, she realized with surprise, was just men. Not soldiers, in spite of their uniforms. Not soldiers as they were used to. These men, unlike Saigo and Spike and most of the rest, didn't look at them with hatred and resentment. These men were musicians first. That they were Japanese and military was irrelevant at the moment. *They don't hate us. They just love music*, Hazel realized. It was a marvelously comforting thought.

She gazed around at the women. Most had their eyes closed, as if to cut out the dreary sight of the camp and imagine themselves wherever they last heard real music played by real musicians. Many were smiling, most had tears rolling down their faces. At the end of each selection, they applauded wildly. Mickey stomped his huge feet and cheered, and they all chuckled at his enthusiasm. They kept the band there as long as they could, begging for encore after encore. But eventually it got dark and the musicians had to stop.

They packed up and climbed back onto their trucks to rattle off into the night. Many of the women, including Hazel, hung around the gate, watching. When the trucks were gone and she could no longer even imagine she heard the sound of their engines, she slowly walked back to the hut. But as she passed the washhouse, she heard a sound and went around behind to investigate.

Jane Kowolski was sitting on the ground, knees up, arms folded, and head bent. Her shoulders were shaking and she was fighting to keep her sobs silent. Hazel sat down and put her arms around her. Jane turned and clutched at her. "Why did they do that to us? Oh, God, why? Isn't it bad enough to deprive us of everything beautiful without giving us a taste like that of what we've lost? It's just like Saigo throwing away the salt in front of Caroline. My musical talent was everything to me. My whole life. My reason for existing. And now that I've lost it, they show me what I've lost, just to remind me."

* * *

The next week had two more high points. The first occurred in the middle of the night two days after the concert. Hazel, her section of floor closest to the door of the hut, was awakened to the sound of someone screaming outside. They were all subject to nightmares and often cried out in their sleep, but this was different. Without coming fully awake, she stepped out the door to determine where the sound was coming from. As she did so, she was nearly knocked down by something that streaked past and brushed against her. Something huge and hairy.

She staggered back into the hut and peered out. The floodlight came on, blinding her for a second, and she heard someone cry, "A tiger. There's a tiger in the camp!"

"Oh, my God!" she exclaimed.

The guards were shouting now; women all over the camp were awake and calling out. The women in Hazel's hut were clustering around behind her in the doorway. The floodlight flickered, went out, came on again, went out again. There was a gunshot, then two more in rapid succession. When the floodlight came back on again, it revealed an extraordinary sight. Hazel gasped and turned to the others, hardly able to speak.

"What's happened?" Sister Maria called from the back of the group.

"There—there was a tiger in the compound. Saigo tried to shoot it," Hazel said. "But he missed and hit a person instead."

"The bastard! The sodding bastard!" Gloria snarled.

"No, let me finish! He hit Spike!" Hazel said.

"Spike? He shot Spike? Dead?" Peggy asked.

"Oh, I dearly hope he's dead," Hazel said. "No, no, no! Quit pushing. We don't dare go out there. He'll shoot the rest of us. Everybody lie down. Pretend we didn't notice."

"Pretend we didn't notice?" Nancy said. "We wake up in the middle of a gunfight in a zoo and you say pretend we didn't notice?" She started laughing and the rest joined in. Hazel hushed them as best she could, but an hour later some of them were still giggling.

They no longer had work outside the camp like the factory work at the previous site, and the Japanese, after a few attempts to use the women as road crews, had given them up as useless. But there was still a great deal that needed to be done to ensure their own survival. A group set out each morning to walk the quarter mile to the nearest stream to bring back water. Another group spent much of each day preparing the meager food they were given and devising ways to make it stretch as far as possible with the addition of fruits, leaves, and roots from the nearby jungle. A third crew went with Mickey every morning to gather firewood.

These out-of-camp jobs were the hardest, but were desirable because they enabled the women who worked them to eat whatever they could find outside the barbed wire. They weren't choosy anymore. Practically anything green that could be torn into small enough pieces to swallow was acceptable. Hazel got on the wood crew as often as she could for the sake of the food and also for the sake of refreshing her senses. Every day they went someplace a little different to find dead wood for burning. It all looked pretty much the same whether they went off into the jungle a few yards up the road or a half mile down, but at least it didn't stink of latrines and unwashed bodies out in the jungle. It was because of this job that Hazel had her second memorable experience of the week.

It was as they were coming back from wood gathering one morning that she noticed something tiny and white in the road just ahead. At first she thought it was a petal from a flower, but as she got nearer, she decided it was something more interesting. Paper. A scrap of paper. She pretended to drop a stick and bent over to pick it up. As she did so, she palmed the little white piece of paper. The next time Mickey wasn't looking, she slipped it into her halter top.

When she got back to camp, she went to the hut. Sister Maria was there, on her knees, saying her prayers. Hazel respectfully bowed her head and waited a moment.

Sister Maria finished and stood up. "You look like the cat that ate the canary, Hazel."

"I found something in the road," Hazel said, fishing the mysterious little find out of her clothing. "Look."

It was a tightly folded scrap of fresh, white paper. As she unfolded it, a coin fell out. Sister Maria picked up the coin and said, "It's an Australian penny. Look at it!"

"Pretty and shiny," Hazel said as Maria laid it on her palm.

"And new. New! Look at the mint date, Hazel. Nineteen forty-five. What does the paper say?"

Hazel's voice was shaking as she read the short message. "It just says: 'Soon. Very soon.' "

Chapter 31

I've discovered something about myself, being so ill and weak so much of the time. I'm not afraid of dying, only of dying for no damned reason. I want my death, as I've always wanted my life, to have made a difference—to change something!

"The problem is, once you get them on the way you want, you can't ever take them off again," Peggy said, studying Hazel's feet.

She had made clunky shoe soles out of a piece of tire and was lacing them onto her feet with the last of the crimson yarn that was once her good knit suit and had been through many reincarnations since. "That's the point," Hazel said with a grin. "It's like a holy vow. I don't intend to take them off until I'm free."

"Free," Peggy snorted. "It's been weeks since you found that note."

"But the natives have slipped other coins in to us. It means something. And haven't you seen how nervous and skittery the guards have been the last few days? All jumpy and whispering to one another all the time. Even Mickey is going around with a face a mile long. Something important is happening. I know it. Peggy, you're not listening to me—"

"Shhh. Look at the guards now. What are they doing?"

Saigo had called to them, and they'd assembled in front of his hut. Mickey brought out a radio, its cord trailing back into the hut. They were talking among themselves until Saigo snapped

362

an order. "Some sort of announcement on the radio they're all to listen to," Peggy said. "Where's Nancy? Maybe she could get close enough to hear."

"She's out with the water carriers."

"Damn."

They got up and, as casually as possible, wandered toward the fence and leaned against it. The guards were all standing in a semicircle, bent forward, listening intently. Saigo's face was frozen in fury. Suddenly, they all stood up very straight and exchanged surprised looks. Then, inexplicably, they all bowed deeply to the radio.

"Must be a real bigshot talking now," Hazel whispered.

"Oh, God! I wish we could hear it."

The unheard voice on the radio went on for some time before the guards bowed again and Saigo turned it off. Then he talked to them for a long time. As they listened, they kept glancing over their shoulders toward the compound. By this time several other women had noticed the odd meeting going on and had joined Peggy and Hazel at the wire to watch and eavesdrop. "What's the powwow about?" Gloria asked.

"I don't know, Dinki, but I don't think it's good for us," Peggy said.

"Look at Mickey," Sister Maria said. "It looks like he's talking back to Saigo." Just as she spoke, Saigo reached up and furiously smacked Mickey in the mouth. The big guard fell back, bowing deeply in contrition.

"If Mickey doesn't like it, neither do I," Gloria said uneasily.

"Then for heaven's sake, don't start any trouble today," Hazel said, feeling distinctly edgy herself. "We don't need to goad them. Especially not Saigo."

They all crept back to their huts, determined to be as near to invisible as they could manage. Two hours later Nancy came in. They fell on her with their worries and Gloria said, "You've got to find Mickey and chat him up! Find out what's going on."

"I already did. He was hanging around the gate looking sick as mud, and I asked him what was wrong. All he'll talk about is a big boom. Bomb, I think he means. Dropped on Japan."

"You don't mean this is the first time in the whole damned war we've bombed Japan!" Gloria said in disgust.

"It's more than just a bomb," Nancy said thoughtfully. "The Emperor himself was on the radio talking about it."

"The Emperor?"

"In person. It's astonishing. He's so lofty. No one outside the highest court circles has ever heard him speak."

"So what did he say?" Gloria asked, not much impressed with this break in tradition.

"Mickey won't say. Saigo told him not to. He's as afraid of the monster as we are."

"Speak for yourself. I'm not afraid of the bastard!" Gloria said.

Peggy turned to her angrily. "Then you haven't learned a single thing in three and a half years! I don't know why that continues to surprise me."

"I wasn't aware that I'd enrolled in a school! So sorry, madam headmistress!"

"*Life* is a school, and you're one of the sorriest students I've ever met!"

"Stop it!" Hazel said sharply. "We're on the same side. Have you both forgotten?"

Peggy turned to her in amazement. She stared at her for a long moment before reluctantly smiling. "Hazel, you wouldn't have dreamed of addressing me in that tone when we started all this."

Hazel didn't reply to Peggy, but spoke to Nancy instead. "Is there anything we should—or shouldn't—be doing?"

"Staying calm and out of their way is all, I imagine. I'll keep trying to pump Mickey, but I don't hold out much hope. When he's given a direct order, he tries to follow it."

The next morning a Japanese official came to inspect them. He was a frazzled, elderly man with a bad limp, a great deal of gold braid on his uniform, and a big patch on the seat of his pants. He wasn't nearly as fascinating to the women as the interpreter he brought along. "Well, twist my knickers! If it isn't Miss Royama!" Gloria hissed to Peggy.

"It isn't!"

She was as much changed as they. Her spiky hair was shorter and spikier than ever and now had a generous swath of gray through it. Dumpy and plump when they last saw her, she was now nearly as emaciated as the prisoners, and several of her flashy silver teeth were missing. "I'm sure it's her. But she looks like she got left out in the rain for a few years," Gloria said gleefully. "Doesn't it do your heart good to see one of them fall to bits that way?"

The official looked them over, Miss Royama following, dead-eyed and tired, in his wake. Then they got back into his car and were whisked away. "So what was all that about, do you think?" Hazel asked. "I'd feel better if it had been Natsume."

"Natsume? Why?" Sister Maria asked.

"I'm not sure. Natsume is a bastard, too, but a more civilized one."

"You just think that because he speaks good English. Anyway, I don't think he's anywhere near here."

"We don't even know where 'here' is," Hazel reminded her. "Much less where he might be."

That afternoon another visitor came. This one was a hefty Japanese corporal who was greeted with enthusiasm. He had a freshly butchered hog carcass and a box of newish lipsticks to drop off. "Good God! What *has* happened outside?" Dr. Millichope said. "And why pork and lipstick? Their mental processes—if you'll excuse the term—never stop surprising me. I better oversee the distribution of that meat or everybody in the camp will be sick to death." In spite of her efforts to convince the cooks to space the meat out over time, it was all served at one meal. It hardly amounted to a quarter of a cup each, but to systems long deprived of animal fats, it was disaster. Long lines formed all night long at the latrine, and there were a few terribly messy accidents. But for once nobody complained.

Hazel was trying another way of tying her tire-tread shoes to her feet the next day when she thought she heard a plane. "Hey! Come out here," she said to her hutmates. "Do you hear something? Dr. Millichope, you've got the best ears. What do you think?"

The old doctor, Beryl Stacton, and Jane Kowolski came to join her outside the hut. "Yes. Yes, you're right. A plane. Just out there," Dr. Millichope said, pointing to the northeast. "Can you see anything yet?"

They shaded their eyes and looked where she'd pointed. Hazel held her breath and could only hear her heart pounding in her ears now. Finally, a distinct buzzing sound. A small plane then. Not big bombers like before. "Damn, it's probably one of theirs," Hazel muttered.

But as the plane drew closer, they couldn't see the rising sun on the wing. Other women had poured out of the huts to see it. It passed over them. They screamed and waved their arms.

"Down here! We're down here! Don't go away!" Gloria shrieked.

The small plane passed, circled, and came back over. This time, something was fluttering down from it. "Papers! Leaflets of some kind!" Hazel said.

The guards had noticed, too. Saigo had rushed into the compound with three of them. He was screaming orders. Nobody, including the guards, paid any attention.

The leaflets drifted down. The women were running around the compound, arms stretched up, each wanting to be the first to catch one. Saigo ran back to his hut and started ringing the *tenko* bell wildly.

"I've got one!" Peggy cried. She stepped up onto the platform Saigo used when he addressed them. "Listen. I'll read it. 'The war is over—' "

An enormous cheer drowned her out for a moment.

"Quiet! Quiet! Let her finish!" Dinki screamed.

Peggy held up the paper and went on: "The war is over. Japan has surrendered. Stay where you are until Allied forces can clear the minefields around the island and bring in materials to construct landing strips to bring you out. Do not leave your camps or antagonize your captors. There will still be fighting. Large bands of roving Sumatran nationalists are a serious threat to you. We'll come for you as soon as we can. God bless you all!"

The last words were almost lost in the happy weeping of the women and Saigo's resumed yelling. This time he had all the guards with him. He ran over and snatched the paper from Peggy, then grabbed her arm and jerked her off the podium. He screamed something in her face and then quickly turned his rifle around and crashed the butt of it into her chest.

"Peggy!" Hazel screamed, pushing forward. Mickey grabbed her and stopped her. She shook him off but found herself with the point of another guard's bayonet at her stomach. Peggy was lying on the ground, doubled over forward, her right arm stretched out at an unnatural angle. She wasn't moving or making a sound. Saigo was screaming at the guards, who were pushing and shoving at the women, herding them into a corner of the compound. "Where's Nancy?" Hazel shouted. "What's he telling them?"

"She ran to find Elise," Gloria said. She was dead white and trembling. "Look at Mickey."

Mickey had his gun pointed at them, but he was sobbing, half turned to Saigo, begging for something. Saigo was shrieking and slapping him, but Mickey went on crying and begging.

"They're going to kill us!" Sister Maria said, crossing herself and falling to her knees.

They were still being pushed and shoved. Three of the guards were corralling them into a corner of the compound while three others went from hut to hut, dragging women and children out of hiding and prodding them toward the group.

"We can't just stand here and die!" Gloria cried.

"We'll have to rush them. It's the only way!" Hazel said.

Jane Kowolski and Nancy Muir were being dragged from the latrine where they'd been trying to hide Elise and Vivian. The girls were crying and clinging to them and the women had their arms around them, doing what little they could to protect them as the guards beat and pushed them.

"If we all run at them at once, they can each get off one shot before we overcome them," Hazel said breathlessly. "That's eight of us that risk being hurt or killed, but it will save the rest."

"I get Saigo. I want to be the one to kill the son of a bitch," Gloria said.

Across the dusty central area, Peggy had moved slightly. "She's alive!" Hazel said to Gloria, and then stopped. In moments Peggy might be the only one of them alive.

"Our Father, Who art in heaven—" Sister Maria was saying. Others around her had gone to their knees to join her in a final prayer.

"Get up, you fools! You can't save yourselves that way!" Gloria said furiously. "Get up and fight for yourselves!"

Mrs. Haver was being dragged out, feet first, from underneath a hut where she'd attempted to hide. She was shrieking hysterically, thrashing and flinging herself against the guard. Another woman ran to her defense and was shot in the stomach. She curled up like a leaf in a fire.

Mickey was still crying and pleading with Saigo, who was dashing back and forth, giving shrill orders.

Suddenly, above the shouting and crying, they heard the sound of a jeep horn. "God! Somebody's here!" Gloria said, grabbing Hazel's arm. "At the gate!" The driver of the jeep had jumped out and was shoving open the gate. A distinguished-looking man got out and walked through, a pistol held high in his left hand.

He fired one shot as he came forward, and the camp fell momentarily silent.

Saigo whirled at the sound of the shot and looked at Natsume with as much loathing as he had for the women.

"Natsume!" Hazel said, clinging to Gloria.

"Don't sound so goddamned happy! He's just a head butcher, come to watch the fun!"

"Shut up, Dinki," Nancy said. She and Elise had pushed their way through the crowd and were now at the front. She waved her hands to shush the rest of them and cocked her head, listening intently. "He's berating Saigo. Natsume says Saigo knew the Emperor reversed the orders that we were to be massacred. He says Saigo's duty was to protect us and he has dishonored the Nippon army, his country, and his Emperor by going against those orders."

Saigo bowed to Natsume. His movements were jerky. His yellow complexion was purple with embarrassment and anger, but he straightened and went to his hut. Natsume barked a few commands to the guards. Mickey dropped his gun and sat down on the ground with his face in his hands.

"Natsume says they are to take their orders from him from now on. They are not to harm us, on orders directly from the Emperor."

"Thank God!" Hazel said.

Natsume approached them. What Nancy had said was spreading through the crowd of women like ripples. Outward from her in rings, they were crying with relief and hugging one another.

"Western women, the war is over. I have much to say to you. Let us have order and decorum, please," Natsume said.

Hazel stepped forward. "May we go to our friend?" she asked, gesturing toward Peggy, who still lay in a heap in the dust a few yards away.

"Three of you may do so. The rest of you should line up in an orderly fashion."

Several women ran over to Mrs. Haver's friend, who was beyond help. Hazel, Gloria, and Dr. Millichope rushed forward and gingerly turned Peggy over. Her face was putty-colored and her breathing was shallow and rasping. There was a flicker of recognition in her eyes before they closed. "We must get her into the shade," Dr. Millichope said. "You girls carry her into the hut."

In the compound the women had formed into straggling *tenko* lines. "You may be more comfortable sitting down," Natsume said. When they had done so, he went on. "The war is over. Emperor Hirohito has surrendered to Allied demands. A great and terrible bomb has devastated two of our great cities, killing tens of thousands of people in a more horrible manner than any weapon before." His clear, carrying voice calmed them. "There is much you will wish to know, and I shall be here to inform you as best I can, but first there are facts you must know for your own welfare. You may not leave camp—"

"We're free now! You can't order us around!" someone shouted.

"I am not giving an order. Your General MacArthur and Lord Mountbatten have given this order. I merely pass it along to you. You may not be aware that many of the natives, now that the war is over, do not wish to return to rule under Europeans. Their resentment might find violent means of expression. You must stay in this camp for your own safety. In addition, I'm sorry to say that you have seen evidence that some Nippon soldiers may be tempted to disobey the Honorable Emperor's orders and attempt to thwart those who are coming to take you home."

"When will we get to go home?" Jane Kowolski asked.

Natsume shrugged. "Days? Weeks? I cannot say. But be assured that neither I nor any other Nippon officer wishes to keep you here an hour longer than necessary."

"Only three and a half years longer than necessary!" a woman at the back of the group jeered.

I've given my life's work to the Emperor and soon will give my life itself, Natsume thought, *but surely this is the most difficult, shameful moment of that life.* He was spared having to give a direct reply to this vulgar comment by the sound of several trucks arriving. They had been just behind him until the last few miles, but his own premonition of something very wrong happening in this camp had caused him to speed forward and leave them lumbering behind. He said, "Western women, I told you all early in the war that your own internal organization and discipline would be vital to your survival. That is more true now than ever. If you will go to your huts in an orderly fashion, I would speak with your camp leaders now."

Hazel was bent over Peggy. "Please, Peggy. Please speak to me. You've got to wake up and live. It's over. We're really and truly free. Even Natsume says so. Peggy—"

Dr. Millichope shook her head sadly and whispered. "Her sternum is splintered. No doubt shards have damaged her heart. It's a wonder she didn't die instantly."

Hazel took the doctor's hand. The nails were turning blue. Hazel's tears dripped onto their twined fingers. "Don't die, Peggy. I need you. We all need you. You son, Jim, needs you."

Peggy's eyelids fluttered. "Jim—" she muttered.

"Yes, Jim! Jim will be waiting for you. It's over, Peggy, and you can go home to Jim."

Peggy looked straight at Hazel. "My diaries—Jim."

"Yes, we'll make sure Jim gets your diaries."

"Promise—?"

"I promise. I'll promise you anything that's in my power to promise, but don't leave me, Peggy."

The older woman shook her head slightly. "People must know—"

She closed her eyes.

Mickey came in, carrying a tottering pile of boxes. He said something fast and cheerful to Hazel in Nippongo. "Go away, Mickey," she said without looking at him.

"Hazer Hammon. Look. Good thing all for womens."

She turned. He was ripping into the boxes and handing Dr. Millichope bandages, quinine, vitamins, hemostats, sutures, towels, mosquito nets, bottles of serum, and packets of sulfa powder. Rising slowly, Hazel took a fresh white sheet from him and shook out the folds before laying it over Peggy. She kissed the dead woman's forehead before pulling the sheet up over her face. Then she bent her head to pray, but no words would come to mind. She was filled with a deep anger so cold and solid that it blotted mere words out. She could think of nothing to say to God except curses.

Natsume looked around in disgust at the half of Saigo's hut that served as the camp office. It was bad enough that the man lacked the Nippon virtues of restraint and self-control, but he was dirty and untidy of person and character as well. The room stank of sweat and urine and hatred. Tomorrow he would have it cleaned out. He glanced through the files, shaking his head with disgust. It would take time to make any sense of them, if it were possible at all.

He sat down carefully, exhausted but reluctant to soil himself by contact with Saigo's chair. It was so hot today. If his dignity didn't demand full dress uniform, he would have liked to shed the coat at least. He closed his eyes and tried to think about snow. He'd done this hundreds of times in the last few years, and occasionally it worked. But not this time. Probably not ever again now that he knew he'd never see snow again. Like his father before him, he had found that he did not have whatever it took to commit honorable seppuku. Perhaps it was genetic; perhaps his early years in America had soiled his soul in some way. Whatever the cause of the failure, he must live. He would "face the music," as the Americans said. Such a foolish phrase. Face war crime trials. For surely they would occur. And he, Etsu Natsume, descendant of respected samurai, would bear responsibility for the acts of dishonorable men like Saburo Saigo.

Karma.

There was a light knock on the door. He went to open it. It was the redheaded young woman. Dreadfully thin and sick-looking, but still very like—

"What is it, Miss Hampton?"

"You know my name?"

"I have an excellent memory. When I found you in my office at the Palembang camp, I made inquiries," he said, then regretted having explained himself. "What is it you want?"

"I was told you had a meeting with the camp leaders. I am one."

"But you were with your friend. Is she well?"

"She is dead."

He nodded. "I see. Her name must be added to the lists."

"The name your army knew her by is false. I wish to be sure her real name is on the list," Hazel had inadvertently picked up his formal mode of speech. It suited the situation and served as a protection against emotion.

"I shall see to it myself," he said, going around behind the desk and taking out a sheet of paper. "What is her real name?"

"Dr. Margaret B. Sutherland."

He looked up slowly. "The author?"

"You've heard of her?"

"Of course. She was—was wise to keep her name a secret. She is on a list of most highly prized captives. There would have been honor to the soldier who captured her."

"Then you have that honor," Hazel said. "Much good may it do you."

"The war is over now, Miss Hampton. You are the victor."

She leaned forward, her palms on the desk. "No, Commandant. That's too easy by far. You can't just say, 'We took your lives and your health and your youth and your mothers and fathers, but you must now forget it because your side won. No hard feelings, okay?' It doesn't work that way. The war may be over, but the losses are forever and the hatred is forever."

"I hope you are wrong. And I remind you that nothing has been done to your people by mine in these last three years that was not done to my people by yours for the hundred years before."

Hazel sighed. "I'm not here for a history lesson."

"What did you come for?"

"I want to ask some questions. No doubt the others asked you earlier, but if there is one thing I have learned in Sumatra, it is not to trust second-hand information."

"Yes?"

"How are we to get in touch with our families?"

"Tomorrow I will start seeing each woman in camp. They will give me their names, nationalities, and next of kin to be informed of their whereabouts. This information will be compiled and handed to the Allied forces."

"And what of those who died?"

"They are on the lists."

"It is important that their families be put in touch with those of us who were their friends."

"That will be up to your own governments."

"I see. Commandant, may I ask you other questions when I think of what they are? I'm very tired and upset—"

"I shall welcome conversation with you, Miss Hampton."

"Where are you from, Commandant?"

He was surprised at the question, but didn't show it. "Nagasaki."

"No, I mean before that. Surely you learned your English in America."

"Yes. I was born in Sacramento, California."

"Thank you. I often wondered."

Out of habit, she bowed to him before she turned to go. As she opened the door, he said, "Miss Hampton, may I have the privilege of asking you a personal question?"

"I suppose."

"Did you ever happen to know a woman named Elizabeth Makepeace?"

Hazel thought for a moment. "No, I don't believe so. Who is she?"

"No one. Just a woman you remind me of. Miss Hampton, believe me, I'm sorry about your friend. If only I'd come sooner—"

"Oh, but you did. You came to us in the first jail and it made no difference. No difference at all."

PART III

Liberation

Hazel woke automatically at dawn, anticipating the *tenko* bell any second. She lay waiting for some time before she realized she wasn't going to hear it. No more *tenko*! Ever again! She turned over, rubbing her cheek against the crisp white sheet she'd rolled up in the night before. She went back to sleep, smiling. When she next woke, it was to the sound of thuds on the roof and an argument raging outside the hut.

"That one's too big! You better get everybody out of the hut first in case the roof falls in," Jane Kowolski was saying.

Gloria's voice came from above. "Don't be such a pessimist! They're just little rocks."

"They're bloody great boulders!"

Hazel went outside. Gloria had organized an assembly line, which was passing rocks along and up a ladder to her on the roof. The rocks were all painted white and smears of the still-wet paint were getting all over everybody. "What in hell is she doing? Has everybody gone mad?" Hazel asked blearily.

"Oh, Hazel, you sleepyhead. Finally awake? We're using the roofs as a giant message blackboard. These three in a row are going to say P.O.W. written out in white rocks so that any more fliers who come along will know we're here. We don't know if the fella with the leaflets reported us."

"Where'd she get the paint?"

Jane looked at her pityingly. "Hazel. After all this time, you still ask these foolish questions?"

"Stupid of me. She hasn't changed a bit, has she?"

"Less than any of us, I would say," Jane mused.

Hazel went off to the latrine and then to the bathhouse, where she discovered that there were actual bars of soap and a few skimpy but clean towels to use. Luxuriating in unfamiliar lather, she stood under the drizzle of the hose and scrubbed off the top few layers of dirt. As she did so, she found herself thinking about what Jane had said. Dinki *hadn't* changed. Diet and circumstances had subdued her slightly from time to time, but she always bounced back, as defiant and troublesome as ever.

But the rest of them—?

Dinki was the exception, wasn't she? Nancy Muir was certainly a different person. Aloof, irritable, and severe at the beginning, she had turned into a friendly, affectionate person. Still a bit stiff in her mannerisms, but only occasionally. Knowing her Mr. Dreyer and having charge of Elise had changed her. Now, of course, she'd lost track of Herbert and would soon have to give up Elise to her own people. And the rest of them, the women she'd learned how to be friends with, would scatter to the four corners of the earth. Would Nancy go back to being as she was?

Will I? Hazel wondered, troubled at the thought. She had come into camp a shy, unsure girl who didn't think very well of herself, a peacemaker who would suffer any amount of personal unhappiness to avoid a confrontation of any kind. It was odd: she could think of that Hazel Hampton as another person, a girl she'd met in the outside world and vaguely remembered. Now she was someone else entirely. The women with whom she'd shared this desperate life had come to regard her as dependable. They respected and liked her. She liked herself, but would Frank?

Frank—?

She could no longer bring his face to mind at all. The photograph she'd had in her billfold had mildewed and disintegrated a long time ago. So had the billfold itself. What would faceless Frank think of her now? Would he understand and accept that she no longer needed someone to make her decisions for her because now she wasn't the least afraid to make them herself and face the consequences? For years she'd been mentally escaping the horror of life in prison camp by imagining the life she'd go back to. Now, suddenly, she was on the brink of actually going back to it, and she was anxious and troubled instead of happy. She'd imagined an immediate wedding. Frank might even come out to fetch her back and they'd be married in Singapore. But, in reality, she couldn't do that. She had responsibilities to take care of first. She had to find her father with only a few insubstantial clues that were years old. And she had to make sure that Peggy's diaries got into her son Jim's hands. There was no question in her mind of packing them up and mailing them off to a stranger. She wanted to hand them personally to Jim Sutherland and tell him about his mother's last years and how much she'd meant to her.

As for the rest of the dream? To settle into a cozy honeymoon house someplace and start having babies and growing irises and joining women's clubs and giving fancy dinners to help Frank's career along? She realized as she stood there, rinsing off under a feeble trickle of murky water from a hose, that she didn't want irises and bridge games and recipes. She didn't even want the babies—right away. Except for some erratic spotting, she hadn't had a real period in two years. She probably couldn't have babies for a while, if ever. But she didn't want to, anyway. She wanted to go to school. Not like a girl, like before, when she went to college because girls of her class did and girls like her who wished to please their parents made an effort to get good grades. No, she wanted to really learn something. Be something. Like Peggy.

"Move it along. You're using all the hot water," Nancy Muir said.

Hazel snapped out of her troubled reverie. "Hot water? We don't have hot water!"

"No, but we will soon," Nancy said, stepping out of her ragged shorts and untying her halter top and gently pushing Hazel out of the way so she could get wet. "Oh, soap! Real soap. Isn't it odd how awfully strong it smells? I never noticed that about soap before." Hazel picked up a towel and started rubbing herself, wondering for the first time exactly when they'd left modesty behind. In the jail at Banka Island they'd gone to great trouble to make screens to undress behind, but now nakedness meant absolutely nothing. They'd all abandoned a terribly basic attitude of their culture, and she'd never noticed it before today. In what other ways had she changed that they didn't even know about? And how would that outside world they'd dreamed about for so long treat them when they'd forgotten the rules of civilization?

She watched Nancy standing under the trickle of water, let-

ting it run over her face. "Nancy? Are you happy? I know I
should be, but I'm not."

Nancy squeezed the last of the soap out of her hair and shook
her head. She didn't answer directly. "Where did you find that
towel? Oh, another. Good. I went outside the fence today. No
reason. Just walked clear around the perimeter of the camp on
the outside instead of on the inside. I liked that. Nobody telling
me anymore which side I have to be on."

"But you're scared, too. Like I am. Aren't you?"

"I'm gaining my freedom and the chance to find Herbert, but
I'm going to lose Elise. Of course I'm scared of that. My only
worth for the last few years has been my value as Elise's 'Aunt
Nancy.' When that's gone, and if Herbert's dead, what am I? A
dried-up old maid with no useful skills."

"But you've learned valuable skills here, haven't you? We
can't have gone through all this for nothing!"

Nancy started putting back on her clothing. "What have we
learned here? I have learned to steal, although I had a head
start—"

"What do you mean?"

"It doesn't matter. I've learned to steal." She started ticking
off points on her fingers. "I've learned to eat very slowly to
make three ounces of rice last half an hour. I've learned to treat
insect bites with bits of rag boiled in palm oil instead of iodine
and bandages. I've learned how to balance two buckets of water
on a pole without spilling it. I'm an expert on creeping under
barbed wire and sneaking through the jungle without making
any noise. I can make a pair of shorts with a rusty needle and
the sleeve of a dead nun's habit, and I'm very good at not seeing
the protein-rich bugs we leave in the rice now for the nutritional
value. I'm skilled, like all of us, at standing at *tenko* for hours
without passing out, and my feet are so tough I can walk for
miles without shoes. So, Hazel, tell me: how is any of that going
to do me any good in the outside world?"

They watched the sky all day. And all the next day and the
next. They saw planes in the distance, or imagined that they did,
but none of them came near. One by one they went to Natsume's
office and told him the name and address of the person they
wanted told of their whereabouts. They were allowed one ten-
word message. Hazel gave Barbara's name and their home address in Evanston. "Mother dead. Me alive. Will find Father.

Love to Frank.'' She felt silly about the ''me alive'' part. It was obvious, but she wanted to use all the ten words she was allowed and couldn't think of another two that said anything half so important.

Gloria sent her allotted message to her new niece and namesake. ''Auntie Gloria coming home. Kiss, kiss, kiss, kiss, kiss, kiss.''

Jane's message to her brother said, ''Coming home soon. Dust off opera scores. Mourn Mother.''

Elise sent her message to her English great-uncle Ralph in Surrey and Nancy sent hers there as well, assuring them that she would continue to care for the girl. She had no one to contact on her own behalf. Dr. Millichope notified her sister-in-law in Edinburgh of her survival. ''She's always hated me. I think the little girl in Kansas would have been happier to hear from me,'' she chortled.

Sister Maria let her mother house know of her whereabouts. Beryl Stacton, not knowing where her husband might be stationed, simply reported herself to the British army without mentioning the child, Jonathan. Audrey refused to send a message to anyone and wouldn't talk about it. Mrs. Haver likewise had misplaced her husband before being captured, so she notified the mayor of Toronto, whom she claimed was her second cousin. ''Dear Lord, she's counting on a welcome-home parade in her honor,'' Jane Kowolski said. ''The bitch!''

Hazel wanted to send a message to Peggy's son, Jim, but had no idea how to go about it. Peggy'd had no idea where he was, and Hazel couldn't guess. She considered contacting Peggy's publisher but couldn't remember which one it was. Nor could she recall that Peggy had ever told her the name of the girl's college of which she was president. Instead, she went back to Natsume and insisted that he put a note to her record that anyone inquiring about her should contact Hazel Hampton of Evanston, Illinois.

They kept watching for planes.

Natsume sent the messages off with a guard and they wondered if they'd ever reach their destinations. Saigo moved in with the other guards and kept out of the women's sight. The daily routine went on without much change. The wood gatherers and water carriers continued to gather and carry, but now the guards went with them under Natsume's orders to protect them from the natives, not Saigo's orders to keep them from escaping.

Hazel started writing bits to add to Peggy's diary.

Jane resumed her singing practice. She'd not done so since their last move. Now she worked at it for hours and hours a day and became more and more depressed. She kept Vivian at her side, just as Nancy suddenly couldn't bear to have Elise more than a few feet away. The girls chaffed at this and got in trouble more often than ever. They found a dead frog and put it in Mrs. Haver's drinking cup. She had a fit and went to Jane in outrage. They shouted at each other for a few minutes and Jane slapped her.

Nancy got her hands on a real deck of cards and tried to teach Mickey how to play canasta without much success. Beryl Stacton made a pair of shorts and a shirt for Jonathan out of a sheet and dyed them purple with some berries she found in the jungle. Audrey got out a pair of high heels she'd managed to hang on to throughout the war and started practicing walking in them.

Gloria started making book on who would be the first in to them. Odds were heavily on the Australians. "Now, it has to be a man and he has to actually have his feet on the ground and be alive to ask his nationality," she warned those placing their bets with her. "We're not going to get into fights over guessing about some guy who flies over and drops more damned leaflets. If a group comes in at once, the bet rests on the highest-ranking one." This was so successful that she also set up a jackpot prize for anyone who correctly predicted the actual city the man would be from. The problem was in the currency of the bets. They no longer had money or anything of much value, nor would Gloria accept any of the sheets, towels, medicine, or soap they'd been given. Hazel put her tire-tread shoes up for an American from Chicago. Audrey bet her high heels on a Londoner. Elise and Nancy together bet the blue headband they shared on a Dutchman from Sumatra itself.

And still they waited.

It was more than two weeks before another plane returned. This time it was a formation of three small American fighter planes. At the first sound of airplane engines, early in the morning, women poured out into the center of the compound. They shouted and waved sheets and soon the small planes swooped over, turned, and swooped back, dipping their wings in acknowledgment and greeting. On the third pass, one plane with an open cockpit flew so low it brushed the treetops. The broadly grinning flier flung something down. A pack of cigarettes with a note tied around. It nearly hit Mrs. Haver, who read the note. "It says, 'What do you need most?' "

"How do we answer?" Beryl asked of the others.

"Get back, all of you," Audrey shouted. As they moved away, she started running around the dusty center of the camp in a most peculiar shuffling fashion. In a moment they realized she was writing in the dirt with her feet.

M-E-N, she spelled out.

"That trashy woman," Nancy Muir said, running along behind, scuffing it out.

Gloria was behind her and to the cheers of a few, she wrote her own message:

BOOZE.

The planes buzzed back over. This time the pilot of each flung a small, hard tube out. When they landed, they were unrolled and discovered to be several issues of *Reader's Digest*. "I think I've forgotten how to read," Sister Maria said. "How are we going to share them?"

"We could tear them up and pass the pages around," Gloria suggested.

"We could have counted on you to want to rip something up the moment we get it, Sister Denk. No, they'd get all mixed up," Mrs. Haver said in her usual superior manner. "We should pick three readers with loud voices to read them aloud for people to listen to. I'll volunteer."

Hazel said, "I hate to admit it, but you're quite right, Mrs. Haver."

They spent the next few hours listening to relays of readers. It was wonderful and frustrating. They didn't get about half the jokes and were perplexed about the people and events mentioned and alluded to.

"Who is this General Eisenhower, anyway?" they'd ask.

"What happened to Hitler?"

"Is Roosevelt still president?"

"Harry S who?"

"I wish there were pictures of the fashions."

"What about Sinatra? Is there anything about Frankie?"

"Oh, no! Carole Lombard died!"

Late in the afternoon they heard a low drone. "Oh, my God,

will you just look at that thing!'' Jane said at their first sight of
the enormous four-engine bomber that was approaching. "How
does anything that big stay in the air? You don't think it's crashing into us, do you?''

The great plane skimmed above them. The bomb-bay doors
were open and they could see men inside, waving at them. They
waved back, happily unaware that the gesture was meant as a
warning to get out of the way, not as a greeting. As it was
directly over them, the men inside started shoving twenty-gallon
barrels out. They fell like bombs. The women scattered, shrieking. One of the barrels plunged through the roof of the kitchen.
Another shattered the small porch of one of the huts. The rest
landed with terrific thuds in the center of the compound. A few
burst open.

As the plane left, the women rushed out to see what they'd
received.

"Bread! Real white bread! Ten loaves!''

"Apples. Oh, my God, apples! I'd forgotten what apples smell
like.''

There were tins of corned beef, one whole barrel full of assorted flavors of chewing gum. Tins of flour, coffee, tea, and
butter. Powdered eggs and milk and cocoa. Hershey bars and
prunes. The barrel that went through the kitchen had been full
of raspberry jam and had burst. The children and some of the
adults were eating it by the handful. They heard the drone of the
plane again, and all ran to the edges of the compound for safety.
This time the first item out was something tied up in mattresses.
Gloria managed to be first to it, and when she got the ropes
untied, she proudly announced that it was a whole case of bourbon with only one bottle broken. "Oh, what a knees-up we can
have tonight!'' she exclaimed.

On the third pass, the bomber dropped another mattress-
padded crate, this one of medicines, and a third that was a whole
box of cosmetics. There was lipstick, rouge, foundation, face
powder, perfume, shampoo, toothpaste, eyebrow pencils. Audrey St. John fell on it and would have kept the whole case if it
hadn't been taken away from her to be distributed. One of the
first in line was Sister Maria.

Dr. Millichope was frantic. "They shouldn't have dropped
all that food at once,'' she complained an hour later. "I've already got eleven people dreadfully ill from stuffing themselves.

One of those little boys who got into the jam is in shock. All that sugar and acid.''

Hazel made sympathetic noises, then ate two candy bars, got so sick she threw them up, and ate two more and went to sleep with another one clutched in her hand which melted all over her.

They had a noisy, happy night, but in the morning they were greatly subdued. The child had died. So had one of the oldest women. There were a great many hangovers, headaches, and terribly upset stomachs. Someone had given Mickey a bottle of the bourbon, and the other guards had taken it away from him and gotten drunk. Several of them had disappeared into the jungle overnight, and the women and children were left only with Natsume, Saigo, Mickey, and two others to protect them.

And the need for protection was suddenly evident.

The big bomber didn't come back, but other Allied planes passed near them. By climbing on the roof of the hut on highest ground, they could squint into the early morning haze and see paratroopers drifting down from the planes. They could also hear the sound of gunfire in the distance. The gunfire went on sporadically all day. By night it was closer. Then it stopped. The next morning it resumed at dawn, but stopped by about ten.

"Hazel, you're a good driver. Why don't we take a jeep and go see what's going on?" Gloria suggested at noon.

"You really are insane!" Hazel replied.

Hazel was taking a nap around three when a shrill voice woke her. "Men! Men coming!"

She leapt up and ran outdoors. Just outside the gate there was a group of about a dozen soldiers. Several of them were being supported by the others. One had a bloody bandage around his head. Another was leaning on a makeshift crutch. They looked battered and tired. In spite of their eagerness to run forward, the women stood silent as Commandant Natsume walked forward and bowed to the men. One of them stepped out of the group, inclined his head slightly, and spoke to Natsume. The commandant bowed again and turned to lead them into the camp.

Hazel was stunned at the sight of them. They were all so big. She'd seen no men but natives and Japanese for months, and except for Mickey, they were all quite small. These men were huge! And so healthy and brawny and strong-looking in spite of their injuries. Nothing like the last sick, emaciated white men she'd seen in the big central prison camp. The man who'd spoken to Natsume stepped up onto Saigo's platform and cleared his throat. Some of the smaller children, those who had never seen a white man, started whimpering in fear. Their mothers hushed them.

The man looked around, apparently shocked at the sight of them, but doing his best to conceal it. He said in thick Australian English: "My men and I have been together since the beginning of this war. We've lost many of our comrades. We've been hurt and angry and homesick. We've endured a lot of casualties, especially in the last few days. But *you* are who we did it all for. You are our wives, our mothers, our girlfriends, and our children. And you are worth it. Every one of you."

No one spoke.

He bent his head, ostensibly to put his hat back on, but he took a quick swipe at his eyes as he did so.

Nobody knew what to say next. There was only the sound of some sniffling and some repressed sobs. Finally, a high, soft voice spoke up. Vivian said respectfully. "Excuse me, sir, but what city are you from?"

He looked perplexed, but smiled a little and said, "Fremantle."

Someone in the back of the group shrieked. "I won! I won!"

The spell was broken. The women surged forward, engulfing their rescuers in hugs and handshakes and questions.

Chapter 33

Within a week the Australians were able to bring in enough troops and trucks to start taking the women and children out. The most seriously ill were first to go. Then the mothers with the smallest children, although Beryl Stacton insisted on staying behind, claiming her child was the healthiest in the camp and did not need immediate medical attention. Since this was so manifestly true, and there were others fighting for her place, she was allowed to remain with Audrey and her friends.

More soldiers came in, and under the direction of Captain Harry Nown, the Fremantler, took over the work of the camp. They carried the water and cut the firewood and cooked the meals for the women. They played with the children, showed everybody the latest dances, filled them in on world events, and just listened to them. They treated their wounds and took photographs of them as though they were worthy, beautiful subjects. They became, in truth, fathers and brothers to everyone.

Finally, toward the end of the second week in September, Harry Nown told them the rest of the camp would leave the next morning. "We'll take trucks to the nearest railway depot. A train will take you from there to the coast, where planes will take you to Singapore. Once there, you'll be taken first to hospital, then assigned to private homes and hotels until you are in touch with your families. All Allied governments have agreed to provide free transport for their people to go home, if they wish. Ladies, we're going to be crowded for space, so bring only your most important personal items. Everything else you need—clothes, food, bedding—will be provided for you."

Hazel woke early the last morning to take a final inventory of what she was taking out. Most important was Peggy's battered suitcase, the lining of which was stuffed with her notes. Inside it was the canteen, likewise filled with tiny bits of paper. She had her once-white silk scarf, now with only her engagement ring, her mother's wedding and engagement rings, and the strand of pearls. Everything else had gone for food and the bribe to the native to try to find Nancy's Herbert. The only meaningful items from internment were her precious maps and a pair of knitted socks which Jane had given her for Christmas two years before. They'd been made out of an unraveled khaki shirt that Gloria had stolen for the purpose. She also saved a halter top that had originally been a dress of old Mrs. Englethorpe's and had passed through several other women before the remaining section of skirt came to Hazel.

She looked over the few pitiful items, closed the suitcase, and used it as a desk to compose a note. "To Whom It May Concern: This is to let you know that Private Masamichi Asakawa has treated the prisoners under his care with as much dignity and kindness as his superiors would allow him. He has been good to the children, has often helped smuggle desperately needed food into internment camp, and has deliberately failed to report transgressions for which we could have been severely punished. If he should come to trial, I hope you will enter this testimony and I will be glad to elaborate on it if you allow me.'' She looked it over, signed and dated it, and gave her home address in Illinois.

Sister Maria came in as she was folding up the note. She'd made a habit out of white sheets. ''I can't get over how you look in that getup,'' Hazel said. ''After all these years of wearing shorts and sun tops, why didn't you just wait until you got to Singapore instead of going to all that work? Certainly your order will have a real habit waiting for you.''

''I'm sure they will. It was the thought of the men. I realized when we knew they were coming that I was content to be a woman among women, but I didn't want to be a woman among men. Do you understand? It doesn't matter. I think God does. I came to get you for the ceremonies.''

''What ceremonies?''

''Mrs. Reid is breaking her plate and wants everybody to watch.''

Hazel laughed. Mrs. Reid had been on her way back to India to join her husband when she was captured. She'd purchased a new set of china back home and had a sample plate along to show him. She'd eaten every meal for three and a half years off that same plate, and swore that when she was free, she would break it. Hazel joined Sister Maria and a crowd gathered around Mrs. Reid's hut. She came out, carrying the plate high. Someone started humming ''Pomp and Circumstance'' and the others took it up. Mrs. Reid put the plate down on the ground and produced a hammer with a flourish. She got the first crack. It broke into four pieces. She passed the hammer around and her hutmates all got a crack at it. ''Ladies, when I get home, I'm doing the same to every place setting in the whole set. I never want to see that pattern again the rest of my life,'' she said.

The Australian soldiers were beginning to move around the camp now, urging the women to bring their things out to be ready to depart. Then they took their things out into the road, but as the first truck came around the bend, Captain Nown said, ''Not this one, ladies.''

The truck stopped and Nown went to the guards' hut to lead

the Japanese away. Commandant Natsume came first. Head held
high, he walked past the women as though they weren't there.
A few yards behind him, Saigo limped along. "You bastard!
You sadistic bastard! I hope they string you up!" Gloria shouted.
Several of the women spat at him as he passed. Two of the
Australian soldiers came forward to hustle him along. The other
guards came next, with Mickey bringing up the rear. Hazel ran
forward and pressed her note into his hand. "Good luck,
Mickey-san," she said softly, then bowed deeply to him.

The others took it up. As he passed by, most of them bowed
to him, the only time they had ever willingly given that sign of
respect to one of their captors. He climbed into the truck and
turned to wave. There were tears rolling down his big face, but
he was smiling.

As the truck taking the Japanese away turned around and
headed down the road, a convoy of transports came up. The
women scrambled aboard, then all had to get back out and be
checked off the roles to make sure nobody was being left behind.
This completed, they crowded back onto the trucks, the engines
roared to life, and they went rattling off down the mountain.

It was a long, jolting ride to the train station, and the train
wasn't waiting for them as it was supposed to be. The women
were all instructed to line up on the platform and not step off it.
At first they were resentful of the strongly worded order, but
soon realized why it had been given. The townspeople had turned
out to gawk at them. They clustered in discontented knots, muttering and gesturing threateningly. Captain Nown and his men
marched up and down the platform in front of the women, hands
firmly on their holstered guns, to discourage any rash actions on
the part of the natives.

Fortunately, it was only twenty minutes until the train came.
They boarded quickly and silently and didn't relax until they
were well away from the town. It was a six-hour journey on hard
wooden seats and another long delay before they were allowed
off at the end. While they were waiting, Elise said, "I heard
something awful, Hazel."

"You did?"

"It's about your lot. The Americans. One of the soldiers was
telling someone why they didn't come for us sooner."

"I should think it was obvious. The natives—"

"No, it wasn't that. He said since the Americans had dropped the bombs that made Japan surrender, they made the Allies wait to start the rescue until your General MacArthur had the surrender ceremony. The soldier said they'd heard Lord Louis was fit to be tied about it.''

"Elise, haven't you learned anything about gossip yet? That whole story is patently absurd.''*

Elise moved away and the wait went on. Hazel noticed that Gloria had been unusually quiet all day. She nudged her with her elbow. "What's up? You mad at the Americans, too?''

"Huh? No, I'm just hating myself.''

"That's new. About anything special?''

"Saigo.'' She said the name with such venom, it gave Hazel goose bumps. "I've spent all these years vowing I'd repay him for the massacre, for Caroline, for Jane, for Peggy. And I did nothing.''

"It's not up to us.''

"But surely it is? Hazel, you're the deep thinker. Haven't you wondered what the hell this has all been about?''

"Does it have to be about something? I'm afraid it's just something that happened—to us, unfortunately.''

"But it should mean something. We survived. That's important somehow. Caroline should have survived. She was a better nurse and a much nicer person than me. And Peggy died! Peggy was—she was an 'important' person. Smart and valuable to the world. But I'm alive and they're dead. There *must* be a reason for that. It must mean something!''

"I know, Dinki, but I don't know what it is. None of us does. Maybe we never will.''

"But we have to!''

"You know that saying—? That God answers all our prayers and sometimes the answer is no. I think it's sort of like that. That He had a reason for this, but He's under no obligation to tell us what it is.''

"But you *do* think there's a reason? That we survived for some purpose?''

"Probably a million of them,'' Hazel said, but she knew she hadn't eased Gloria's mind. This was the sort of moral question that Gloria had spent her life oblivious to and now was mired in. Nobody could help her out.

* * *

*The story was true.

By dark they were checked off yet another list and were taken in trucks to a row of barracks, where they were given sheets, pillows, soap, towels, underwear, and a fresh khaki shirt and skirt each. "I thought we were going to Singapore today," Gloria complained to Captain Nown.

"Tomorrow morning."

They were driven to the airfield shortly after dawn. Hazel, Gloria, Nancy, Jane, and Vivian went outside to wait in a shady place under some trees. "You look nice, Dinki," Hazel said.

Gloria twirled around, showing off her uniform. She'd washed it out and stiffened it with some rice water. It was still dingy, but a great improvement over what she'd been wearing for years. Her cheerfulness was almost usual and only Hazel noticed the faintly troubled look behind the usual flip facade. "You look nice, too, Hazel. Like the first time I saw you—remember? Except now your hair is short and you're awfully skinny and you've got those sores on your face, but they're healing nicely and—"

"Dinki, stop! Your idea of a compliment always backfires."

Her words were drowned out by the engines of a plane that had landed and was taxiing toward them. It stopped just on the other side of the fence. It was a big Australian passenger liner converted to temporary military use. A ramp was wheeled out, the door opened, and two Western women and three Japanese officers came down the steps.

"Will you look at that?" Jane said. "Those are nurses in uniforms with slacks. Slacks! Oh, the world has changed! Dinki, what's wrong?"

Gloria was making funny noises. Shading her eyes and squinting she said, "Those women aren't nurses. Look at the one with the bandanna around her hair."

"Yes? Anybody we know?" Hazel asked.

"Jesus! Don't you ever look at the illustrated papers? It's Lady Louis! Lady Mountbatten—here in Sumatra!"

"Come on! What on earth would she be doing here? Dinki, I think you're imagining—" She stopped, as Gloria wasn't paying any attention.

The group in question had moved away and another woman was coming along behind. Gloria goggled. "If I haven't gone completely crazy, that's—yes, it is! It's Matron Eagleton!" She ran forward and the others came close behind out of sheer curiosity. "Matron Eagleton, is it really you?"

The plump, middle-aged nurse held out her arms and hugged Gloria, then held her back and looked her over. "I told you I'd come to bring my girls out, didn't I, Sister Denk?"

"The others—what about the others?"

Matron Eagleton's smile faded. "I lost sixty-five girls. Twenty-six of them survived that I know of. I still can't account for Sister Cassini and Sister Warbler."

"I'm sorry, Matron, but Sister Cassini died at the very beginning and Sister Warbler was killed a few months ago. A Jap named Saigo—"

She was getting red in the face, and Matron Eagleton stopped her. "Now, now, Sister Denk. There will be plenty of time for your report. Let's get you and your friends back to Singapore so we can start sorting everything out and get you all back to health and back to your families."

"Sister Denk, need I remind you again that you are a patient at the moment!" the nursing sister on one of the Alexandria women's wards said vehemently.

"There isn't a thing wrong with me that a steak and a date with a good-looking Aussie bloke wouldn't cure."

"Just the same, until the doctor officially releases you, you've got to stay in bed."

"But Sister—"

"Dinki, shut up and do as she says. You spent three years complaining about never getting to lie around in a soft bed," Hazel said. "Now you've got the chance, so do it!"

"Aren't we touchy today?"

"Yes, we are," Hazel replied repressively. Her irritation sprung from the fact that she was as eager as Gloria to *do* something. In spite of the early arrival of the plane the day before, there had been delay after delay and they didn't reach Singapore until just after dark. From the airfield, they'd all been whisked straight to the hospital without anyone paying the least attention to what else they might want to do or see. Not that Hazel knew what she'd have done, given the choice—she just wished she *had* been given a choice. This particular brand of freedom was starting to look a great deal like imprisonment.

At the hospital they'd been given a wonderful dinner, soft white cotton pajamas, and even softer beds with huge, fluffy pillows. Most of them had gotten on the floor with their bedding during the night, however, complaining that the soft bed was uncomfortable. An orderly had come through about midnight with a big bottle of something chalky to calm their stomachs. He hadn't even needed to be told that they'd all eaten too much; he'd been dealing with ex-prisoners for several weeks now and knew their ways. Because of that, he also took away a number of pork chop bones, bread slices, and baked potato skins they'd hidden to eat later.

"So when's this doctor going to see us, then?" Gloria was still disputing the nurse's edict.

"Look here, Sister Denk, you of all people should know that we have a great many desperately ill people here. He must tend to them first, and you if and when he has the time."

"Perhaps we could help?" a quiet voice said from the doorway. Three women in civilian clothes were hovering, waiting to get the sister's attention.

"Yes, you can certainly be of more use to them than I can. Ladies, your visitors are from the W.V.S.—Women's Volunteer Services. This is Mrs. Maxwell—"

The lady addressed, a plump, fiftyish woman in a navy and white polka-dot dress, took over and the sister fled gratefully. "Please, ladies, call me Eunice. This is Mavis Smith—" A little, sparrowlike woman in black with startlingly blue hair bobbed a nod. "And Harriet Vane—just like Peter Wimsey's girlfriend." The tall, awkward woman in a baggy apricot cotton dress smiled. "We will each take charge of ten of you. Or rather, let ten of you take charge of us. We're here to help you in whatever way you'll let us. Running errands, taking you places, harassing the authorities for news of your families, sorting out your bank accounts if you had any here, sending telegrams—anything that you need, that we're able to do. Now, first thing, we'll get the names and most pressing needs of each ten. Shall I start here?" she said, stepping over to Hazel's bed.

"How very good of you to do this," Hazel said.

"Well, there's a need. R.A.P.W.I. is swamped."

"R.A.P.W.I.?"

"Repatriation of Allied Prisoners of War and Internees is what it stands for, although some have started saying it means Retain All Prisoners of War Indefinitely. The sorting out is a huge job. They've located nearly one hundred twenty thousand of you now in Japan, Borneo, Java, Sumatra, Shanghai, Hong Kong, and the Dutch East Indies. And every one of you has so many needs—official and unofficial. What is your name, dear?"

"I'm Hazel Hampton—"

"Oh, yes. I saw your name on the list and thought what a pretty name it is. You sound American."

"Yes, from a city near Chicago."

"Married?"

"No. I was to have been, though."

"So you want to make sure your fiancé is notified—?"

"Well, there's two other things I need more urgently. I stayed behind because my father was missing. Somewhere between Singapore and Penang. His name is Ronald Hampton."

"I'll start checking the lists immediately. What is the other thing you most need?"

"I need to notify my friend's son of her death and that I've brought out her diaries."

"Shhh—oh, dear. My loyalties are getting mixed, but I would suggest you don't make official mention of these diaries until you have made a copy. You see, there will be war crime trials, and I'm afraid the diaries might be confiscated."

"Peggy would have appreciated the irony of that," Hazel said with a sad smile. "Very well. I appreciate the warning. The war crimes people are more than welcome to a copy, but not the original. But it is most important than her son know to contact me."

She gave what information she had to Eunice Maxwell, who seemed to take it in stride that the facts were all rather fuzzy. Mrs. Maxwell then moved on. It wasn't until she'd left that Hazel learned her own interest in the internees. "Her husband was a tin-mine executive," the nurse told her later. "He sent her out to India to safety but didn't get out himself. He was beheaded at Changi. She volunteered the very day she found out. Said since she couldn't help him, it was her duty to help others."

"Oh, poor Mrs. Maxwell!"

"Don't ever say that to her. And don't call her Mrs. Maxwell. She really wants to be Eunice to all of you. Must get on to the others. Be sure you keep putting that salve on the rash on your arm. It's coming along nicely."

Eunice came back late that afternoon. She pulled out a note-pad and said to Hazel. "No luck with your father yet. Doesn't mean a thing. There are dozens of different lists and they're not cross-referenced as well as you might think. I'll keep working on it. I did have marvelous luck with Jim Sutherland. He was demobbed from the British army in June, went back to the States, then went out to Hawaii to wait for the end. Apparently had some trouble getting clearance, but he left there last Tuesday for Singapore.''

"He's in Singapore? Now?"

"Somewhere. Don't worry. I'll find him."

"I believe you will! You're a perfect wonder, Eunice."

She went on her way, dispensing what news she'd found. Gloria was disappointed that Eunice couldn't make the doctor come see them so they could be released, and Nancy was unhappy to hear that there was no news of Herbert Dreyer. Jane's news was equivocal; Vivian's mother had been reported to have survived her initial injuries and been moved to another camp, but after that there was no record of her yet. Beryl's husband was in India and on his way to Singapore. Beryl managed to pull enough rank to get herself and Jonathan temporarily released to run an errand with Eunice.

Hazel ended up sitting on the sun porch with Audrey that afternoon. "Did Eunice find out anything for you?" Hazel asked her.

"I didn't ask her to."

"But why not? Don't you have family or friends to contact? You must have a great many friends worried about you."

Audrey was doing her nails. She lifted one languid, newly lacquered hand and waved it about to dry. "Friends? What would they want with me now? Look at me. Or are you as blind as that old doctor?"

"You'll be all right. You're putting on weight and your skin looks better already. As soon as you get dentures to replace your missing teeth—"

Audrey laughed bitterly. "Oh, I'll be a beauty, won't I? With my false teeth and crocodile skin and dyed hair. Just a beauty."

"Audrey, I know you were very beautiful, but take it from somebody who wasn't—your friends, the real ones, won't care. People love each other for what's inside, not what they look like."

"Still quite the little Girl Guide, aren't we? Shoulder to the wheel. Honor thy father and mother. Early to bed, early to rise. You stupid thing! Don't you know a whore when you see one?"

Hazel realized with a curious detachment that she'd lost her fright of raw emotions, having experienced so many. "That was only to take care of Jonathan. Everybody understood."

"You're more of a fool than I knew. I went into the war a high-class whore and came out an ugly, low-class one."

"But I thought—"

"Oh, the stories. You heard them, did you? The exalted father who left me the inheritance. That was good, wasn't it? I worked hard at getting that going, then it just kept on like a perpetual motion machine. Amazing, really. I started the story off with him as an earl. He became a duke on his own. Listen, Girl Guide, my father—the real one—was an alcoholic bricklayer and self-proclaimed minister in the slums of London. I grew up in conditions almost as bad as the camps, except that it was cold in the winter. When I was ten, my father started raping me every Friday night. A year later my brother got into the act. That's when I left home."

That *did* surprise Hazel. "You can't mean this! But you were so elegant—the way you dressed and talked and everything."

"Learned it all myself. I got a job as a kitchen skivvy and worked my way up to a lady's maid."

"But a lady's maid doesn't make much money."

"She does when she tells the mistress she's pregnant with her son's child. They bought me off and I used every shilling of it to create Audrey St. John. Courtesan *extraordinaire*."

Hazel leaned back in her chair, trying to absorb all of it. "Did you really have money? You seemed wealthy."

"Oh, I was. I certainly was. My brain's as good as my body was."

"But you wrote all those checks to people in the camps—"

"That I did, Girl Guide. About a thousand pounds more than I had. Of course, some of the poor dears will find their consciences and feel guilty cashing them, and others have died, Thank God. I'll have something left. Enough to live modestly as an ugly spinster. Or maybe I'll get lucky and find some girl with potential and teach her what I know and then share in the profits. I don't know."

"What about Jonathan?"

"What has Jonathan got to do with anything?"

"He's your child."

"He popped out from between my legs. That's all. I never wanted him and I don't now. He's Beryl's child. Period."

"But you do care about him. I know you do."

"Nobody cares about anybody but themselves. Even you. The sooner you recognize that fact, the better off you'll be in this world."

"You're very wrong. I even care about you. God knows why."

Audrey put her hand over her eyes and mumbled. "Go away, Girl Guide. Get the hell away from me."

Chapter 34

Jane Kowolski had her head tilted back and the doctor was peering down her throat with an otoscope. "No serious damage," he said, putting down the instrument and going around the desk to sit down. "There's some scar tissue on the left vocal cord. Not enough that the normal person would ever notice the difference or care. But as a singer—well, I'm afraid there's not much to be done."

Jane smoothed down her skirt and forced a polite smile. "You're saying that I'll never recover the voice I once had."

"I'm afraid so, but that doesn't mean—"

"You don't have to reassure me, Doctor. I've expected to hear this for some time now." How brave and mature she sounded when all she wanted to do was sit on the floor and howl in misery. "I just needed to know for sure, so that I could plan things accordingly."

"What *will* you do?"

"Teach, I imagine. Isn't that what all performers do when they aren't quite up to performing standards? I might even like it. I've been responsible for another woman's child during internment, and I've learned that there is real pleasure, some-

times, in someone else's accomplishments when you've
influenced them.''

"That must be little Vivian."

"That's right. You've met her."

"A few minutes ago. You have, indeed, done a fine job. She's
a bright, mannerly little girl and in far better health than many
I've seen. Plenty of food and she'll be as right as rain. I haven't
seen the blood test results yet, but I expect an excellent report.
Did her mother die in camp?"

"I haven't found out yet. I was washed up on the beach with
her and never saw her mother. The W.V.S. woman is trying to
trace the rest of her family. I appreciate your time, Doctor,'' she
said, rising.

"When you get back to the States, you should see a specialist.
There may be some new surgical technique that may help you
that I'm unaware of."

"Are Vivian and I approved to leave the hospital now?"

"Anytime that R.A.P.W.I. and the W.V.S. or you yourself
find someplace to go. You know you're entitled to free passage
home, but there is a wait for transport."

"Thank you. Yes, I know."

Jane headed back toward the ward, but decided she couldn't
face her friends yet. They'd all been trying to buck her up before
the examination, telling her what good news she was bound to
get. She wasn't adjusted enough to her disappointment yet to
tell them about it and see them try to deny it. Instead, she went
out on the hospital grounds and walked aimlessly. They were
free to go now. But where? With what? Her brother had wired
two hundred dollars to her, two hundred dollars she imagined
he could ill afford, and she would have to make it last as long
as possible. Even if she could get a booking on a ship tomorrow,
she couldn't leave Vivian.

Vivian was her great worry. How could she ever make herself
give up Vivian? And most likely to an aunt or cousin or somebody who had no idea what the child had been through. They
wouldn't be able to comfort her nightmares, nightmares rooted
in a life no outsider could understand. Maybe not even believe.
How would Vivian herself adjust to a real world she didn't even
remember? She'd grown up on smuggling and beatings and filth
and starvation and with only women for companions. In how
many horrible ways might it all have marred and warped her for

life? Jane had no doubt that they, she and Vivian together, could get back to normal. But Vivian by herself? With strangers?

A nun drifted past in a rustle of starch and Jane paid no attention until she heard Sister Maria's familiar voice. "Lost in your thoughts or have I disappeared into this thing?"

"Maria? It's you. In a real habit!"

"The Mother Superior herself brought it to me. It feels very stiff and peculiar and terribly hot. I'll get used to it soon, though."

"What are you still here for? I thought you'd had your examination this morning."

"I did, but there was something in my blood test. Some parasite they have to identify. But I feel fine. You looked so sad, Jane, that I almost didn't speak to you. What's wrong?"

They walked over and sat on a bench in the shade of a tree. "Oh, Maria, you're about the only person I could say this to, but I'm not liking freedom very much. I like the food and not having to bow and be terrified all the time, but the one thing about it I never appreciated was having to make decisions about my life. The only thing we had to worry about in camp was to stay alive, and that clears your mind wonderfully, I've discovered. Now I'm just muddled and feel very confused and stupid."

Sister Maria patted her hand. "First, the doctor told me we're all muddled. It's physical. The lack of protein makes the sheathing on our nerves recede or erode or something, and the nerve ends don't match up like they're supposed to. Proper diet will take care of it, but remember how we all kept forgetting things toward the end?"

"Did we?"

Maria laughed. "The other thing you should know is that you're not the only one. Several of our friends have confessed the same thing to me. For some reason, I'm 'safe' to talk to, especially since I got this habit. It seems that nothing that we look forward to for so long and with such desperation can quite live up to our expectations. I think we all imagined that we'd come back out as we went in. Just pick up precisely where we left off. But we've lost so much. Audrey's worst example in physical terms, but we've all lost—oh, innocence? Trust? Faith?"

"Faith? You don't include yourself?"

"Oddly enough, I wasn't talking about myself. And I didn't mean religious faith. I mean that faith that people on the whole are pretty nice and that no matter how bad things look, every-thing will work out somehow. That kind of faith is as important to your mental outlook as faith in God, I think.''

"What about you, Maria? Has this jeopardized your voca-tion?''

"I suppose. But I'll be fine, I think. Mother Superior brought me a habit and she had a priest come and confess me and is arranging for my medical treatment. I don't have the same kind of decisions to make that the rest of you are facing. I'm con-tent—grateful—to let her. When I'm healthy and rested I'll have to take a spiritual inventory, but there's plenty of time for that. God isn't rushing me.''

"Will you keep in touch? I'll miss you.''

"Probably not, Jane. We all feel that now, but I suspect as time goes on, we'll all associate each other with the worst part of our lives and won't want to be reminded.''

"I've been looking everywhere for the two of you!'' Beryl Stacton said, rushing across the lawn toward them. Her face was flushed and she was smiling. "I have an announcement to make and I want everybody to hear it. Come on.''

They allowed her to drag them to the ward where she'd al-ready ordered Audrey, Hazel, Nancy, Elise, Vivian, Claudia Millichope, and Eunice Maxwell to stay put. "You didn't tell them, did you?'' she asked Eunice.

"We tried everything from torture to bribery and she wouldn't say a word,'' Hazel answered. "Now that you've all but ce-mented us in place, what is it all about?''

Beryl picked Jonathan up and nuzzled his cheek before say-ing, "Eunice was kind enough to take me out to see my old house. The one we lived in before the invasion. Except for a bomb crater in my hydrangea border, it's in perfect shape. Some Jap officials used it for an office and took remarkably good care of it. Both cars are even in working order.''

"Thrilled for you, of course, darling,'' Audrey drawled sar-castically.

"And well you should be, because we're all going to move into it today, or as soon as we're released.'' There was a flurry of polite refusals to accept such hospitality, but the refusals weren't convincing and Beryl wouldn't listen to them. "One of Eunice's jobs is to find places to put us when we're released. Hotels and private houses and such. If we don't all go to my house, we'll be scattered all over Singapore and I'll still end up

with a houseful of people. I'd rather it were you lot than
strangers.''

The move was made by late afternoon. Neither Dr. Millichope nor Sister Maria came with them. Both were still under
observation, and when Sister Maria was released, she would go
to the convent. As Hazel went to tell her good-bye, she sensed
it would be the last time they saw or spoke to each other. While
they had been close of necessity in the camp and come to like
each other, they had little in common in the lives they were going
back to. Hazel was both sad and oddly relieved at this realization.

Claudia Millichope would, however, be joining them until
she could get passage to Scotland, where she intended to live
with her sister-in-law and try to get a job teaching tropical medicine at the University of Edinburgh. Such a post had been offered to her before the war. "I don't know," she told Gloria.
"My eyesight was merely failing then. Now I'm nearly blind.
Worse, I've had more practical experience in the last few years
than anyone could ask, but I'm entirely out of touch with the
research.''

Beryl herself drove Audrey, Jonathan, Elise, and Vivian
home. Eunice took Hazel, Gloria, Nancy, and Jane. "Could we
stop at the cathedral for just a minute?" Gloria asked.

"Why, of course," Eunice said. Her passengers, knowing
Gloria far better than she, looked at one another with amazement.

When they walked into the cathedral, they were even more
perplexed. While the rest of them went to pews at the back to
have a moment of meditation or prayer, Gloria ignored the religious aspect of the vast building and instead, hustled down the
side aisle to the organ. A man tried to stop her and they watched,
curious, as she spoke to him and gestured. He nodded and the
two of them disappeared. In a few minutes Gloria was back with
several wads of scraps of paper. "I'm ready. Let's go."

"*She's* ready," Jane groused. "I hope you're feeling spiri-
tually refreshed," she said when they got back in the car.

Gloria looked at her with surprise. "Oh, did you think I
wanted to go pray? Not bloody likely. God and I aren't speaking
just now. No, I had to get these names. The ones Caroline and
Sister Cassini and I hid here." She explained about the hospital
having run out of death certificates and the nurses making lists

of the dead. "I'll need stationery, too. To start writing to the families. Do you suppose Beryl will have some?"

Hazel looked out the car window at Singapore and mused on what a peculiar person Gloria Denk really was. So rebellious and irritating and insensitive most of the time; and yet, her first act upon release was to get her lists so she could write to the families of men who'd died in the invasion. The prisoner Dinki she'd known for so long and the nurse Sister Denk must be very different people, and it was annoying to discover she'd known only one of them—the less admirable of the two.

When they got to Beryl's house, their hostess was waiting at the front door. "The children are out playing—probably in the bomb crater since it seems so 'homey' to them—and Audrey is taking a long bath. I've got beds made up for all of you, and gin slings waiting for everyone. Welcome!"

Looking at the big stucco house that was so like the one they'd been renting before the war, Hazel felt a sudden wave of something like claustrophobia—or was it ordinary homesickness magnified to an oppressive degree? In spite of the attractive surroundings and the servant bobbing little bows and carrying her pitiful bags up to the elegant bedroom, Hazel suddenly was frantic to go home to Evanston. She didn't want to ever see a tropical plant again, or taste a gin sling, or hear the sound of parrots in the garden. Nor did she—at that moment, anyway— ever want to see or hear any of these women again. Not even the ones she liked best.

She wanted to be alone in her big bedroom in Illinois. She wanted to bundle up in furry slippers and the heavy quilted robe her father had given her for her birthday and stand at the window, looking at the lake in the cold winter moonlight. She wanted to walk across the crunchy lawn after the first frost and throw snowballs when the snow came.

But even that was impossible to really return to, she realized with a deep sense of sadness. She wasn't a girl anymore and never would be again, and Mother wouldn't be in the kitchen baking cookies and planning bridge parties. Mother was buried in the jungle. And maybe Father, too.

She got up and dressed early the next morning, determined to fling herself at R.A.P.W.I. and not let go until they'd turned up her father's name. As she came down the steps, however, she met Beryl coming up. "There's someone to see you, Hazel. A young man."

"Frank?" she said, her heart leaping into her throat.

"No, Jim Sutherland. He's in the morning room, but you should take him to your room to speak privately. The children have taken over the whole house."

"Yes, of course."

She paused at the door to the morning room, trying to dredge up some extra emotional strength. As she walked in, a lanky, sandy-haired man with very pale blue eyes and a deep tan stood up. "Miss Hampton?"

"Yes. Mr. Sutherland—"

"Don't worry. You don't have to tell me. R.A.P.W.I. already did. My mother's dead."

"I'm so sorry. More than you can know. Your mother was the most wonderful person I've ever known, and I have so much to tell you. Please, come up to my room. I have something to give you."

He followed her up the stairs.

"Close the door, or the children will invade. They're mad for Western men." She handed him the battered suitcase, having already removed all her own belongings from it. "Inside the lining and stuffed into the canteen inside it are your mother's diaries. Actually, they're a long letter to you. Or they started that way."

"I see." He'd gone pale under the tan. She could see his resemblance to his mother in his eyes and the firm set of his jaw.

"I have to go somewhere for a few hours. Maybe all day. Why don't I leave you here with it? Beryl won't mind. There's a bath next door and I'll ask that your lunch be sent up. I'll also send the majordomo up with some tools to get into the canteen."

"I don't want to run you out—"

"You're not. The room is yours for the day. Of course, you can take it all away if you'd rather—"

"I'd rather read it here, thank you."

Hazel paused at the door. "She kept it at risk to her life. Besides what it will mean to you, it's—well, it's *important*."

He set the suitcase down and came and took her hand. "I know it is. Do you want to stay and read it with me?"

"No, it's meant for you—first."

* * *

It was a day spent harassing R.A.P.W.I. to no avail. Or practically so. Passed from one clerk to another and another, she discovered that they had a Charles Hampson in a hospital in Butterworth and a Donald Hammond in a military camp in Thailand, but no Ronald Hampton anywhere. "He couldn't have just disappeared!" Hazel exclaimed in irritation to the last man she talked to. And immediately she realized what a foolish thing that was to say. Of course he could have just disappeared. Thousands of people died in the invasion without any record of their death. "What will I do if I don't ever find any record of him?" she asked.

"It's early days yet, Miss Hampton," the exhausted, overworked R.A.P.W.I. official said. "We're still turning up camps in the jungles. A lot of the Japanese made it their first order of business to destroy the lists they kept of the prisoners."

And their second order of business was to destroy the prisoners themselves, she thought bitterly. *If Saigo had had his way, I'd be dead now.* "Thank you. I'll be back tomorrow."

When she got back to Beryl's, Nancy was just coming out. "Any luck?"

"None. I asked about Herbert Dreyer, too. Nothing. I'm sorry."

"We'll find them. They let Dr. Millichope out. She's in the room next to yours and Jim Sutherland is waiting in the garden for you. He's a nice young man. Just what you'd expect Peggy's son to be like."

"You've talked to him, then?"

"Only for a few minutes. He's very anxious to talk to you."

Hazel went first to her room to freshen up. She felt a little silly about it, but vanity was returning. She didn't want to look like a skinny, sick hag. She studied herself in the mirror and was fairly pleased. The malnutrition sores on her face were nearly healed now, and a bit of powder covered the scars fairly well. She'd put on an amazing amount of weight. More than twenty pounds. She was up to a hundred and three now. She wet her hands and ran them through her short, curly hair, trying to dampen down the fuzziness.

When she walked into the garden, Jim Sutherland had Jonathan on his lap. Vivian and Elise were sitting at his feet, listening raptly. When he saw Hazel, he deposited Jonathan on the ground and stood up. "I was about to send out a posse for you. Kids, get along. I'll finish the story later."

"I'm sorry. I wanted to give you plenty of time. Did you read them all? Were you able to get the bits in order?"

She took a seat across from his. There was a pitcher of lemonade on the umbrella-shaded table and two glasses. He poured one and handed it to her. "No and no. The handwriting is so tiny and cramped that some of it didn't make much sense. But I skimmed it all and read some of it very carefully. It was like having her talk to me."

"That's what she wanted, Mr. Sutherland."

"Would you mind if I called you Hazel? I've been reading about you all day long and feel that I know you very well."

"Please. It seems strange to call you Mr. Sutherland. I've known you as Jim for years," she said with a smile.

He took a sip of lemonade. "Tell me about the end."

"Are you sure you want to know?"

"I'm sure I don't, but I must."

"There was a plane dropping leaflets."

When she finished, he didn't speak for a long time. Finally he said, "You mentioned that she kept the diary at risk of her life."

"Yes. She kept telling me how important it was that there be a record of what happened to us so it couldn't happen again."

"And your life was a risk, too. You put it at risk for her—and for the diaries."

"Oh. She wrote about that?"

"At length. I read it carefully. I owe you a lot."

She set her glass down and thought for a long moment. "You owe me nothing. Peggy owed me nothing. We saved each other's lives countless times and put them in danger just as often. All of us. You see, the rules were different. In normal life, if you're careful and good and do what you're supposed to, you greatly increase the likelihood that nothing bad will happen to you. But in the camps, everything was tenuous and capricious. On the occasion you're talking about, I took an action that resulted in punishment. But other times—oh, countless other times—we did nothing and got punished just as severely. It made taking risks meaningless toward the end. Peggy knew she was in danger, reading the leaflet. But she might just as well have been killed for doing nothing, and she knew it. Caroline Warbler was."

"I sensed all that—in a way. As fluent as my mother is in print, though, it's different hearing someone talk about it. She—

she loved you a great deal, you know. She wrote of what an admirable young woman you'd become. Even glancing through, I saw your name often."

"Peggy was probably the most important person in my life. Maybe even more than my parents. Not so much what she did or said, but just what she was."

"An irascible, stubborn, outspoken, bossy woman!" he said with a grin.

Hazel laughed. "All of that! And she'd have loved hearing you say so."

"What about you, Hazel? The diary said you'd been separated from your father before the invasion."

"Yes. I've been nagging the R.A.P.W.I. people all day. No luck. They have nothing about him."

"That doesn't mean anything."

"That's what they say. But all those years in camp I guess I imagined I'd walk out and say 'Where's my father?' and somebody would tell me. I'm nearly mad with impatience."

"Maybe I can help. I spent most of the war unsnarling paperwork. May I try?"

"I'd be grateful. Could you help us find someone else? Herbert Dreyer's his name."

"Sure. Who's he?"

Hazel told him briefly about Nancy and Elise and Herbert.

"I'll see what I can do. What about the rest of your family? Have you been in touch with them?"

"My mother died in the camp. I understand my sister's on her way here. I've sent telegrams to my fiancé, but I haven't heard from him yet. Of course, I have no idea where he's stationed. The last time I heard from him, before the invasion, he'd joined the navy but had some sort of ear problem that was probably going to mean no overseas duty, but that might have been cured or overlooked. He could be anyplace or he could be—"

"I'm sure he's fine. If he's affluent enough, he may be on his way, too. It costs a fortune to get here, but it can be done if you can put up with the red tape. Tell me, there was something I was trying to read this afternoon that I couldn't make sense of. Something about you and a pig."

"Oh, yes. I'd almost forgotten that. Saigo's huge pig. . . ."

By the time she'd finished the story, which had led to another story and yet another, it was getting dark. "You look tired, and I've made it a long day for you, Hazel. I'll go now."

"The diaries—?"

"You aren't ready to let go of them, are you?"

"That doesn't matter. They're yours."

"Not entirely. I'd rather go back to my room at the Adelphi and think about what I've read today and come back tomorrow to read more. If that's all right—?"

"More than all right. It's wonderful. Thank you for understanding, Jim. Those hundreds of little bits of paper are all I have left of a dear friend. My parting with her was so abrupt—"

"I understand." He got up and started strolling slowly around the side of the house toward the front drive. He took her hand and tucked it through the crook of his arm. "I'm amazed at how well I feel I know you, and yet we only met this morning."

"Oh, but I met you years ago."

"I wish you had. I'll see you tomorrow."

Hazel felt her face grow strangely warm. *I'm blushing*, she thought as she watched him climb into a borrowed military jeep and wave good-bye. *I haven't blushed for four years!*

Chapter 35

The next morning, instead of donning one of the ubiquitous khaki shirts they'd been issued, Hazel borrowed a white blouse and bright red scarf from Beryl, whose wardrobe (for reasons none of them could fathom) was still in the closets and drawers where she'd left it. Since most of her old clothes, purchased for a much plumper woman, didn't fit her anymore, she was thrilled to give them away. The blouse was much too large for Hazel, too, but she tucked the excess into her skirt and didn't care. She went down to breakfast and found Nancy and Gloria at the table.

Gloria was intently munching very buttery toast with one hand while writing with the other. She had a stack of letters already finished and addressed. Some had buttery smudges on them.

Nancy was reading a letter, or, rather, staring at it. "Bad news?" Hazel asked softly.

Nancy looked up. "Depends on your viewpoint. R.A.P.W.I. sent it over. It's a copy of a letter they received. It seems Elise's great-uncle Ralph, living in Surrey, has asked friends of the family who sat out the war in Australia to try to find Elise and bring her back with them. Apparently he got word about the rest of the family. This is their letter expressing the friends' eagerness to help. They'll be here in a few days."

"Nancy, I'm so sorry. But—"

Nancy stood up abruptly and said, "Oh, Hazel, do be quiet! I know! I shouldn't have gotten my hopes up. I shouldn't have fooled myself that I'd get to keep her. She'll be better off with her own people. Et cetera bloody cetera! I don't need to hear it." She stormed out of the room.

"Hell!" Hazel muttered. "Why do I always say the right thing at the wrong time?"

Gloria reached for another piece of toast. "I didn't hear you say anything."

"But I was going to say just what she thought I was."

"If the words don't actually pass your lips, they don't count against you. Always remember that, Hazel. Toast?"

"No, thanks."

"Who would have thought any of us would ever turn down food? Are you going out? Could you mail these for me?"

"I don't know when. I'll leave whenever Jim Sutherland gets here. I want to leave him alone with the diaries."

"I didn't get a look at him, but from what I heard, no girl in her right mind would go off and leave him alone. Awfully good-looking bloke, they say."

"I guess so. He's healthy. To our eyes right now, I think that's all it takes to be handsome."

"Don't kid yourself. I still know the difference, and so do you."

Nancy was back at the doorway. "Hazel, I'm sorry for what I said," she said brusquely. "Do you want to go see the R.A.P.W.I. people with me? Eunice is on her way over."

"As soon as Jim Sutherland gets here."

"He just arrived."

Hazel hurried to greet him. The hallway was as busy as a hotel lobby. He was sitting out of traffic on the bottom step in the front hall. "Jim, how nice to see you. This is Nancy Muir—"

He stood up and shook her hand. "We met yesterday. You're the lady looking for Herbert Dreyer, aren't you? I checked with the officials before I came over. Nothing new on him or Mr. Hampton today so far."

"Still, it can't hurt to make nuisances of ourselves," Hazel said. As she spoke, there was a sharp rap on the front door. She turned to cross the hall and open it, but Audrey was coming through and got there first. A terribly dignified British army officer in full regalia stood there. He had fair hair and a pencil-thin mustache. "This is still the Stacton home, isn't it, miss?"

Audrey gaped at him for a moment. "Y-yes, it is."

"Will you tell Mrs. Stacton that her husband is here?"

"Tell Mrs. Stacton—yes, of course," Audrey said.

"Who is it n—?" Beryl was coming down the steps. "Dennis?"

"Beryl?" He was clearly astonished. Hazel was puzzled at his reaction, then she cast her mind back to Beryl as she'd first met her—a prissy, plump, pale woman who looked a good ten years older than the thin, tanned, self-assured Beryl coming down the steps. No wonder he was having trouble coming to grips with the situation.

"Come in, Dennis," Beryl said coolly. "The army said you were on your way, but I didn't expect you quite so soon. How fit you look." She summoned a maid and said, "Is that room at the south end of the hall prepared for the brigadier if he decides to stay? Good. I know you like the view from there, Dennis, although the garden is in very sad shape. Do come into the study and tell me how you've been." She turned and walked off toward the study.

"Beryl?" he said again before trailing after her with what dignity he could muster. It wasn't much.

Audrey was still standing at the door. Hazel had momentarily forgotten Audrey's connection with Dennis Stacton. Now she wished that someone had slapped him senseless for not recognizing his former mistress. The mother—though he didn't know it and might never know it—of his only child. "Audrey, he's a stupid man—"

"Oh, bugger off!" She plunged through the doorway and disappeared.

"Twice in fifteen minutes," Hazel said with a disgusted shrug.

"What in the world was all that about?" Jim asked.

"You mustn't mind us, Mr. Sutherland. We've gotten used to treating each other nastily," Nancy Muir said. "We're enmeshed in a hideously complicated snarl of relationships. We'll all have to be sent to etiquette classes before we're fit for society. I'll wait outside, Hazel."

"The woman who snapped at me is Audrey St. John. You'll meet her in the diaries—" Hazel said to him.

"But I already did, I thought. Am I mixing her up with somebody else? Mother's diary described her as a swanky beauty."

"I'm sorry to say you're not mistaken. She was, and that's just part of the problem. Jim, go read. I'll see you later."

"Come back, early, will you? I'd like to take you to dinner. I made reservations at Raffles. They're crowded to the rafters with other P.O.W.s, but if you don't mind that—"

"Not in the least. But may I bring Nancy and Elise along? Nancy's had bad news this morning."

"Bring along as many as you want. In fact, I'd like to meet as many of the women in the diaries as I can."

Beryl preceded Dennis into the study and sat down behind what had been his desk. "I understand you were posted to India," she said calmly.

His face was red. He sat down hard. "Beryl, is that the only greeting you have for me when I come home to my own wife and my own house?"

"Perhaps it has been a while, but if you'll check the deed, I think you'll find that this is *my* house, Dennis."

His jaw fell. "Beryl, is this really you? What's happened to you?"

"The war is what's happened to me. Three and a half years of filth and brutality and hunger, Dennis. And a number of other things as well, most of which were your fault."

"Steady on, old girl—"

"Don't you 'old girl' me! You're a military man; you knew the situation better than most. If you'd cared anything for me, you'd have sent me to safety, or at least tried to. Instead, you shoved me onto a doomed boat on the last day, and only when it was your commander's order. It must have been hard on you when I didn't turn up at my destination, not knowing what had become of your 'old girl,' not able to spend my money without me, and not being able to have me declared dead.''

"Beryl, I never thought—"

"No, I don't believe you did. But I've thought. A great deal. And I've come to a few conclusions. The first is that I don't much care if I ever see you again after today." She'd been formulating this speech ever since the day she'd helped Audrey St. John carry her fancy suitcase that her, Beryl's, money had purchased. Her husband's blubbering astonishment and humiliation were all she'd hoped for. "You see, Dennis, I realized in the camp that I'd let you spend my money on your women and drag me to the most godforsaken places on earth, in the hopes of two things in return: your love and a child. Quite simply put, you welshed on your part of the bargain. You're a bounder, Brigadier Stacton. I never had your love, and by the time I was captured, I'd realized it. In a prison camp you learn how to face the most unfaceable truths without flinching. But these last three hellish years have given me one thing you never did—a son.''

"What?" He stood up so quickly, his chair fell over backward with a loud crash.

"I have a son. His name is Jonathan Stacton. Jonathan for my father, who tried to warn me against marrying you when I was a silly girl.''

"You don't mean you—"

"He was born under Japanese rule in a filthy hut with rats in the rafters and swarms of roaches on the rotting plank floor, not a proper hospital. There were no documents, so I am applying for one now. He's my child. The child of my body. That's what the birth certificate will say.'' She crossed her arms on the desk and leaned forward, looking up at him with a cold smile.

"Hazel, do you realize that the first camp we were in—after the Banka Island jail, I mean—must belong to Elise now?'' Nancy asked as Eunice Maxwell weaved expertly through traffic.

"How odd. Yes, you must be right. It was the coolie quarters of her father's plantation, and she's the only one left in the family. Imagine, Elise is the 'lady of the manor,' or will be when she's an adult.''

Nancy stared at her. "No, I don't think you see quite what I meant. I meant, Elise is now a wealthy girl. An heiress."

"She'll handle it all in a levelheaded way. Don't worry."

"Oh, Hazel. You can be so dim! She's rich. That means my chances of convincing her family to let her stay with me are even more remote than they might otherwise be. I'm dirt poor and I can't even blame it on the war. They'd think I just wanted her money."

"You *didn't* think you could fight her family for her custody, did you? Oh, Nancy—"

"Not fight them. No. But I'd hoped since she's nearly of age anyway and doesn't know any of her people, she might want to stay with me and they might be willing to allow it. But the money makes that impossible."

"Here you are, ladies. I'll come back for you in two hours. Good luck," Eunice said, coming to an abrupt stop in front of the R.A.P.W.I. headquarters.

The office was crowded and it was impossible to continue a personal discussion, not that Hazel had any idea what more there was to say about the matter. Nancy had always seemed to have a more down-to-earth view of reality than any of them. She was surprised to realize that even Nancy could dream something so impossible. "Beryl got Audrey a ticket on a ship that sails tomorrow afternoon. Did you know?" Nancy asked.

"No. How did she manage it?"

"I imagine a lot of money and some pretty hard string-pulling was involved. She tried to get Dr. Millichope on the same ship, but couldn't. Poor Claudia was hoping to get away."

"What will Audrey do?"

Nancy shrugged. "Something pretty awful, probably. By the way, I heard some interesting gossip. About Mrs. Haver."

"I hope it's to her detriment."

"Her husband's. Remember all that stuff about what an important, rich man he was. Well, he was caught, too. And the men in his camp murdered him for collaborating with the enemy. Apparently, he stopped two other men who were planning an escape and they were beheaded for it, so he was killed."

"I don't suppose they'll have the big parade in Toronto for her after all," Hazel said. Then: "What a callous person I've become. I ought to feel sorry for her."

"I can't imagine why. She was a bitch."

When they finally reached the head of the line, the clerk, who recognized them, said, "Miss Hampton, nothing of your father. Sorry."

"What about Herbert Dreyer?" Nancy asked.

He leaned forward and said, "Now, don't get your hopes up, but there is a chance—a mere chance—that we've found him. There's a man on my list who was brought from Sumatra, dreadfully ill. His mates don't know him as anything but Herb. He's not well enough to give his name. It's not much, Miss Muir, but—"

"Which hospital? Where?"

"No, don't sound so happy about this. It's not really very likely—"

"Write down the address. Quickly!"

They didn't wait for Eunice, but Nancy got a taxi by the simple expedient of stepping directly in front of one and demanding that they be accommodated—to the considerable alarm of the previous passengers. Nancy was out of the taxi before it had come to a full stop, and Hazel was left to pay the driver and trail along in her wake. While she waited for Nancy to return, she occupied herself making phone calls, trying to alert Eunice Maxwell as to what had become of them.

Nancy returned in half an hour. She looked limp. "Was it Herbert Dreyer?" Hazel asked.

Nancy slumped into a chair next to her. "Yes. What remains of him. Malaria, a septic leg wound, amoebic dysentery. He's unconscious. Has been for several days."

Hazel started to formulate something encouraging to say, then thought better of it—for once. "I found Eunice. She's on her way to fetch us."

There was another surprise waiting at Beryl's. "A Mr. and Mrs. Lord are waiting to see you and Elise," Beryl told Nancy.

"No! Not so soon! Where's Elise?"

"In the bath. She and Vivian tried to make a fish pond out of the bomb crater and turned themselves into mud balls."

"I'll see the Lords. Would you send Elise in as soon as she's dressed?"

"Certainly." Beryl laid her hand on Nancy's arm for a moment before turning and going up the stairs.

The Lords were horsey, gap-toothed, pleasant people who looked more like brother and sister than husband and wife. "Miss Muir? Oh, we're so delighted to meet you," Mrs. Lord said, leaping up and hugging Nancy violently when she came in the room. "We hear you've taken wonderful care of our little Elise. Just a dreadful experience for all of you."

Our little Elise, Nancy thought. "She's not the child you remember."

"Quite a young lady now, I imagine," Mr. Lord said heartily. "You were friends of the de Groots?"

"Of Hannah's," Mrs. Lord said. "Her parents knew mine, and when she was sent off to school, she spent all her holidays with us. We were like sisters. In fact, we'd just visited them a month or so before the invasion. I begged Hannah to bring the children home to England with us, but she wouldn't leave Horst. Just what happened to them?"

Nancy felt a nasty urge to shock these nice, complacent people. "Mr. de Groot was shot to death in front of Hannah and the girls for moving a chair. Annie died of a lung infection, and her body was dug up by wild dogs. Hannah cut her jugular with nail scissors."

Mrs. Lord sat down abruptly and slapped her hand over her mouth. "Oh—oh, dear. I had no idea. No idea at all," she murmured, turning white under her tan.

"I'm sorry. I shouldn't have been so blunt. But if you're going to take Elise, you should know what she's been through. That's part of her life."

"Quite right, Miss Muir," Mr. Lord said. He looked sicker than his wife.

"When may we see her?" Mrs. Lord asked, fanning herself with a magazine she'd picked up off the table.

"She'll be along in a minute."

"Miss Muir, Elise's great-uncle feels strongly that you should be—well, let us say 'rewarded' for your care of the girl."

"Do you mean 'paid off,' as though I'd been a governess who's no longer needed?"

"Please. No offense intended."

"I didn't take care of her in the expectation of monetary gain."

"Quite. Quite. But please don't ignore an old man's desperate need to express his gratitude. To whom but you can he express it?"

"Yes, I see what you mean," Nancy said, her indignation evaporating.

"Will you come back with us? We've booked a ticket for you."

"I'd like to do that, but I have an obligation here. My—my fiancé is desperately ill. You've already gotten passage?"

"Got damned lucky. Four first-class tickets. If you can't come along, what about one of the other ladies from the camp?"

"Yes, there is one. Dr. Claudia Millichope is most eager to return, and Elise is very fond of her. You do know, don't you, that your government will reimburse you for their tickets. When will you leave?"

"Tomorrow afternoon."

"*Tomorrow!* Oh, no! Not so quickly!"

Mrs. Lord laid the magazine down and came over to put her arm around Nancy's bony shoulders. "Miss Muir, I know it must seem that way to you, but to us, and to Elise's family, it's already been a terribly long time. Almost four years. If we were to give up these tickets, it might be months and months before we could get others. They're as scarce as hen's teeth."

Nancy dragged a handkerchief out of her skirt pocket and blew her nose. "Yes. I know. I know."

The door burst open and Elise dashed in. "Aunt Nancy! Hazel told me you found Mr. Dreyer! Oh—! Mrs. Lord. Mr. Lord."

"The Lords have come to take you home, Elise," Nancy said.

Mrs. Lord enveloped Elise in another of her overwhelming hugs. Elise was straining to turn her head and look at Nancy.

"I'm sorry I hadn't told you yet, Elise. I got the message only this morning, and I had no idea things would move so quickly. They're taking you back to your great-uncle Ralph."

"Me? What about you?" Elise said, struggling free of the embrace.

"Dr. Millichope is going with you. I'll stay here with Mr. Dreyer."

"Oh, of course. I'm sorry. I didn't think. When he's well, will you both come?"

"Possibly."

"Elise, how tall you've become!" Mrs. Lord said. "You can wear my frocks until we can buy you your own. And we'll have to start planning some shopping in London. Your great-uncle wants to throw a big welcome-home party for you—"

Nancy saw Elise's eyes light up at the mention of party clothes.

"If you'll excuse me, I'll go tell Dr. Millichope of your kind offer."

"Do you think maybe a pink dress? A sort of shimmery pink? With a ruffle around the neckline. I've always wanted a dress like that—"

Hazel didn't invite anyone else to dinner and Jim Sutherland didn't question her. They had dinner at Raffles and then danced for a while. Hazel was surprised and a little alarmed at how very much she liked being in a man's arms. But after the first dance she said, "Jim, would you mind if we left here? It's so crowded and I'm sick to death of crowds."

"I should have realized. The diaries are full of Mother's complaints about the lack of quiet or privacy. Do you want to go back to Mrs. Stacton's house?"

"Good Lord, no! It's like a hotel there, too."

"How about a ride?"

They drove out into the suburbs, and Hazel directed him to the house they'd been living in before the invasion. There was little left of it. They stopped the jeep in the drive where Johnny Leighton had parked his fancy new sporty car the night the bombing started. "My mother's room was up there and we stood in the window that night—"

"You must miss your mother a great deal."

Hazel considered. "More now than in the camp. She was so elegant and sparkling. But when we became prisoners, she changed. Disintegrated. Not just physically. But I do miss the woman she was before the war. I've never had a day that I didn't miss my father, though. We were very close."

"And your sister?"

"I love my sister."

Jim smiled. "But you didn't miss her?"

"She'd have driven me mad in the camps. She couldn't have stood it."

"And your fiancé? Frank?"

Hazel didn't answer, and after a few more minutes Jim started the jeep and drove slowly back down the rutted, neglected driveway.

Chapter 36

The Lords came to Beryl's house to pick up Claudia Milli-chope and Elise and, when it was discovered that Audrey was to be on the same ship, they offered to take her as well. In an effort to be considerate, they came quite early, so that the part-ings wouldn't be rushed. It was the worst thing they could have done. No one wanted the pain drawn out any longer than nec-essary. Jane, Vivian, and Hazel stood around, feeling awkward as the good-byes were said and repeated in variations.

Gloria hung on to Dr. Millichope like a child. "Now, don't go on deck without someone to hold your arm, and be careful of getting a chill. It's been so long since you've been in a cool climate. Do you have some warm wools along? Oh, Claudia, what will I do without you?" she finally sobbed.

Dr. Millichope held her, patting her back and smoothing her hair. "You'll do just fine, Dinki dear. I need some help getting into the car."

Elise and Nancy held hands, hardly speaking at all. Elise was wearing a new dress Mrs. Lord had purchased that morning and brought along for her. It was a splashy pink and white print with a matching wide-brimmed hat. With her hair curled and a hint of lip rouge, she looked so grown-up it broke Nancy's heart. "You had better get in the car, too. The traffic might be heavy and you don't want to make everybody late," Nancy said.

Elise turned and hugged her fiercely. "I love you so much, Aunt Nancy."

She took the girl's head in her hands and forced a smile. "And

I love you, too. But distance won't make any difference. You know that.''

"You'll visit us. Promise!"

"I'll try."

There was a great bustle as Mr. Lord declared they must get going. Beryl approached Audrey and held out her hand. "Best of luck, Miss St. John—Audrey. Let me know if there's anything you need. Jonathan and I will be coming back to England in a few months. I could look you up if you'd like.''

"No need. Thanks ever so,'' Audrey drawled. She didn't ask to see Jonathan again, and Beryl didn't offer to have him brought out.

There was another round of hugging as Jane, Vivian, and Hazel bid their final farewells, then Mr. Lord engaged the gears with a clash and they were gone. As they walked back to the house, Hazel said, "Beryl, you said you and Jonathan are going back to England?''

"In a while. I don't want to rush him into yet a third kind of life too suddenly. And I've got to sell this house and arrange for the shipping of all the furniture and paintings. It will be some time. Don't feel you must rush away.''

"Thank you, but that wasn't what I meant. What about your husband?''

"I'm divorcing him," she said calmly. "Nancy, would you like to use one of the cars to make your hospital visit today?''

Nancy pulled herself together and said shakily. "Thank you very much, but I don't know how to drive.''

"Nancy, would you like me to come along?'' Hazel asked. "I could do the driving.''

"I'd be most grateful. But what about Mr. Sutherland?''

"He's reading the last of the diaries today. I can't resist the temptation to read over his shoulder if I'm here. I'd like to go with you.''

They spent the last of the afternoon sitting at Herbert Dreyer's bedside. He was barely alive. His skin looked like crinkly yellow paper, and his breathing was so faint it was almost imperceptible. When the orderly came to change his dressings and the bedclothes, Nancy and Hazel went into the hallway. Nancy leaned against the wall and closed her eyes. "I can't bear the thought of his dying without ever knowing I was here with him.''

Hazel started to say something comforting about how she was sure he was going to get well, but swallowed the words.

* * *

The next morning Jim said, "I ran into a man I served with in France last night in the hotel lobby. He's working with R.A.P.W.I. I was talking to him about the confusion over prisoners, and he mentioned that he'd heard there was a group of men just being brought into a hospital across the strait. Apparently there was some snafu with the lists of names and some were lost. I thought, instead of waiting for them to straighten it out, you might like to drive up there and ask about your father."

They were on their way in half an hour. As they neared the rebuilt causeway, Hazel was taken aback. She told Jim about the scared young soldier with whom she'd stood watching the pipers cross before the old causeway was blown up. "I wonder what happened to him," she said. "There are so many I wonder about. The boys in Dinki's truck she was bringing down the peninsula; the rest of the women and children from the boat your mother and I were on. I met your mother in the toilet. Did you know? She was flushing away her passport and the covers from some books of hers."

By the time she finished telling him about their first few days, they'd reached their destination. Jim briskly cut through several layers of the nursing and orderly staff before finding the matron of the ward they wanted. He explained their errand, promised they would not disturb the patients unduly, and ushered Hazel onto the ward. These men, the matron explained, were from various camps in Thailand and Burma. Most had been starved, tortured, and worked nearly to death on road crews.

Hazel went down one side of the ward, then came back along the other, walking to the head of each bed and studying the face of the man in it. Her stomach was churning by the time she got back. These men made Herbert Dreyer look like the picture of health. Most were so skeletally thin it was almost impossible to believe they could be alive. Many had terrible injuries. Most had innumerable round scars Hazel had come to recognize as cigarette burns. One man had mutilated fingers, all the nails having been torn out by his captors. They all looked incredibly old, though she knew most were probably in their twenties and thirties. The older men had all died long before.

"You didn't find him?" Jim asked softly.

She swayed and he put his arm around her shoulders. "No. I don't know. Oh, Jim—"

"Here. You sit down. I'll be back in a minute."

Hazel all but fell into a chair and leaned forward for a long moment, letting the blood come back to her head. When she sat back up, feeling cold all over but sweating, she saw that Jim was going from bed to bed and speaking briefly to those men who were awake. As she watched, he leaned closer to one, then looked up at her and gestured for her to join him.

"Hazel, this is Ed Percy."

The man was sitting up, bandages wrapped around his throat. He spoke in a coarse, half-strangled whisper. "Ronald's Hazel? I should have known you with that hair. Just like his."

"You know my father?" Hazel said.

"Knew him, miss? He was the best friend I had in this war. I broke my leg when I was captured. The dirty Jap bastards were going to shoot me, and he got right in there and told 'em he'd carry me so I wouldn't slow down the march. And he did it. Propped himself under me like a living crutch. He died the first year. Sorry. I thought you knew. I turned his name in."

Hazel put a hand out on the edge of the bed to steady herself. "I think I did know in my heart, Mr. Percy. But I hoped—"

"Here, sit down. You can't hurt me with a little jiggling."

"Where were you?" Jim asked.

"Burma. Least that's what they tell us now. We didn't know then just where we were. We built a goddamned railroad. That's how Ronald died. On a bridge. He was up top and three of the sodding Japs were drunk as lords and decided it would be a lark to use him for target practice. Sorry, miss. Guess I shouldn't have told you that. I forget how nice people—"

"I was in a camp, too. I know."

"I'm glad Ronald never knew that. He kept himself going by talking about how his girls were safely home. He thought sure you were. But you gotta look at it that he didn't have to suffer what the rest of us did, dying sudden and early on and not knowing you'd been captured, too."

"I know."

"Your mother and sister? Did they make it?"

"My mother died in the camps. My sister escaped to the States and is due back here any day."

Mr. Percy started coughing, a racking, hideous sound. Hazel bent her head and waited until he'd caught his breath, then rose and took his hand. "I'm glad I found you, Mr. Percy, and I thank you for telling me about my father. It's better, knowing for sure."

When they left, Jim handed her into the jeep and sat for a moment before starting it. Hazel stared straight ahead at the hospital building. "I lied," she said slowly. "It *isn't* better knowing." She balled her fists and put them on her knees. "I even do it to myself, try to say something optimistic and encouraging in the face of everything to the contrary. I ought to be put in a sack and drowned. Audrey was right. I *am* a bloody Girl Guide."

Jim put his hand over one of her fists. "Not such a bad thing to be, Hazel."

When they returned, late in the afternoon, Gloria and Nancy were sitting on blue and white striped canvas sling chairs in the garden. Gloria leapt up at the sight of Hazel and ran over. "My, my, my! This must be Peggy's son!"

"And you have to be Dinki. I'd have known you anywhere," Jim said with a smile.

"Would you really?" Gloria preened for a second, then thought it over. "What do you mean by that?"

"Just that I'm glad to meet you."

Gloria was satisfied. "Hazel, I saw the most wonderful thing today. I was sick you weren't all with me. My sister cabled some money and I went to Robinsons to get some clothes and on the way, the taxi had to stop for a whole bloody gang of captured Japs being put on trucks to be taken to Changi. The best place for them, if you ask me, where they kept so many of our people. Do you know how many nurses—"

Hazel ran a hand through her hair impatiently. "Is there a point to this, Dinki?"

"You bet there is. One of the Japs was dragging along, and the soldiers gave him a great shove and he turned around and I saw his face. Saigo. It was the bastard Saigo! I hope they send them all back to Japan and finish bombing the damned place—"

Nancy struggled up out of the lawn chair awkwardly. She said, "You're a great fool, Gloria Denk. You've known fewer than a dozen Japanese and you're judging a whole people by them."

"Are you trying to defend Saigo and those other sadistic bastards?"

"Of course not. But they're not typical of their people. I know the Japanese well and most of them are—"

"Their people started this war, in case you've forgotten."

"Not all of them."

"A bloody great lot! Saigo and his thugs didn't take most of East Asia all by themselves!"

"They were obeying their Emp—oh, what difference does it make? Hazel, you look awful. Is it Dinki's charm or something else? Where have you been all day?"

Hazel glanced at Jim, then said, "I found a man who knew my father. He saw him die in the first year."

"Oh, my God!" Gloria said, throwing her arms around Hazel. "Why didn't you ram a garden tool down my damned-fool throat and shut me up? I'm so sorry."

"Yoo-hoo! Hazel? Are you there?" Beryl called from one of the windows at the side of the house. "Telephone!"

Hazel disentangled herself from Gloria and ran inside. "Hello?"

"Hazel? Is that you? Is that really you?"

"Barbara! Where are you?"

"Raffles. I'll just freshen my powder and change my clothes and I'll be right there."

Hazel glanced out the window at Gloria gesturing as she told Jim something. "No, let me come there. What room?"

Barbara told her. "Have you found Daddy?"

Hazel paused. It wasn't news for the phone. "No, not yet. What about Frank? I haven't heard from Frank."

"He's fine. Just fine. Hurry, Hazel."

Jim drove her. As he pulled up in front of the hotel, he said, "I'll go back to the Adelphi and I'll be there all evening. Call me if you need a ride home or anything."

"You're not coming in with me?"

"It's a family event. I'm not family."

"Jim, you've been my 'family' for years and years. Please come with me."

"That's nice, Hazel, but—"

"I'm not being nice. I'm asking—asking for your support. I'm scared."

"What on earth of?"

"Telling her? Seeing her? I don't know. But I'd like to have you with me, if you don't mind."

Ignoring the hotel employee who said he couldn't leave a jeep right there, Jim got out and came with Hazel. She paused at the hotel room door. Jim nodded encouragement and she rapped lightly. The door was flung open a second later by her sister. Barbara looked wonderful. Sleek, plump, healthy, beautifully dressed and groomed. "Hazel? Can that be you?" She hugged her carefully, as though afraid she might break. "What did they do to you? You look awful!"

"I—"

"So skinny. My word, I wouldn't have thought it was possible. You look downright haggard. And your hair—your beautiful hair is gone! That was your best feature."

"It will grow back, I'm told," Hazel said dryly. "And I'm positively rolypoly, I've gained so much weight."

"What about your skin? It's so rough and dark—"

Jim stepped into the room and put his hand lightly on Hazel's elbow. "The mind reels at the thought of what she must have looked like before, because she's clearly one of the most beautiful women I've ever seen as she is now. How do you do. I'm Jim Sutherland."

Hazel stared at him and felt part of a terrible load slip away. "Oh, I'm sorry. Barbara, Jim is the son of my very closest friend in the camps. She kept diaries and I've been helping explain some of the gaps in them to him."

"Sit down. Both of you," Barbara said. Typically, in spite of Singapore's vastly overcrowded conditions, she'd gotten not only a room, but a suite. They took the two chairs by the window, leaving her the sofa, behind which was a long table with a tray of materials to fix drinks. Barbara fixed three without asking anybody's preference, and Hazel noticed that her hand was shaking as she poured. Some gin splashed on her silk dress and she didn't even notice. She handed each of them a drink and sat down with exaggerated grace, "You know, I thought you and mother were dead."

"I can see why you would if you heard anything outside about the conditions of the camps."

"No, I mean I thought I *knew* you were dead. I got a telegram from the government."

"What?"

"That ship you said you were taking—"

Hazel cast her mind back with an effort. So long ago. Another life, another person. "Oh, yes. The one with the meat lockers. They wouldn't take us on and the launch found another boat to take us. A big yacht."

"Then you don't know about the 'meat locker' ship, as you

call it. It was in a convoy of three and hit a mine. It blew to bits right in front of everybody. Only a handful of people were saved. It was in all the news, Hazel.''

''I let my subscription lapse!''

''I'm sorry. I didn't mean it to sound that way. But you see, I knew you and Mother were on it. And your names were on the official list of passengers. You were declared to be drowned at sea almost four years ago.''

''Oh. I see. You really did think we died then. My God, what a shock it must have been for you to get my message!''

''More than you can imagine—'' Barbara drained her drink and got up to fix another. ''Tell me about Mother.''

''She died in the first camp. Malaria—or something. It was hard to tell without any sort of medical help just what it was. She died peacefully during a camp concert.''

''And Father? What have you found out about him?''

''Barbie, I didn't tell you on the phone, but I have bad news. Daddy died early on as well. A quick death,'' she added, knowing her sister was not one to bear the details. Maybe someday, but not now.

Barbara bowed her head and put a handkerchief to her nose. ''I see. I thought you were keeping something from me. I could tell by your voice. We really are orphans, Hazel. But at least we have each other.''

''Barbie, tell me about Frank. Where is he? Does he know I'm all right?''

''Wait. Wait!'' She got up and got a third drink. Hazel exchanged an alarmed glance with Jim. ''Hazel, there's something I have to tell you, and it's too awful to know where to start or how to say it.''

''Frank's dead.''

''No!''

''Yes, he is, and you're trying to soften the blow.''

''Listen to me for once and let me say this my way. When I heard the news that your ship had sunk and got the telegram and everything, I called the navy and found Frank stationed in New Orleans. He came home and helped me. We had a memorial service and everything—''

Hazel leaned back, letting the words wash over her, merely waiting for Barbara to confirm that Frank was gone.

''—beautiful day and everybody who'd ever known us came. Frank took care of everything. Selected the music and wrote up the announcement for the newspaper and all of that. I was dev-astated, Hazel. Absolutely helpless. I can't tell you how much it meant to me. Anyway, Frank called his commanding officer and explained—of course, Aunt Corny and Uncle Joe were more than willing to help me out, but they wanted me to move in with them and—'' She took a sip of her drink. "Frank got temporar-ily reassigned to the Chicago area to help me. We were both a great comfort to each other. At first all we talked about was you, Hazel. Frank was heartbroken. So was I. But people can't be sad all the time, and Frank's really charming and—''

Hazel sat up straight, her heart suddenly thudding in her throat. "Barbara—what are you trying to say?''

She set her drink down on the floor and stood up. Walking across the room, weaving slightly, she opened the door to the bedroom. A moment later, Frank walked through it.

"Hello, Hazel,'' he said. "I'm awfully sorry.'' His voice was strangled with emotion.

Hazel had stood up and was staring at him. "You—you two—?''

"I hadn't quite told her yet, honey,'' Barbara said. She held out her left hand, waggling the fingers frantically to show a flashy pair of rings. Her voice cracked as she said, "Hazel, Frank and I were married two years ago. We're expecting a child.'' She sounded positively horrified at the prospect.

Hazel was drifting toward the door, not looking at them. "I—I have to go now,'' she said mechanically.

Jim got to the door ahead of her and opened it.

Frank came forward. "Now, Hazel. I know it's an awful shock, just like it was to us when we got your message, but I want to explain. You have to understand, Hazel. You owe us that, at least. A chance to really explain. And there's a lot to talk about. All kinds of things that need to be sorted out. Ha-zel!''

She was already in the hallway.

Jim started to pull the door shut, but paused and said to Frank, "Amazing. I've known you for only thirty seconds and already it's apparent that you're a first-grade son of a bitch. Some people make such strong first impressions.''

Chapter 37

"Do you want to go back to Mrs. Stacton's?" Jim asked.

Hazel shook her head.

He drove along the shore until the traffic was very sparse. Neither of them said anything. Finally, turning down a deserted road, they came to a beach. It had once been a private swimming beach but now the Mediterranean-style home on the slight rise behind it was empty and deserted, the windows boarded up. Jim stopped the jeep, got out, and came around to Hazel. "We'll walk," he said firmly.

She climbed down and followed him slowly. They walked for about five minutes until they came to a sheltered spot that was clear of debris. Hazel sat down cross-legged, facing the sea. Jim sat beside her. "You can scream if you want," he said casually. "There's nobody to hear you and it might feel good."

Hazel leaned against his shoulder. "I like the sound of the waves. It makes me think of home. My bedroom window faced the lake and in the summer, late at night when there wasn't any traffic left, I could just hear the water lapping. When I was little, I told myself it was God whispering to me, but I could never understand the words."

Jim moved his arm, draping it over her shoulders.

"Did I make a fool of myself, Jim?"

"No. You behaved with alarming dignity. I, on the other hand, almost succumbed to the urge to beat the shit out of your Frank."

"Not *my* Frank. Barbara's Frank. How extraordinary. Of all the reunions I imagined over the years, I never came close. I worried that he'd meet someone else, fall in love. But with my sister? My own sister?''

She turned to him and looked at him for a long, puzzled moment, then moved closer and kissed him. Then kissed him again, harder. Surprised, he put his other arm around her and she slowly fell back onto the sand, pulling him along. She started fumbling with the buttons of his shirt. ''Please, Jim—'' she whispered.

They undressed quickly and made love furiously, heedless of the surroundings, the circumstances, or the sand. All the sexual energy that had been pent up for four years in Hazel suddenly had come to the boiling point. Technique, affection, and foreplay were irrelevant; she desperately needed release. And it came violently, her body climaxing in spasms that were nearly painful in their intensity. Gasping and whimpering, she clung to him long after they were both spent.

He rolled sideways when he finally relaxed her grip on him. ''I think I got sand up my nose,'' he said.

She sat up slowly, wrapping her arms around her knees. After a long moment she turned to him again and said, ''Nice girls don't do that sort of thing. Why don't I feel guilty? Or even shocked at myself?''

''Nice girls who've been through what you have are entitled to do anything they want. The rules are suspended.''

''Jim, I am sorry—''

''Nothing to be sorry about. We both needed something. We were able to supply it for each other. That's all. That's what friends are for. Now put your clothes on. You have unfinished business.'' He shook the sand out of her panties and bra and handed them to her.

''I can't go back there,'' she said, standing up and putting them on slowly.

''You have to sooner or later, and you might as well get it over with now. Like it or not, Frank is your brother-in-law and will be for a long time.''

''Tomorrow. It's too late tonight.''

''It's only nine. You're getting that shirt on inside out.''

''Jim—this is stupid to ask, but were they both fat or am I so used to emaciated people that everybody looks fat to me?''

''Do I?''

''No.''

''That's your answer.''

* * *

"Hello. We're back," Jim said cheerfully.

Barbara, her eyes red and puffy, opened the door. "I'll tell Frank," she said listlessly.

Hazel walked in behind Jim and sat down again by the window. He took a place across from her and leaned forward to whisper, "You look perfect. Like a woman who just had a damned fine bang. Keep that expression. It scares the hell out of people."

Hazel laughed.

Frank walked in, looking upset and offended at the laughter. "I'm glad you came back. We've been calling the house where you're staying. Hazel, when that ship went down, we got a telegram—"

"Yes, I know. Barbara told me."

"If I'd known—" He glanced uneasily at Barbara and cut off the phrase. The rest of it hung unspoken in the air, but everyone could hear it. *If I'd known, I wouldn't have married Barbara.*

Hazel suddenly felt a heart-wringing pang of sympathy, but for them, not herself. Poor Barbara—it must have been awful enough for her, knowing she was Frank's second choice, a stand-in for his dead fiancée. But now, to have the dead return—?

"Well," Frank said, trying to recover ground, "I don't know what would have happened if we'd known the truth."

Barbara came around and collapsed on the sofa. Frank sat down and put his arm around her. The gesture was tentative. He was obviously in misery. For a second Hazel felt sorry for him, too. He really believed she was dead, the government had said so. What was he to do? Remain faithful to her memory the rest of his life? Romantic, but unrealistic.

Barbara said, "The point is, what are we to do now?"

"I'd say everything has already been done," Hazel said. "We all get used to it somehow."

"No," Frank said, taking his arm back and leaning forward on his knees. "There are a great many legalities to be sorted out."

"Legalities?" Hazel asked. It was the last thing she expected to hear.

"Well, your father's death, for example. We'll need documentation. Do you have that? And your own death has to be—well, reversed. You see—"

"Frank, could you stop being a lawyer for just a little while?"

Hazel asked. *Why did I never notice what unattractive eyebrows he has,* she wondered. Still, maybe Frank had the right idea: talk about practical matters while the emotional ones simmer.

"Perhaps you'd like to know where Hazel's been?" Jim said.

Hazel felt a momentary urge to smack him, and Frank gave him a baleful look as though he'd almost managed to forget his presence and was now unpleasantly reminded of it. "Yes. Of course. Were you here, in Singapore? At that place—ah, Changi?"

"No, Sumatra. I have maps I made. I'll show them to you later. We were at several different places. First, we were taken to a jail on Banka Island. There were hundreds and hundreds of us there and the conditions were awful. At least we thought they were then. Later we learned what awful really meant. Many of the women died there at first, mostly from injuries they'd gotten when their ships were wrecked or from their immersion in the sea—"

"Hazel, please—" Barbara said.

But Hazel had waited a long time to share this. "Many of them had been in the sea for hours and hours, and the bombing had caused terrible internal injuries. Ruptured abdominal organs. But those of our group who survived were taken on a long journey up to a plantation near Palembang. We lived in the coolie quarters and eventually the woman whose husband owned the plantation before the war was brought to it as a prisoner, too. She had two daughters. The little one died before long and Hannah—that was the mother—killed herself. But the other girl, the older one, survived and—"

Barbara put her hands over her eyes for a moment, then said, "Hazel, this is too awful."

"Yes, it was, but the point is, it got more and more awful. If we'd known we'd someday be eating rice with the bugs still in it for the protein and—"

"Please! Hazel, I know this is on your mind and it was all awful, but don't you realize that we went through a lot, too? War is hard on everybody. Why, the rationing alone was enough to make us wild. A limit on how much butter and milk you could buy and—and the shortages! Buying decent clothes was a nightmare. For a while I was down to two pairs of nylons and thought I'd never get any more. And Frank, poor Frank, was stationed for most of the war in New Orleans. Do you have any idea how hot and muggy it can get in New Orleans in the summer? Dangerously hot!''

Hazel stared at her in amazement. "Do you mean to say you think our experiences in the war were—were the same?''

Barbara seemed to hear herself for the first time. "God! No, Hazel. I don't know why I said anything so stupid. I'm so upset! Hazel we have to—to do *something* about this.''

"About what, Barbara?''

"Us! All of us!'' she said frantically. "You. Me. Frank.''

Hazel stared at her. There was clearly nothing to be done but get used to it. It seemed so obvious. "Barbara, I don't know what to say. It can't be undone. Any of it.''

Jim stood up quickly. "I just realized that Hazel and I missed dinner. I'm hungry. Come on, Hazel. We'll talk about all this tomorrow. When everybody's had time to rest and think.''

"But Hazel—'' Barbara exclaimed.

Hazel put her arms around Barbara. She was shivering. "Barbie, I'm glad to see you again. We'll fix everything somehow.'' She glanced over her sister's shoulder and noticed Frank staring at her with an agonized expression.

For the second time that evening they made a hasty departure. This time Jim drove straight for Beryl's house. They went in the back door and he headed for the kitchen. "It wasn't an excuse. I *am* hungry,'' he said.

She trailed along and watched as he found a bowl of leftover fried chicken. "Want some?'' he said through a mouthful.

"No, I don't want anything to eat! What on earth did you make me go back there for? Don't you realize how painful this all is for me? That man was my fiancé! I got myself through the whole war imagining the day we'd be happily reunited. Can't you see how terrible this is for me? But you fling me in there, let me be devastated all over again, and then drag me back out just so you can stuff your mouth with chicken. Are you a madman?''

"You needed to go back. Can't you see that? Is there any milk here? This chicken is dry.''

"Needed to go back? For what? And how dare you think because we had sex that you have some right to barge in and run my life. Who invited you to interfere?''

Dinki stuck her head through the door. "Is this a private fight, or can the public get into it?''

"It's private. Get out of here,'' Hazel snapped.

"But I'm hungry, too."

Hazel grabbed a piece of chicken and flung it across the room. Gloria caught it and disappeared.

Jim sat back and let out a whoop of laughter. "I love your prison-camp manners! It gives a whole new meaning to 'pass the chicken.' "

Hazel's eyes filled with tears. "You think I'm funny, do you? You've been laughing at me all evening. The worst night of my whole life and you're amused by it. How smug and superior of you. You're despicable, Jim Sutherland. I asked you to come with me as a friend and, after witnessing my complete humiliation, all you can do is laugh." She was crying in earnest now, tears coursing down her face. "I wish I had died in the camps."

She put her hands over her face and sobbed. Jim got up and put the food back in the refrigerator. He got a drink of water, then handed her his handkerchief. "Here. Mop up."

When she'd gotten herself to the sniffling stage, he said, "Now, if you can stop being the Queen of Tragedy for a few minutes, you can listen to some truth. The real thing. No jokes. Years ago a girl named Hazel Hampton from Evanston, Illinois, was in love with a young man named Frank. He probably wasn't so stiff and dull then, at least I hope not."

"That's not fair to Frank. He's in a terrible position. Have you no sympathy for him?"

"Not much, but I'm glad *you* do. Sympathy is a step in the right direction."

"What does that mean?"

"Nothing. Just listen to my story. Young Hazel was a gawky, awkward, timid girl. Shy, unsure of herself, dying to hand her life over to somebody who would tell her how to live it and what to do with it."

Hazel looked at him sharply. "What the hell do you know!"

"I know a lot about you. More than you knew then. My mother told me—in the diaries. She was a very perceptive woman. I trust her assessment. So this Hazel got caught by the Japanese—and she died."

"Oh?"

"Yes. She died. While poor old Frank was sweltering in New Orleans and sitting out the war in a chair, Hazel ceased to exist. And instead, this new person came into being. Also, coincidentally named Hazel Hampton, but nothing like her. This Hazel is a gorgeous, strong-minded, bossy woman who throws food at her friends.''

This was so close to what she'd thought herself—about the old Hazel being a different person—that it infuriated her all over again. ''You just know everything, don't you? We met only a few days ago and you barge in, telling me—''

''Not a few days. Years. I've read Mother's diaries and I've known you girl and woman, as she did.'' He started laughing. ''Can you just picture how Frank would have reacted if Barbara heaved a chicken breast at him?''

Hazel fought the smile, but it won.

''Barbara's perfect for him. Your Frank needs a wife who will sit at his feet and adore him. Or, at least, will have the good sense to pretend to adore him. I can't imagine you sitting at anybody's feet. You could have before the war, but now you know what servitude is and you'll never willingly submit yourself to it again.''

Hazel got up and poured herself a drink of water. ''The memory of Frank, the anticipation of a life with him, was what got me through.''

''Fine. He served a worthy purpose. I'll give him credit for that. Grudgingly.''

''And now you're telling me I don't love him? That I don't need him?''

''You know you don't.''

''Because I'm a bossy, opinionated woman who throws food. Pretty well put myself out of the marriage market entirely, haven't I?''

He considered. ''I don't know. My mother was bossy and opinionated and I'm living proof that she found a husband. I don't recall any food-throwing, though. Do you want a husband, Hazel?''

That brought her up short. She thought for a moment. ''No, as a matter of fact, I don't believe I do.''

''You can destroy their marriage, you know.''

The truth of that was as shocking as bucket of cold water in the face. Hazel thought back to the look in Frank's eyes, and Barbara's trembling. ''I think just being alive may have done so—''

''Not necessarily.''

''But what is there to do? And why the hell does everybody

make me feel this is all my fault? I didn't do anything but survive."

"It isn't your fault, but it's up to you to solve it."

"Well, since you seem to have all the answers, how do I solve it?"

"You have to absolve them, Hazel."

She was about to say, 'What the hell does that mean?' when the meaning started to become clear. "It is, isn't it? I have to convince them it's really all right with me."

"Is it? You have to convince yourself first."

Hazel felt herself relaxing, joint by joint. A smile started somewhere deep inside. "Yes—yes—it *is* all right. Frank's right for Barbara. But not for me. Not anymore." She paced around the kitchen, realizations swamping her. She felt a deep, sincere sympathy for Frank, but wasn't that proof itself of the distance she'd come? If she still really loved him, she'd be in too much agony to spare sympathy. "You know, I thought I was liberated when the Aussies came to the camp. But that wasn't freedom. *This* is! I'm really free now. You know, Dinki's been upset about finding a meaning in what we went through."

"And you've discovered it?"

"Not for anybody but me. But maybe God put me in that awful prison in order to free me. I know that sounds stupid, but it could be. See, because I was trapped, I couldn't marry Frank, and because I couldn't marry Frank, Barbara could, and all of that makes me free to do whatever I want with my life." She laughed at herself. "On second thought, I don't think God would arrange a world war to break my engagement."

Jim grinned at her. "What *do* you want to do with your life, Hazel?"

She sat down and looked at him with dawning amazement. "It's up to me now, isn't it? It's really and truly up to me!"

"So? What are you going to do first?"

She thought for a minute. "First, I'd like to offer you my services."

"Which services exactly?" he said with a leer.

"Editorial," she said primly. "I'd like to help you get your mother's diaries in order and ready for publication."

"Your help would be invaluable. I appreciate the offer—in fact, I was prepared to go to extraordinary lengths to extract it from you. But Hazel, you know what this means? Weeks, probably months of working closely together. Very closely."

"Yes," she said slowly. "That's probably quite true, Jim. But we can't work all the time. We might have to stop occasionally and—oh, maybe go to the beach?"

He cocked an eyebrow at her. "We might find the time."

🪷 *Epilogue*

Hazel Hampton returned to Evanston to help edit Peggy's diaries, which were published to national critical acclaim in 1947. She married Jim Sutherland the same year and followed in the footsteps of her illustrious mother-in-law by getting her doctorate in education at Northwestern University while raising three children (Margaret, b. 1948; Elise, b. 1949; and Ronald, b. 1952). Dr. Hazel Sutherland, Mrs. Robert Landsdowne, and Mrs. Herbert Dreyer were responsible for founding, in 1956, the Sutherland Christian Women's College in Palembang, Sumatra. Dr. Sutherland and her husband now live in retirement in Evanston, Illinois, in the home where she grew up.

Gloria Denk testified at the war crimes trials in Tokyo before returning to Australia. Enrolling in medical school, she dropped out a year later and suffered a mental breakdown. After six months of treatment and another six months recuperation at home with her sister in Sydney, she returned to medical school, where she eventually received degrees in obstetrics and tropical medicine. She suffered a stroke and died in 1978 in Mexico City, where she was a guest lecturer at a seminar sponsored by the World Health Organization.

Nancy Muir remained in Singapore for nearly a year, as housekeeper and companion to Beryl Stacton, until Herbert Dreyer was released from the hospital. He had lost his left leg and had sustained severe liver damage, but they married the day after his release and moved to California a month later, where he lived an active life for several years as a citrus broker. Mr. Dreyer died of a heart attack in 1953. Nancy Dreyer moved to Sumatra in 1955 with Mr. and Mrs. Robert Landsdowne and died there in 1967.

Elise de Groot completed her secondary education in England and upon the death of her great-uncle immigrated to the United States, where she lived with Mr. and Mrs. Herbert Dreyer in Los Angeles while attending college. She earned a degree in home economics in 1952 and married Robert Landsdowne, an architect, the following year. Mr. Landsdowne donated his skills to the planning of Sutherland Christian Women's College and Mrs. Landsdowne gave the land, which was her former family home, to the college. The Landsdownes and their child (Anne, b. 1957) live in Palembang, Sumatra.

Audrey St. John returned to England and opened a boardinghouse in Worthing, England. Within a few years she was clashing with local authorities, who insisted that she was running a brothel. After a series of legal battles she closed the boardinghouse and was found dead on the beach in January 1951. An autopsy revealed advanced breast cancer and a high alcohol content in her blood. She left everything she owned, which amounted to several small pieces of property, some jewelry, and a thousand pounds, to Jonathan Stacton.

Jane Kowolski remained in Singapore for three months after liberation. She could locate none of Vivian's relatives, and since no one came forward to claim the child, the authorities were finally convinced to let her take Vivian back to the United States. She legally adopted her two years later. They lived in New York City, where Miss Kowolski gave singing instruction and soon was in great demand as a teacher of some of the finest soprano voices of the 1950s. When Vivian married in 1960, Miss Kowolski retired to Santa Fe, New Mexico, married a widowed landscape painter in 1962, and has continued teaching until the present.

Sister Maria left the religious order a year after the end of the war, and took a job teaching in a private elementary school in Singapore. She died in 1949 after a long, undiagnosed illness, thought to have been acquired in internment.

Dr. Claudia Millichope returned to Edinburgh. She began teaching the following year, but repeated bouts of pneumonia and the complete loss of her eyesight resulted in her almost immediate retirement. She died in a nursing home in 1948.

Etsu Natsume committed suicide in his cell at Changi shortly after receiving notice of the death of his wife in the bombing of Nagasaki.

Saburo Saigo was tried and executed for his brutality to the women under his command. The primary witness to the February 1942 massacre on Banka Island and the murders of Caroline Warbler and Margaret Sutherland was Gloria Denk.

Masamichi Asakawa was repatriated to Japan, where he worked as a security guard at a Tokyo hotel until his retirement in 1988. He now lives with a great-niece and her family in Yokahama.

Beryl Stacton remained in Singapore for a year with Nancy Muir, then took her son, Jonathan, back to England and raised him quietly in Clifton-upon-Dunsmore. She contributed a large sum toward the Sutherland Christian Women's College in Sumatra and died on her eighty-first birthday in 1976 as a result of injuries suffered in an automobile accident.

Jonathan Stacton is a successful stockbroker in London. A faded photograph has pride of place on his office wall: it shows a group of emaciated, tattered women and children posed at the gate of a prison camp and was taken by an Australian soldier on the day the camp was liberated. Across the sky at the top of the photograph are a few handwritten words: "Guests (!) of the Emperor."

Bibliography of Major Sources

Diaries and First Person Accounts

Crouter, Natalie. *Forbidden Diary: A Record of Wartime Internment, 1941-1945.* New York: Burt Franklin and Co., 1980.

Gilkey, Langdon. *Shantung Compound: The Story of Men and Women Under Pressure.* New York: Harper and Row, 1966.

Goodman, J. M. *MD—POW.* New York: Exposition Press, 1972.

[Nursing Sister] Betty Jeffrey, *White Coolies.* London: Angus and Robertson, 1954.

Keith, Agnes Newton. *Three Came Home.* Boston: Little, Brown and Co., 1946.

Lawton, Marion. *Some Survived.* Chapel Hill, N.C.: Algonquin Books, 1984.

Lim, Janet. *Sold for Silver.* Cleveland: World Publishing Co., 1958.

Lucas, Celia. *Prisoners of Santo Tomas.* London: Leo Cooper, Ltd., 1975.

Priestwood, Gwen. *Through Japanese Barbed Wire.* New York: Appleton-Century Co., 1943.

Valentine, Douglas. *The Hotel Tacloban.* Westport, Conn.: Lawrence Hill and Co., 1984.

van der Post, Laurens. *The Prisoner and the Bomb.* New York: William Morrow and Co., Inc., 1971.

Weinstein, A. A. *Barbed Wire Surgeon.* New York: The Macmillan Co., 1948.

General Information

Arthur, Anthony. *Deliverance at Los Banos*. New York: St. Martin's Press, 1985.

Barber, Noel. *A Sinister Twilight: The Fall of Singapore 1942*, Boston: Houghton Mifflin, Co., 1968.

Benedict, Ruth. *The Chrysanthemum and the Sword*. London: Rutledge, 1967.

Blair, Clay, Jr., and Joan Blair. *Return from the River Kwai*, New York: Simon and Schuster, 1979.

Caffrey, Kate. *Out in the Midday Sun: Singapore 1941–45—The End of an Empire*, New York: Stein and Day, 1973.

Kerr, E. Bartlett. *Surrender and Survival: The Experience of American POWs in the Pacific 1941–1945*. New York: William Morrow and Co, Inc., 1985.

Knox, Donald. *Death March: The Survivors of Bataan*. New York: Harcourt Brace Jovanovich, 1982.

McBryde, Brenda. *Quiet Heroines: Nurses of the Second World War*. London: Chatto and Windus, Hogarth Press, 1985.

Olson, John E. *O'Donnell: Andersonville of the Pacific*. Privately printed, 1985.

Owen, Frank. *The Fall of Singapore*, London: Quality Book Club, 1960.

ABOUT THE AUTHOR

Janice Young Brooks is the award-winning author of twenty books, most of them historical novels. She has also written a nonfiction history textbook and is the author of several mysteries under the pseudonym Jill Churchill.

She is a member of MENSA, Sisters in Crime, and is president of Novelists, Inc., a professional association of published authors. Brooks lives with her husband, two children, one dog, and too many cats in a suburb of Kansas City.

NEVIL SHUTE...

At His Best